"THEY'RE ALL DEAD," WILLEM SAID.

"Who's dead? You're not making any sense."

"The Supreme Court, they're all dead."

"You mean one of the justices died?"

"No, I mean they're all dead! The full court was in session, and there was some sort of blast."

"Contact the NSA, and tell them we need everything they've got on this. Set the Joint Chiefs up in the situation room and let them know I want a briefing ASAP," President McDonald ordered.

• • •

THE CHAIRMAN OF THE JOINT CHIEFS OF STAFF, Admiral Zacharias, kicked off the meeting. "I have a tentative assessment of the event. We haven't identified them yet, but a small band of terrorists stole a Potomac river tour boat, and used it to launch three cruise missiles, which took out the Supreme Court building, and all the justices. We believe they had at least one other target, but one of the missiles malfunctioned, killing everyone on board."

"So it was a terrorist attack?"

"Without a doubt."

REBELLION

TOR BOOKS BY KEN SHUFELDT

Genesis
Tribulations
Rebellion

REBELLION

KEN SHUFELDT

TOR

A TOM DOHERTY ASSOCIATES BOOK
NEW YORK

REBELLION

A Tor Book
Published by Tom Doherty Associates, LLC
175 Fifth Avenue
New York, NY 10010

www.tor-forge.com

Tor® is a registered trademark of Tom Doherty Associates, LLC.

ISBN 978-0-7653-7071-6

Tor books may be purchased for educational, business, or promotional use. For information on bulk purchases, please contact Macmillan Corporate and Premium Sales Department at 1-800-221-7945, extension 5442, or write specialmarkets@macmillan.com.

First Edition: June 2014

Printed in the United States of America

0 9 8 7 6

To my lovely wife, and best friend, Leslie.

Who knows whether the gods will add tomorrow to the present hour?

—HORACE

PART 1

CHAPTER 1

Eastern New Mexico, northern Texas, and the Oklahoma panhandle had been under a winter storm warning, but the ferocity of the late-October blizzard had taken everyone by surprise.

Lyndon and Betty Drury were dirt-poor sharecroppers in the Oklahoma panhandle, and as the brutal north wind buffeted their drafty old farmhouse, it shuddered and groaned in protest.

Betty was taking a quick shower before they went into town to catch a movie, so Lyndon switched on the TV to see what the weather was going to do.

Betty was almost nine months pregnant with their first child, and if the weather was going to get worse, Lyndon was going to try to talk her out of making the forty-mile round-trip into town.

Betty hadn't wanted to worry Lyndon, but she'd been having an occasional contraction all day. As she was getting out of the shower, she doubled over in pain, but unlike the previous contractions, this one didn't want to let up.

"Lyndon, I think my water just broke," Betty yelled as she slumped to the floor.

"Hold on, I'm coming," Lyndon assured her as he tried to keep the panic out of his voice.

When he came rushing in, he almost fell when he slipped on the wet bathroom floor.

"Careful, you're going to bust your butt. We've got plenty of time yet."

"Are you sure you're all right?" Lyndon asked as he helped her up.

"I'm sure."

However, as she was toweling off she had another strong contraction.

"Maybe we should get going," she said softly, as she tried to mask the pain.

As he helped her into the bedroom, she asked, "What did the weatherman have to say?"

"He said we're in for a real blue norther, and to stay home unless it was an emergency."

"I think this qualifies."

Lyndon was hovering, so she suggested, "Why don't you get the truck warmed up, while I get dressed?"

Lyndon had his warmest coat on, but he was shivering when he reached their decrepit old truck.

"Come on, you piece of shit, start," he exclaimed as he pumped the gas and turned the key.

As it slowly turned over, he prayed for a little good luck.

It finally started, but it only ran for a few seconds before it backfired and quit.

"Oh hell!" He pumped the gas and tried again. When the engine roared to life, he exclaimed, "Oh thank God."

When he was sure it was going to stay running, he rushed back inside.

"Take a good hold of my arm, the steps are really slick," Lyndon advised.

"It looks like the weatherman got one right for a

change," Betty commented, as they struggled through the blinding snow.

Their house sat at the end of a dirt road, and it was filled with ruts.

"Take it easy," Betty groaned as the pickup swerved and bounced its way toward the highway.

It only took him a couple of minutes to reach the pavement, but by then Lyndon was getting anxious. When the old truck slid up onto the pavement, he floored it.

"I can hardly see the road," Lyndon complained as their old pickup struggled for traction.

"Slow down," Betty implored.

Jeff Reeder lived just down the road from the Drurys, and he was trying to get home before the worst of the storm hit.

"Oh shit," Jeff screamed as he lost control of the semi. He never had a chance to react as his truck skidded across the centerline and struck the driver's side of the Drurys' pickup.

Lyndon was wearing his seat belt, but he died instantly when the truck crashed into them. Betty hadn't buckled up, because it hurt her swollen belly, and the horrific force of the impact catapulted her through the windshield and out onto the snow-covered pavement.

Jeff hadn't been wearing a seat belt either, and the impact had propelled him across the cab of the truck.

Momentarily unconscious, it was several minutes before he crawled down from the cab of his jackknifed semi. Jeff knew he'd hit something, but he was still disoriented, and the whiteout conditions were making it hard to see. He wandered aimlessly, until he heard someone whimpering in pain. He couldn't see more than a few feet, but he kept moving toward the cries.

"Oh God, what have I done?" he exclaimed when he saw Lyndon's mangled body pinned in the wreckage.

There was no doubt that Lyndon was dead, but when Betty made another anguished cry, Jeff forgot about him, and rushed to help her.

"Hold on, Betty, I'll call the ambulance," he screamed when he saw her bloodied, mangled body lying in the snow.

As he fumbled for his cell phone, he threw up all over his shoes. He spit to clear the bile out of his mouth, and dialed 911.

"This is Jeff Reeder, and I need the ambulance west of town on FM 1125," he said, with panic in his voice.

"Calm down," the 911 operator told him. "What's going on?"

"I just hit the Drurys head-on."

"Any injuries?"

It took him a couple of seconds to get the words out. "Lyndon's dead, and Betty is in bad shape."

"OK, how far out are you?"

It was snowing so hard that Jeff had to get within a few feet of the mile marker to see it. "We're at mile marker eighteen, and you need to tell them to hurry."

The phone went quiet for several seconds before the operator came back on. "The ambulance is on its way, but it may be awhile, because the roads are getting slick as hell. Try to keep her warm, and if she's got any bleeding, put some pressure on it. Call me back if you've got any questions."

Jeff took his coat off and covered her as well as he could. Her cries had turned to an occasional whimper, as Jeff tried to get the gashes on her head to stop bleeding. As the wind howled around them, the snow was getting heavier. By then he was shivering so badly he could hardly think. *Shit, she'll be dead before they get here if I don't do something,* he realized.

He returned to his truck and dug out two sets of old, greasy, insulated coveralls he had stuffed behind the seat. His hands were so stiff he could barely get the coveralls on. He didn't know how he was going to get the other pair on Betty without hurting her, but he knew he had to do something.

As he was getting down out of the cab, he heard one of the tarps covering the trailer flapping in the wind, and thought, *Damn it, I should have thought about that sooner.*

He quickly cut one of the larger ones off, and started dragging it toward Betty. The tarp almost took him with it a time or two, as the wind caught it, but he finally managed to get Betty covered up. The cold had helped slow the bleeding, but he knew she wasn't going to last very much longer if the ambulance didn't get there soon.

He redialed 911. "Where are they?" he asked frantically.

"They should be there anytime now," the dispatcher told him.

Normally the ambulance only carried an EMT, but Jim Johnson had been the doctor on duty, and he'd decided to ride along.

"Oh crap." Tim Warner, the ambulance driver, screamed as he hit the brakes to keep from hitting Jeff's truck. "Everybody all right back there?" Tim asked.

"Yes, but what the hell was that?" Dr. Johnson asked, as he got up off the floor.

"I damn near ran into the wreck," Tim explained.

"Let's get to it," Dr. Johnson called as he opened the back door.

"What happened?" Dr. Johnson asked, as Manny Perez, the EMT, and Tim put the stretcher down beside Betty.

"I hit a patch of ice," Jeff explained as he tried to choke back the tears. "I've tried to keep her warm, but I didn't know what else to do."

Dr. Johnson pulled the tarp back and got his first look at Betty's mangled body. He patted Jeff on the back, and told him, "Doesn't look like there was much else you could do."

He was about to ask about Lyndon, when he caught sight of their pickup. *At least he didn't suffer,* the doc thought to himself.

After Dr. Johnson gave Betty a quick examination, he stabilized her neck with a collar, and motioned to Manny. "Help me slide her onto the stretcher."

When Manny had secured her to the stretcher, Dr. Johnson, told them, "Let's get her in the ambulance. I know the conditions suck, but we need to get her to the hospital as fast as you can," he called to Tim.

Tim flipped on the lights and siren, and hauled ass. They'd only gone a couple of miles when Dr. Johnson yelled, "You'd better pull over and park. I've got to deliver the baby."

"Here?"

"I'm afraid so. Betty's dying, and it's the only chance the baby has."

"Manny, get the kit ready, and I'll cut her clothes off."

It didn't take long to do the C-section, but Betty died as he was removing the baby boy.

"Damn it, she's gone."

"How's the baby?" Manny asked.

"He'll be fine, but this really sucks. Would you mind recording the time? I'll need it for the death certificate."

As Manny noted the date and time (October 28, 2028, at 6 p.m.), he thought about how bittersweet the poor little boy's birthday was going to be.

Dr. Johnson clipped the cord and wrapped the newborn in the warmest blanket they had, before he told Tim, "You can get going, but there's no need to hurry."

When they reached the hospital, Betty's OB/GYN was waiting. "What the hell happened out there?" Dr. Winslow demanded.

"Lyndon and Betty were in a horrible wreck, and they're both dead," Dr. Johnson explained.

"Oh God. What about the baby?"

"I managed to save him."

"Good work, but what a tragedy. They were so looking forward to raising John David."

"They'd already named him?"

"As soon as they found out it was a boy."

"What's going to happen to him?" Dr. Johnson asked.

"It's hard to say. Neither of them had any living relatives, so I guess it'll be up to the state."

CHAPTER 2

When they discharged John David, the Oklahoma Child Protection Services sent him to live with an old couple who were willing to serve as foster parents.

Leroy and Emma Bolton were already in their sixties when they took John David in. They were good honest people, but Leroy was a hard man, and never paid much attention to the boy.

John David's life had been uneventful until he started school. On his first day, some of the older boys had started picking on him.

Leroy was in the front yard cutting the grass, when he saw John David come running up, with the bullies hot on his trail. When the boys saw Leroy, they quickly turned and ran the other way.

Leroy grabbed John David by the arm and growled, "Were you running from them boys?"

"Yes, sir, I was. I was afraid they were going to beat me up."

Leroy never said a word as he took off his belt and beat John David bloody. When he finished, he turned him around and warned, "Boy, don't let me ever see you run from anyone again."

Leroy expected John David to cry and run into the

house to Emma, but to his surprise, John David looked him in the eye, and said, "Yes, sir! I understand."

John David had nightmares of what the next day might bring, but he never said a word about it when Emma handed him his lunch and sent him out the door.

After school, John David was sneaking down the alleys, hoping the boys wouldn't see him.

Just when he thought he had it made, they found him.

There were six of them, and they were all older and bigger than he was. He knew he could outrun them, but there was no way he was going to take another beating.

His heart was racing madly as he looked around for something to defend himself. He was about to give up and make a run for it, when he spotted a pile of tree limbs. He could hear them shouting threats at him as they grew closer, but he was surprisingly calm as he picked up a branch, stomped on it to break it down to size, and turned to face them. When the gang of boys reached him, they started laughing and taunting him, as they circled around him menacingly.

They were really enjoying themselves until John David let out a bloodcurdling scream, and started swinging his homemade club like a broadsword. His attack took them by surprise, and before long they were running away, bloodied and bawling like babies.

John David was trembling as he watched them run for it, but it wasn't from fear. He didn't realize what it was at the time, but he'd grow to love the feeling of an adrenaline rush.

Once he was sure they were gone, he threw the bloody stick down, and went on home. When he walked up the driveway, Leroy and Emma were outside working in her flower beds.

"How was school, dear?" Emma asked.

"Fine," he lied. Hoping she couldn't see that he was still trembling, he asked, "Do you have any chores for me?"

"Not today, but I do have some fresh-baked cookies on the kitchen table. Just don't eat too many, it'll spoil your supper."

"Ha, nothing could spoil that boy's appetite," Leroy grumbled. "He eats like a horse."

Emma looked at him and shook her head. She loved him dearly, but his time in the military had soured his outlook on life. He'd spent most of his career leading a Black Ops team, and he was a changed man by the time he'd retired. He'd never been willing to discuss it, but occasionally he would talk in his sleep, and she would catch a glimpse of the horrors he'd experienced. She'd often thought of leaving him, but after all those years, it was just too much trouble. She wished she could do a better job of protecting the boy, but she knew Leroy would never tolerate anything but what he viewed as proper behavior.

John David went inside, and thirty minutes later, the six boys' mothers showed up in front of their house. When he saw them stop and start getting out of their SUVs, Leroy stood up and took off his gloves. As he walked toward them he grumbled, "I wonder what the hell they want." He'd only gotten halfway there when one of the mothers started screaming at him.

"I want you to do something with that juvenile delinquent you've taken in," Rose Parker screamed at him.

"You need to calm down," Leroy advised.

"We will not, he attacked our boys for no reason," Betsy Jenkins declared.

"He did, did he? Well, let me tell you this. It was probably your damn kids that chased him home from school yesterday, and I gave him a real thrashing for running from them. I told him never to run from anyone ever again, so I guess you can blame me for your brats getting what was coming to them."

One of the other women was starting in on him, when

he cut her off, and said, "Look, if you don't like it, you can tell your husbands to come back down here, and I'll kick their asses too. Now get the hell out of here. I've got more important things to do than stand here jawing with you."

John David had heard the commotion, and was watching from his bedroom window. When the mothers left, he'd expected Leroy to come in and beat him again, but Leroy went back to helping Emma.

Leroy didn't mention it until they sat down for dinner. "How many of them were there?" Leroy asked.

"Six."

"Classmates of yours?"

"No, sir, they're older than me."

"You listened. That's good."

They never discussed it again, but from that day forward Leroy treated him differently. Not that he was any easier on him; in fact, he seemed to expect even more.

The next Saturday afternoon, the bullies' families got together for a barbecue at the Parkers' house. Rose Parker and the rest of the women were drinking screwdrivers, while the men were in the backyard waiting to cook the steaks.

"I still can't believe the way that old fart talked to us," Rose Parker complained.

"Me either," Betsy Jenkins agreed. I told Billy what he said, but he blew me off."

"Same here," Genevieve Fisher chimed in.

When Rose had finished preparing the steaks, she took them to the backyard. The men were laughing and swapping tall tales as they swilled beer after beer.

"Here are your steaks," she told her husband, Jeff. "Instead of sitting out here getting shit-faced, you losers should be jumping on old man Bolton's ass for talking to your wives the way he did."

"It wasn't that big of a deal," Jeff told her.

"No big deal? Your sons got beat all to hell, and he as much as called you all cowards."

"He did what?" Billy Jenkins asked.

"He told us to get the hell out of there, and that if we didn't like it, we should send you all over there, and he'd kick your asses as well."

"Well, that's crap. If that gets around, we're going to look like complete dumb-asses."

"Maybe we should go over and have a talk with the cantankerous old bastard," Jeff Parker challenged.

"Let's do it," Billy agreed. "The girls can cook the steaks while we're gone."

They all grabbed a couple of beers, and piled into Jeff's SUV. When they got to Leroy's house they swaggered up on the porch and knocked loudly.

"Can I help you?" Emma Bolton asked, a little concerned to find six obnoxious drunks on her front porch.

"Where's your old man?" Jeff demanded.

"Leroy and the boy went to the grocery store for me. If you'd like to wait, they should be back in a little while."

"Let's go, boys. We can catch him there."

As they sped off, Emma wished Leroy had a cell phone so she could warn him.

The grocery store was only a couple of blocks away, and when Leroy and John David came out, they were waiting by his old car.

"What's up, boys?" Leroy asked.

"We need an apology out of you, or we're going to teach you and that snot-nosed kid of yours some manners," Jeff said.

"You boys look like you've been drinking. You'd be better off to get back in your car and go on home."

"Piss off, old man," Billy Jenkins challenged. "You're not talking to our wives now, and you and that juvenile delinquent need to learn some manners."

One of the bag boys had seen the fight about to start,

and had run back inside the store. "Jeff Parker and some of his buddies are starting shit with Leroy," he told the store manager.

"Oh hell, they've got no idea what they're getting into," Marvin Meyers responded. "Call nine-one-one."

When Marvin ran outside to see if he could break it up, most of the people in the checkout lines followed.

"I'm only going to ask you one more time," Leroy warned the six men. "Get back in your car, and get the hell out of here."

"The hell we will," Jeff screamed, as he took a swing at Leroy.

Leroy seized Jeff's right arm and flipped him into the side of the car. When the rest of them saw Jeff hit the vehicle, they made their move.

"Boy, get back out of the way," Leroy ordered.

Marvin was still a hundred feet away when Leroy pitched Jeff. "Shit, too late," he commented, as he stopped to watch.

John David had moved to the other side of the car, and he watched in amazement as Leroy spun and kicked the next closest one in the balls.

"You old bastard," Billy Jenkins screamed as he made his move on Leroy.

Leroy slammed him to the ground, and drove his fist into the center of his chest.

The fight was over in less than three minutes, and the six men were sprawled across the parking lot. Two were out cold, and the rest were screaming in agony from their injuries.

"You all right, Leroy?" Marvin Meyers asked as he walked over.

"No problems here, but you might want to call the ambulance for these assholes." Leroy looked over at John David. "Load the groceries, and get in the car."

"Yes, sir," was all John David could say.

After John David loaded the groceries, he sat in the front seat, reliving how easily Leroy had handled six men half his age.

It was a small town, so it only took a few minutes for the EMTs and the police to arrive. Chief Long stopped to talk with a couple of the bystanders, before he walked over to where the EMTs were treating the injured men, and demanded, "What the hell were you drunken assholes up to this time?"

"The old man jumped us," Jeff Parker said.

"That's bullshit," one of the bag boys yelled out. "They were out here waiting on him, and Mr. Parker took the first swing."

"You need to shut your mouth," Jeff threatened.

"No, you need to shut up," Chief Long advised.

By then the town's two patrol officers had shown up, so the chief told them, "Get all the witnesses' statements, while I visit with Leroy."

An hour later, they'd taken the six men to the hospital, and Chief Long had finished comparing notes with his men.

"Leroy, I'm sorry this took so long. If you wouldn't mind following me back to the station, we'll get the assault charges filed, and get Judge Blackburn to slap a protection order on their asses."

"No need, I won't be pressing charges, and I don't need a restraining order."

"Why not? It's an open-and-shut case."

"I don't think they'll be bothering me again."

The chief chuckled. "I'll bet that's right. You got them good."

By nightfall, the stories of the brawl had spread over the entire county, adding to Leroy's reputation as a war hero, and someone you didn't want to mess with.

It doesn't matter if you lose the fight, you can't ever tolerate a man disrespecting you. However, it goes both ways. You've got to show respect as well, and you've got to protect the ones who need it, and always stand up for what's right.

—LEROY BOLTON'S WORDS TO LIVE BY

PART 2

CHAPTER 1

The confrontation was soon forgotten, and John David didn't cross paths with the boys again until the sixth grade.

Frank was the oldest of the group, and a born bully. His dad was the town's banker, and like his dad, he thought he was better than everyone else.

The six of them cornered John David in the gym, and this time he never had a chance. They beat him so badly that one of the boys got scared. "Stop it. He's had enough," George Fisher screamed.

"Bullshit! This little prick is going to learn that he doesn't ever want to cross me again," Frank Parker declared.

John David was already unconscious, but Frank kept kicking him. When didn't react, he started stomping him, yelling, "Get up, you little bastard."

Luckily, George had the good sense to grab one of the coaches. When Coach Wesley saw Frank stomping JD's head, he ran over and grabbed him. "Stop it, you idiot, you're going to kill him."

When the coach got a look at JD, he told George, "Go and get Mrs. Robinson, and tell her to call nine-one-one before she comes."

When the paramedics arrived, the lead EMT took one look and said, "We need to get him to the hospital, right now!"

While they were loading him into the ambulance, the school nurse, Mrs. Robinson, called John David's parents.

"Mrs. Bolton, this is Sue Robinson, the school nurse. John David has been injured, and they're transporting him to the hospital."

"Was he in an accident?"

Mrs. Robinson hesitated before she answered, "No, I'm afraid he got hurt in some sort of fight. Coach Wesley might be able to tell you more, but right now you should hurry, because I think he's badly hurt."

"We need to get to the hospital," Emma said.

"What's wrong, has the boy been hurt?" Leroy asked.

"He's been in a fight, and the school nurse said he was in bad shape."

Coach Wesley had followed the ambulance to the hospital, and he met Emma and Leroy when they walked in.

"They've already taken him to surgery," Coach Wesley said.

"What's wrong with him?" Emma asked.

"I'm not sure. Dr. Henry only spent a few minutes with him before he rushed him into surgery. He said he would send a nurse out to give us an update when he knew more."

"What the hell happened?" Leroy asked.

When Coach Wesley saw the expression on Leroy's face, he knew he needed to choose his words very carefully.

"Now Leroy, before you go off half-cocked, it was just a fight among boys," he lied.

"Tell me about it, and you'd better not bullshit me."

A shiver ran down the coach's back as he realized he'd made a mistake lying to him.

"I don't know the whole story, but here's what I do

know: six boys jumped him in the gym, and when it got out of hand, George Fisher came and got me. When I got there, Frank Parker was stomping on his head."

"Six of them! That sounds like the same pack of cowardly little bastards he got into it with a few years back."

They'd been waiting anxiously for over four hours, when Dr. Henry finally came out to talk with them.

"He's in recovery. I think he's going to be fine, but he's going to be laid up for quite a while."

"We were terrified when you didn't send the nurse out," Emma told him.

"I'm terribly sorry, but his injuries were far more extensive than I'd first thought. He has a severe concussion, a broken collarbone, and all but three of his ribs are broken. He would have been out a long time ago, but his brain started swelling, and I had to put a drain in to relieve the pressure."

"Just a kids' fight, huh," Leroy muttered.

He'd said it very softly, but the coach could see the raging fury in his eyes.

The coach started to warn him not to overreact, but he decided to keep his mouth shut. "I'm glad he's going to be all right, and if there's anything I can do to help, please call on me," Coach Wesley offered as he was hurrying away.

"When can we see him?" Emma asked.

"You can go on in, but I've got to warn you, he looks bad," Dr. Henry cautioned.

When Leroy saw the boy, it was all he could do to keep from going berserk. John David's face was so swollen that they could barely tell where his eyes were supposed to be.

"Bastards."

When Leroy pulled the sheet down to get a look at the rest of him, he saw the incision where they'd put a pin in his collarbone, and his stomach was black and blue from where they'd stomped him. Emma gasped and almost fell down before Leroy grabbed her and helped her to one of the chairs.

"He's going to be all right, mother."

"How could they do that to him?"

"It can be a cruel world."

MOST OF JOHN David's wounds healed quickly, but it took him over nine weeks to get to where he didn't get dizzy when he tried to stand.

Frank's father had convinced the school board it was simply a fight that had gotten a little out of hand, and the boys got off with a few days of after-school detention.

"It's just not fair," Emma complained when they found out. "They beat him like a dog, and all they got was detention."

"I'm afraid it's the way the world works sometimes," Leroy told her.

"What if that damned banker's kid does it again?"

"He might, and that's why John David's not going back to school until he can take care of himself."

"What about school?"

"You're going to homeschool him for a while."

"I can do that, but he's going to miss out on so much."

"It won't be forever, so just do as I ask."

Leroy couldn't sleep that night, so he got up and went into the living room to think.

As he sat there in the dark, thinking through what he needed to do for the boy, he found himself wishing that he had enough humanity left in him to be a real father to him. He hadn't ever faced the truth before, but he was bitter about the whole military experience. The government had ruined his, and countless others' lives, in its ill-fated attempt to force democracy down everyone's throats.

Get over yourself, you old bastard, he thought to himself. *There's not one damn thing you can do about*

the past, but you can sure as hell get the boy better pre-
pared to deal with the coming shit storm than you were.

Leroy had a large shop in the backyard, and when
John David was well enough, he took him out back to
talk. When they walked in, John David was surprised to
see that Leroy had converted the shop into a gym.

"Boy, are you afraid to go back to school?"

John David hesitated before he replied. "Maybe a little."

"Good, fear is a natural thing. If a man tells you that
he's never afraid, he's either a liar, or someone who'll get
you killed. Walk with me, and I'll explain what we're
going to do."

"What's all this for?" John David asked.

"I'm going to teach you how to take care of yourself."

"I sure didn't do very well last time."

"Not your fault, but you won't have to worry about
those jerks for a while. Emma's going to homeschool you
until I'm sure that you're ready to face them."

Leroy was an expert in several disciplines of martial
arts, and had been a colonel in the Special Operations
Command, so he had an immense amount of knowledge
to share. Since he was just a kid, Leroy tried to bring
him along slowly. But John David absorbed the training
like a sponge, and before Leroy realized it, he'd taken his
training much further than he'd intended. There were
many days that John David went to bed with bumps and
bruises, but he never complained.

"Leroy, you need to take it easy on the boy," Emma
admonished, after she'd dressed a particularly nasty
contusion on John David's shoulder.

"Nonsense, the boy is doing fine. I would never hurt
him on purpose, but the training I'm giving him is pretty
intense."

"He's not a soldier, why are you being so hard on
him?"

"Life's hard, and besides that, he's damn good at it."

Leroy was doing what he thought was right, but if the OCPS had known what he was up to, they would have taken John David away.

When Leroy felt he was ready, he started teaching him about firearms. "This is a Sig Sauer .40 S&W," Leroy told him. "Pay attention, because I'm going to show you how to field strip it, and I'll expect you to be able to do it blindfolded."

"Why would I need to do that?"

"Because you never know what conditions you'll find yourself in. If you're going to carry a weapon, you've got to be completely familiar with it."

When John David understood the weapons and range safety, he started taking him out to shoot. There wasn't an actual shooting range in the county, so they used an old abandoned caliche pit outside of town.

"Take your time. You don't pull the trigger, you squeeze it," Leroy instructed.

From his very first shot, Leroy could tell John David had an eye for it. They went to shoot at least three times a week, and by the time John David was thirteen years old, he was a crack shot with a rifle and a pistol.

In between the firearms and martial arts training, Leroy would teach him strategy and combat tactics.

"What am I supposed to do with all of this?" John David asked.

"Someday you'll have to lead men, and you need to be ready."

"Lead men? Does that mean you think I should be a solider like you?"

"Not necessarily. God knows I hope you won't, but with where our country is going, I'm afraid you may need this to survive."

Leroy had his own set of rules when it came to life, and he did his best to impart them to John David. He had many rules, but he had a few overriding principles that he never stopped drilling into John David's head. He'd tell him, "Son, it doesn't matter if you lose the fight, just remember that you can't ever tolerate a man disrespecting you. However, it goes both ways. You've got to show respect as well, and you've got to protect the ones who need it, and always stand up for what's right. The other thing is, never tolerate a liar. It doesn't matter whether it's a man or a woman; if they lie to you, they're not worth the powder to blow them to hell."

Like all young people, his emotions often raged within him, but Leroy was trying to teach him how to compartmentalize them.

The few people he had contact with thought he was shy, and somewhat introverted, but it was just his way of dealing with the almost overwhelming loneliness he felt.

A few months before John David's fourteenth birthday, they were sparing like they did every day. Leroy had always held back so he didn't hurt the boy, but before he realized it, he was going all out.

Damn, he's gotten good, Leroy observed, and it was at that moment, he realized he'd screwed up. "Let's take a break," Leroy told him. "We need to talk." They got a bottle of water from the fridge, and sat down on the mat.

"John David, I've trained and worked with some of the finest soldiers that ever lived, and even though you're still a young man, you're the best I've ever seen."

"Thank you, sir."

"You're welcome, but therein lies the problem. I've been so focused on trying to get you ready to meet the physical side of life that I've forgotten you're still a boy."

Puzzled, all John David could say was, "I appreciate everything you've done for me."

"I know you do, and in a way I may have helped you. However, I've given you a set of skills that carry great responsibility." Leroy saw that John David didn't have a clue what he was talking about. "What I'm trying to say, is that you need to guard against overreacting, or you could really hurt someone."

"I understand."

God, I hope so, Leroy thought to himself. Leroy wasn't afraid of much of anything, but he was terrified he might have unintentionally ruined the boy's life.

They still worked out every day, but Leroy found himself spending more and more time just sitting and talking with John David. He'd taught him every physical skill he knew, but he was feeling a tremendous sense of urgency to try to get him mentally prepared.

THE WEATHER HAD just turned cold, and Emma had made a special dinner to celebrate John David's fourteenth birthday.

"Emma this looks wonderful," John David told her.

"Happy birthday, my boy," Leroy said, as he patted him on the back. "Emma tells me you're doing great with your studies, and I've never trained anyone who was better than you are right now."

Leroy only rarely gave him a compliment, so it meant a lot to him. "Thank you, sir."

For once they seemed like a normal family, as they enjoyed the fine dinner Emma had prepared. When they finished, Emma asked, "I've got your favorite dessert. Do you want it now, or do you want to wait for a while?"

"That's a silly question to ask a growing boy," Leroy said, with a rare chuckle.

When Emma walked back in from the kitchen, Leroy had an odd look on his face. "You feeling all right?" she asked, as she set the devil's food cake down.

Leroy struggled to answer, but all that came out was a horrible gurgling sound. After what seemed an eternity, he managed to lurch to his feet, but he lost his balance, and fell face-first into the cake.

"My God, what's wrong?" Emma screamed.

Leroy never answered, as he slid off the table.

"Call nine-one-one," Emma shouted frantically.

The hospital was just down the road, so the ambulance arrived within minutes.

"What's going on, Emma?" the paramedic asked, as he rushed through the front door.

"Leroy's had some sort of attack," Emma said with a sob.

Leroy was still alive when they first arrived, but after they'd worked on him for several minutes, the lead EMT told his partner, "Move back. His heart has stopped, and I'm going to try shocking him."

They worked on him for another twenty minutes, before the paramedic stood up and said, "I'm so sorry Emma, he's gone."

Emma couldn't respond before she broke down crying, and left the room.

"We'll take care of him, you'd better see to Emma."

"I will, and thanks for trying," John David told him.

IT TOOK ALL of her meager savings to bury Leroy, but Emma managed to get through it.

At first Emma tried to get by on just her Social Security checks, but she soon realized she needed a job. She hadn't worked in years, and she couldn't have picked a worse time, because the national unemployment had just hit 13 percent.

"President Montfort promised us more jobs, but they sure haven't shown up yet," Emma complained.

After several weeks, she finally managed to land a waitressing job down at the diner.

"John David, I'm sorry, but we're going to have to cut your studies back to half a day. I'm just too tired to do more."

"Nothing to be sorry about, and that will give me

more time to help out a little more. I'll take over the laundry and make sure the house stays clean."

"I hate that you have to do it, but thanks," was all she could say.

CHAPTER 2

Emma was working all the hours they'd let her have, and for a while they managed to eke out an existence. However, toward the end of the summer, she had to admit she couldn't handle it all.

"I'm so sorry, but I've got to send you back to public school," Emma said.

"It's all right, I'll get by," John David assured her.

When the new school year started, John David enrolled in high school, but they made him take a series of tests before they would let him start classes.

"Good work, I've never had anyone ace the achievement test," Mr. Campbell, the freshman math teacher, remarked.

"You're Leroy and Emma's boy, aren't you?"

"Yes, sir, although Leroy is dead."

"I'm so sorry, I knew that. Emma's done a fine job of homeschooling you. I was going to offer to tutor you, but you won't be needing it."

That afternoon, the teachers were sitting in the lounge, discussing the first day back at school. "I had the strangest thing happen today," Mr. Campbell commented. "The Drury kid aced the state achievement test. I've never had anyone do that. Hell, I couldn't do it."

"He did the same thing in my science class," Mrs. Rosewood chimed in. "I'm kind of ashamed of myself," she continued. "I accused him of cheating, and when he denied it, I had him take the graduating seniors' exit exam. I sat there while he took it, and he aced it as well. I apologized, but he didn't seem to care."

John David had continued the daily training regimen Leroy had taught him, but he needed more.

"Emma, would it be all right if I tried out for football?" John David asked as they were eating dinner.

She didn't want him getting hurt, but she knew he needed some sort of male role model, and an outlet for his seemingly endless supply of energy.

"I suppose so, dear, but you'll still have to take care of your chores. I'm going to need your help more than ever, now that I've got a part-time job down at the drugstore."

"No problem, but I hate that you're having to work two jobs. If you'd let me, I could get a part-time job."

"No, sir, we'll get by somehow. You need to concentrate on your schooling."

The next day, John David showed up in the locker room to see if the coach would let him try out. The team was already out on the practice field, but he found the head coach in his office, finishing up some paperwork.

"Sir, my name is John David Drury, and I'd like to try out for the team."

"What grade are you in, and what position do you play?" Coach Driscoll asked.

"I'm a freshman, but I don't know which position, because I've never played football."

Great, another loser that I've got to waste my time with, he thought to himself. However, as he looked the boy over, he liked what he saw. He was just a freshman, but he looked like he would go to at least two hundred, and by the looks of his arms and neck, he was in great shape.

"Get with the manager, and he'll get you fixed up with some gear. When you get suited up, come on out, and I'll try to decide what to do with you."

When John David came trotting onto the field, the coach thought, *I like the way that kid moves.*

"Douglas, get over here," Coach Driscoll yelled to his senior tailback.

Bryan Douglas was the fastest man on the squad, but he liked to loaf in practice, so the coach decided to kill two birds with one stone.

"You two line up on the goal line. Douglas, you lazy dog, he'd better not beat you."

When the coach blew the whistle, John David was slow to respond, and Douglas had him by five yards in the first twenty.

"Doesn't look like a running back," the coach commented to his assistant, Jerry Flood.

"Maybe not, but he's catching Douglas."

By the fifty-yard line they were neck and neck. Douglas tried to pick up his pace, but John David cruised by him, and beat him by seven yards.

"Damn he's fast," Coach Driscoll remarked.

The coach could see he had raw talent, but he didn't know anything about the game.

"I need this kid," Coach Driscoll declared. "I'm putting you in charge of teaching him the fundamentals, and the playbook."

"Why me?" Coach Flood whined.

"Because I told you to, and if it means staying late, you'd better do it. I need you to get him ready quickly, because we've got some tough games coming up, and we're short of running backs."

He whined about it, but Coach Flood stayed after

practice to mentor John David. At first he'd thought it was a complete waste of time, but by the third week, he'd made tremendous progress.

"You're not going to believe this, but there's not much else I can teach him. I've never seen anyone pick up the game quicker. You show him once, and he's got it. Hell, his techniques are as good as anyone we have," Coach Flood gushed. "I wouldn't be afraid to play him right now."

"Are you just saying that to get out of staying late?" Coach Driscoll asked.

"Nope, he's ready."

After practice, Coach Driscoll called John David over.

"Son, I'm going to let you suit up tomorrow night."

John David was so excited that "thanks" was all he could say.

"THE COACH IS letting me suit up," JD told Emma.

"That's wonderful, dear, but you be careful."

"Oh, I won't get to play."

They had suffered a rash of injuries, and the local newspaper had made them huge underdogs. However, on the second play of the game, it looked like their luck was finally changing, when Bryan Douglas broke free on a sweep. He had a clear path to the end zone, but as he crossed the forty-yard line, he stepped wrong. When he dropped to the turf, they could hear his screams all the way across the field.

"What the hell," Coach Flood screamed.

"Damn it, I think he's blown out his knee," Coach Driscoll exclaimed, as he sprinted across the field.

"Stay down son," Coach Driscoll ordered.

After the team doctor made a quick check, he told them, "I'll have to do an MRI, but I think he's torn his ACL and his MCL."

Once they had Bryan in the ambulance, Coach Driscoll yelled, "All right, Drury, you're in."

His first two carries were unremarkable, as he tried to get over his jitters, but on his third try, he broke through off tackle, and sprinted toward the corner of the end zone. The safety was a three-time all-state senior, and he had the angle on John David. Coach Driscoll didn't think John David even saw him, but when the safety caught him at the three-yard line, John David made a cut directly into him, and ran him over.

"My God, did you see that?" Coach Flood screamed. "I told you the kid could play."

JD went on to score three more touchdowns that night, and by the next morning, the video of him running over the safety was all over the Internet.

Even though it was several games into the season when he first got to play, John David made the all-district team. When football season ended he went out for basketball, and the results were just as spectacular.

Jeb Turner, Emma's boss down at the diner, was a huge sports fan, and he followed JD's every move.

"JD ended up averaging twenty-one points a game," Jeb gloated. "That's never been done by a freshman. I hope you know how special an athlete he is."

"I don't know much about sports, but he's a fine young man," Emma responded.

"What's he going to run in track?"

"I don't think he's going out for track. He's looking for a part-time job to help out."

"He's got to go out, we need him. How about I give you some more hours, and double your pay?"

"That would definitely help."

Jeb's faith in John David had been rewarded, when he'd dominated the state track meet in the 100, 200, and the 400 meter sprints, and led them to the team state track title.

His sophomore year had been more of the same, but a couple of weeks before the end of the spring semester, he had another run-in with Frank Parker.

John David was shooting baskets in the gym, when Frank and his cronies came sneaking through, on their way to cut class.

"Look at the big bad jock," Frank remarked.

Frank was more than a little envious of John David, because he was a straight-A, honor society student, and a local sports hero.

Frank made a couple more rude comments, and when John David didn't pay him any attention, he yelled, "Hey dip-shit, I'm talking to you."

Frank was a big boy at six foot five, and two hundred and seventy pounds. He was a bully by nature, but un-like most bullies, he was damned tough, and he loved terrorizing people.

"Boys, should I teach him another lesson?" Frank asked, thinking his boys would egg him on like they always did.

"You're on your own with that," George Fisher told him. "He ain't done nothing to us. Let's go before one of the teachers catches us cutting class again."

None of his little rat pack had ever had balls enough to buck him before, and he didn't like it.

As John David went up to tip in a missed shot, Frank jumped up and slapped the ball away.

"You'd better pay attention when I talk to you, or I'm gonna stomp your ass again," Frank blustered.

John David looked him in the eye, and hit him with a stiff left jab, followed by a vicious right cross, which knocked him back on his ass.

Pissed at being embarrassed in front of his boys, Frank jumped up. "You're going to regret that."

When Frank rushed him, John David slid to the side, and hip tossed him across the gym floor.

Frank couldn't believe how easily John David was handling him, but he got up and came at him again. As they continued tussling, one of the boys ran to spread the word about the fight.

John David knew he could end it whenever he wanted, but he was enjoying toying with him.

After almost twenty minutes, the big man was huffing and puffing, as he struggled to get up off of the floor.

By then there were over a hundred kids, and a couple of the coaches, watching the fight. No one tried to stop it, because they were all enjoying seeing Frank get his ass kicked.

John David wasn't in a hurry to end it, but he could see Frank wasn't going to last much longer. When he dropped him with another vicious right hand, it took Frank several seconds to get up.

Exhausted, he put his hands on his knees to try to catch his breath.

"Not such a big man now," one of the bystanders taunted.

When Frank looked up to see who it was, he realized how many people were watching. Almost insane with embarrassment, he grabbed Jimmy Little, and demanded, "Gimme your knife, you little prick."

Jimmy pulled a switchblade out of his boot, and Frank grabbed it.

"Don't be stupid, Frank," George Fisher said.

When Coach Flood saw the knife, he started running toward them, and screamed, "All right, break it up before someone really gets hurt."

Frank let out low guttural sound and charged John David.

I've had enough of this asshole, John David decided. He stood his ground until Frank was close, and then he spun on one leg and caught him with a powerful round-house kick to the side of the head. The savage blow knocked Frank out, and when he hit the floor, sweat and blood splattered in all directions.

The coach kicked the knife out of Frank's hand and yelled, "Some of you men get over here and help me hold him down."

Coach Flood put his knee in Frank's chest, but when he saw he was out cold, he called, "Never mind. I don't think the big dumb asshole's going anywhere. Will one of you run and get the school nurse?"

Disgusted, George Fisher turned to the rest of their little gang and said, "I don't know about the rest of you, but I'm done with his bullshit."

They all nodded in agreement, and started walking away.

"John David, why don't you hit the showers, and we'll talk about this later," Coach Flood instructed.

The nurse used some smelling salts to revive Frank, and after she'd checked him out, she said, "He's all right, he just got his bell rung."

She handed Frank an ice pack and instructed, "Hold that against your head for at least thirty minutes."

They helped him up, but he was unsteady on his feet. Coach Flood took him by the arm to steady him. "Come with me."

Coach Flood didn't know what to expect when he escorted Frank into the principal's office. He'd tried to discipline Frank several times over the years, but his dad had a great deal of clout in their little town, and the principal had always been reluctant to follow through with it.

"Take a seat, Mr. Parker," the principal ordered.

"I didn't do anything, that maniac attacked me. I think he hit me with a two-by-four or something,"

Frank Parker whined, as he pressed the ice pack against his head.

"Nice try, asshole," Coach Flood interjected. "I saw the whole thing, and you were the one who started it, and when you got your ass kicked, you pulled a knife on him."

Principal Estep had Frank's records open in front of him. "I see you just had a birthday; tough luck for you. You're old enough to be tried as an adult."

"So what, my father isn't going to put up with any crap out of you," Frank said.

"We'll see about that. I'm tired of your bullshit, so we're going to press charges on you, and your father isn't going to be able to buy your way out of it this time."

CHAPTER 3

Like all boys his age, John David had become interested in the opposite sex. However, unlike most boys, John David only had one girlfriend, Susan Roberts.

By the end of their sophomore year they were inseparable, and most of the town believed they'd get married.

The popular parking spot for young lovers was down by the lake, and John David and Susan were no exception. One Saturday night, they were making out in the front seat of her mother's car. The windows were completely steamed over, and when they came up for air John David told her, "I love you more than life itself."

"You know I feel the same way," she said as she ran her hand along his thigh up to his crotch.

"Are you sure?" he asked breathlessly.

"Oh yes," she said, as she started unbuttoning her dress.

Since they both wanted to go on to college before they got married, they were very careful not to get her pregnant, but once they got started, they went at it like bunnies.

Several months later Emma sat John David down to talk.

"I know I should have had this talk with you a long

time ago, but we need to have the talk. If you know what I mean?" Emma asked nervously.

"It's all right. I'm fine. We've had sex education in school."

"Are you sure?"

"No problem, everything's fine."

Since he was a good-looking kid, and a star athlete, several of the other girls hit on him, but he loved Susan more than life itself. So no matter how hard they flirted, he never showed any interest.

Money was still scarce, so the summer before JD's junior year he got a job on the wheat harvest. The night before he had to leave, John David and Susan were lying on a blanket, talking.

"I hate being gone all summer, but we really need the money."

"I hate it worse than you," Susan told him. "You'd better call me as often as you can."

"You'd better stay away from those other boys."

"Hey, you're my sweetie, and nothing could ever change the way I feel about you. I'm sure going to miss nights like this." She giggled, and started stripping.

John David's crew started in south Texas, and followed the wheat harvest as it moved north. They worked long hours, so the summer passed quickly for John David. He wrote to Susan religiously, and he called her every chance he got, but it wasn't enough for either one of them.

Finally the harvest was winding down, and they were supposed to be done cutting in a couple of weeks.

"Can I take the truck to town?" JD asked. "I want to give Susan a call and let her know when we're heading back."

"Sure, and while you're there, pick up some oil," Charlie Thompson told him.

* * *

"ANYTHING ELSE WE can do for you?" Rob Tompkins, the auto parts manager asked.

"No, that's everything. Is there a pay phone anywhere close by?" JD asked.

"Collect call?"

"Yeah why?"

"You can use the phone in the office, as long as it's collect."

"I promise it is, and thanks."

"WE'RE SCHEDULED TO cut our last field in ten days, so if we don't break down, we should be pulling in to town on August seventh," JD told Susan.

"Oh goody. I've missed you so much, and I can't wait to see you again," Susan said.

"Not as much as me, and seeing you isn't all I missed."

"Don't worry, I'll take care of that."

"Love you, but I'd better be getting back, we're supposed to hit it pretty early."

"Love you too," she responded.

The next morning they were up before the sun, and as they were about to pull back into the field, Travis West, the owner, drove up.

"Hi, boys, I thought I'd come by and give you a hand."

"I wasn't expecting you until next week," Charlie said as they shook hands.

"I know, but I flew up to talk with my uncle, so I thought I'd swing by."

That afternoon the temperature set a new record, and they could see the supercell thunderstorms building in the distance.

"Damn, those clouds look bad," Charlie commented.

"They sure do, and it looks like they're headed our way," Travis observed. "Let's get the equipment out of the field."

They'd just gotten everything onto the pavement, when the storm swept over them.

"Shit, this is the worst I've seen," Charlie exclaimed when a softball-sized hailstone shattered the windshield.

"I just hope there's not a tornado in this mess," Travis shouted so he could be heard above the noise.

Thankfully the ferocious storm blew through quickly, and they got out to survey the damage.

"My God, there's nothing left." Charlie gasped as he surveyed the flattened field.

"It didn't do us any favors either," Travis observed, as he looked the equipment over. "I'd be surprised if they don't total everything."

After they discussed it with the farmer, Travis told Charlie, "Well, that's a hell of a way to end it, but we're done for this year."

They'd gotten the local glass place to come out and install new windshields, and when they finished, they started loading the combines.

"It looks like you've got everything under control, so I'm going on back," Travis told Charlie.

Two-a-day football practices were due to start, and being a huge fan, Travis didn't want JD to miss any practice.

"John David, would you like to ride back with me?" Travis asked.

John David had never flown before, but he jumped at the chance to get back early. By the time they landed it was almost 7 p.m., and John David rushed home to get cleaned up. After he'd showered, he visited with Emma for a few minutes, before he asked, "Can I use the car?"

Emma could see how antsy he was to see Susan.

"Sure, but take it easy, it needs new tires."

Susan's house was only a few blocks away, and as he knocked on her door, he was growing more excited by the second.

"I'm sorry, she's not home," Susan's mom explained. "Betty and some of the girls came by, and I think they all went to the drive-in."

He stopped at the gate to pay, and then he drove up and down the rows until he spotted Betty's car. He parked beside her and got out. When he didn't see Susan, he asked Betty, "Is Susan at the concession stand?"

Betty got that deer-in-the-headlights look, before she stammered, "John David! Yes, she just left. I'll run over and let her know you're back."

"Don't bother, I'd rather surprise her."

"No really, let me go and get her for you."

JD thought she was acting strangely, but then again, he'd never really understood girls. "I got it."

He hadn't gotten very far when he saw Betty hurrying down the back row of cars, toward Larry Jameson's car. Larry was his best friend, so he decided to go over and say hi. When Betty saw him coming, she turned back to cut him off.

"Please give her a chance to explain, and don't do anything stupid. After all, you were gone all summer."

He was about to ask what the hell she was talking about, when he saw Susan in a passionate embrace with Larry.

"Please stop," Betty pleaded, before John David picked her up and set her aside.

When Larry heard the commotion, he looked up, and spotted John David coming toward them.

"Oh shit," Larry said as he hurriedly locked the doors. He paused to take a couple of deep breaths before he got out to face John David.

Before John David even realized what he was doing, he'd smashed through the window with his elbow, and smacked Larry in the side of the head.

"Please stop," Susan pleaded.

If John David heard her, it didn't slow him down, as he pulled Larry through the shattered window and started punching him in the head. He'd hit him several times before Susan grabbed his arm and screamed, "You've got to stop."

Thinking that someone was butting in, John David spun around to knock the crap out of them, when he realized who it was. He froze, and stood there shaking from the adrenaline coursing through his body. Susan didn't know what to expect next, but she could see the agony in his eyes. After several seconds, he dropped Larry's limp bloody body, and walked away without a word.

Luckily, Larry hadn't been seriously injured, and even though his parents pushed him to, he'd refused to press charges. School started the next week, and John David was still trying get his emotions back under control. He was crushed by Larry, and Susan's betrayal, but his response had terrified him. Susan tried everything she could think of, but John David never spoke with her again.

Their first football game of the year was in two days, and they were trying to put the finishing touches on their offense. Larry had been trying desperately to mend his relationship with John David, but he wasn't getting anywhere. Frustrated by John David's unwillingness to even discuss it, Larry tried to force the issue.

"Look, asshole, you need to grow up," Larry exclaimed. "Neither of us intended to hurt you, it just happened." When John David didn't answer, he tried a more direct approach. He grabbed John David by the face mask, put his face up next to his, and yelled, "How long are you going to stay mad at me? You need to get over it, and remember that I'm your best friend."

John David's blow to the side of Larry's helmet was so vicious that it fractured his helmet, and knocked him out cold. John David looked down at what had once been his best friend, took off his helmet, dropped it on the turf, and walked away. Coach Driscoll ran after him, while Coach Flood checked on Larry.

"Son, you get back here," Coach Driscoll screamed. "You can't be doing shit like that." John David just kept walking. The coach grabbed him by the shoulder and spun him around. "I'm talking to you, boy," he screamed.

The coach wasn't the sort of man who took any crap from anyone, but when he saw the cold fury in John David's eyes, he turned him loose and stepped back, as a shiver ran down his spine. The coach had intended to kick him off the team the next day, but John David never showed up again.

Without athletics to anchor his life, John David struggled to get his life under control. He still went to school, but other than responding to a teacher's direct questions, he never spoke to any of his classmates again.

A couple of weeks later, Emma showed up to work, and Jeb Turner waved her back to his office.

"Don't bother to clock in."

"What's up, Jeb?"

"Emma, I'm very sorry, but I have to let you go."

She thought she was going to pass out from the shock, but she managed to stammer, "Why? I thought you were pleased with my work."

"It's not that, I'm paying you way too much money for what you do, and my niece needs a job."

"I'd take a pay cut," she offered.

"I'm sorry, but my mind's made up. Here's your last check, and feel free to use me as a reference."

The drive home was a blur, as she tried to figure out how they were going to survive.

"Did you forget something?" John David asked when she returned.

"No, I got fired," she said with a sob.

John David put his arm around her. "Don't worry, we'll figure out something."

Emma fixed a cup of hot tea, and sat down to talk it over. "I hate to ask, but do you think you could find a part-time job to help out?"

Relieved to have something else to focus on, John David told her, "Of course. You should have let me get one a long time ago. Maybe it will keep my mind off of how bad I've screwed up."

"I've got faith in you, you'll figure it out. Just remember, if your grades start suffering, you'll have to quit."

"Deal. I won't let you down again."

CHAPTER 4

Before the incident with Larry Jameson, John David could have gotten a job anywhere.

After several weeks of futility, he finally managed to get an interview down at the pool hall. Rex Allen, the owner, knew his reputation, but he'd decided to give him a job anyway. Partly because he'd known Leroy, and partly because his reputation wasn't all that good either.

"OK, JD, the job's yours. It pays ten dollars an hour, and you can shoot all the pool you want for free," Rex told him.

"I've never played, but thanks."

At first Rex thought he was just another punk kid, but he soon realized JD, as he liked to call him, was a hard worker, and would do anything he asked. At one time Rex had been a pool shark, and one of the better players on the unofficial pro circuit, but his eyesight had gone bad and he'd had to quit.

One day after John David had finished for the day, Rex walked over and said, "Rack them up and I'll teach you how to play."

Rex enjoyed the challenge of teaching him how to play, and they got into the habit of shooting a few games every day after work.

He wasn't the shooter he once was, but Rex was still way better than most. At first he'd beaten JD easily, but within a few months he could only occasionally beat the boy. Just for grins, he had Bud Chambers, one of his old running mates, drop by to see how JD would match up. Bud stomped him the first couple of games, but once JD got over being nervous, he started winning.

They'd been playing for several hours when Bud came over and sat down beside Rex. "Sorry, but this kid's too damn good for me. How old is he anyway?"

"Sixteen, I think, why?"

"Sixteen! Have you thought about taking him out on the circuit?"

Rex grinned. "Why do you think I had you drop by? I'd appreciate it if you didn't say anything about the boy."

"No problem, but let me know the first time he plays, so I can get some money down."

A couple of weeks later, Rex set up a game in Fort Worth, to try their hand with the big boys.

Slick Willy, as he liked to be called, was an arrogant son of a bitch, but Rex knew if JD could hold his own with him, he had the chops to play with anyone. They met at a strip club on the outskirts of town that occasionally hosted the big-money shooters. It only had four tables, in a private section of the club, but they were of impeccable quality.

When they walked in, Slick Willy asked, "Who's the kid?"

"This is JD."

"Where's your shooter?"

"You're looking at him."

"Are you shitting me? You want me to shoot this snot-nosed kid?"

When Rex saw the fire in JD's eyes, he put his hand on his shoulder. "I'm not joking, and I've got the money to prove it," Rex told him, as he opened his briefcase to show him the stacks of hundred-dollar bills. "It was ten grand a game, right?"

"You're backing the kid?"

"Yes, I am."

Slick Willy shrugged. "It's your money, so let's get to it."

The game was nine-ball, and as they lagged for the break, Rex was starting to get nervous. He'd only been able to scrape up three hundred thousand dollars, and he knew it could be gone quickly if the kid wasn't on his game.

The soft click of their pool cues was followed by Slick Willy's exclamation, "Damn fine lag, kid. You break."

As Rex watched JD walk up to break, he hoped he wasn't pushing him too fast. He knew JD could play, but Slick Willy was a stone-cold gambler, and a master at disconcerting his opponents.

Rex expected JD to be nervous at first, but when he made the nine ball on the break, he thought they just might have a chance. As JD continued shooting, Willy was sitting in a chair to the right of the table. His expression never varied as he watched JD run rack after rack. He just sat there and smoked his cigar as he waited for his turn to shoot.

After JD had finished off the nineteenth rack, with a really difficult three rail bank shot, Rex watched in disbelief as Slick Willy took his cue apart and put it back in its case. He felt for the comforting weight of his .45 in the small of his back, but as he quickly surveyed the room, he knew they wouldn't stand a chance if things turned nasty. Instead, Slick Willy walked over to JD, held out his hand, and said, "Kid. You're too damn good for me; I'm a gambler not a fool."

They spent the rest of the summer playing around the tri-state area, and by fall, JD had won almost a million and a half dollars for Rex. Rex hadn't wanted JD worrying about the money during a game, so win, lose, or draw, he'd guaranteed JD three thousand dollars every time he played. JD would give Emma most of what he earned when they got back, and she never asked where he got the money.

JD was still a growing boy, and by the time he turned seventeen, he was six two and a rock-hard two hundred and twenty-five pounds. He'd continued honing the skills Leroy had taught him, but he always worked alone, so no one had any inkling of his prodigious abilities. As JD's reputation grew, it had become increasingly difficult for Rex to set up a game. Frustrated, Rex started reaching out to some of the well-heeled amateurs who thought they could play. After several phone calls, he'd managed to get a game with a rich oilman from Borger, Texas.

Big Bob Tower, as he liked to be called, wasn't nearly as good as he thought, but he had a buttload of money. Bob had a rather sordid reputation, so Rex arranged some additional security. When they arrived at the bar, the owner, Helen Gomez, met them in the parking lot. As they embraced, she whispered, "It's been too long."

They'd been an item when they were younger, and they'd stayed friends over the years. She knew him well, so as she stepped back, she told him, "I don't want any trouble, so leave your gun in the car."

"I've heard some bad stories about Bob."

"All true, but my guys know to keep an eye on Bob and his boys."

"OK, but I'm going to feel naked," Rex grumbled as he slid his .45 under the seat.

It was Saturday night so the place was packed. Word of the game had gotten around, so Helen had moved one of the pool tables to the center of the gigantic dance floor, so more people could watch.

"Take it easy on him at first," Rex instructed. "We don't want to scare him off."

JD walked over to shake Bob's hand. "I thought you'd be older," Bob commented.

"I get that a lot. What's your game?"

"Eight-ball freeze out," Bob declared confidently.

"Great, let's lag for the break."

For the first few games JD did his best to make it look like a match, but he soon got caught up in the flow of the game. As JD moved confidently around the table, making shot after shot, Big Bob was growing increasingly agitated.

Bob leaned over to one of his men and commented, "The little shit can play, but no snot-nosed kid is going to make a fool out of me.

"Let's double the stakes," Bob blustered, as JD started to break.

Rex knew better, but before he could stop him, JD responded, "No problem here."

JD was really feeling the flow, and even though Rex kept trying to get him to back off, Bob never had a chance. JD ran several racks in a row before he finally missed.

Bob was desperate to win a game. So after he'd made a good run, he purposely froze the cue ball behind his two remaining balls. "Gotcha now," he crowed.

Under the rules of eight-ball freeze out, you lose if you're shooting the eight ball, and either pocket scratch, or miss hitting it.

JD took a quick look at the leave, pointed to the right corner pocket, and called, "Eight ball in the corner."

"Bullshit, I'll bet you another twenty-five grand you don't make it," Bob challenged.

"You're on."

"Oh hell," Rex muttered.

The eight was frozen to the rail on the other end of

the table, and you could hear the buzz from the crowd as JD stepped up to take the seemingly impossible shot. Rex crossed his fingers and hoped for a miss.

JD played a four-rail bank shot, and when the cue ball came off the final rail, it gently cut the eight ball into the pocket he'd called. That put Bob down three hundred and fifty thousand dollars, but it was the crowd's screams of approval that pushed him over the edge. The money was no big thing to Bob, but he was furious at being embarrassed in front of his friends. He was madder than hell, but since JD was still a kid in his eyes, he decided he'd kick the crap out of Rex. When he went for Rex, JD stepped between them and hip tossed him. Stunned, it took Bob a few seconds to recover, and when he did, he growled, "You need to learn some manners, you little shit."

Bob Tower was a bear of a man, at six foot six and over three hundred pounds, and Rex was scared to death when Bob let out a bloodcurdling scream and charged.

"Where the hell are bouncers?" Rex muttered. His eyes darted around the room until he finally spotted them on the far side of the dance floor, trying to push their way through the crowd. "Never should have let her talk me out of my gun," he groused.

As Rex was panicking, JD made no attempt to get out of the way. He bounced on the balls of his feet a couple of times, and when Bob was close enough, he spun and hit him with a roundhouse kick to the head. The force of the blow stopped Bob dead in his tracks, and he let out a low moan as he dropped to the hardwood floor, out cold. Rex was stunned by the speed and ferocity of JD's attack, but Bob's sidekicks weren't. One of them pulled the biggest knife Rex had ever seen, and started toward JD.

"Look out, he's got a knife." Several of the onlookers screamed.

When the goon made a swipe at him with his bowie knife, JD slapped his arm away, and broke his right knee with a snap kick. The blow shattered the thug's knee, but he managed to stay on his feet, as he screamed obscenities at JD. When he didn't drop, JD's right arm snapped out in a blur. When his open palm shattered the man's nose, it exploded in a spray of blood. The thug screamed, cupped his nose, and fell to the floor, writhing in agony. Expecting the rest of them to jump him, JD turned to face them. However, the rest of Bob's henchmen didn't want any part of him.

"We don't want any more trouble. Just let us get Bob and Jeff, and we'll get the hell out of here."

"Do it."

It took four of them to pick up Bob, before they started pushing through the crowd to the front door. When Helen and her men finally managed to reach them, she told them, "Sorry, we got hung up."

Rex was about to chew her ass out, when she glanced at the door and warned, "You two had better get going. If I know Bob, they'll be back with guns." JD started putting his cue back in its case, and Helen prodded them again. "You should get going, and it'd be better if you go through the kitchen; I'll have my boys slow them up enough for you to get gone."

They had just made it to Rex's pickup truck, when Bob's men came running out. Rex almost panicked when he thought the truck wasn't going to start, but the engine finally roared to life. As they fishtailed out of the parking lot, they peppered Bob's men with gravel.

When they crossed the Canadian River bridge, JD glanced back. "I think they're coming after us."

"Not to worry, this old truck may look worn out, but it can move." Rex floored it, and the truck lunged forward when the super charger kicked in.

"Good God, you weren't kidding when you said this old piece of shit could get it," JD said, laughing.

Rex never slowed down as they blasted through Stinnett, and thirty minutes later they were back in Oklahoma.

"That was quite a ride," JD said as the pulled into town. "How come you never me told me it would run like that?"

"No reason, I just never thought about it. If you think that was something; you should see my Corvette."

"I've read about those, but Ford and GM were long gone by the time I was old enough to want a car."

"Let me check on a couple of things, and then we'll run out to the barn," Rex said.

The Quonset hut was filled with all sorts of junk.

"What is all this crap?" JD asked as they worked their way through the piles.

"Stuff, honestly I have no idea anymore, but my baby's back here," Rex said as he pointed to the tarp-covered vehicle. "Grab the other end, and help me uncover it. Be careful, don't let it scuff the paint."

They laid the tarp down, and Rex opened the hood to the cherry-red Corvette.

"It's a 2010 ZR1. It's got a 6.2 liter, 638-horsepower, L-59 supercharged V8, and right from the factory it had a better power-to-weight ratio than any of the high-dollar Ferraris, Lamborghinis, and Porsches," Rex explained with pride.

"How'd you come by a car like this?"

"In another life, I used to rebuild cars and resell them."

CHAPTER 5

After their run-in with Bob, Rex decided they'd better lay low, but he knew JD still needed to make some money.

Rex was definitely an entrepreneur, but he was no stickler for the law. Among his many endeavors, Rex was the area's biggest bootlegger. When he'd first started, he'd made the runs himself, but now he farmed out the driving.

JD didn't have a car, so Rex had Sam Blevins build him one. It was a late-model US Motors sedan, and it looked stock in every way, but it was far from it. It was powered by a turbo-charged 4.3 liter V6 engine that pumped out four hundred horses. It could easily hit one-sixty, but with the NOS (Nitrous Oxide System) it could top two hundred.

JD knew how to drive, but Rex spent weeks teaching him the ins and outs of how to stay alive running booze for a living. After several weeks of instruction, he capped his training off with lessons on how to execute a J turn, as well as the bootlegger's turn, in case they tried to jack his load.

"All right, I think you know enough not to get yourself killed," Rex declared. "I've programmed the GPS with the route I want you to follow. Just drop the stuff off, collect the money, and get back here."

While school was in session, Rex was paying him a hundred bucks a run, and letting him make three or four runs a week. When summer arrived, Rex had JD making a run, and sometimes two, a night.

"I've got a quick run down south for you, and when you get back we'll shoot a few games," Rex told JD.

"Love to. I haven't had a decent game in weeks."

The drop had gone off without a hitch, and on the way back he had the windows down to enjoy the cool night air. He was just loafing along at a hundred, when he spotted two sets of headlights coming up behind him. When they got close, one of them pulled out to pass him. He slowed down to let him go on by, but when the car was only a few car lengths ahead of him, it swerved back over into his lane. For a split second he thought it was just someone messing with him, but when he saw it decelerate, he knew something was up.

Rex had covered this type scenario, so he knew just what to do. He jerked his car to the left and hit the accelerator. His car leaped forward and when he rammed the blocker's car, it went into a violent spin and left the road. As he started pulling away from the other car, he saw several flashes of light in his mirror, and then his back glass exploded.

"Damn, I think they're shooting at me," JD exclaimed. He triggered his NOS system, and the violent acceleration pressed him back into his specially fitted bucket seat. By the time the NOS ran out, he was running 200 mph, and his pursuer's headlights had faded away into the night.

It was a little after 9 p.m. when he pulled into the dirt parking lot behind the pool hall, and Rex walked out to greet him. "What the hell happened to your car?" Rex asked when he saw his shattered back window.

"Two carloads of assholes tried to jump me on the way back. I spun the blocker, just like you taught me, but then the other one started shooting at me. What's going on Rex?"

"Sorry, I guess I should have mentioned it at the time, but I didn't think they were stupid enough to bother you. I had a call from our friend Bob the other night, and he wants a chance to get his money back."

"So let's play him again, but I still don't understand why his men were shooting at me."

"He thinks you cheap-shotted the last time, but who knows with Bob. He's about half crazy, but crazy or not, it's bullshit that his men were shooting at you. I'll give him a call and find out what he's up to."

When Bob answered, Rex lit into him. "You crazy bastard, what the hell are your men doing shooting at JD? I thought you were a man, not some sneaky back-stabber."

Before Bob could even answer, Rex continued. "Just keep quiet and let me finish. I don't give a shit if you've got all the money in the world. If you hurt that boy, there won't be anywhere in the world you can hide."

"He caught me with a cheap shot the last time, and I mean to have my revenge," Bob ranted.

"You silly bastard, you're the one who started the whole thing. So what do you want?"

"I'm not going to be satisfied until I kick his ass."

"You want to fight a seventeen-year-old kid? What the hell will that prove?"

"I'm sick and tired of everyone down here reminding me of how he kicked my ass. So I'm going to prove it was a fluke."

JD had been listening, and he told Rex, "Tell him I'll fight him anywhere, anytime."

Rex wanted to tell him to shut up and let him handle

it, but he knew what Leroy had beat into him. He knew JD wasn't going to let Bob run his mouth about him.

"All right, where do you want to hold this little revenge session?" Rex asked.

"We're going to hold it in the Borger event center, and I'm going to have it broadcast as a pay-per-view event on the local cable channel."

Big Bob still hadn't paid up from the pool match, so Rex asked, "What's in it for JD, and why should we trust you again, you welching bastard?"

"Double or nothing, and I'll put the money in an escrow account."

Rex thought to himself, *The arrogant bastard, I hope the kid kicks his ass.* He said, "OK, fine. Just let us know the date and time and we'll be there, but you'd better not pull anymore shit."

Bob had been one of the local badasses when he was a young man, and after he'd struck it rich in the oil field, he'd become obsessed with reaching an elite level in martial arts. He'd spent almost a year training at the Rilion Gracie training center in Curitiba, Brazil, where he'd blossomed into one of their best students. There'd been no doubt about his talent, but his volatile temper had done him in when he'd killed a fellow fighter over a woman and had to leave the country in a hurry.

WORD OF THE fight had spread quickly, and it was sold out in just a few days.

Normally the local police would have stepped in and stopped a fight between a grown man and a seventeen-year-old kid, but Bob had his thumb on the police.

JD hadn't told Emma what was going on, but she knew, because almost everyone in town had come by.

When fight day arrived, Rex and JD didn't talk too much on the way down. Rex was amazed at how calm he seemed to be. When they reached the event center, one of the security guards took them in the back way, so they wouldn't have to deal with the crowd. When JD started unpacking his gym bag, he found a note from Emma. He wasn't particularly sentimental, but he had to wipe the tears away after he finished reading it.

"What's wrong, did something happen?" Rex asked.

"Everything's fine, Emma just put a note in my bag, and I guess I had forgotten how much she loves me. Leroy never allowed us to show much emotion, but I always knew she was there for me."

As fight time drew near, Rex was becoming increasingly uncomfortable with the situation.

"Look, Bob just wants to show the world you got lucky. None of this is worth getting hurt over, so if it gets too rough, tap out."

"Don't worry about me, I can take care of myself."

"I know, but there's no telling what sort of crap Bob will pull."

Leroy had trained him well, and the calm determination Rex sensed was real. JD realized he could be seriously hurt, maybe even killed, but he truly believed in Leroy's overriding view of life and death. He used to tell him, "Boy, when it's your day to go, and God is ready to call you home, it don't matter where you are, or what you're doing, he's gonna take you. However, it works the other way as well. If it isn't your day, you're as safe as in your mother's arms. So don't waste a minute worrying about it, because there isn't one damn thing you can do about it."

A few minutes later the security guard stuck his head in and announced, "It's time."

As they made their way down the aisle to the ring, Rex exclaimed, "What the hell?" when he saw the chain-link fence enclosing the ring.

"Bob, what's this bullshit?" Rex asked.

"I don't want the little shit trying to get away."

"Let's go, JD, we're out of here," Rex told him, as he grabbed his arm.

JD shook his hand off. "Don't worry about it, let's just get it over with."

In an attempt to give the match a little credibility, Bob had hired a professional referee from one of the extreme fighting organizations. After the referee covered the rules, they went to their corners to wait for the bell.

Rex didn't know how the rest of the spectators felt, but when they closed the gate to the cage, locking them inside, he felt a sense of foreboding.

When the bell rang, JD and Bob moved to the center of the ring. Bob wanted to end it quickly, so he was a wild man when he attacked, but JD managed to withstand his first flurry of blows without any real damage. JD spun around Bob's left side, and delivered a vicious kick to his side.

"Good one, but you're going to have to do better than that," Bob said as he rubbed his side.

They traded kicks and blows for the rest of the round, without any real harm to either one of them. When the bell rang, JD dropped his hands and turned to go back to his corner. Bob waited until his back was turned, and hit him in the back of the head with a vicious punch. Stunned by the blow, JD pitched forward on the canvas. Bob laughed as he sauntered to his corner, with a shit-eating grin on his face.

"Cowardly bastard," Rex screamed, as he crawled through the ropes. "You all right?" he asked, as he helped JD to his feet.

"Give me a moment and I will be," JD told him as he wobbled toward his corner.

Enraged at the blatant foul, the referee ran over to Bob's corner. "One more stunt like that, and I'll stop the fight," the referee screamed at Bob.

Bob looked down at him with scorn, and said, "Get the hell out of my face. I'm gonna tear this boy a new asshole, and you just need to stay out of the way."

"I'm not going to stand for this; I'm ending it right now."

Bob growled, "If you do, you won't live to get out of town. Now stay out of the way, and don't interfere, or you'll regret it."

Shaken, the referee walked over to JD and Rex and said, "If it was me, I would try to walk out right now. The crazy bastard just threatened me, and I'm not going to get killed over this, so you need to watch out for yourself."

"Understood," JD said. "Just do like he said, and don't get in our way." The referee gave JD a funny look, and walked away shaking his head.

"Damn it, I'm sorry I ever got you involved with Bob," Rex said. "I'd heard a lot of stories about him, but I never thought he'd go this far."

"Don't worry about it, and no matter what happens, don't try to interfere."

The second round started out much like the first one, but as the fight progressed, JD's kicks and blows were starting to take a toll. JD wasn't nearly as big, but he was incredibly strong, and a lot quicker. Every time Bob would launch a kick or throw a punch, JD would beat him to it. By the end of the round, Bob had several red welts on his body, and as he struggled to catch his breath, blood was bubbling out of his nose and mouth. As Bob lumbered back to his corner, Rex thought that he had the look of a beaten man.

"I think you've got him," Rex said.

"Maybe, but he doesn't strike me as a quitter. Leroy always warned me that desperate men do desperate things."

When they started the last round, Bob came out in a

mad rush. JD slipped his charge, and caught him with a savage kick to the ribs, followed by a snap kick to his knee. In excruciating pain, Bob dropped to one knee near his corner.

"Finish him," Rex yelled.

JD knew he should, but he hung back to let him get up. It wasn't because he felt sorry for him; he just wanted to make sure Bob wouldn't ever threaten him again. When Bob lurched to his feet, he leaned against the chain-link gate.

"Take this, boss," one of Bob's men said, as he pried the gate open enough to slip him a large knife.

JD had already seen what was happening, before the crowd started yelling, "Look out, he's got a knife."

To his credit, the referee moved to cut Bob off. JD was afraid he'd stab him, so he grabbed the referee and threw him out of harm's way.

"Boy, I'm gonna gut you like a fish," Bob growled, as he limped toward JD. As Bob tried to corner him, JD kept his distance, until he had a sense of how well Bob could still move. Bob was limping badly, but he managed to get close enough to make a vicious swipe with his knife, but JD was way too fast. He finished off Bob's damaged knee with a leg sweep, and Bob let out a guttural scream of agony as he crumpled to the canvas. Crippled, he thrashed around on the canvas until he finally managed to get back up.

"You're a dead man," he screamed as he lunged forward to stab JD.

Trained to react, JD's right hand was a blur when it snapped out, catching Bob flush in the throat. The blow dropped him like he'd been shot, and as he thrashed around on the canvas, JD returned to his corner. The crowd was screaming their approval as the referee counted him out and walked over to where JD was waiting.

"You put a real ass kicking on the arrogant asshole,"

the referee said as he raised JD's hand in victory. "I guess I'd better make sure he's all right," the referee commented, when Big Bob stopped thrashing around. When the referee bent down to check Bob, he immediately screamed, "Medics, I need medics in here right now."

When EMTs rushed into the ring, the cheers died away to dead silence. Once it became evident Bob was dead, the police moved into the ring.

"You're going to have to come with us."

"What the hell, why are you hassling him?" Rex asked.

"It looks like he killed a man to me, and Bob's sister is married to the chief of police, so he's not going to let this pass."

For a brief moment JD had considered trying to fight his way out. However, Leroy had trained him to be observant, and as he studied the three officers, he could see that they were hoping he would try something, so they could kill him and be done with the whole thing.

The next day they held a pretense at a grand jury, and JD's trial was set for the next month. Rex couldn't get them to set bail, and he had no illusions about how the trial would play out if he didn't do something.

WHEN THE DEPUTIES led JD into the courtroom, he was astounded to see it was standing-room only.

"All stand for the Honorable Judge Watson," the bailiff announced.

"What's this, where the hell is Judge Brambly?" the prosecutor asked his assistant.

"You can all be seated," Judge Watson told the courtroom. "I know you were expecting Judge Brambly, but the attorney general has assigned me to try this case," he announced.

"How did you get this done?" Larry Shaw, JD's lawyer, whispered to Rex.

"I've still got a few contacts downstate."

"I've got a pretrial motion that I'm going to rule on before we begin," Judge Watson announced. "In all my years on the bench, I've never worked a murder trial where there was a complete video of the crime. I don't know why the prosecution is objecting to the video, but we'll watch it, and then I'll make my ruling. Bailiff, please escort the jury into the next room."

AFTER THEY'D WATCHED the video, the judge banged his gavel and announced, "We're going to take a two-hour recess, while I think about what I just witnessed."

Judge Watson had just sat down when one of the Texas Rangers the governor had sent along for security came in.

"We've just received another warning from one of the undercover operatives."

"Is it credible?"

"Without a doubt. I'd say this young man's life is about to be cut short. There are some very bad people after him."

"All tied to the man he killed?"

"Him, and the scumbag sheriff we're investigating."

"OK, thanks. I may need your help after I make my ruling."

"No problem, that's why we're here. Just let me know what you need."

"Would you tell the bailiff that I need to see the defense team?" Judge Watson asked.

"WE'VE HAD ANOTHER threat, and the judge would like to see you in chambers," the Texas Ranger whispered to the defense team.

"I hope you don't mind, but I brought Rex Allen with me," Larry Shaw said. "He's a family friend, and he's got some background on a previous attempt on John David's life."

"No problem, as long as you trust him," Judge Watson replied. "I'm not going into how we know, but there has been a hit put out on John David."

"It's not the first time they've tried to kill him," Rex interrupted. "They shot up his car a few weeks ago. That's what led him to take the fight against Bob Tower."

"Why didn't you file a complaint?" the judge asked.

"The circumstances would have made a report problematic."

"Well, no matter," Judge Watson told them. "When we reconvene I'm going to dismiss all the charges against him, but that's just going to make it easier for them to kill him."

"I could try to hide him out," Rex offered.

"That might work for a while, but these people won't give up as long as they think he's still around," the Judge said. "He really needs to leave here and never come back. But before we address that, maybe you can tell me what a teenager is doing fighting a man like Bob Tower?"

When Rex finished giving him a summary of how JD had been raised, and the details of how the fight had come about, the judge asked, "How would he feel about going into the army?"

"He wouldn't have any problem fitting in," Rex said.

"Normally it would take a few weeks to get him into the system, but Colonel Martinez and I were classmates at West Point, and I think I can get him to pull a few strings."

While they pulled JD into a private room to make sure he was all right with the plan, the judge called his friend. After a brief conversation with the colonel, he called them back in.

"I've made all the arrangements," Judge Watson told them. "Was Mr. Drury all right with the plan?"

"He wasn't that happy about it, but he understood," Larry Shaw explained.

"It's not a perfect solution, but it beats letting them murder him. I'll give you a few more minutes to brief Mrs. Bolton, and get her to sign the permission papers, before we reconvene. I'm going have the Texas Rangers make all the travel arrangements, and they'll be providing a security detail."

When the judge came out, the bailiff declared the court back in session. Before Judge Watson could get started, the prosecutor stood and said, "Your Honor, I move—"

The judge cut him off when he slammed his gavel down and ordered, "Take your seat." Judge Watson didn't try to mask his anger. "I can't believe you filed murder charges against this young man. When they contacted me, they warned me this was probably a railroad job, but this is a travesty.

"John David Drury, please rise. You have the court's profound apologies, and I'm dismissing all the charges against you."

The prosecutor jumped up to object, but the judge cut him off. "You need to sit down, and shut up, and don't run off because I've got some rangers who'd like to have word with you. Members of the jury, you are dismissed as well. Thank you for your time, and I apologize for your inconvenience."

Emma was waiting in the rangers' SUV when they led Rex and JD out. They had two other teams for security, and on the way to the airport, Emma and JD finally got a chance to talk. Emma tried to put her feelings into words, but she just couldn't do it. As they neared the airport, JD could see she was almost in tears, so he put his arm around her. "Emma, there's nothing you have to explain or apologize to me for. I should have told you this a long time ago, but you're the only mother I've ever known, and I love you. As far as Leroy goes, he was just the way he was. I can't say that I ever loved him, but I do owe everything I am to him. So don't feel bad about not protecting me, it turned out fine." Emma sobbed softly and put her head on his shoulder, and for the first time in decades, she was at peace.

As JD was about to board the plane, Rex pulled him aside. "Don't worry about your mama, we'll make sure she gets home all right."

"Thanks."

As they announced last call for boarding, Rex held him up. "I know you need to go, but I need to pass something by you. If it's all right with you, I'd like to give Emma all the money we won off of Bob."

JD got a huge grin on his face as he grabbed Rex up in a bear hug. "You can never know how much that means to me."

As JD was leaving he told Rex, "If you ever need anything, just give me a holler, and I'll come a-running."

"Good-bye, my young friend. Write if you get the chance, but if I were you, I would stay out of this part of the country. The judge was right; the people around here have long memories."

When it is a question of money, everybody is of the same religion.

—Voltaire

PART 3

⟨∞⟩

CHAPTER 1

Years before John David had been born, Barack Obama and the Democrats had swept the Republicans out of office, forever changing the landscape of American politics.

The upheaval that followed allowed the Tea Party to grow into a credible political force. However, as the years passed, the turmoil had been unabated, which provided the opportunity for the Federalist Party to be reborn.

The politics of consensus building and collaboration had never been easy, but with four political parties, it had become virtually impossible. Corporate bankruptcies had reached an all-time high, but it wasn't just the large corporations that were struggling to survive.

Jacques Montfort's family had made their immense fortunes in biotech, but their real passion was wine. They'd owned the largest vineyard in Napa Valley for five generations, and their wines were world famous.

Jacques and his wife, Marie, were sitting on their veranda, sampling a glass of wine from their latest crop. They had a magnificent view of their vast vineyards, but they were having a hard time enjoying it, as they were going through the latest P&L from their accountant.

"This can't be right," Marie lamented. "How can we still owe eight hundred thousand in taxes?"

Jacques's father, Leopold, was the patriarch of the family, and he just happened to overhear her outburst. "We've stood for this bullshit long enough, and this time we're going to do something about it," Leopold shouted to them through the open patio door. As he hobbled out onto the veranda, he launched into a tirade. "The deficit, and unemployment are at all-time highs, and these nitwitted politicians don't seem to be able to do a damn thing about it."

Jacques cringed, because even though Leopold was getting up there in years, he could still be hell on wheels when he got on a roll. Jacques jumped up to help his father, and as the old man plopped into the chair with a thud, he groaned. "Damned arthritis."

"OK, you're pissed, and so am I, but what can we do about it?" Jacques asked.

"You're going to run for president. That's what," the old man said with absolute conviction.

"President? Get real. I've never even run for class president. No one is going to vote for me."

"You might be surprised. The country is fed up with the career politicians, and I think the time is right for a move like this. Besides, most of what it takes to win an election, comes down to money."

"I suppose you're right, but you're talking a lot of money."

"Well, we've got a little money, and with the help of some of our friends, I think we can swing it."

To say that they had a little money was a bit of an understatement. The annual list of the world's richest people had just been published, and the Montfort family occupied eight of the top ten positions. For the fourteenth straight year, Leopold was leading the list, with an estimated net worth of over a hundred billion dollars.

"Think back to when Jimmy Carter won the presidency. The country was in turmoil and desperate for change, and I think we're in the same set of circumstances," Leopold recounted.

They cussed and discussed it for hours, before Jacques finally relented. "All right, Father. I'll do it, but I still don't think I'll have a snowball's chance in hell."

THEY ENDED UP spending an extraordinary amount of money, but Leopold had been right about the political climate.

Jacques's election represented another rift in the political landscape, as he joined George Washington as the only other independent candidate ever elected.

The first few weeks had been a blur, but by the sixth week, Jacques thought he was starting to get used to the pace. He'd just sat down to eat breakfast with Marie, when Alfred Kinsey, his chief of staff, came rushing in.

"You're in a hell of hurry this morning," President Montfort commented.

"You need to take a look at this," Alfred told him.

"Can't it wait?"

"I don't think so," he said as he handed him the printout.

When President Montfort finished reading it, he almost threw up. "Good God, tell me this is just a bad joke."

"I wish I could, but these are copies of what they're going to announce after the markets close."

"Shit," President Montfort exclaimed. "I sure didn't see this coming. General Motors and Ford declaring bankruptcy on the same day isn't going to do much for the markets or the economy. I don't suppose there's any way we could get them to delay the announcements for a day or two?"

"I'm afraid not. The SEC would be all over them and

us. Besides, they've already filed the paperwork with the bankruptcy court in New York, so it'll be public record by tomorrow morning."

"It was just a thought. OK, I need you to get Larry Ellis over here right away."

"He's chairing the quarterly Federal Reserve meeting in Boston."

"Doesn't matter, have him catch the first flight out. Once I figure out what I'm going to do, I'll need the two of you to put substance to it."

As the president continued thinking through the situation, he asked, "If it turns out that I need some sort of legislation to pull this off, do you think I can count on the support of our congressional partners?"

"Considering the mandate you just received, I think they'll be inclined to go along with whatever you suggest, as long as it lets them save face for not addressing the issues sooner," Alfred Kinsey said. He put his hand on the president's shoulder. "But I've got to warn you. You're going to have to come up with something quickly. Because if you let the last two American car companies go under, there'll be hell to pay."

Later that evening, they got back together to begin strategizing. The president had immense respect for Kinsey, so he asked, "What are your thoughts on the subject?"

Alfred had suspected the president would ask, so he'd thrown together a summary of the situation, and some tentative thoughts on a course of action.

"I've laid out a strategy that might work. If we act quickly, we can help them put together the funding for their prepackaged bankruptcy plans. They'll be appreciably smaller when we're done, but it should allow them to survive," he said as he handed the president his notes.

"I hear you, but General Motors went through the

same thing several years ago, and it wasn't a long-term fix. Let me have thirty minutes to look it over, and then we'll discuss it."

ALFRED RETURNED JUST as he was finishing.

"Your strategy might let both of them survive for a few more years, but let's face it, there are simply too many car companies in the world, and ours aren't competitive anymore."

"What are you thinking?" Alfred Kinsey asked.

"We need to force them both into Chapter 7 bankruptcies, with the government agreeing to do an asset purchase. That would allow us to jettison all of their debt and toxic assets, and then we can merge the best parts, to form one viable company."

"An interesting proposition, but which management group would you use?"

"We've got to bring in an outsider to lead it, because I wouldn't trust either one of them not to repeat their mistakes. It needs to be someone who has a keen sense of the overall economy and business, but not necessarily the car business."

"It sounds like you already have someone in mind."

"Do you remember Charles Whitman?"

"Wasn't he the economist you met with at the Wharton School of Business fund-raiser?"

"That's him. John Stasi, one of my biggest contributors, wanted me to spend some time with him. He didn't come right out and ask, but I think he wanted me to consider him for a leadership position in the OMB. After talking with him, I could see why. He was the youngest person to graduate from Wharton's MBA program, and he's been working for the Hudson Institute for several years, as their top strategist."

"Sounds too academic to me, and what makes you think he could run a company?"

"He's extremely bright, and not afraid to think out-side of the box; besides, he couldn't do worse than the bozos running them now."

THE NEXT DAY, the president called Charles Whitman to pitch him the job.

"Mr. President, I'm honored you would think of me, but I've never run a company of any size, and this will be an immense undertaking."

"I can understand your reluctance, but I'm convinced you're the man for the job. So what do you say, will you do it?"

"Let me sleep on it, and I'll give you my answer in the morning."

When the president's phone rang at 6:45 the next morning, he didn't know what to expect. "Good morning, Charles, have you come to a decision?"

"I'll do it, but I'm going to ask you to be patient while I put it together, and I've got to warn you that I may not succeed."

"Understood, and I give you my word that I'll back you to the hilt. All I ask is that you keep me in the loop."

BESIDES BEING A financial genius, Whitman was an avid student of history. So he realized he faced an insur-mountable task if he tried to go it alone.

"Is Whitman ever going to get moving?" the Speaker of the House whined. "I've got constituents who are go-ing hungry and want to know if they're going to have jobs."

The Speaker was from Michigan, so the president knew he was taking heat from all sides.

"I promised Charles I'd let him have enough time to do the job right, and I'm going to keep to my word," President Montfort said.

"I understand, but our people are desperate."

"I tell you what, I'll give him a call, and get back to you with an update."

When he hung up, the president told Alfred Kinsey, "I hope Whitman is about ready to get moving, because I'm not sure how much longer I can hold these vultures off."

"I had real reservations when you chose him, but I like him more every day. It's almost textbook the way he's modeling his approach after Lee Iacocca."

"Good to hear, but what changed your mind?" the president asked.

"I got to sit in on one of his staff meetings, and he may be a better delegator than Iacocca, and I didn't think that was possible. He's pulled the best talent out of both companies, and he's even pulled in a couple from the old Chrysler leadership."

"I'm glad you're coming around. Would you mind getting him for me?"

"Sorry to bother you, Charles, but I need an update," President Montfort told him.

"I understand completely, and thank you for your patience. Your timing is perfect, because I was about to give you a call. I'm happy to report that I've completed the team, and we're ready to get to work. I just e-mailed you the draft of the announcement. Look it over, and if you're all right with it, I'll send it out tomorrow morning."

"That's great news. I'll take a look, but I'm sure it's fine. Keep me updated, and let me know if we can help."

The new company was named US Motors, and the first two years had been just as brutal as Charles Whitman had anticipated.

However, when they reported their earnings for their third year, they'd surprised the market with a small profit, and given a positive outlook for the coming year.

When the news broke, the president gave Charles a call. "Congratulations on a job well done," President Montfort said.

"Thank you, but we're not out of the woods yet."

"I understand, but you need to stop and enjoy the moment. God knows we haven't had much to celebrate lately."

"True enough, and I've got to admit that I'm excited about our new fall lineup. Speaking of celebrations, congratulations on a second term."

"Thanks, but if you think you have challenges, you should see the crap that I'm trying to make sense of. You've managed to resurrect at least a semblance of the car industry, but I can't say the same for the rest of the economy. Every time I think I've gotten a handle on it, something else goes to hell."

"Honestly, I could never understand why anyone would want the job," Charles told him.

"I hope you don't mean that, because Alfred Kinsey and I were just talking about what a great president you'd make."

"No way. I've got no interest in politics."

The president laughed and remarked, "Neither did I. However, you should at least consider it. The country could use a man like you."

CHARLES WAS A valued contributor to the Salvation Army, and Craig McAllen, the president of the Salvation Army, came by to pick up his yearly donation, and to thank him.

When Charles handed him a check for two million dollars, it took him by surprise. "Charles, you have no idea how many people this will let us help."

"Never an issue, I'm sure there are a great many people in need."

"You really don't know how much this means, do you?" Craig questioned.

Charles thought about it. "No, I guess I don't."

"Would you be willing to let me show you?"

"Sure, if it's not too much trouble."

"It would be my honor, and I promise that you'll never forget it."

Craig picked him up early the next morning.

"Where are we headed?"

"We're going to meet the Adult Protection Service at one of their cases."

"Adult protection, I've never heard of it," Charles remarked.

"I figured, but I want to show you what happens when someone falls through the cracks in the system."

When they pulled up in front of the dilapidated old house, Charles remarked, "All the windows are broken out."

"Yes, they are, and it looks like the front door has been kicked in."

"Surely there's no one living here?"

"I'm afraid that's why we're here. Good, here comes the APS team."

After they'd introduced themselves they walked up on the porch.

"Careful, the wood's rotten, so watch where you step," Officer Stamens cautioned.

"Hello, this is the Adult Protection Service and we're coming in," Officer Stamens announced, as she pushed the remnants of the front door aside. The front room was littered with every manner of filth.

"Good God, what's that smell?" Charles asked.

"It could be any number of things," Officer Stamens said. "Is there anyone here?" he called.

"Back here," a plaintive voice called out. They made

their way back to the bedroom, and when they walked in, all they could see was her head sticking out of the pile of blankets and old clothes.

"Mrs. Goldman, are you all right?" Officer Stamens asked.

"I'm alive," Hattie Goldman answered weakly.

The only heat she had was a propane space heater, and she had every blanket she owned piled on top of her.

"Hattie, I need to take a look at you, if that's all right," Officer Stamens requested.

"OK, but be quick about it."

When Officer Stamens pulled back the pile, she saw that Hattie's body was covered in filth and scabs, and the stench was horrific.

"Oh my God," Charles exclaimed.

Officer Stamens had to cover her nose with a handkerchief before she could continue. "Are you bleeding?"

"Maybe a little, down there," Hattie told her, embarrassed at being seen in that condition. All Hattie had on was an old flannel nightgown, and when Officer Stamens pulled it up to get a better look, she could see the blood on the bed between her legs.

"How long has this been going on?"

"Not sure, but it's been getting worse for a week or two."

"Can you get up?"

"Not for a couple of days."

"How have you been eating and drinking?"

"Some of the neighbors come by a couple of times a week to bring me some food and water."

Officer Stamens covered her back up and dialed 911. "This is Officer Stamens with APS, and I need an ambulance at 1432 Oak, ASAP."

After the ambulance had taken Hattie away, they got into Craig's SUV to talk for a few minutes.

"God, that was awful," Charles commented.

"Happens almost every day," Officer Stamens replied.

"How can that be?" Charles asked. "There are all sorts of agencies to help people like her."

"If only that were true," Craig told him. "This is the sort of thing we deal with every day of our lives. It's not just old people, or children either. This country has abandoned many of its citizens, and there isn't anything in place to save them."

"I never knew," was all Charles could say.

CHAPTER 2

While Charles Whitman had been busy with US Motors, John David was on his way to boot camp.

When JD's plane landed at the Columbia Metropolitan Airport, a corporal from Fort Jackson met him.

"I'm Lance Corporal McClusky; do you have any luggage?"

"Nope, all I've got is what I have on."

"Just as well, they would make you mail it home anyway. You look kind of young to be joining the army."

"Maybe, but the judge convinced me it was in my best interest."

"One of those, huh," the corporal said. "They'll get that out of you in no time."

JD knew what he was thinking, but he didn't bother trying to explain. It was a short ride to base, and when the gate guard recognized the corporal, he waved him through.

I wonder what the hell I've gotten myself into this time, John David mused as they drove through the sprawling base.

When they arrived at the administration building, the corporal took him to the personnel office. "What can I do for you?" the young woman behind the counter asked.

"I just arrived, and I'm not sure what I'm supposed to do," John David explained as he handed her the envelope the judge had given him.

After the clerk read the papers, she handed them back. "You need to take these down to room one twenty-one. Give them to the sergeant, and he'll take care of you."

The sergeant didn't know what to do, so he asked the lieutenant.

"No problem, Colonel Martinez told me you were coming. I'll get you sworn in, and then the sergeant will take you over to the reception station."

John David spent two days in the processing center before they assigned him to his recruit battalion. He was in with three hundred other recruits, and some of them struggled with the transformation from civilians to soldiers, but it was almost second nature to him.

When his squad had their first APFT (Army Physical Fitness Test), Sergeant Porter had been impressed by John David's performance. As their training progressed, his performance had been excellent, but he really excelled when they made their first trip to the firing range. After they'd finished firing from the various positions, Sergeant Porter started grading their targets.

"Damn, Drury sure can shoot," the sergeant commented to the corporal recording their scores. "Every one's in the bull. I've never seen anyone shoot a score like that with these old worn-out pieces of shit. Mark him down as an expert, but it doesn't do him justice."

If his marksmanship had impressed, Sergeant Porter was in complete awe after they started their hand-to-hand combat training.

"What do you think of Drury?" Lieutenant Stevens asked.

"Oh good God, I've never seen some of the moves he was using. For a moment, I thought I was watching a Special Ops instructor."

"Excellent. I was going over the aptitude tests, and I've never seen scores like his. I'm thinking of flagging him for OCS consideration. Would you recommend him?"

"Even though he's only seventeen, I've never seen a recruit who was any more self-confident, and yet he's not a pushy asshole like most of the athletes we get in here."

"How do you know he's an athlete?" Lieutenant Stevens asked. "I went through his file last night, and there's literally nothing in it."

"If you'd ever seen him in action you wouldn't have to ask."

"It's settled then. Get me your letter by the end of the week, and I'll get the recommendation put together."

Most of the men liked John David, and went to him for help. However, Lonnie Masters was the exception. Unlike John David, he had an extremely high opinion of himself, and was used to being the center of attention. He'd graduated summa cum laude from the Virginia Military Institute, and the president of VMI had personally recommended him for the Army War College, after OCS.

A couple of weeks before graduation, their company had been selected to act as guinea pigs for a new obstacle course. The course had turned out to be far too difficult, and Lonnie Masters and John David were the only ones who managed to finish. John David had beaten Lonnie by a wide margin, and even though it was quite an accomplishment to have finished at all, Lonnie was pissed.

"I suppose you think this proves you're better than me?" Lonnie asked.

When he saw the fury in Lonnie's eyes, John David tried to smooth it over. "Look, it was just an obstacle course run, so lighten up." He didn't want it to escalate, so John David turned to walk away.

Lonnie's blow to the side of his head momentarily stunned him. When he hit the ground, Lonnie pounced, but John David managed to tie him up, until his head cleared. When it did, he quickly escaped from Lonnie's grasp, and stood up. "What the hell do you think you're doing?" John David asked.

"I'm going to show you who the better man is," Lonnie said as he charged him.

This time John David was facing him, and instead of hitting him, he simply hip tossed him across the grass. Embarrassed by how easily John David had handled him, Lonnie scrambled to his feet and charged again. Lonnie came at him time after time, and each time JD would use a different technique on him. They'd been going at it for almost five minutes, when John David decided he'd taken enough shit from Lonnie. The next time Lonnie attacked, he slid to the side, and caught him with a powerful kick to his lower back. The kick broke two of Lonnie's ribs, but he was too stubborn to quit.

You'd think the arrogant bastard would catch on, John David thought to himself. When Lonnie came at him again, JD delivered a vicious kick to the side of his head. Out cold, Lonnie dropped like a rock.

Sergeant Porter had seen the fight start, and had decided to let them settle it among themselves. However, when he saw Lonnie go down, he was afraid he'd made a terrible mistake. When he was unable to revive Lonnie, the sergeant decided to call for help. "I need an ambulance at the Charlie company barracks," Sergeant Porter told the operator.

FORTUNATELY, THE LIEUTENANT had already submitted the paperwork for John David's OCS nomination.

When Lonnie's grandfather, a retired Air Force general,

found out about the incident, he flew down to make sure John David was properly punished.

"I want this Drury court-martialed," General Masters demanded.

"Calm down," Colonel Martinez cautioned. "His sergeant is on his way over, and once I know the facts, I'll decide what to do."

"Unacceptable," the general blustered. "I demand that you punish this criminal immediately."

What an asshole, the colonel thought to himself. However, he knew the general was still well connected, so he told him, "Look, if you want, you can sit in while I interview the sergeant."

When Sergeant Porter arrived, he realized he might be in deep shit, but he wasn't going to lie to cover his own ass.

"Take a seat, Sergeant Porter," Colonel Martinez ordered. "Tell me everything you know about the incident that injured Pfc. Masters."

"It was an assault," General Masters corrected.

The colonel looked at him, and said, "Sir, you need to let me handle this. You're here only as an observer. Go ahead, Sergeant."

"We'd just returned from the new obstacle course, and Pfc. Masters and Pfc. Drury were having a discussion. I was too far away to hear what was said, but Pfc. Masters seemed upset. When Pfc. Drury turned to walk away, Pfc. Masters struck him from behind."

"Liar, he attacked my grandson," General Masters screamed.

"I'll not warn you again," the colonel cautioned. "Continue, Sergeant."

"They rolled around on the ground for several seconds before they got back up. When they did, Pfc. Masters attacked Pfc. Drury again, and Drury hip tossed him. The fight continued for several minutes, until Pfc.

Drury kicked Pfc. Masters in the side of the head, and knocked him out."

"Go on, what happened next?"

"When I couldn't revive Pfc. Masters, I called the ambulance and had him taken to the infirmary."

The colonel thought for a moment. "Why didn't you stop it?"

"In retrospect I probably should have, but Pfc. Masters had been mouthing off to Drury for quite a while, and I thought I'd let them settle it like men."

The colonel could see that the general was about to go ballistic, so he said, "Thank you, Sergeant, that will be all."

The general waited until the sergeant had left, before he started in on the colonel. "The man's a liar; there's no way that Drury could take my grandson in a fair fight."

"I'm sorry, sir, but it sounds like he got what was coming to him. I won't be punishing Pfc. Drury for defending himself."

"We'll see about that," the general threatened as he stalked out.

CHAPTER 3

Lieutenant Stevens had tried to get John David directly into OCS when he graduated, but with General Masters's complaints, and the army's budget at an all-time low, he was lucky to get him on the waiting list. So after boot camp, John David received his first duty assignment in São Paulo, Brazil.

The detachment's mission was to help the Brazilian government track down and capture or kill Generalissimo Eduardo Castellans, the leader of the insurgents. The US didn't have a base in the area, so John David had to take a commercial flight. After his plane landed in São Paulo, he was getting his gear from the baggage carousel, when he saw the sergeant walk up.

"I'm First Sergeant Stapleton. Are you Drury?"

"Yes, First Sergeant."

"Great, grab your gear and follow me."

They were quartered in an old hangar beside the main runway, so it was a short drive.

"This is it," Sergeant Stapleton told him. "Grab an open bunk, and stow your gear. The captain holds a daily briefing at 1930, and you'll need to be there. If you're hungry there's a cafeteria in the airport. The keys to the jeeps are on the wall beside the bulletin board."

When JD took his seat at the meeting, he quickly counted the other men in the room. He'd been a little surprised to learn that there were only twenty men in the squad, including him. A few seconds later, the first sergeant came hurrying in. He pointed to JD, and motioned for him to stand.

"Gentlemen, this is the newest member of our little group, Corporal John David Drury. Please make a point to introduce yourselves, but right now I need you to listen up, while I bring you up to speed on what's going down. I just got out of a briefing with the local commandant, and he thinks they've located General Castellans in the southern portion of the Brazilian rainforest." The sergeant knew the men would be wondering where the captain was. "Captain Morgan will be leading the mission tonight, but he's busy arranging for transport. Time's short, so I'm going to keep this brief. We're scheduled to take off at 2100. We'll be joining up with a detachment of the Brazilian Special Forces. According to the intelligence reports, the rebels number less than a hundred men, but make sure you've got plenty of ammo, and your night-vision gear. Any questions?

"No? Be out on the runway by 2030. "Sergeant Chavez, Drury is going to be in your squad. Make sure you get him fixed up with the gear he needs, and try to keep him alive."

So much for getting settled in, JD thought to himself.

They didn't take off until almost 2200, in a helicopter that looked like it had seen better days.

"Sorry, but this was all I could get," Captain Morgan said as they lifted off.

"It beats walking," First Sergeant Stapleton remarked. "Did the pilot give you an ETA?"

"He said if he doesn't have to dodge too many storms, we should be there by 0030."

"We're cutting it kind of close, aren't we?"

"We are, but the damn thing wouldn't start," Captain Morgan said disgustedly.

Their pilot managed to dodge the worst of the storms, but several of the men got airsick due to the extreme turbulence. As they approached their destination, they ran into another storm.

"I'm going to try to land, but you'd better hold on tight, because I can't see a damn thing," the pilot warned.

The ground didn't come into sight until just before they touched down, but the copter only bounced a couple of times as it skidded to a stop in the mud.

"Well done," Captain Morgan commented to the pilot. "First Sergeant, get everything unloaded while I check in with the colonel."

He found the colonel huddled under a tarp they'd set up to shelter them from the downpour.

"Welcome, Captain Morgan, your men will be leading the assault," Colonel Ernesto told him.

"You do know that I only have twenty-two men, including myself."

"I do, but I need you to step up and get it done." The colonel didn't explain, but he wanted to take the general alive and he wasn't sure he could trust his men to do it.

"Yes, sir. Anything else?" Captain Morgan asked, wondering what the hell they'd gotten themselves into.

"I'd like to take the general alive if possible, but no matter what, we've got to make sure he doesn't slip away again."

"Understood," Captain Morgan responded. "How big of a force does the general have with him?"

"The last estimate put the number at ninety. They're not supposed to have anything but small arms, but I wouldn't put much faith in that."

"Why?"

"Because I think the general has infiltrated our intelligence organization."

Great, the captain thought to himself. "When are we jumping off?"

"I've delayed it until 0230. These damn storms have put us behind schedule."

Captain Morgan took a few minutes to reconnoiter the encampment. It turned out to be a collection of hastily constructed huts, surrounded by a roughly hewn field of fire.

"It's about two hundred yards of open field to the camp, but if we can take out the sentries, I think we'll be all right," Captain Morgan told the team. "First Sergeant, you've got the left flank. Sergeant Chavez, you've got the right flank. I'll take the rest of the squad up the middle. Check your gear, and make sure your headsets are working."

The storms had blown through, and the moonless sky was filled with stars. Their night-vision gear let them pinpoint the sentries' positions, and at precisely 0230, Captain Morgan whispered into his mike, "Take them down and move out."

Their silenced M110 SASS rifles allowed them to kill sentries without raising any alarms. They'd been counting on the element of surprise, but they were less than halfway when several flares suddenly illuminated the camp. As the flares drifted overhead, they watched in horror as the sides of the huts on the perimeter fell down, revealing several heavy machine guns.

"Get down," Captain Morgan ordered.

They hit the ground, but other than the random logs scattered across the expanse, there wasn't any real cover. JD was behind one of the logs, trying to get as close to the ground as he could. The gunfire was deafening, as the machine guns chopped their meager cover to bits. He felt the fear and adrenaline coursing through his body, as the flying wood chips stung him, and for a split second he was afraid he was going to panic. But just as quickly, he flashed back to one of Leroy's favorite sayings: *"Boy, anybody who tells you that they're not scared in combat, is either a liar or a fool. Besides, if it's not your day to die you'll be fine. If it is, it wouldn't matter if you're lying at home in your featherbed, God would find you."*

As they started to return fire, the captain radioed Colonel Ernesto for help. "We're pinned down, and we need some covering fire."

The Brazilian Special Forces immediately opened fire in response. Colonel Ernesto had two hundred heavily armed commandos, and their withering crossfire began shredding the machine gun positions. When Captain Morgan saw it was having an effect, he ordered, "Let's move out." Firing as they went, it only took another forty-five seconds to reach the huts. The first one was riddled with bullet holes, and everyone inside was dead. After a cursory check, Captain Morgan ordered, "Nothing left here, move out."

The enemy's rate of fire had slowed, but when Captain Morgan rounded the corner of the next hut, his squad was caught in a vicious crossfire.

When he saw the captain's team go down, First Sergeant Stapleton took over. "Keep moving, we've got to take out that gun," the sergeant ordered over his headset. "Chavez, let's focus on the large hut in the center."

They were starting to take heavy fire again, and Sergeant Stapleton was about to order Sergeant Chavez's squad to take cover, when a barrage of RPGs hit the first sergeant and his men, killing them all.

Sergeant Chavez was down to the new kid, Drury, and Corporal Bellamy, their radio operator. The sergeant used his grenade launcher to take out the last machine gun, and ordered, "Follow me, and stay close."

When they reached the general's hut, Sergeant Chavez kicked the door in, and yelled, "Remember, take the general alive if possible." When he entered, he was firing as fast as he could, but he was met with a barrage of automatic weapons fire. The impact of the bullets drove him back out the door, and when JD glanced down at the sergeant's bloody corpse, he wasn't even recognizable.

Corporal Bellamy yelled, "Hang back and give me cover." Bellamy went in low, firing his shotgun as he went, but he met the same fate as the sergeant.

John David didn't have any more clips for his machine gun, so he tossed it aside, drew his sidearm, and dove through the door. There was only one bodyguard left alive, and JD put two rounds into him as he rolled up on one knee. His eyes darted around the dimly lit room, until he spotted the general trying to pull his pistol as he stood up.

When JD pointed his pistol at the general's head, he slumped back into his chair and said, "Well, I guess you've got me, but don't think this will change anything."

A little surprised he spoke English, and with a British accent, JD told him, "That's not my concern. Now stand up and turn around."

After JD had disarmed him, he bound his hands with the plastic handcuffs they all carried, and shoved him outdoors into the now quiet night.

The hut was surrounded, and as the colonel motioned for his men to lower their weapons, he ordered, "Bring him over here, and we'll take over. Where's Captain Morgan, and the rest of your team?"

"I think I'm the only one left."

"Unfortunate, but you've done a fine job," Colonel Ernesto said.

The colonel took the general by the arm. "So my old friend, we meet again," Colonel Ernesto whispered as they were walking away.

"I'm not your friend, and as I told you when we last

met, I'll see you in Hell," General Castellans screamed. The general jerked free, jabbed his right boot heel into the ground, and kicked the colonel under the chin.

JD jerked the general to the ground, and warned, "You need to cut that shit out."

Colonel Ernesto's men reached them within seconds, but when they rolled the colonel over, JD could see the gaping wound left by the knife blade in the tip of the general's boot.

"I told that bastard I'd kill him one day," General Castellans gloated.

The colonel's second in command never said a word as he walked over and pumped three rounds into the general's head, spraying blood in JD's face.

"Sorry about that," the XO apologized, as he helped JD up.

After the Brazilian medics verified the colonel and the general were beyond help, one of them asked, "How about letting me take a look at those wounds?"

JD hadn't realized he'd been hit, but after the medics had cleaned and bandaged his wounds, they loaded him on a medevac helicopter, and airlifted him back to the city. He spent two nights in the hospital in São Paulo, before he was ordered back to the States.

WHEN HE GOT off the plane in Miami, Lieutenant Thomas met him.

"Welcome back, Corporal Drury. Here are your orders, and a plane ticket for your next flight."

"Thank you, sir, but where am I going?"

"Sorry, I'd forgotten you hadn't been briefed. "They've moved you up on the list for OCS, and you start school in two days. We need to hustle, because your next flight takes off in twenty minutes."

As John David sat staring out the window, he was

wondering what lay ahead, and if he would be up to the task. Leroy's words came rushing back: *"Boy. You can do anything you're truly committed to, so don't ever doubt yourself."*

CHAPTER 4

When John David arrived, there was a soldier holding up a placard with his name on it.

"I'm Corporal Drury."

"Great to meet you, I'm Steve Lester," he said as he held out his hand. "You got any luggage?"

"Just what I carried on."

"Good deal, let's get going. I overheard the general and his staff talking, and that sounded like a hell of a firefight," Steve said as he pulled away from the terminal.

"It sure was."

"So, you were the one who captured the general?"

"Yes, but I just happened to be in the right place at the right time."

"Whatever, that's sure not the way I heard it."

Steve took JD directly to the headquarters building. "This is Madge, the general's secretary, and she'll take care of you. Good luck, and I hope that the next time I see you, I'll have to salute."

"Take a seat, I'll be right back," Madge told him with a big smile. A couple of minutes later she returned and said, "Please follow me, the general is ready for you." When they reached the general's office, she opened the door. "Go on in, they're expecting you."

JD was surprised to see several senior officers standing in front of the general's desk talking. JD snapped to attention and saluted. They all returned his salute, and then General Russo ordered, "At ease, soldier. Come on over, we'd like to talk with you for a few minutes." The general met him halfway, held out his hand, and bellowed: "Congratulations on a job well done. It's too damn bad about the rest of the team, but the Brazilian government couldn't be more pleased."

"Thank you, sir."

"I've read the action reports, and it sounded like it got pretty hairy. How many times were you hit?"

"Seven, but none of them were much more than flesh wounds."

The general nodded knowingly, and asked, "Is it true you'd only been with the detachment for a short time?"

"It was my first day in the country. My plane landed at 0900, and we left on the mission that evening."

"Incredible. I'd intended to give you the medal the Brazilian government sent, and a Purple Heart, but you were never there, according to the State Department. However, I've added a classified entry to your personnel file, and trust me, the word will get around, in spite of the damn bureaucrats. Tell us a little bit about yourself," General Russo requested.

As JD shared some of his life story, the general stopped him to ask, "Was your stepdad Leroy Bolton?"

"Yes, sir."

"Did he ever mention that he was in the military?"

"He never said much about it, but yes, he was a colonel, and served mostly in the Special Ops."

JD continued his story, but the general was thinking back to the day Leroy had saved his life. They talked with JD for almost an hour before the general announced, "We had better let him go and get settled in."

General Russo led him to the door. "Good luck in OCS, and I'll be keeping an eye on you."

For a change, OCS was uneventful. JD graduated at the top of his class, and General Russo was there to congratulate him.

"Well done, my boy," the general said as he shook JD's hand. "I knew you could do it, but your performance was more than outstanding."

"Thanks, it was a challenge, but I've learned a lot."

"Walk with me for a moment. You don't have to accept, but I've pulled some strings with an old classmate of mine, and I've gotten you an assignment to the 75th Rangers. It's one of the most elite regiments the army has, and I once commanded it."

"Thank you, sir, it would be an honor."

"When we're alone, it's Doug."

JD didn't know what to say, but he managed to stammer, "Thank you, Doug."

They talked for almost thirty minutes, before the general said, "I'd love to talk longer, but I've got to be going. I'll keep in touch, and don't ever hesitate to give me a call if you need anything."

JD THOUGHT HE knew what to expect, but the training at Fort Benning, Georgia had been the most intense he'd ever experienced.

However, he'd gutted it up, and had again excelled. In what seemed like no time at all, he'd graduated, and had been selected to join the Regimental Special Troops Battalion.

The years seemed to fly by, as they sent JD all over the world, on some of the toughest missions imaginable. He'd progressed through the ranks on his own merit, but having a highly respected flag officer as a mentor hadn't hurt. By the time he was twenty-six, he'd been fast-tracked to lieutenant colonel, and was leading his own command.

True to his word, General Russo had followed, and at times guided, JD's career until he was due to retire. When the time had come, he'd made a point to have JD flown in to attend his retirement party, and to introduce him to another friend of his.

JD's flight was almost forty-five minutes late. The general had sent his driver to pick him up, and when he stepped off the plane the sergeant saluted and said, "Let me put your bags in the trunk and I'll take you directly to the officers' club."

The party had already started, so when JD walked in, he started looking around for General Russo. They spotted each other about the same time, and General Russo waved JD over.

"Great, you made it," General Russo said as he shook JD's hand and patted him on the back.

"This is Lt. Colonel John David Drury, the young man I've been telling you about. JD, this is Major General Jeffries, a good friend of mine, and I hope that he'll become a good friend of yours."

"General Jeffries, I can't tell you what an honor it is to meet you. I've read all of your papers from the War College," John David said as he shook General Jeffries's hand.

John David turned back to General Russo. "Doug, I'm going to miss you. I would have never gotten to where I am if it hadn't been for you."

"Nonsense. I've never seen a more gifted solider, and I'm sure you're going to go far. However, just to make sure, I've asked Walter to keep an eye on you for me."

JD didn't know what to say, but General Jeffries saved him. "Doug has been telling me about you for years, but I never understood why he took such an interest, until he got me to start reading your mission reports. At first I thought he was feeding me a bunch of fairy tales, until I verified a few of them."

"It does seem like I'm always in the middle of something."

Even as he said it, JD thought back to the events that had shaped his life, and realized just how true the statement was.

JD AND GENERAL Jeffries stayed in touch over the next couple of years, and as General Russo had hoped, they'd become good friends.

When John David's team completed their latest mission in Rabat, Morocco, they boarded a flotilla of fast attack subs off the coast of Africa, on their way to Diego Garcia.

"I've got General Jeffries on the video conference for you," the sailor told JD. JD hadn't talked to the general in several months, but he knew it wasn't going to be a social call.

"Good to see you, General."

"Same here, my boy. Sorry to get right to it, but the shit has hit the fan in South Africa, and I need your team there right away."

"Yes, sir, what's the mission?" JD asked.

"A group of terrorists from Mozambique has managed to infiltrate the country, and recruit enough of the local dissidents to carry out a coup attempt. Pretoria, Cape Town, and Bloemfontein have already fallen, and what's left of the government has taken refuge in a small town on the north shore of Saldanha Bay. I need you to get down there, stabilize the situation, and make sure President Okonkwo regains control."

"We'll do our best."

"You always do."

JD briefed his team before he attempted to contact President Okonkwo.

JD's sub surfaced just long enough to rendezvous with a stealth helicopter from a carrier task force that was loitering a hundred miles off the coast. The chopper dropped him off in a small park, near where President Okonkwo was holed up.

"I can't thank you enough for coming," President Okonkwo said, as they shook hands. "How big of a force do you have with you?"

"I'll have nine hundred and fifty men, but they're not in the country yet."

"That's all! What can you hope to accomplish with so few men?"

"My mission is to take out the terrorists' leadership, return you to power, and that's exactly what I intend to do."

The president liked his enthusiasm, but he wasn't sure that he understood the situation.

"They have over ten thousand men in Cape Town alone, and I don't have any men that I can spare."

"We'll have the element of surprise, and my men are quite good at what they do."

They talked for a few more minutes, before JD called for the helicopter pick him up.

"It looks like we're screwed," the president commented to his aide as the chopper took off. "Make sure my aircraft is standing by. I don't think they have a chance in hell, but I'll stay until I'm sure they've failed."

The copter took JD to their jumping-off point, about five miles off the coast. As the helicopter slowed to a hover over the bay, the submarines started surfacing to offload his men. When the subs had put a couple of their rubber boats into the water, JD yelled to the pilot, "Thanks for the lift," and jumped.

"There's the colonel," Lieutenant Herrera called out. "Let's go get him."

"Good to see you, Colonel," the lieutenant said as he pulled Colonel Drury into the boat.

As their boats approached the beach, Colonel Drury's headset came to life. "Come straight in," the local CIA contact instructed.

"Roger that," JD responded.

The CIA had a convoy of M35 transport trucks waiting to take them into the Capitol. When they'd beached the boats, JD ordered, "Get the men loaded, we need to be out of here in twenty."

While Lieutenant Herrera was getting the men on board the trucks, their CIA contact pulled JD aside. "The rebel commanders are holed up in the main parliament building."

"What can we expect on the way in?" JD asked.

"We haven't seen any fighting since the president's men made a run for it."

"That's good. Are you going to lead us in?"

"Sorry, we've got another mission, but I've programed a GPS with the best route into the city," he said as he handed the unit to JD.

"You need anything else, Colonel?"

"Nope, I think you've got us fixed up. You'd better get going. It's hard to tell when this will go to hell."

JD was riding in the lead truck, and the roads were virtually deserted until they reached the outskirts of the city. "Slow down, there's a roadblock ahead," JD instructed.

When they were a hundred yards out, he ordered, "That's close enough, stop here." He tapped the back window, and ordered, "Team two, dismount and take them down."

Six snipers jumped out of the back of the truck, and thirty seconds later the guards lay dead. Once the guards were neutralized, they rammed through the barricade and continued toward their destination.

JD was following their progress on the GPS screen. "That's close enough, you can stop here. Lieutenant Herrera, I need you up front."

JD spent a few minutes surveying the situation, before he laid out their plan of attack. "I haven't seen any tanks or heavy weapons, and there are approximately forty guards on this side. I'm going to assume a similar number on the other side."

"That shouldn't be an issue," Lieutenant Herrera said.

"Position your sniper teams, here, here, and here, to provide covering fire," JD instructed. "When I give the word, take two squads and cover the left flank; have Lieutenant Williams take two squads and cover the right flank. I'll take the rest of the men up the center. Any questions?"

"I'm good."

When everyone was in position, Colonel Drury ordered, "Fire."

They were laying down a murderous crossfire, and JD waited until the survivors made a run for it. "All teams move out," he ordered.

As they charged the building, the snipers were continuing to fire. The snipers killed most of the guards, but a couple of them managed to scramble back inside and lock the bulletproof glass doors.

"Blow the doors," JD ordered.

As JD's men rushed to set the charges, one of the guards remembered to punch the panic button, and the alarm was almost deafening. They slapped the small plastic explosive charges on both sides of the double doors and blew them off their hinges. The building was a hub-and-spoke design, and as they jumped over the shattered doors, they could see the rebel forces rushing down the hallways toward them.

"Alpha team, deploy on the north side of the building," JD ordered over his headset. "Delta, you take the south, and we'll clear out the main hall."

The rebel guards put up a short but spirited resistance, but they didn't stand a chance against JD's men.

"Sergeant Lopez, take your men and go and help out the alpha team," JD ordered. "Sergeant Morley, you're with me. The rebel leaders are supposed to be in the auditorium, and it should be down this way."

They'd positioned fifty of their fiercest fighters to protect the auditorium, and it took JD's men twenty minutes to fight their way through the fanatical guards. The auditorium had twenty double doors leading into it. When they reached the center, JD pointed to a door and ordered, "This is where we'll enter. Sergeant Morley, blow that door open, and be careful, they're true fanatics."

The sergeant's men set several explosive charges on the heavy metal doors and detonated them. When explosions blew the doors into jagged pieces, Sergeant Morley charged through the shattered opening with his squad following close behind. The last man had just made it through the opening, when a series of massive explosions blew him back out into the hall. The explosions blew the rest of the doors off their hinges, and knocked everyone off their feet. As JD picked his way through the carnage, he could see the bloody ball bearings rolling down the polished marble floor.

"Damn fanatics. They'd rather blow themselves up than be captured," he lamented.

With their leaders dead, the coup started collapsing, and by the end of the week President Okonkwo had regained control.

A few days later, General Jeffries contacted JD. "Well done," he congratulated.

"Thank you, sir. It got a little Western at times, but we got it done."

"I need you back in the States ASAP."

"What's up?"

"I'll brief you when you land."

THEY'D JUST LANDED at Langley Air Force Base in Virginia, when JD's satellite phone rang.

"I'd intended to brief you today, but the situation has changed, and I won't be needing you right away," General Jeffries explained. "However, I've just been named to the Joint Chiefs of Staff, and I've got something else in mind for you. So just hang loose until I call for you."

"Will do, sir, and congratulations on your appointment."

AS PART OF his new assignment, General Jeffries was working with Charles Lutz, the director of the CIA.

"Charlie, I'd like for you to take a look at this young man's service record. I know you have an opening in SAD (Special Activities Division of the CIA), and I think he would make a good addition to your team."

Charlie spent almost a half hour going over JD's service record, and then he noticed the notation for a classified section. He signed on to his terminal and called up the entries.

"I see what you mean. Quite impressive, but why the special interest from you?"

"It started out as a special request from General Russo when he retired."

"He'd taken him under his wing when he first went to OCS. I didn't figure it out at first, but the man who raised JD had saved his life, and he was trying to repay the debt. But none of that makes any difference, because he's a truly outstanding young man."

"That's evident from his record. I tell you what, let me think about it overnight, and I'll give you a call in the morning."

It turned out to be two days later before Charlie got back to him.

"Sorry, I got caught up in budget meetings. I can't see any reason not to take him. With the economy as bad as it is, our budgets are sure to take a big hit. So I had better get all the good men I can."

"Thanks, and I don't think you'll ever regret it. I'd like to keep in touch with him if you don't mind."

"Hell, General, you're on the Joint Chiefs of Staff, who am I to tell you who you can talk to."

The end justifies the means.

—Niccolò Machiavelli

PART 4

CHAPTER 1

Charles Whitman was normally a very reserved person, but his new role had forced him into the sometimes harsh public spotlight to tout his company. US Motors's rebirth had made him one of the most successful and recognized men in the country, except in one area. He'd never had a close personal relationship.

President McDonald knew Charles was up to his ears in a union negotiation, but he decided to give him a call anyway. "How's it coming?" President McDonald asked.

"Slow and painful. You'd think we were back in the heyday of Detroit, by some of their outlandish demands."

"Some things never change, but I've got faith you'll work it out. I just wish I could say the same. I can't seem to push forward on anything."

"Like I've told you, I damn sure wouldn't want your job."

"I understand. Thank God I've only got eight more months of this hell, but that brings me to why I called. Our country desperately needs a man of your talents in the White House, and before you say no, just promise me, you'll at least consider it."

Charles hesitated before he answered. "I'll think about it. That's the best I can do."

"Thanks, and I know you'll come to the right decision, for you and the country."

The contract negotiations had reached an impasse, so they took a couple of days off. When they got back together, the union had added a new lawyer to the team.

"This is Victoria Cangelosi, and she's taking Stan's place as the lead counsel," John Stasi, the president of the UAW announced.

"It's very nice to meet you, Victoria," Charles Whitman told her.

"Same here, and I've heard nothing but good things about you," Victoria commented.

Victoria was a drop-dead-gorgeous Sicilian beauty, and as the talks had ebbed and flowed, Charles had found himself paying more attention to Victoria than the negotiations.

Damn, that's a fine-looking woman, Charles thought to himself. *I wonder if she'd go out with me?* As he sat there trying get up enough courage to ask her, he thought, *What the hell, nothing ventured, nothing gained.* When they quit for the day, Charles walked over to Victoria. "I'm not trying to place you in an awkward situation, but would you have dinner with me tonight?"

"I'd love to. Do you want to meet, or will you pick me up?" she responded without hesitation.

Surprised, it was several seconds before he managed to blurt out, "I'll pick you up at eight. You're staying at the MGM Grand, aren't you?"

Struggling not to giggle, she told him, "Yes. I am, and I'll meet you in the lobby."

It had been several years since he'd dated, and as he changed for dinner, he found himself growing excited by the prospect of spending the evening with Victoria. He picked Victoria up at her hotel, in one of the new models they'd just started shipping. It was stretched to limo size, and at the president's insistence, armored.

"This is nice, one of yours?" Victoria asked.

"It is, but it's had a few modifications." It had a full bar, so they had a drink on the way to the restaurant. When the limo pulled up in front of what looked like an old mansion, Victoria commented, "Oh goody, the Whitney, I love this place."

When they walked in, Barnaby Jones, the owner, recognized them, and started their way. The waiting area was packed, but Barnaby moved smoothing through the crowd.

"Good evening, Ms. Cangelosi. Mr. Whitman, everything is prepared as you requested."

The Whitney had once been a mansion, but they'd renovated it into what many considered the finest restaurant in Detroit. They'd converted the various rooms to themed dining areas, and Barnaby led them to what had once been the library, where he seated them at a table by the fireplace.

"Enjoy, and if there's anything you need, please ask."

"I've never seen it this empty," Victoria observed.

"I asked Barnaby to make sure we weren't disturbed, so he cleared it for us."

As they talked, it was like they'd known each other for years. They had a wonderful dinner together, and it turned out to be the first of many. Neither of them had ever taken time for a serious relationship, but it was definitely a case of love at first sight for both of them.

The labor negotiations had continued at a snail's pace, and they'd spent every moment they could together. Victoria was smitten, but she couldn't believe how shy he was around her, and that he hadn't tried to bed her yet.

* * *

THE NEGOTIATIONS HAD been brutal, but at the end of the seventh week, they'd finally hammered out an agreement.

"I'm glad that's finally finished," Victoria declared as Charles signed the contract.

"Me too, but I sure hate to see you go," Charles said.

"I'm not leaving right away. Daddy asked me to take a look at the MGM's books. They've been trying to sell it to him for months, but he said the price seemed too cheap."

Clearly relieved she wasn't leaving, he said, "Wonderful. Does it mean we can have dinner again tonight?"

"Absolutely." She paused. "And breakfast, if you'd like?"

SHE'D WORKED AS slowly as she could, but three weeks later, she'd wrapped up her due diligence, and was getting ready to return to New York. The night before she was supposed to leave, they were sitting at their usual table at the Whitney, and Victoria noticed Charles was unusually nervous.

"What's wrong? You seem agitated."

Charles reached into his jacket pocket, but he dropped the box as he fumbled to take it out. "Damn it. I've never been this nervous." Embarrassed, he retrieved it, and got down on one knee beside her chair. "I'm horrible at this sort of thing, but would you be my wife?"

Victoria looked down at one of the most powerful men in the United States, and said, "Get up you silly man, of course I'll marry you." She stood up and took both of his hands to help him up. As they stood in the middle of the crowded dining room, kissing like the lovers they were, they didn't seem to notice that everyone in the room was clapping.

The next morning they were eating breakfast in her

room, when he asked, "When would you like to get married?" Expecting her to say the spring or later.

"How about this Thursday?"

"Wow, great by me, but I figured you'd want a huge wedding, with all the bells and whistles."

"No way. After you fell asleep, I called Daddy to tell him the good news, and ask him if we could use the wedding chapel at one of his hotels in Vegas."

"Damn, girl, you sure don't mess around when you make up your mind. I'll book our flights."

"No need, Daddy has one of his Gulfstreams coming for us."

When they landed at McCarran International, their plane taxied over to the Signature FBO.

The engines hadn't even wound down, before an armored limousine drove out onto the tarmac to pick them up. When the driver opened the rear door, he told them, "Go ahead and get in, we'll take care of your bags."

When the hulking bodyguard bent over to grab a bag, his impeccably tailored suit gapped open, and Charles caught a glimpse of his large-caliber pistol.

"That man is carrying a gun."

"Of course he is," Victoria said. "He wouldn't be much of a bodyguard without one."

When they arrived at the casino, the hotel manager and his staff immediately swarmed them.

"Welcome back, Ms. Cangelosi," Stephan Walberg, the hotel's general manager said.

"Good to be back."

"I can't tell you how honored we are that you're holding your wedding here, and I think you'll be pleased."

"I'm sure I will. This is my fiancé, Charles Whitman."

"It's an honor, Mr. Whitman."

"If you'll follow me, I'll show you to your rooms."

The private elevator to the penthouse was flanked by

armed security, and it whisked them directly to the pent-house.

"No door?" Charles asked.

"None needed," Stephan said. "Other than the one-way emergency exits, the elevator is the only way in or out, and it's always guarded. Your suite covers the entire floor, so there's no chance of anyone disturbing you. Give me a call when you're ready to come down, and I'll have my men escort you to the wedding chapel."

Once they'd showered and changed clothes, Victoria called Stephan. "We're ready."

"You might as well make yourselves comfortable. Victor's plane had to detour around some weather, and he's running about an hour behind schedule."

"No problem, just let me know when he arrives."

An hour and a half later, Stephan called back. "Your father is in the lobby, so you can come down whenever you're ready."

UNLIKE THE HUGE wedding Charles had expected, the only people in attendance were her father, and a few of his associates. After the brief ceremony, they returned to their suite, where Charles finally got to meet Daddy.

"I've been looking forward to meeting you, sir," Charles Whitman said as they shook hands.

"Same here, my boy. My little girl sure seems to have taken a liking to you."

"As I have for her."

"I've followed your work, and I've got to say that I've been highly impressed," Victor said. "I never thought anyone could rebuild the auto industry, but you've done a hell of a job."

"Thanks, but at times, I had my doubts as well." Charles almost admitted he'd heard a lot about Victor's business dealings, but he thought he'd let sleeping dogs lie, because Victor was rumored to be the most powerful crime boss of all time.

"I trust the accommodations are acceptable?" Victor asked.

"They're magnificent." Even *magnificent* was a bit of an understatement, because Victor had given them a top-floor penthouse, and it was sixteen thousand square feet of over-the-top opulence. They made small talk for almost thirty minutes, before Victor got up to leave.

"I'll be going now. You two enjoy your honeymoon, and if you need anything, just ask."

THEY WERE TALKING over breakfast, when Victoria first learned Charles was toying with the idea of running for president. They'd spent the rest of the day discussing the pros and cons of it, until she finally got frustrated.

"You sure are a hardheaded devil," Victoria declared. "I know you really want this, so get off the damn fence and run. I'll help, and I think you'll be surprised at how well you'll do."

"OK, I'll give it a go, but I'm counting on you to not let me screw it up."

She giggled. "The only thing you're going to screw is me. Now come here."

"You can be such a crude little thing, but I guess it's what I love most about you," he said as he picked her up and tossed her onto the bed.

CHAPTER 2

Charles had struggled at first, but as she'd promised, Victoria stepped in to help.

"I hope I can raise enough money to get the matching funds," Charles said.

"You won't be taking the matching funds, too many strings," Victoria declared.

"How's that going to work? I'm a political unknown."

"Trust me on this, it'll be all right."

Charles got caught up in the grind of the campaign, and hadn't thought much about the money, until they held their first finance meeting.

"Did you see the first month's contributions?" Charles asked.

"I did, and a hundred million isn't a bad start," Victoria said.

"A start? I'm beginning to see why you told me not to take the matching funds."

As they crisscrossed the country making campaign stops, Charles was starting to get into it. At first the turnouts had been light, but it hadn't taken long for the crowds to grow to standing-room only.

After what seemed like an endless series of speeches and gatherings, election day had finally arrived.

At Victoria's insistence, they had returned to Los Vegas to wait out the election results. Victor had set them up in the same luxurious penthouse they'd used for their honeymoon.

"I still can't get over how incredible this is," Charles said.

"Daddy said it was the least he could do, and that he was terribly sorry he couldn't be here with us. He had some urgent business to attend to in DC, but he said he would call you in the morning."

The sitting area in the master bedroom had a two-hundred-inch flat-screen TV, so they curled up on the couch to watch the election commentary. Neither of them was saying much, as they waited for the results to start coming in. Finally, Charles broke the silence. "I don't think I've ever been this nervous. I'm not really expecting to win, but I find myself wanting this more than anything in my life, other than you."

Victoria was not a shy woman, but she blushed as she hugged him. "I don't know how you do it, but you always seem to know the perfect thing to say. However, I think you're underestimating yourself, because Daddy was feeling good about your chances."

Finally, the polls began to close, and the networks started making their early projections. At first Charles couldn't believe it. He was winning, and not by a small margin. By the time he received the call from his opponent conceding the election, he'd won virtually every state.

"I told you," Victoria said. She gave him a big kiss and asked, "How does it feel to be the next president of the United States?"

"I'm not sure I could describe it. It's almost as good as the first time we made love."

"Well, you're about to relive that moment."

"Do you think we have time?"

"What are they going to do, leave?" she asked, as she started stripping.

THE TIME SEEMED to fly by, and before they realized it, Charles had been sworn in, and they were living in the White House. However, Charles's euphoria had been short-lived.

"Did you watch CNBC this morning?" Victoria asked.

"Of course, and I can't believe there's no good news, but I'm going to change that."

"If anybody can, it's you."

He knew the massive deficits had to be addressed, so he forced through drastic funding cuts to virtually every government program. Next, he got Congress to revamp the tax code, to raise more revenue. By the end of his first year, it was evident that the cuts, and additional revenue hadn't been enough to turn it around.

He'd just finished reading the year-end numbers. "Damn, I'd hoped it wouldn't come to this."

He knew he couldn't wait any longer, so he called in his chief of staff, Leonard Montage, to begin work on the next phase of the effort. He'd already written it up, but it was risky, because their lobbyists were legendary for their ability to make or break any politician's career, even a president's.

After Leonard had read the proposal, he warned, "They're really going to come after you if you slash the military's budgets."

"Agreed, but given the current state of our economy, I don't see how we can continue being the world's policeman."

"Have you discussed this with Victoria?"

Most presidents would have been offended, but Charles had known Leonard for a long time. "You know I have. We discuss everything."

"Very well, I'll deliver it myself, but you'd better be damn sure you're ready for the shit storm that's sure to follow."

It had taken every ounce of political capital the president could muster, but he'd managed to ram the cuts through.

When the military started making the mandated reductions to their overseas commands, there was a huge uproar from the various nations around the world that depended on the United States for protection.

A couple of months later, the president got an urgent call from the secretary general of the UN, Gabriel Arrobas.

"Mr. President, I've delayed the decision as long I could, but your actions left me no other recourse. Our need for troops is at an all-time high, so I've asked the Chinese government to step in to help out."

"I understand completely. It pains me to admit it, but the state of our economy just wouldn't allow us to continue. I understand your reluctance to call on the Chinese, but at this point, they're the only ones who could do it."

"Don't get me wrong, I'm thankful that they've agreed to step up, but I'm not naïve enough to think there won't be a price to be paid."

President Whitman's drastic measures had helped, but they still hadn't been enough.

After studying the situation for several months, he came to a reluctant conclusion.

"Please tell me you're not seriously considering doing this," Victoria pleaded.

"I'm between a rock and a hard place. I've already raised taxes, and cut everything I can think of. Besides, I think I can hold my own with them."

"I know you're a great negotiator, but you're negotiating from a position of weakness, and Daddy has always said it's a formula for disaster."

"I can't believe your father has ever dealt from a position of weakness, but I get the point. I'd be happy to listen, if you have any bright ideas?"

She thought for a moment. "No, I guess you're right. We're screwed, and not in a good way."

THE NEXT DAY they took Air Force One to Bonn, Switzerland, to attend the quarterly G8 finance meeting. It took six days of almost around-the-clock talks, but President Whitman got them to grant most of the accommodations he was seeking.

The night before they were scheduled to sign the agreements, he and Victoria were dining alone for the first time in days. She was reading the agreements as they ate. "This really sucks. You've had to give away a lot."

"True enough, but it should give us some breathing room."

Many pundits called the agreements the most one-sided they'd ever seen, but they opened the floodgates for cheap European money. At first there had been a firestorm of criticism in the press, but several months later it looked as though his desperate gambit had succeeded. The large multinational banks and investment firms were healthy again, the stock market was booming.

The timing couldn't have been better, because President Whitman's approval ratings had gone through the roof, and he'd easily won reelection. The United States was slowly regaining its stature in the world's economic community, and it looked like he was going down in history as one of the most successful presidents of all time.

The moral test of government is how it treats those who are in the dawn of life, the children; those who are in the twilight of life, the elderly; and those who are in the shadows of life, the sick, the needy and the handicapped.

—HUBERT H. HUMPHREY

PART 5

CHAPTER 1

Eighteen months into his final term, President Whitman decided it was time to address the fundamental issues that had led him to run for president.

"I let you talk me out of bringing this up during the last election, but I think the time is right," Charles said as he handed Victoria his plan.

She didn't bother reading it before she laid it aside.

"Look, I know you and your father don't agree with me, and it's never been formally recognized as the tipping point. However, the recession of 2007 was the start of the downturn that devastated the engine of the economy, our middle class."

"Actually, I agree with you on that point," Victoria said. "It's your approach to fixing it that I take issue with. What you're proposing is very close to socialism."

"To some extent you're right, but most of the programs aren't intended to be permanent. Think of it as a way to jump-start the economy."

"I'm not sure you'll ever convince me, but I'll help if you need me to."

The stock market was booming, but many aspects of

the economy were sicker than ever. The latest unemployment numbers were out, and President Whitman had scheduled a meeting to go over them.

"How's it look?" President Whitman asked.

"Unemployment is at thirteen percent, but I believe the number is horribly understated," Leonard Montage said.

The president pulled his proposal out, and handed it to Leonard. "I'm convinced it could be another ten points higher. I've been working on this for some time, and I would like you to go through it. When you're ready, let's discuss it."

When Leonard finished, he was stunned. He'd known the president for many years, but he'd never recognized the depth of his empathy for the underprivileged.

Leonard often used Victoria as a sounding board when he wasn't on the same page with the president. "Have you seen your husband's newest quest?" Leonard asked.

"Of course, but it's not new. Up to now, I've been able to talk him out of it, but this time he's adamant."

Eight days later the president walked into Leonard's office and asked impatiently, "Have you read my notes yet?"

"Several days ago, but I haven't been able to decide whether it's the right thing to do."

"Forget right or wrong, can you help me?"

"Are you absolutely sure?"

"I've never felt more strongly about anything in my entire life."

Leonard could see the passion burning in the president's eyes, and thought, *What the hell, we might as well go out in a blaze of glory.* Later that day, Leonard reached out to Victoria.

"I'm about to start working on the legislation, and I should be finished by the end of next week."

"Great, thanks for the heads-up," Victoria said.

They went through several rounds of revisions before Leonard sat down with the president one last time.

"You've done your normal masterful job," President Whitman said.

"Thanks. When would you like me to submit it?"

"Right away."

Leonard delivered the legislation just before lunch, and that evening the leaders of the House and Senate met for drinks to discuss it.

"Have you had time to go through Whitman's proposal?" Jerry Chambers, the Speaker of the House asked.

"I've read it, and I assume you got the same call I did?" Larry James, the Senate majority leader asked.

Jerry nodded and he took another sip of whiskey.

"This could mean the end of our political careers."

"I didn't get the feeling he cared."

"True enough, and I guess it's time we pay the devil his due," Larry said, before he drained his glass of whiskey.

To the surprise of virtually all the prognosticators, they rammed the president's bill through in one marathon session. Leonard was in the Senate observing, and when the final vote was taken, he called the president. It was two in the morning, and Victoria answered. "What's up Leonard?"

"The just passed his bill," Leonard reported.

"Good deal, it means a lot to him."

"You don't seem surprised," Leonard observed. "I have to ask. How did you pull it off?"

"Me! I didn't do anything."

"Understood. Would you mind giving him the good news?"

"First thing in the morning. Good night, Leonard, and thanks."

Unbelievably excited, President Whitman had Leonard schedule a prime-time telecast to sign the bill.

As President Whitman waited for his cue to begin, he suddenly realized that however it turned out, he was about to change the course of history.

"My fellow Americans, it's my great pleasure to sign this monumental legislation into law," President Whitman proclaimed. "It's rather complicated, so if you'll bear with me for a few minutes, I'll try to give you an overview. I've tried to draw on the lessons learned from Franklin Delano Roosevelt's New Deal, as well as Lyndon Baines Johnson's Great Society, and his war on poverty. Before all of you naysayers start pointing out the problems, I'll be the first to admit that all the programs had some issues, and I expect that these new initiatives will as well. However, I truly believe they'll go a long way toward addressing the key issues that we are faced with today, which are: affordable housing, job creation, eradicating hunger, and adequate health care for everyone. You may ask, how we're going to pay for all of this? My answer to you is: How can we not pay for it? I do understand that there will be valid concerns about the cost and complexity of the programs. So let me start by assuring you that we're not going to set up a whole new bureaucracy to administer the programs. Unlike the previous bailouts and subsidy programs, we're going to ensure that the funding reaches the people who need it, not the labyrinth of fat cats and financial organizations, which have sucked it up in the past. As the old saying goes, the devil is always in the details.

"To address the lack of affordable housing, the FHA will be rolling out new mortgage guidelines. Depending on the borrower's income level, it'll provide mortgages at extremely low, or zero interest rates, as well as an upfront subsidy to lower the principal. For those of you with existing mortgages, we'll provide refinancing and principal reduction, to bring your mortgages in line with the new programs. Anyone who has already paid off their mortgage will receive a tax credit of fifty percent of the value of your home, which can be used over a period of up to twenty years.

"We've supposedly had comprehensive medical care in place for decades, but it has never been effective. This bill provides the necessary funding to ensure everyone receives the care they need. We're aware it's going to exacerbate the shortage of doctors. Short term, we'll provide a fast path certification for national interest, and E1B visas to allow foreign doctors to fill the gaps. As a long-term solution, we will fund the expansion of every medical school in the country, along with full-ride scholarships to everyone who qualifies.

"The rampant unemployment and underemployment situation requires an aggressive strategy. First, we're providing four trillion dollars in grants and zero-interest loans to jumpstart rebuilding our manufacturing base, and small business creation. I'm fully aware the WTO is going to accuse us of unfair subsidies, but we're going to make 'Made in America' a good thing again.

"Sadly, we've allowed our transportation infrastructure to deteriorate to the point where it's in danger of becoming unusable. It's a monumental task, and the government couldn't possibly pull this off without help. The NTSB will immediately begin flowing the necessary funding to state and local governments so they can begin refurbishing our airport, highway, and railway systems. This will not only help us rebuild our infrastructure, it will provide millions of new jobs. Until the new jobs kick in, we'll be providing a graduated subsidy to anyone making less than three times the poverty level. The subsidies will range from five hundred dollars a week to as much as fifteen hundred dollars a week, depending on the size of your family.

"The last change, and my personal favorite, is that we've abolished the IRS, and the existing tax codes, and instituted a national sales tax. To ensure the sales tax doesn't unfairly effect the lower income segments of our population, we'll be issuing sales tax exemption cards to everyone that qualifies.

"I know I've probably raised as many questions as I've answered. However, we've just launched a new Web site, America_Reborn.gov, and it has the details of every program that I've just mentioned, and links to sign up for any of the initiatives you're interested in.

"In closing, I would ask that each one of you make the commitment to do everything in your power to help me rebuild this great nation of ours.

"Good night, and God bless all of you."

CHAPTER 2

There were many start-up issues, but surprisingly the people had embraced the process.

"Did you watch the evening news?" Victoria asked as they were getting ready for bed.

"No, I was in a defense briefing," President Whitman said. "What did I miss?"

"They were doing interviews with people from all across the country, and I have to admit, I've never been more proud of our country. Time after time, they had families sharing their stories about how much better their lives were.

"The changes you've instituted have made a great number of people's lives worth living. I'm so proud that you had the strength of character to make the changes, in spite of everyone, including me, telling you they would never work."

Charles took her in his arms and gave her a big kiss. "I couldn't have done it without you and your father's help."

She giggled and took his hand. "Come to bed, and you can thank me properly."

* * *

BY THE END of the first year, the economy was surging like never before, and America was on its way back. When President Whitman was convinced the changes were going to achieve his goals, he called Leonard in.

"See if you can arrange a meeting with Secretary General Arrobas for the first week in February."

"No problem, but he's going to want an agenda."

"Tell him I'd like to discuss the US taking back some of the peacekeeping duties."

Surprised that he'd want to take on the burden again, Leonard asked, "Why in the world would you want to get into that mess again?"

"I'm concerned the Chinese are growing too powerful."

"Probably true. I'll get right on it."

Shortly afterward, the old saying, "Nothing remains constant except change itself," proved to be brutally true.

"What the hell's going on?" President Whitman asked, as he watched the stock market drop another 5 percent.

"I don't understand it," Leonard Montage said.

"It looks like the automated trading programs are dumping everything. Most of the built-in circuit breakers have already tripped, but it hasn't seemed to slow the decline. I've spoken with all the exchanges, and they're going to suspend trading for the rest of the day."

"Call some of your friends and see if any of them have a handle on what's happening," President Whitman instructed.

The president's request jogged Leonard's memory. "I doubt that this has anything to do with what's going on, but I got a really odd call from Ferdinand Stubbens."

"What did the cantankerous old bastard want?" the president asked.

"He wouldn't tell me what he wanted, but he was worked up enough that I think you should give him a few minutes."

"Do I have to?"

"Of course not, but he is our ambassador to China."

"OK, I'll do it."

"Good, you've got an opening at 0900 tomorrow."

IT WAS ALMOST 3 a.m. when Leonard heard someone banging on his front door. He often got calls in the middle of the night, but it was highly unusual for them to come by. Thinking it must be really important; he threw on a robe and rushed downstairs.

The knocking was growing louder as he reached the entryway. "Hold your horses, I'm coming," he yelled.

He turned the alarm off, and jerked the door open, expecting to see one of the president's Secret Service details. Instead there were three masked men.

Terrified, he tried to slam the door in their faces, but they rushed through the door, slamming him back into the entryway. Thinking it was a robbery, Leonard pleaded, "Take what you want, just don't hurt us." When his wife heard the commotion, she came rushing down the stairs.

DC had always been a dangerous city, so the president had made them install a safe room when Leonard took the job. "Get to the room," Leonard screamed.

She turned to run back upstairs, but one of the men shot her in the back. The bullet's impact drove her forward, and her lifeless body slid down the stairs, until one of her legs got hung up in the railing. Leonard lunged at the killer, but a bullet to the head put an end to that.

"Damn it, you got brains all over me."

They dragged Leonard's lifeless body out of the way, and closed the door. None of them said a word as they moved to carry out their assignments. The man who'd shot Leonard went directly to the study and started stuffing the papers from Leonard's desk into the sack he was carrying. The second intruder rushed upstairs, where he ransacked their bedroom for what cash and jewels he

could find. Meanwhile, the third man used a small explosive device to blow open the floor safe in the entryway coat closet.

They'd been in the house less than five minutes when
the team leader ordered, "OK, time's up, get your asses
in the car."

THE NEXT MORNING, President Whitman was growing
impatient, as Lee Child, Leonard's assistant, was pouring his third cup of coffee.

"See if you can find out where everyone is this morning."

"Will do," Lee responded. "Is there anyone in partic-
ular you're looking for?"

"I was supposed to have a nine a.m. meeting with
Ambassador Stubbens, and where the hell is Leonard?"

Thirty minutes later, Lee returned. "Sorry for the delay, but when I couldn't contact Leonard I had the police do a welfare check."

"Is everything all right?"

"No, sir, they just reported that Leonard and his wife
have been murdered."

"My God, what happened?"

"They don't have any details yet, but the captain I
spoke with said it looked like a botched home invasion."

"Get James Fenimore in here, right now!" the president barked.

"I want you to get me a copy of everything the DC
police have," the president told the head of his Secret
Service detail.

"This is outside our jurisdiction," James Fenimore
said. "They're going to bitch if I try to get involved. Besides, from what I've heard so far, they don't have much
to go on."

"Let them bitch. If they were doing their jobs, shit like
this wouldn't be happening all the time. If they won't co-

operate, get Jenkins with Justice to help out. While you're at it, find out where Ambassador Stubbens got off to. He was supposed to meet with me this morning."

It took him a couple of days to round it all up, but surprisingly, the police didn't take issue with the request.

"Here's everything they have so far," James Fenimore said as he handed the president the case file. After the president read the one-page summary he said, "You were right, they don't have shit." The president slid the folder into his desk drawer. "I don't understand why they would have targeted him, they weren't wealthy people."

"It's hard to say," James Fenimore said. "You know as well as I do that shit like this happens all the time in DC."

"Thanks for getting this, and I hope I didn't ruffle too many feathers."

"It turned out to be no big deal."

"Have you found out what happened to Ambassador Stubbens?"

"Not a trace. He had the hotel concierge book a car for eight a.m., but he never showed. We had them open his room, and all his stuff was still there, but there's no trace of him. We'll keep looking, but I don't hold out much hope."

As they were lying in bed that night, President Whitman told Victoria, "The police don't have shit on Leonard's case, and we still haven't been able to locate Ambassador Stubbens."

"If you'll get me a copy of everything you've got, I'll see if Daddy can find out anything."

A couple of weeks later, Victor Cangelosi called Victoria back with an update.

"I'm very sorry, but we haven't been able to identify the bastards who killed Leonard and his wife. The police may be right that it was a random home invasion, but those kinds of people usually can't keep their mouths shut, and there's absolutely nothing on the street."

"How about the ambassador?"

"Charles might want to take a look at what he'd been up to, because it looks like a pro hit to me."

"I'll let him know, and thanks, Daddy."

"Anytime, sweetie."

THE LOSS OF his friend and closest advisor had devastated the president, but he had plenty of other worries to take his mind off the loss.

While President Whitman struggled to make some sense out of it, the financial Armageddon had continued. The president's team couldn't determine the cause, but the same horrific scenario had played out day after day, week after week, until the stock market finally stabilized at a level that hadn't been seen since the 1930s. No matter what President Whitman tried, nothing worked.

"How much frigging money have we dumped into the banks so far?" the president asked Meg Palmer, his new chief of staff. She had taken over shortly after Leonard Montage had been killed, and he felt fortunate to have her.

"A little over six trillion so far."

He was used to dealing with huge sums of money, but the enormity of this was a bit overwhelming, even for him. "Damn!" He lowered his head, and closed his eyes for a moment. He looked up at Meg and remarked, "I know this sounds bad, but I'm sure as hell glad my term is about done."

As Meg listened to him, she was struck by how much he'd aged. When he'd taken office, at the age of forty-one, he'd been the youngest president ever, but now he looked closer to seventy than he did to fifty. She wished she could think of something to say, but there really wasn't anything, and it was about to get worse. She'd just reviewed the inflation reports that would hit the press in the morning, and they were unbelievable. Once she'd briefed the president, he got the stock exchanges to open two hours later than normal.

Early the next morning, President Whitman begged the congressional leaders to step up and help him save the country, but he couldn't muster enough votes to pass anything. When sweet-talking them didn't work, he tried threats, but after an hour and a half of futile attempts, it had become apparent he wasn't going to get anything but partisan bickering out of them. Frustrated at their lack of courage and vision, he decided to go back to the White House and regroup.

HE SPENT THE rest of the day soul-searching, and by the time they were getting ready for bed that night, he was totally frustrated.

"Since I can't get the cowardly bastards to commit to a damn thing, I'm just going to keep a low profile and ride it out until we can go back home," Charles said.

Victoria's dark brown eyes flashed with anger, as she said, "The hell you are. I'm meeting Daddy in Vegas tomorrow morning, and then we're going on to California for the week; while we're out there, I'll get him to fix it." He tried to hide it, but she saw the look of disgust on his face. "Look, I know you don't like to use him, but he can get them to do what you need done."

"I hate owing him."

"You worry too much. Daddy doesn't need anything from you, and besides, how do you think you got elected?"

"You don't need to remind me, but you know I wouldn't have run if I'd known he was going to rig the election."

She smiled mischievously. "I know. That's why I didn't

tell you. I knew you would make a great president. You just needed the chance, and I have no intention of letting these gutless bastards ruin your legacy." As he looked at her, he was reminded of how much he loved her, and how glad he was that she was on his side. Victoria could be just as ruthless as her father, but she loved him more than life itself. Seeing they could debate it all night, she told him, "Enough of this, come to bed and make love to your wife."

CHAPTER 3

The president was working in the Oval Office when Meg Palmer walked in. She coughed softly to get his attention, and when he saw the look on her face, he asked, "What's wrong?"

She took a deep breath. "Victor Cangelosi's Gulfstream went down in the Sierra Nevada mountains this morning."

"My wife, is she all right?"

"I'm so sorry," she said as she put her hand on his back. "Victoria and her father were killed in the crash."

President Whitman's sobs of undisguised agony almost broke her heart.

After a couple of minutes, he managed to compose himself enough to ask, "Why hadn't we heard about this before?"

"They didn't file a flight plan, so no one noticed when they didn't arrive in San Francisco. Some of her father's people finally called to report them missing. Once they started looking, it took the CAP a couple of hours to locate their plane. They said it looked like it exploded in midair. The terrain is very rugged where they went down, but they've already verified there weren't any survivors."

* * *

AFTER THE FUNERALS, President Whitman disappeared from the public's view. Everybody believed he was grieving over his wife's death, and that was some of it, but he'd given up.

As the presidential election approached, President Whitman felt he owed it to his party, so he offered his help. The convention was in three weeks, and since he hadn't heard anything from the election committee, he had Meg Palmer contact them.

"When do they want me at the convention?" President Whitman asked.

He hated conventions, but since it was being held in Detroit, he was looking forward to seeing his hometown again.

Meg looked at him, not quite sure how to break the news.

Seeing her hesitate, he asked, "They don't want me there, do they?"

"I'm so sorry."

"It's not a complete surprise. I knew Brooks was trying to distance himself from my administration."

"Does Gutierrez still have a twenty-point lead?"

"No, it's up to thirty-three." She could see it was depressing him, so she changed the subject. "Have you decided where you're going to live after you leave office?"

"I have. We were going to move back home to Detroit, but there's too many memories there, so I've decided to relocate to Hawaii."

"I've always wanted to live there myself," Meg said wishfully.

"You're welcome to come along. I'll need an assistant, and you could help me set up my library and handle my speaking engagements."

"Let me think about it," she offered. Even though there was no way she would ever consider it.

A few months later, the Republican nominee for president, (Lucky Louie) Gutierrez, and his advisors were gathered around a bank of TVs to watch the election results come in. The previous night's preelection polls had him in the lead by thirty points, so the champagne was chilled, and the press was in position to cover his acceptance speech. You could feel the excitement in the room as the networks started giving their exit poll projections. However, as the final numbers began posting, the mood began to shift.

"Jeffery, find out what's going on," Lucky Louie bellowed. "These numbers can't be right."

"Will do," Jeffery Woodbine, Louie's longtime friend and manager responded.

When Jeffery returned, Lucky Louie immediately knew something was wrong. "You look like you've seen a ghost," Lucky Louie observed.

"In this case, looks aren't deceiving, because I've just seen the ghost of your presidency. You were right; there was something was wrong with the numbers. Bill McDonald is winning by an even wider margin than the networks are reporting."

"Quit bullshitting me, no one had even heard of him a year ago."

"Judging from the people I've talked with, it was a backlash against the incumbents. However, spending a billion dollars on campaign ads alone probably didn't hurt either."

"So you're telling me I need to make a concession speech, instead of a victory speech?"

"You can wait a couple of hours if you'd like, but that's the reality of it."

* * *

PRESIDENT WHITMAN HADN'T bothered watching the election night proceedings, and he'd just sat down for breakfast when Meg came rushing in.

"Mr. President, I've got the final election numbers for you."

He put his coffee down and asked, "How much did Gutierrez win by?"

"He didn't win."

"We won?"

"No, sir, Bill McDonald won, and by a wide margin. Some of the House and Senate numbers are still being compiled, but it looks that along with the presidency, they've won almost all the available seats in the House and the Senate."

"Unbelievable. I know we'd discussed the possibilities, but this is beyond reason."

It took President Whitman a few days to digest the reality of the Federalist's landslide victory, but when he did, he realized it might present an opportunity to pass some of the legislation the country so desperately needed. He'd come to depend on Meg, so he called her in to discuss it.

"Since many of those Congressional ingrates are lame ducks like me, maybe they'll listen to reason and help me pass a few of the bills we so desperately need," President Whitman said.

"I haven't seen any indications they're ready to deal with the cold, hard reality of their situations," Meg Palmer advised. "But who knows, maybe they'll listen to reason. They're in session all week; I'll get them to schedule some time for you."

PRESIDENT WHITMAN GAVE a rousing speech, but without Victor's influence to grease the way, it turned out to be the same old partisan bickering.

A few weeks later, Meg Palmer handed him the daily briefing report.

"Just net it out for me."

"The number of Chapter 9 bankruptcies set a new record again this month. In addition, the OMB projects that there could be another thousand municipalities that will file within the next sixty days."

"Damn, this is already worse than the California debacles."

"It gets worse. The unemployment numbers hit twenty-five percent, and Texas just announced they're furloughing half of their state workers."

"I know you just talked to the leaders of both Houses, do you think they're ready to listen to reason?" the president asked.

"Not a chance in hell," Meg Palmer said. "The clueless bastards won't even agree to meet with you to discuss it."

"Then I guess I've shot my wad."

INAUGURATION DAY FINALLY came, and as Bill McDonald was waiting for the chief justice of the Supreme Court to arrive, he was reflecting on how he'd gotten to this point in his life. An avid student of history, he realized his presidency was going to be more than a little unique. He was the first president from the Federalist party since John Adams in 1797, and just the second unmarried president. James Buchanan had used his niece to fill the role of First Lady, but as far as Bill McDonald knew, he didn't have any living relatives. He'd only been a few days old when they found him on the steps of an orphanage in San Francisco. He'd never been adopted, so he'd bounced around foster care until he was old enough to be out on his own.

He might have had a rough start in life, but once he

got going, his life had seemed blessed. He'd gotten into Stanford through the generosity of an unknown bene-factor, where he'd blossomed into a brilliant student. Then during his junior year, he'd been selected for a highly coveted internship with Geely, the Chinese car company. From then on, he'd spent every summer in mainland China, learning the ins and outs of the Chinese way of doing business. After graduation, Geely had chosen him to coordinate their growing presence in the United States.

It's funny how life works out, he thought to himself.

EARLIER IN THE day, President Whitman had gathered his belongings, and left the White House for the last time. He'd considered attending the inauguration, but it was McDonald's day, and he was quite frankly tired of the whole Washington scene.

As President Whitman flew high over the Pacific to-ward Hawaii, he pulled out the folder of material Meg Palmer had handed him as he boarded the aircraft. He'd been deeply disappointed when she'd turned down his offer, and he found himself wondering if his interest might have been more than professional. Pushing the thought aside, he started studying the data. Shortly after the election, he'd asked her for an analysis of where Bill McDonald's campaign funds had come from. Under nor-mal circumstances, it should have been a simple task. However, the money trail was highly convoluted. It had taken all of her considerable talents, but Meg had finally unwound the labyrinth of contributions.

He thought back to his campaign, and chuckled at his own hypocrisy. When he'd finished the report, he was shocked at the enormity of the deception.

He hadn't been going to watch the inauguration, but his curiosity got the better of him. He was watching the broadcast in Air Force One's briefing room, and as the scene popped up on the hundred-inch high-definition TV, he remembered the excitement, and pride he'd felt when he'd first taken the oath of office. When the telecast was over, he turned the TV off, and reread the information Meg had given him.

By the time they touched down in Hawaii, he'd decided to give the file to the chief justice of the Supreme Court. He was a close friend, and would know what to do with the information.

His Secret Service detail whisked him away to the luxurious beachfront home he'd inherited when Victoria and her father were killed. The staff rushed out to meet him when he arrived.

"Dinner will be in an hour," Anthony Genovese, Victor's longtime butler, informed him.

"I know you've gone to a lot of trouble, but it's been a long day, and if it's all right, I'd like to eat in my sitting room."

"Of course. You should have everything you need, but don't hesitate to ask if we've missed anything."

"Thanks."

"What time would you like breakfast?"

"Six thirty would be fine. I've had some urgent business come up, and I've decided to fly back to the States in the morning. Would you mind booking me a flight?"

"No need, I'll have one of the Gulfstreams standing by."

"One of the Gulfstreams. I'd trade every penny of Victor's immense fortune for just one more day with Victoria."

As he'd done every night since her death, he said a prayer for Victoria before he went to sleep.

When he didn't come out for breakfast, one of the Secret Service agents went to check on him, and found him dead in his bed, one month before his forty-ninth birthday.

* * *

MEG PALMER WAS cleaning out her office when she received the news of his untimely death. She wasn't into conspiracy theories, but the timing and circumstances seemed suspicious. She placed a quick call to Larry Oakley, the chief justice of the Supreme Court.

"Yes, sir, I appreciate you making the time for me. I'll be there within the hour." She took the only other copy of the information she had given the president, slid it into her briefcase, and hurried downstairs. When she reached the ground floor, she hailed a taxi on the other side of the street. When it stopped, she waited until the sign flashed walk, before she stepped into the crosswalk.

There was a black SUV parked just down the block, and as she started across the street, it accelerated away from the curb. When she heard the roar of its engine, she looked over at it and froze. When it hit her, the impact threw her over the hood and into the windshield. The security personnel from the nearby buildings reached her in seconds, and even though they'd immediately started CPR, they couldn't revive her. During the confusion, no one noticed a well-dressed man pick up her briefcase and stroll away.

CHAPTER 4

When President McDonald sat down at his desk in the Oval Office, he was reflecting on how his first official function had been to attend his predecessor's funeral.

"It's a shame to die so young, but at least he doesn't have to deal with this shit anymore," he muttered. He started leafing through the various reports on his desk, and after an hour and a half, he thought to himself, *This is even worse than I'd feared. I just hope I can turn this mess around.*

His chief of staff, Willem Martell, interrupted his introspection. "Here are the rest of the reports you requested."

"Thanks. Why don't you go home for the night. It's been a long day."

"It has. I'll see you first thing in the morning."

He'd hoped to find at least a sliver of good news, but as he studied the data he was aghast. The tidal wave of chapter 9's had continued to grow, and like President Whitman before him, he was struggling to understand how it could have gone south in such a hurry. When he finished, it was time for the late news, and even though he knew better, he decided to watch it, hoping there might a bit of good news. However, that wasn't to be, and as he quit for the evening, he realized he would have to be at the top of his game to turn the tide.

The next morning, he was back at it by 5 a.m.

President Whitman's deal with the G8 had revolved around them buying massive amounts of the US debt, but the report he'd just read put the Chinese's share of the US debt at over 80 percent.

"I wonder how the hell that happened," President McDonald wondered aloud.

After he'd spent the morning studying the myriad of problems facing the country, he knew he had to stabilize the economy before he tackled the rest of their issues.

"I need to persuade the Chinese to help bail us out of this mess, but I don't have much to offer," President McDonald admitted.

"I thought you might come to that conclusion. You might want to consider this," Willem said as he handed him a folded-up piece of paper.

The president read the list and said, "This is pretty radical. Where do you come up with this shit?"

"I know number three is a real issue to them, and the rest are well known problems."

Having worked with the Chinese for many years, he was on a first-name basis with many of the Chinese business and government leaders. He decided to call Geely's chairman of the board, before he reached out to the government leaders.

"Good day to you. This is Bill McDonald, and I would like to talk with Chairman Huang, if he has a moment."

"President McDonald, congratulations on your election. This is Lu Yang, your old assistant."

"Lu Yang, my apologies for not recognizing your voice."

"None needed, sir, and it will be my pleasure to connect you."

"Mr. President, congratulations," Chairman Huang told him when he answered.

"Thanks."

"So what's up?"

"As I'm sure you know, the US is in a terrible financial crunch, and I wanted to see if you could help me set up a meeting with the premier."

"What a coincidence. Premier Lin Sen and I just met on next year's budget, and his top priority is to clean up some of the problems we've had with your country. I'll give him a call in the morning."

"Outstanding, just let me know what he says."

A few days later Dong Huang called President McDonald back. "The premier is speaking at the UN next week, and he's agreed to take a meeting with you."

"I can't thank you enough."

"Never a problem, and I hope it all works out."

President McDonald called Willem Martell in to arrange his travel, and get his opinion on his tactics.

"Well, do you think I've got a shot?"

"If you offer what we discussed, I'm sure they'll be willing to step up."

The president was a little surprised by his absolute conviction, but he was often spot-on when it came to reading the Chinese.

"How am I going to sell it to Congress?"

"We'll cross that bridge when the time comes."

"I sure hope so, because if this doesn't work, I've got no idea where to turn."

The president met Premier Sen in one of the meeting rooms at the UN.

"Thank you for taking the time to meet with me," President McDonald said.

"Normally, I wouldn't, but Dong called in a favor."

"He's a good man, and I'll try not to waste your time," President McDonald assured him.

The president spent the next thirty minutes explaining his issues, and his proposals. They went back and forth for several hours before the premier told him, "It's agreed then. I'll write off ninety percent of the bonds we hold. In exchange, I'll expect a complete download of the patent office files, and make sure we get everything, not just the issued patents. Also, I need your assurance that we won't be stopped from using them in any manner we choose."

"Is that it?" President McDonald asked, with no idea how he could hold up his end.

"There is one more thing. You need to repeal the ridiculous financial rules your Congress put in place."

"I'll need a little time to pull this together."

"You've got a week."

By the time Premier Lin Sen boarded his plane for the trip back to China, he couldn't have been more pleased. He'd gotten everything he'd hoped from President McDonald, and the UN had accepted his offer to allow the Chinese government to assume a more dominant role in the UN.

"How'd you do?" Willem asked.

"He went for the deal," President McDonald said.

"Good, I've prepared the bill to overturn the financial restrictions. I don't think we should risk sending the files electronically, so I've arranged for a courier to deliver the hard drives to the embassy."

"What happens when they start using the data?"

"I'm still working on that."

Two days later, the president walked into Willem's office and asked, "Did you see the evening news?"

"Yes, I did, but they're wrong, it's not going to take months to get it through Congress."

"I hope you're right, because we're going to be in deep shit if the premier backs out."

To the pundits' surprise, the proposals sailed through Congress in only three days. The president immediately called Premier Sen with the good news, and within the week, the Chinese began to flood the country with cheap money, and started making acquisitions.

CHAPTER 5

A year later, the weather had turned unseasonably warm for March, and President McDonald decided to read his daily reports in the Rose Garden. As he sat sipping a cup of hot tea, he was reading Willem's summary of the deluge of patent infringement lawsuits working their way through the courts. When he finished, he made a mental note to discuss the situation with Willem. As he moved on to the economic reports, he was invigorated by what he read. The GDP was finally growing, and unemployment had dipped under 10 percent for the first time in many months. He was almost finished, when Willem Martell came rushing out.

"Slow down, Willem, you're going to hurt yourself."

"They're all dead," Willem said.

"Who's dead? You're not making any sense."

"The Supreme Court, they're all dead."

"You mean one of the justices died?"

"No, I mean they're all dead! The full court was in session, and there was some sort of blast. WTTG had a news crew on location, and they got some unbelievable footage of the explosion."

"Contact the NSA, and tell them we need everything they've go on this. Set the Joint Chiefs up in the situation room, and let them know I'll want a briefing ASAP," President McDonald ordered.

Three hours later, President McDonald sat down in the briefing room for his first sit rep. As he surveyed the room, he could see that every intelligence and military organization was represented.

The Chairman of the Joint Chiefs of Staff, Admiral Zacharias, kicked off the meeting. "I have a tentative assessment of the event. We haven't identified them yet, but a small band of terrorists stole a Potomac river tour boat, and used it to launch three cruise missiles, which took out the Supreme Court building, and all the justices. We believe they had at least one other target, but one of the missiles malfunctioned, killing everyone on board."

"So it was a terrorist attack?"

"Without a doubt."

They worked the situation until 3 a.m. and by then everyone was exhausted.

"Let's take a break," President McDonald told the group. "We'll meet back here at 1300, and I'll need to know whether this was an isolated incident or the start of something bigger."

When they got back together, the admiral had a clearer picture of the situation. "We've identified the crew of the yacht, and they were being led by Victor Camilla."

"That name sounds familiar," President McDonald commented.

"It should, he used to be the top hit man for Venezuela's secret police. He dropped out of sight a couple of months ago, and we thought he was dead."

"Venezuela!" the president exclaimed. "There's going to be hell to pay if they're behind this. This is now strictly need-to-know," he warned. He turned to Willem Martell. "I need to buy some time. Make sure this looks like an unfortunate accident."

Willem opened a map of the city's utility services.

"There's gas service in the area, so we'll blame the explosion on a leaky gas main."

"Great, and when you're finished, I need you to start compiling a list of potential replacements for the justices."

By the next morning, there were numerous articles in the press about the tragedy, and what a unique opportunity President McDonald had been presented. The consensus was that the confirmation process could take over a year once President McDonald made his recommendations.

Six days later, Willem handed President McDonald his handpicked list of candidates.

"What's this?" the president asked.

"It's the list of potential replacements you asked me to compile."

"No way!" the president exclaimed. He scanned the list. "I'm vaguely familiar with a couple of these, but I've never heard of the rest. Did you already vet them?"

"Of course. Their credentials and backgrounds are above reproach. I admit that most of them are relatively unknown, but they've all got strong judicial backgrounds."

"I believe you, but I'm afraid it'll further elongate the confirmation process."

"Not with the mandate you currently enjoy."

The president knew Willem's attention to detail was impeccable, so he told him, "Good job. Go ahead and submit them, and we'll see what happens."

To THE AMAZEMENT of everyone, including the president, the entire list had breezed through the legislature in a matter of weeks.

When the President received the news, he rushed to share it with Willem.

"Great work, Willem, but I still can't believe it was that easy."

"Thanks, and I guess I was right about the mandate."

Willem handed the president a briefing folder. "I hate to kill the buzz, but we just received the CIA's assessment of the attack on the court, and their current thinking about the ongoing risks."

"It's about time," President McDonald declared, as he opened the folder and started reading the cover page.

"The director of the CIA asked for a meeting to discuss it."

"Absolutely," the president responded. He leafed through the document to get a sense of the size. "Come back in a couple of hours and we'll discuss the timing."

The president had hoped the report would leave some room for doubt, but they'd unearthed incontrovertible evidence that the SASR (South American Socialist Republic) had perpetrated the attack.

His blood ran cold as he read their threat assessment. The projected spiderweb of deep cover SASR operatives, and the possible scenarios they could be contemplating, painted a terrifying picture of their future.

President McDonald had never understood the unbridled hatred the president of Venezuela, Hugo Chávez, had held for America. He'd never been successful in his many schemes against the United States. But he'd succeeded in forming the republic shortly before his death, and it had been in a constant test of wills with the US ever since.

When Willem returned, he asked, "Would you like me to schedule a meeting?"

"Not yet. I don't want to fly off half-cocked, and risk the situation escalating into a full-blown war."

His back was turned, so the president couldn't see the scowl on Willem's face, but it had been replaced by a smile before he turned to the president. "Very well. Just let me know when you're ready."

CHAPTER 6

Willem hounded him, but it took President McDonald two more days to reach a decision.

"The director is here," Willem announced, pleased that he was finally going to do something.

"Charles, I appreciate your patience, and I've determined the course of action I want to take," President McDonald said.

"Great, what do you have in mind?" Charles Lutz, the director of the CIA asked.

"I want you to take out the SASR embassy in Santiago, and make sure they know it was us."

"No problem, I can have a team on the ground in twenty-four hours, but what else, drone strikes, assassinations, or maybe a kidnapping?"

"No, that's it. I don't want to start a war, I just want them to know that we'll hit back."

Willem was livid, but he managed to hold his tongue until the director left. "That's it?" he demanded, almost screaming. "They wiped out the Supreme Court, for God's sake."

"You need to calm down. It's my decision, and that's all I'm going to do."

Willem was still muttering curses as he walked away.

* * *

AFTER SEVERAL MONTHS of calm, President McDonald was beginning to believe his response had achieved its goal. However, in late August, the SASR struck back with a vengeance.

When Willem Martell burst into the Oval Office, the president could tell the shit had hit the fan.

"What's going down?"

"There have been a series of explosions in New York."

"Accidental?"

"Initial assessments indicate terrorists. The first incident occurred at 0805, and it took down the George Washington Bridge. The second at 0810, and it collapsed the Holland Tunnel."

The president's stomach churned when he realized they'd struck at the peak of the morning rush hour.

After the president read the sit rep, he instructed, "Get the team in here, and I need one of our people on the ground, ASAP."

In a little over an hour, the White House situation center was filled to standing-room only.

"We still don't have the full picture, but there have been a series of explosions that destroyed the George Washington Bridge and the Holland Tunnel," Admiral Zacharias informed the group.

"How many casualties?" General Jeffries asked.

"I seriously doubt we'll ever know the exact number, but it'll make Nine-eleven look like nothing more than a bloody nose," Admiral Zacharias declared.

"Why the hell didn't we see this coming?" President McDonald asked.

"Obviously I don't have the answer to your question, but some of it has to do with the lack of resources," Admiral Zacharias responded.

They discussed their options for a few minutes, before the president motioned for quiet. "I'm declaring New

York City a disaster area. Willem, make sure FEMA jumps on this with both feet. I don't want them screwing around like they have in the past."

"I'll make sure there's no misunderstanding," Willem said as he placed the call.

The president surveyed the room and asked, "Do any of you have a gut feeling on whether this will be the end of it?"

"I'd be shocked if they weren't planning more attacks," Admiral Zacharias said. "We should raise the alert level to Imminent, and either close, or severely restrict access to as many bridges, and tunnels as possible."

"If we do, it's going to paralyze most of the country, and there's a good chance it'll set off a nationwide panic," Major General Jeffries warned.

"Probably true, but I'm going to go with the admiral on this one," the president instructed. "Issue the Imminent alert, and include the appropriate mandates for the bridges and tunnels."

THE PRESIDENT WATCHED them feverishly working the situations, and after almost fifty minutes, he was beginning to think the worst was over.

"I just received a report of more attacks," Admiral Zacharias announced. "They hit the Big Dig twenty minutes ago, and—"

"How bad?" the president interrupted.

"Two of the tunnels have totally collapsed, and they're expecting massive casualties, but it gets worse. They've also hit the San Francisco Bay area. They've brought down several sections of the Oakland Bay Bridge, and the Golden Gate Bridge has suffered heavy damage."

"Oh my God!" the president said.

Willem motioned for the president to meet him in the hall. "Mr. President, I think it's time for you take control of the situation."

"Okay, but the admiral's people are already doing everything possible."

"You need to take operational control of all the National Guard units, as well as the state police."

"Can I do that?"

"Yes, if you declare a national emergency."

"How does that work?"

"First you send a formal declaration to Congress. I've already drawn up the paperwork, all you need to do is sign it. Then we'll do the necessary press releases to get the word out."

"That it?"

"Yes, and I've already given the leaders of both Houses a heads-up."

The president briefly pondered the ramifications of Willem's proposal.

"OK. Do you have a pen?"

Once he'd signed it, Willem gave it to the courier, and they returned to the War Room.

"If I can have your attention, the president would like to say a few words," Willem Martell announced.

"I know you're all very busy, so I'll be brief," President McDonald told the group. "I've just declared a national emergency."

"Good move," Admiral Zacharias commended.

"I know you're struggling to find enough resources, so I'm activating the National Guard units, and placing them under General Jeffries's command. The president turned to Admiral Zacharias. "I need you to contact every governor and let them know what's going on. Then you can help General Jeffries put a security plan in place for every major city."

"I'll begin coordinating resources with the governors immediately," General Jeffries said.

"No, sir, you misunderstand me. You're to take complete operational control."

"Mr. President, I mean no disrespect, but that's not how it's supposed to work."

"It is now. Now get to it," President McDonald barked.

Even though they were both sitting in the same room, the president was tapping furiously on his iPad as he chatted back and forth with Willem.

Admiral Zacharias was about to ask the president if there was anything else he needed done, when the president looked up and said, "General Jeffries, I'm also placing the state police units under your direct control."

The president paused to read the latest text message from Willem.

"You need to get this done by this afternoon, because I've got a press conference scheduled at nine p.m. eastern."

AN HOUR BEFORE he was scheduled to go on, President McDonald and Willem were sitting in the Oval Office preparing for the telecast. Willem had written his speech, and this was his first chance to go over it.

"I'm declaring martial law?" the president asked incredulously.

"Yes, sir, I think it's the prudent thing to do, and it places you on a better footing for having taken control of the National Guard units, and the state police."

"OK, but are you absolutely sure this is all legal?"

"It'll be fine."

BY THE NEXT afternoon, every governor had filed lawsuits to block the president's actions.

"I was afraid of this," the president told Willem. "I just had a conversation with the White House counsel, and he said there's no precedent for what I've done. You assured me this would be all right."

"It's not going to be a problem. I've arranged for all the lawsuits to be combined, and the Supreme Court will hear the case on Wednesday."

"How in the world did you pull that off?"

Willem just smiled, and went about his business.

As Willem had predicted, the Supreme Court upheld the president's actions.

Even with the combined manpower from the state police and the National Guard, General Jeffries was struggling to regain control.

"We've got to get a handle on this," President McDonald admonished the team.

"I've finally got some good news," Admiral Zacharias reported. "The CIA has located several of the terrorist cells."

"Great, what are we going to do?" President McDonald asked.

After several seconds of uncomfortable silence, General Jeffries spoke up. "We got a detachment in Africa that would be perfect for the job."

"Good deal, get them moving," the president ordered, relieved that they could finally take action. When he saw the concerned look on the general's face, he asked, "Is there something else?"

"We've never used a Special Operations force on a domestic mission. Are you prepared to deal with the collateral damage?"

"If they can get these attacks stopped, I'll deal with anything."

Two days later, Colonel Drury and his men landed at Andrews Air Force base in Maryland.

"JD, it's good to see you again," General Jeffries said.

"It's good to see you as well, sir, but what's the hurry? We needed more time to get the rebel situation under control."

"We've got bigger problems than a rogue warlord or

two. How much do you know about what's been going on here in the States?"

"Almost nothing. We've been in the field for months, with very little outside communication."

"Have your XO take care of your men, and I'll bring you up to speed."

When the general finished, JD exclaimed, "My God, that's horrible. What do you need me to do?"

"I've brought you back to eradicate the cells we've located."

"When do we start?"

The general handed him a laptop. "Everything you need to know is in here. If we need to give you any updates, I'll send a courier."

"We'll do our best," JD told him as he turned to go.

"That's why you're here."

The needs of the many outweigh the needs of the few.

—Leonard Nimoy's Spock in
Star Trek II: The Wrath of Khan

PART 6

CHAPTER 1

JD caught up with his men in one of the hangars near the end of the main runway.

"I need to go through the intel the general gave me, so get the men fed and settled in for the night," JD told his XO, Captain Blume.

"No problem. Is there anything I can do?"

"Thanks, but I don't understand the situation yet myself. I'll let you know if I need to postpone, but I should be ready to brief you by 0800."

JD got through the data quicker than he'd anticipated, so he managed to get a few hours' sleep.

When Captain Blume walked in, he was carrying a tray of food. "I know you didn't get to eat last night, so I brought you some breakfast."

"Thanks, I'm starving."

JD ate as he laid out their first mission. "The first group is located in Overland Park, which is a suburb of Kansas City. According to the CIA, there are at least twenty-two of them, and they're living within a few miles of each other."

"How about transportation?" Captain Blume asked.

"General Jeffries has wrangled a CIA jet to drop us off at a private airstrip near their location."

As JD pointed out the addresses on the map on his laptop, he could see the concern on Captain Blume's face. They had 101 men when they deployed to Africa, but injuries and combat fatalities had reduced the team to 65 men.

"I know, we're going to be spread thin, but as long as the groups aren't any larger than their projections, we should be all right."

"It is what it is."

AS THEY BOARDED the jet, JD said, "This sure is better than that worn-out piece of shit we got last time. I thought we were going down for sure when the engine exploded."

"Yeah, me too, but we got a little R & R in England," Captain Blume told him with a grin. "And the barmaids sure were cute. I guess we should be thankful we're Special Ops. Just think what we might have ended up with otherwise."

Once they were airborne JD stood up and told the team, "You can get out of those uniforms." While they were changing into civilian clothes, JD continued. "Remember, we've got to keep a low profile, we don't need any press."

THEY'D PREPROGRAMMED THEIR GPS units, so they were ready to go when they landed. Their jet taxied into an unmarked hangar, and when it stopped, JD yelled, "All right, boys, let's get to it.

When JD saw the nondescript vehicles lined up on the tarmac, he remarked, "Good deal, I was afraid they'd show up with a bunch of black SUVs."

After they'd loaded their gear, JD told the group, "You all know your assignments, and when you're finished, get back here ASAP. I'd like to be wheels up by

2100. All right, let's move out, and don't forget to leave the staging materials behind."

When they exited the expressway, and pulled up to the gated community's entrance, JD said, "Damn, the terrorist business must be doing well."

As they stopped in front of a two-story Mediterranean-style villa, JD reminded them, "It doesn't matter who it is, if they come out of the house, kill them."

At precisely 1530 they made their move, and as JD was hustling up to the front door to kick it in, he spotted the line of cameras covering the approaches to the house.

"Heads up, they've got a surveillance system," JD warned.

When JD reached the front porch, he saw that the door was far more substantial than he'd expected. He used some of the det cord he was carrying to blow it open, and when the explosion shattered the massive steel-reinforced door, it had momentarily stunned the guard in the foyer. As JD rushed through the opening, he put three rounds into the dazed guard, and moved down the hall.

There were supposed to be four operatives in the house, but when the explosion went off, it seemed like there were people running everywhere. JD's men did as they were ordered, and as the terrorists came running out, the 7.62mm rounds from their silenced HK 417s cut them down without mercy.

Once JD had cleared the first floor, he started up the ornate spiral staircase. When he reached the top of the stairs, a bullet splintered the railing beside his left hand. Before he could return fire, the man ducked back into one of the bedrooms and slammed the heavy oak door shut.

Once JD had checked the other rooms, he returned to

where his assailant was holed up. The terrorist heard JD approaching, and fired several large-caliber rounds through the door.

JD blew a hole in the door with his machine gun, and pushed a grenade through it. The explosion blew out the windows, and shredded everything inside.

JD kicked the splintered door out of the way, and moved cautiously into the room.

"Stupid son of a bitch!" JD exclaimed, when he saw the remains of the man's wife and two children. JD verified everyone was dead, and went back downstairs.

"We killed seven, Colonel," Sergeant Brown reported.

"Did anyone get away?"

"No, sir."

The sergeant could see the colonel wasn't himself. "Is there something wrong?"

"Nothing I can change. The damn fool had his family with him."

"That sucks," Sergeant Brown said. "All right, men, spread that stuff around, and let's get the hell out of here."

The team quickly planted the drugs and money strategically around the first floor.

JD AND HIS men spent the next two months crisscrossing the country, taking out cells.

"I've got another mission for you," General Jeffries informed JD.

General Jeffries hadn't personally tasked a mission since the first one, so JD knew something was up.

"OK, but what's different about this one?"

"The CIA has just identified a large cell in southern California, and they've hired one of the local gangs for protection."

"That's different. What sort of manpower are we talking?"

"The CIA isn't sure. It could be more than a hundred men."

"Damn! I could use some air support."

"We've talked about this. Aircraft would draw too much attention, but I could give you some Predators."

"It's better than nothing, but it doesn't solve my biggest issue."

"What else do you need?" the general asked.

"Is there any way you could get the LA SWAT to help out?"

"I know the chief of police, and the terrorists blew one of his precinct headquarters last month, so I think he'll be happy to help out."

Since the terrorist cell's headquarters was located in an industrial area, JD scheduled the attack at 1900 to mitigate the civilian casualties.

The chief had been pissed, and had sent his best SWAT commander, along with two hundred men and six Lenco BearCat armored vehicles.

As the SWAT teams started moving into position, JD deployed his men around the perimeter of the warehouse to provide covering fire. At 1900 JD ordered, "Take them down."

After the snipers killed the sentries, JD radioed the SWAT commander. "The guards are down, and you can move out."

The BearCats were supposed to breach the warehouse doors, and as they roared to life and lurched forward, JD hadn't been expecting any serious resistance. However, they'd only gotten halfway when the terrorists hidden on the roof started firing shoulder-fired antitank missiles.

"Commander, you need to pick it up," JD ordered.

"We're moving," the SWAT commander responded.

The terrorists had cut gun ports into the sides of the

building, and they were laying down a murderous field of fire.

"Colonel, we're taking heavy fire," the SWAT commander reported.

JD could see they were going to be wiped out if he didn't do something.

"Pull your men back to the staging areas, and hold there," he ordered.

JD used his satellite phone to contact the Predator ground control center at Davis-Monthan Air Force Base in Tucson. "This is X-ray, Mike, Alpha. Launch all missiles, authorization code One, One, Victor, Two."

A few seconds later, the Predator's hellfire missiles started hitting the building.

The terrorists had been stockpiling munitions, and the entire building mushroomed into a towering column of fire and smoke. "Holy shit," JD exclaimed.

One of the drones was broadcasting the engagement back to General Jeffries, and a few seconds later JD's phone rang. "Yes, sir, that's right. The warehouse and half the block are gone," JD confirmed.

"I'll give the chief a call. You need to get with the SWAT commander and make sure his people keep their mouths shut," General Jeffries instructed.

"Will do."

By the next morning, the general and the LAPD chief of police had managed to fabricate a gang turf war cover story.

General Jeffries called to update President McDonald on the mission.

"Great job," President McDonald told him. "How many more cells do we have left?"

"That was the last one that I'm aware of."

"God that's good to hear, but you'd better keep Colonel Drury's team on standby."

"You can count on that, but I'm hopeful that we've seen the worst of it."

"Me too, but I'm going to get the CIA to give us an update."

CHAPTER 2

It took them a few days to compile it, but Willem Martell had a big grin on his face when he handed President McDonald the CIA's update.

"Congratulations, I believe you've done it," Willem said. "The CIA doesn't believe there are any credible threats left."

The president didn't even bother to read it. "Good, maybe now we can return our attention to the economy."

"Possibly, but since we're still under the martial law decree, I think the time is right to deal with the SASR."

The president frowned and asked, "What did you have in mind?"

"I've taken the liberty of preparing some preliminary thoughts on the subject."

He'd made sure Willem had complete access to the classified information he needed, but he was often surprised by the detail included in his notes. When President McDonald realized how many pages there were, he said, "You'd better give me a couple of hours." As he dug into the material, it was evident that it was far more than just notes. The seventy-five pages of material detailed a comprehensive plan for invading South America. The president took the time to read it twice, before he called Willem back in.

"This is incredible. How did you come up with all of this? You've got stuff in here I would have to make a special request to get."

There was a hint of panic on Willem's face, but he quickly recovered. "Much of it is highly classified, and I had to use your access codes to get to some of it."

The president started to admonish him, but he only had himself to blame for not reining him in years ago. "I'll need to spend some more time with this, there's way too much for me to digest in one sitting. Let's discuss it over breakfast."

PRESIDENT MCDONALD WAS an early riser, but Willem was already sitting at the table when the president came down.

"I've decided to take your recommendations," President McDonald said. However, I do have great concerns about some of it. We'll be taking quite a chance if I commit all of our military assets, and I can just hear the UN whining when we pull the rest of our troops."

"I understand your trepidation, but isn't it about time the US thought about its own safety first?"

"I guess you're right, let's get to work."

They spent the rest of the morning discussing how he should approach the legislature, and after several hours they'd hammered out his presentation.

President McDonald convened a secret joint session of Congress to present his evidence, and ask for a formal declaration of war.

Once they were all seated, he passed out copies of the evidence against the SASR.

"The information being passed out is what we're going

to discuss today," President McDonald announced. "I'll give you a few minutes to read the summary of the documents, and an overview of what I'm proposing."

The president gave them thirty minutes before he stepped up to the podium to make his pitch. President McDonald had one of those voices that could fill a room, and everyone could feel his passion as he spoke.

"Not since Pearl Harbor has there been a more cowardly act of treachery and aggression. As the evidence clearly shows, the SASR planned and executed these acts of terrorism to try to inflict as much terror and damage as possible against innocent civilians. Even though we believe we've successfully eradicated the first wave of threats, there is every reason to believe they won't stop until they've brought our country to its knees." He paused to take a deep breath before he continued. "I will not stand by and let these criminals destroy our way of life. So I'm asking that all of you stand with me, and unite against this threat to our freedom, and issue a declaration of war against the SASR."

President McDonald moved back from the podium, and began scanning the crowd for some sign he'd gotten through. For just a moment his heart sank, as they sat there in silence.

First one, and then another, began jumping to their feet, clapping, and screaming their support. His heart swelled with pride, as the entire room rose to their feet, screaming their approval. After the uproar continued for several minutes, he stepped back to the podium and said, "Thank you so much for your support, and now let's get this done."

It wasn't that anyone disagreed in principle, but being politicians, it still took them many hours of contentious debate before they ratified the declaration of war.

It was almost midnight when the president got back

to the White House, but Willem was there waiting when he walked in.

"Well done," Willem said.

"Thanks, but most of the work was yours. Would you arrange for the Joint Chiefs to come in tomorrow?"

Willem had already contacted them, but he said, "Certainly, I'll have them here at 1400."

Everyone had arrived early, and by the time the president walked in, there were several heated conversations going on. However, the room fell silent when he sat down.

"I know you're all very busy, so I'll get right to it," the president said. "I'm sure what I'm going to cover is going to raise many questions, but please hold them until I've finished."

As he spoke, all of them had been furiously taking notes, but no one said a word when the president finished. After an embarrassingly long silence, Admiral Zacharias finally spoke up to say what they all were thinking.

"No disrespect, but you can't be serious. Even if we abandon all of our current commitments, there's no way in hell we can pull this off."

"I'm deadly serious, and if you're not up to the task, I can sure as hell get someone else to lead this."

"That won't be necessary, but I would like to go on record that this is a monumental mistake."

The admiral wasn't quite ready to let it go. "Do you really believe you can get Congress to go along with this?"

"I've met with Congress, and they've already signed off on a declaration of war."

Shocked that he hadn't already heard of it, the admiral nodded in resignation, and like the good soldier he was, he went to work on the plan.

During the four months it had taken them to pull the troops back, the admiral's team had managed to work out most of the details, except one. Their strategy called for a direct assault, but due to the cutbacks from the previous decades, they lacked the resources to mount an amphibious assault. He knew it wasn't going to be well received, but the admiral scheduled a private meeting with the president, to go over their findings.

"I'm sorry, but as you can see, there isn't any realistic chance of success," Admiral Zacharias reported.

The admiral was expecting the president to push back hard, but the president surprised him. "I get it, but give me a few days, and I'll see if I can help out."

After he finished his meeting, the president called Willem in to discuss the admiral's assessment.

"What are you going to do?" Willem asked.

"I need you to arrange a call with Calderon. I'm going to try to persuade him to let us move our troops through his country."

The president of Mexico took President McDonald's call, but he wasn't willing to help.

"I don't know what to do now," President McDonald admitted. "He was my last chance. I even had the DIA take a look at the admiral's analysis, and they agreed with his assessment."

Willem frowned, and remarked, "That's not good, but maybe Calderon will come around."

"Wishful thinking, I'm afraid. The man's a self-serving asshole, but I don't know why I'm surprised, since he was once one of the largest drug lords in Mexico."

At Willem's insistence, the president had put off telling the admiral he'd failed, and two days later, President Calderon called back.

"I've thought about your request, and I've decided it's in the best interests of my country to cooperate. I'll allow your forces safe passage through our territory."

The president started to ask him what had changed, but he decided he didn't give a shit."

"Thank you so much, and as I mentioned before, I'll personally guarantee your country's safety."

When he got off the phone, he called Willem to let him know the good news. He'd expected Willem to be ecstatic, but he didn't seem surprised.

To hell with him, the president thought to himself. "Get the admiral on the horn. I want to give him the good news."

"You heard me correctly," the president assured him. "The president of Mexico is going to let us to move our troops through his country. He's even agreed to let us use their airfields to stage our aircraft."

The admiral had hoped the invasion was going to fall through, but he soldiered on. "Great, I'll get moving. We should be ready within the month."

Once they had their forces staged along the Mexican and Guatemalan borders, they launched the attack.

The SASR had plenty of warning, but the campaign had gone as planned, until they reached the Costa Rican and Panamanian borders.

"I've got General Jeffries for you," Willem announced.

"The SASR has hit us with a massive counterattack," General Jeffries reported.

"How bad?" President McDonald asked.

"We've managed to stop them, but we've taken heavy casualties."

The general was expecting the president to ask about the numbers, and what they needed, but instead he asked, "How long before you can get moving again?"

General Jeffries was caught off guard by the question, but he managed to stammer, "Impossible to say. Hell, we were lucky to hold."

"Keep me updated," the president requested as he hung up.

SEVERAL WEEKS LATER, General Jeffries had managed to mount a counterattack, and the president was sitting in the Oval Office waiting on an update. When Willem walked in, he could tell it wasn't good news. "They've had to break off the attack," Willem reported.

"What happened?"

"They had more reserves than we thought, and the general thinks someone tipped them off."

"Damn it, we've got to get moving." He looked at Willem. "I know you've read the report, what are your thoughts?"

"It's time to transfer the National Guard units to General Jeffries," Willem suggested.

"If I send them in, how are we going to maintain order?"

"You know as well as I do that the intelligence reports are always overstating the threats," Willem said. "It's an acceptable risk."

THE PRESIDENT THOUGHT about it for over a week before he gave in to Willem's prodding.

"OK, let's do it," President McDonald ordered.

"Excellent, I've taken the liberty of drawing up the orders."

Of course you have, President McDonald thought to himself.

HE KNEW, AS president of the United States, it was his responsibility, but more often than not, his strategies were coming from Willem.

Admiral Zacharias had tried vehemently to talk him out of it, but the president stood his ground.

It took several weeks to move the National Guard

units to the front, but they had made an immediate impact.

The SASR forces had fought like madmen, but the US
forces had slowly driven them back through Panama.

CHAPTER 3

For the first month the president had been pleasantly surprised by the lack of issues, but the lull ended abruptly.

"I need your team in Chicago, ASAP," General Jeffries ordered.

"We just landed in Dallas, but we can get refueled, and be there by noon," Colonel Drury responded. "What's up?"

"All hell's broken loose. We've had seven terrorist attacks this morning, but the most urgent is in Chicago. An undetermined number of terrorists have taken control of the Willis building."

"Is the Chicago PD involved?"

"Other than cordoning off a perimeter around the building, they've been instructed to stay out of it. I've lost track. How many men do you have with you?"

"I'm back up to eighty men, but only thirty of them are fully trained."

"This is our top priority, so let me know if there's anything you need," General Jeffries instructed.

When JD's team landed, they were met by thirty black SUVs. The windows were heavily tinted, and the FBI agents from the local field office were driving.

They didn't say a word as JD's men loaded up, and in less than five minutes the caravan was doing more than a hundred miles per hour, as they sped down the Kennedy Expressway toward downtown.

The local police had cleared the way, so they didn't have to slow down until they reached the police roadblock, a couple of blocks away from the building.

As JD was walking toward the ad hoc command post, he could see several plumes of smoke rising in the distance.

"I sure am glad to see you, because we're up to our ears in shit," Captain Ferguson of the Chicago PD declared. "General Jeffries has ordered me to give you whatever you need, so all you have to do is ask."

"Thanks. What's with all the smoke?" JD asked.

"They shot down three of the helicopters I brought in to assess the situation."

"Gunfire or missiles?" JD asked.

"Missiles.

"I just can't believe I got them all killed," the captain lamented. "I've never dealt with this sort of threat."

"Don't beat yourself up. There's no way you could have anticipated it. It doesn't look like we're dealing with a spur-of-the-moment operation. Got any idea how many there are?"

"Ballpark at best. One of the security guards reported seeing over a hundred and fifty men before they killed him."

"How the hell did they get that many men into the area without someone spotting them?"

"They came in on tour buses, so no one realized what was going down until they started blasting their way through the lobby security."

"I'll need to see a copy of the building's architectural drawings, and anything else you think might help," JD requested.

"Thought you might," the captain said as he handed JD the plans.

As JD studied the drawings, he realized they faced significant problems. There had been taller buildings built since, but at 108 stories and 1,451 feet, the Willis building was still one of the tallest structures in the world.

When JD felt he had all the available information, he called Captain Blume and Sergeant Brown over, to start laying out their plan of attack.

He spread out a map of the area. "I need you to position our snipers here, and here. The shots are going to be from well over a thousand yards, so make sure they have the fifty cals."

"What's the mission?" Captain Blume asked.

"The terrorists have men stationed on the roof, and in the SkyDeck levels of the building. We'd have to use helicopters to get at the ones on the roof, so let's focus on the observation decks."

The snipers split up, and the SUVs dropped them off on opposite ends of the street. They made no effort to disguise their intent as they unloaded their equipment in the middle of the intersections.

The lookouts should have spotted them, but since they were on the 103rd floor, they'd assumed they weren't in any imminent danger.

"Take them out, and while you're at it, see if you can take down the enclosures," Captain Blume ordered.

The snipers fired as one, and the lookouts never knew what hit them. The impact from the Barretts' armor-piercing fifty-caliber slugs were devastating, and the pristine glass of the SkyDecks were soon splattered with blood and bits of flesh and bone.

As the sentry's blood flowed across the clear glass floor, they turned their attention to the glass ledges. The three observation points were four and a half feet wide, and were made of three half-inch-thick sheets of tempered glass that had been laminated together. They were built to hold five short tons of weight, but they weren't designed to withstand the impact of multiple armor-piercing slugs.

In less than sixty-seconds, the snipers had blown away the key support points of the glass panels, and the terrorists' bodies, and what was left of the ledges, plummeted to the street below. When the first two enclosures fell, they turned their attention to the third one in the center.

They hadn't bothered to man that one, and with both teams firing as fast as they could, they made quick work of it.

"The observation points have been neutralized," Captain Blume reported.

"Understood, have your men start sweeping the building's windows for more of the intruders, and if you spot any, take them out."

"How are we supposed to tell them apart from the civilians?"

"Just use your best judgment."

Captain Ferguson overheard JD's instructions, and interrupted JD before he could continue. "What the hell was that? You can't be shooting civilians."

"We won't intentionally kill any noncombatants, but we don't have time to waste trying to sort them out. Now shut up and let us do our jobs."

JD didn't like treating the captain so brusquely, but he couldn't allow him to start second-guessing him. As JD scanned the building with his field glasses, his mind was racing through his meager options. He assumed they had more missiles, so he didn't want to waste any more helicopters, and there was nothing remotely high enough to afford them a decent line of fire into the upper stories of the building.

"Guess we'll have to do it the old-fashioned way, a

floor at a time," he muttered under his breath. He was about to give the order to start clearing the building, when he got a call from General Jeffries on his encrypted satellite phone.

"What have you got, General?"

"NSA just finished deciphering a message to the terrorist commander. He's been ordered to ready what we believe is a multimegaton nuclear device, and await further orders. We don't know how long they're going to wait, so you'll need to do something quickly."

JD hesitated before he asked, "To be clear, what exactly, are you asking me to do?"

"Whatever it takes. They can't be allowed to detonate the weapon," the general replied tersely.

"Understood."

JD knew what he had to do, but it was going to be the hardest thing he'd ever asked of his men. He switched to the secure channel on his headset and asked, "How much C4 do we have with us?"

"We have thirty blocks, but if that's not enough, there's a large supply at the Great Lakes Naval Station," Captain Blume responded.

JD called General Jeffries. "I need a lot more C4, and Captain Blume thinks there's a large supply at the naval station."

"He's right, and I can have it there within the hour. Anything else you need?"

"Just a little luck."

Captain Blume was also his demotions expert, so he pulled him aside and handed him the building's plans. "The terrorists have a nuke, and we've got to stop them. While we're waiting on the C4, I need you to map out where we need to plant the charges."

"Oh dear God!" Captain Blume exclaimed. "You're not joking, are you?"

"Afraid not."

"I'll get to it." Captain Blume said, sick to his stomach at what he was being ordered to do.

The nine tubes that made up the first fifty floors of the building were for all practical purposes nine separate buildings. So Captain Blume knew that he needed to take them out simultaneously.

It took thirty-five minutes for the C4 to arrive, and by then the captain had determined where to plant the charges.

"How much C4 is there, and what type of detonators did they send?" Captain Blume asked.

"Four tons, and the detonators are the new smart, ultra-low-frequency models. They included a programmable controller as well," Sergeant Brown reported.

"Now that we've got plenty of C4, where do we put it?" JD asked.

Captain Blume had them gather around, so he could show them where to plant the explosives. As he talked, none of them said a word, until Sergeant Brown asked, "We're going to drop the building?"

JD stepped in to answer, "We are. They have at least one nuke, and we can't allow them to detonate it, because it will kill millions."

"We'll kill thousands of innocent people," Sergeant Brown pointed out.

"Can't be helped. You have your orders, get to it," JD ordered.

When the terrorists had moved to the 103rd floor, they'd disabled all the elevators, and booby-trapped the stairwells. They'd left a contingent of heavily armed men on the first floor, so Captain Blume sent two ten-man teams in to clear them out. A vicious firefight ensued, and when the rearguard realized they'd lost, they detonated their explosive vests.

When the rest of the team entered the lobby, it was a gruesome sight, but they didn't have time to mourn. They worked feverishly, but it took them almost thirty minutes to plant the explosives.

"The charges are in place, and active," Captain Blume reported, as they came running out of the building.

"Sergeant Brown, you're with me," JD ordered. "Captain, take the rest of the men and head back to the airport."

Once Captain Blume had left, they moved back to the police roadblock.

"What are you doing back here, was it getting too hot for you?" Captain Ferguson asked sarcastically, still pissed at how JD had treated him.

Ignoring the captain, he told Sergeant Brown, "Set the controller up on the hood."

The controller resembled a laptop, so the captain took another swipe at JD. "What's that for, you going to write home to momma?"

"It's ready," Sergeant Brown advised.

JD said a quick prayer for the poor souls in the building, and triggered the charges. When the C4 went off, the first floor disappeared in a wave of fire and dust. A couple of seconds later, the sound from the explosions hammered their eardrums. For an instant, it looked like nothing else was going to happen, and then the building began to implode.

"You maniac, what have you done?" Captain Ferguson screamed.

A tidal wave of dust swept toward them, and in less than thirty-seconds they were completely enveloped. It took several minutes for the dust to clear, and JD and the sergeant were long gone. When Captain Ferguson realized they'd left, he started screaming. "Put out an all-points bulletin on those murderous bastards, and do it right now."

A few seconds later his cell phone rang.

"Yes, sir, I understand. I'll take care of everything, General. You can count on me."

That night, the evening news reported a terrorist attack had collapsed the Willis building, killing everyone inside.

CHAPTER 4

JD and his team spent the next three months ferreting out the resurgent terrorists. Several of the encounters had turned out to be bloody affairs, but none rivaled the mess in Chicago.

They'd just completed a mission outside of Atlanta, and General Jeffries had flown down to debrief JD. When they finished, the general pulled out a flask of whiskey, and a couple of shot glasses. He filled them and handed one to JD.

"That was great work, but I'm afraid I can't let you and your men have any downtime."

"We're used to it."

The general downed his shot, and poured himself another. "The salvage crews finally uncovered the weapon in Chicago."

"Really! To be honest, I'd about given up hope it even existed," JD admitted.

"They had a black market, fifty-megaton Pakistani nuke, and it would have killed millions."

"I'd be lying if I didn't admit that helps, a little."

They bumped their shot glassed together and downed the fine Kentucky bourbon. The general refilled their glasses, and got around to why he'd really come.

"I may need your team to help out General Little."

"No problem, but I don't have enough men to make much of a difference."

"Not to worry, you won't be on the front lines. I'm searching for some high-value targets for your team."

"Just point them out, and we'll get it done."

President McDonald was growing desperate, as the press continually questioned his decision to use the National Guard troops.

"I've got to do something to improve security," President McDonald lamented. "I'm considering recalling the National Guard."

"Even if you wanted to, it's no longer possible," Willem said.

"And why not?"

"They suffered heavy casualties, and General Jeffries was forced to integrate them into the regular army units."

"The general should have consulted me first."

"He did ask, about two weeks ago. I thought it was a no-brainer, so I went ahead and gave him permission in your name."

President McDonald scowled, and grumbled under his breath. "I'm about tired of you taking so many liberties."

"Was there something you wanted to say?" Willem asked.

"What's done is done. However, in the future, I would appreciate a heads-up."

"Certainly, and I meant to tell you, it simply slipped my mind."

The president nodded, but he didn't believe a word of it. He shrugged it off, and asked, "I suppose you have some thoughts on the security situation?"

"I do. It's time to ask the UN for some peacekeeping

forces. The United States has always been there for the rest of the world, and it's about time they reciprocated."

The president briefly mulled it over. "That's not a bad idea. I'll call Secretary General Arrobas this afternoon."

After the secretary general listened to the president's plea, he told him, "You'll have to give me a little time."

"Understood, and I'll appreciate anything you can do."

When they hung up, the secretary general reached out to the Chinese leader, Premier Sen.

"Mr. Secretary, it's been a long time," Premier Sen remarked.

"It has, but I'm afraid it's not a social call."

"How can I help?"

"President McDonald has requested UN troops to help stabilize the security situation in his country," Secretary Arrobas explained.

"No problem, I'll get to work on it right away. I'll let you know when I have a firm timetable for their arrival."

Shocked, it took a couple of seconds for the secretary to respond. "Many thanks, and I'll pass the good news along to President McDonald when I hear back from you."

EARLY THE NEXT morning, the secretary general received an e-mail from the premier, detailing the proposed troops movements.

"Damn that was quick," he muttered. When he'd finished reading it, he called President McDonald.

"We'll have the troops you requested in place in six weeks, if that will work for you," Secretary General Arrobas said.

"That's great news. How in the world did you get it done that fast?"

"I was shocked myself, but it didn't turn out to be a big deal."

A MONTH AND a half later, there were over a million troops spread out across the US.

When President McDonald finished the daily sit rep, he told Willem, "I know it's too early to declare success, but we haven't had a major incident in over a month."

"It's looking promising, but as you said, it's too early to declare victory."

The next day, the Michigan State Police had been responding to a suspected terrorist attack in downtown Detroit, when the incident occurred. No one knew who fired first, but the heavily outgunned state police had taken thirty casualties before it was over.

Over the next two weeks, there had been a half dozen more incidents, and the public's tolerance for foreign troops on US soil was growing thin.

When President McDonald finished reading the synopsis of the latest incident, he declared, "That's it. I'm going to ask Arrobas to recall the troops."

"I realize you've got to do something, but pulling the UN troops out would be shortsighted," Willem cautioned.

"They're much better equipped to handle the ongoing terrorist threats than the state police."

"If you've got a better idea, I would love to hear it."

"I think you should disband all the state police units, and probably the police departments, at least in the major cities."

"Why would I do such a thing? The people are already calling for my head for bringing the troops in."

"Two reasons. Capability, and money. Their troops are much better suited to deal with the terrorists, and the UN is footing the bills."

"You're probably right, but I'd better discuss it with

Vice President Murray before I pull the trigger. He was really pissed when I didn't brief him before I asked for the UN's help."

"I really think we need to go ahead and move on this."

"I hear you, but the VP will be back from New Orleans late tonight, and I'll meet with him first thing in the morning."

PRESIDENT MCDONALD WAS an early riser, so he was in the Oval Office by 5 a.m. the next morning.

Willem usually didn't make an appearance until around seven thirty, so the president had scheduled his meeting at five thirty, in hopes of getting some one-on-one time with the VP.

He'd come down early to get some work done, and when he realized it was already 5:45, he muttered, "That's odd, Murray's always early for meetings." He was about to have one of his Secret Service agents find out where he was, when Willem came strolling in.

"You're up and around kind of early," the president kidded him.

"I'm afraid I've got bad news. They found the vice president dead in his bed this morning."

"My God, that's horrible. Do they know what happened?"

"They'll do an autopsy, but the doctor said it looked like a heart attack."

THE DAY AFTER the vice president's funeral, President McDonald sat down to pick Murray's successor. To get started, he jotted down the names of the people he thought would be up to the task. He'd come up with ten names, and as he went back down the list, he decided to add Willem's name.

Willem sometimes got on his nerves, but he was a

known quantity, and the reality of it was, he'd been more of a vice president to him than the real one.

It took him the rest of the day, but he finally pared the list down to two names. He'd composed the e-mail to Congress with both names, intending to edit one of them out, but he just couldn't make up his mind. *Oh what the hell,* he thought to himself. *I'll just flip for it.*

He'd been carrying his lucky 1899 silver dollar for years, so he took it out and flipped it. He'd done it a thousand times, but he fumbled the catch, and it rolled under his desk. "Nice catch, dip-shit." Frustrated and tired of thinking about it, he hit send on the e mail and muttered, "Let them sort it out."

THE PROGNOSTICATORS HAD Joseph Mayberry as the leading contender, but everyone had expected a protracted debate.

The first day's debate had indeed been rancorous, and President McDonald had gone to bed that night expecting an ugly, long drawn out process.

The next morning, he'd been shocked to learn that during a marathon all-night session, they'd confirmed Willem Martell as the new vice president of the United States.

After breakfast, President McDonald went to find the new vice president. "Congratulations."

"Thanks, and thank you for nominating me."

THAT AFTERNOON, THE chief justice of the Supreme Court swore Willem Martell in as the vice president. After the brief ceremony, they met back in the Oval Office to discuss the security situation.

"I suppose you still feel strongly that we should disband the state police, and the metropolitan police departments?" President McDonald questioned.

"Even more than before, but I don't suppose you've seen the latest incident in Houston?"

"No, not yet. What's happened now?"

"The Houston police were trying to break up a food riot, and it turned ugly. They're not sure who started it, but you know those Texans and their guns. Anyway there were twelve civilians, six police officers, and two UN troops killed."

Clearly frustrated, the resident groused, "Wonderful, like I needed any more bad news." He didn't want to do it, but he couldn't think of an alternative. "All right you win. If you'll draw up the orders, I'll sign them. Did you see the Fox News last night?" he asked.

"I did, but you can't pay too much attention to those losers," Willem advised.

"That's easy for you to say. They're calling me everything from a traitor to a maniac. Not only that, there have been riots in almost every major city."

"You're probably not going to want to do this, but the Chinese commander, General Sung, has requested that you make a personal appeal to the public to stop the rioting."

The president had been considering something along those lines, so he said, "I'll do it, but I doubt it will do much good."

"Excellent, I'll get it set up."

"Hearing you say that just reminded me. Who do you think should take your old job?"

"If it's all right with you, I'd like to continue filling that role as well."

The president was surprised to say the least. "OK by me, but you're going to be awfully busy."

"It's no problem, I want to do it."

Willem got the networks to schedule the president's speech for a primetime Saturday night slot. Thirty minutes before, President McDonald and Willem met to go over his notes.

"What's this bullshit?" the president asked. "I'm not going to threaten our people."

"I know it comes across like that, but you'll be saving lives, because the general isn't going to back off."

The president had thirty minutes, but he wanted to keep his message short and to the point. "My fellow Americans, it's with a heavy heart that I stand before you tonight. Our country is under attack from all sides, and our resources are perilously low. When I asked the UN for help, I never envisioned the types of tragic incidents, and unnecessary deaths that have occurred, but the UN troops are not our enemies, and . . .

"Oh to hell with it. I'd seriously considered having the UN troops removed, but we've got to face reality. We simply don't have the wherewithal to fight a full-blown war, and provide domestic security. However, security cuts both ways, and the UN troops have every right to protect themselves.

"General Sung, the commander of the UN forces, has warned that he's going to authorize an expanded use of deadly force, if the violence continues.

"Please, I beg you, listen to reason, and stop the riots, before we have any more unnecessary deaths, on either side. I give you my word that once the war is over, the peacekeepers will leave. Thank you and good night."

"You had me worried when you went off on that tangent, but that was very well done," Willem Martell said.

"It was still bullshit, but maybe it will save a few lives."

CHAPTER 5

"I'd hoped President McDonald's broadcast might help, but there have been six more major incidents today," Major Ma reported. "Do you want me to issue the shoot to kill orders?"

"No, we'll let it play out for a bit," General Sung instructed.

"Very well," Major Ma replied, somewhat surprised at the general's restraint.

AFTER FOUR MORE weeks, the violence had continued unabated, and after an emergency session of the UN Security Council, they reached out for more help.

"General, I know we've already asked for more than you expected, but we've got to do something to restore order," Secretary Arrobas pleaded.

"What do you have in mind?" General Sung asked.

"We believe more troops is the only answer."

"I'm not able to make that commitment, but I'll talk with the premier, and call you right back."

An hour later General Sung called the secretary general back.

"The premier has agreed to send me another million men," General Sung reported.

"Unbelievable news, please pass along my thanks."

* * *

Six weeks later, General Sung called Major Ma in for status update. The major's photographic memory and genius-level IQ had made him the general's go-to guy.

"The last contingent arrived last night," Major Ma reported.

"What's that bring us up to?"

"Two million six."

"That should be enough. Now you can issue the shoot to kill orders."

It had taken a few months, but the huge influx of troops, and the new level of brutality, had finally tamped the violence down.

"Did you see your latest approval ratings?" Willem asked.

"I did. Now if we could just get some traction in Central America."

"Speaking of that, did you get a chance to read General Jeffries's recommendations?"

"Finished it last night," the president said. "Give him the green light, I don't see that we have much to lose by trying."

General Jeffries had already moved JD and his team to Central America, in anticipation of getting his operation approved.

"I've got a mission for you," General Jeffries announced.

"Great, I was beginning to think you'd forgotten us," Colonel Drury responded. "Are the Chinese out of control again?"

"No, for a change it's completely unrelated to our domestic problems. We're going to try to disrupt the SASR command structure. We've located General Escobar's temporary headquarters. He's staying in a villa in the Ensenada de Utria National Park."

"I know the area, but it's several hundred miles from here. How are we supposed to get there?"

"You'll be using some of the prototype stealth Ospreys. I've just sent you all the available intel, but you need to hurry, because he doesn't stay put for very long."

"We're on it," Colonel Drury assured the general.

Sixteen hours later, JD and his team were on their way into Colombia.

JD had needed more personnel to pull off the mission. He'd added a 30-man squad of army rangers to the team, but at the last moment he pulled in 150 more. They reached the coast just after dark, and JD had the pilots land on a deserted beach, not far from the general's villa.

"Just hang here until I call," JD told the pilots.

As they double-timed toward the villa, JD told Captain Jennings, the ranger commander, "Once we're inside, my team will secure the general while you take out the rest of their officers. Have Lieutenant Sheridan and the second wave hang back to provide covering fire if we need it."

"No problem. You want any prisoners?"

"No, the general is all we're after."

They were expecting lax security since it was so far behind their lines. They used their silenced M110s to take out the guards, before JD led them up the stairs in front of the magnificent villa. They'd just reached the top of the stairs when they started taking fire from the trees.

"Lieutenant Sheridan, split your force and take them out," JD ordered.

The enemy hadn't been expecting a second group, and the battle-hardened rangers made quick work of them.

General Sanchez had taken an entire floor for himself, and as JD led his team up the staircase, Captain Jennings's men spread out and started kicking in doors. The third floor was heavily guarded, but after a short but vicious firefight, one of JD's men pitched a stun grenade into the general's room.

JD found the general disoriented, and kneeling beside his bed. JD disarmed him, and ordered, *"En tus pies."* (On your feet.)

"Please don't kill me," the general begged in impeccable English.

JD holstered his pistol and jerked him to his feet. He bound his hands with plastic handcuffs, and pushed him onto the bed. "Sit there and don't make any trouble," JD warned.

"Take a look around and see what you can find," JD ordered.

"Colonel, I've got a floor safe in the closet."

"Blow it out of there and we'll take it with us," JD ordered.

It took four of them to carry it, and as they lugged it down the stairs, JD called the Ospreys in. "Lift off in five," JD notified the rangers still sweeping the villa.

They cut the safe open when they landed, and JD started going through the contents. When he didn't find anything of value in the papers, he moved on to the laptop they'd found. Most of the data wasn't worth anything, but one folder was encrypted with a heavy-duty military-grade cipher, and none of JD's normal tools would open it.

"Get me the geek," JD ordered.

"What you got, boss?" Lindsey asked.

"You're never going to get the military protocol thing, are you?" JD asked.

"Probably not, but what have you got?"

JD handed him the laptop and said, "See if you can get into this folder."

Twenty minutes later, he was back. "I can't read

Spanish, but this must be some serious shit, because it's the best encryption I've ever seen outside of the NSA."

There were only two documents in the folder, and they were both marked with the SASR's highest security classification. JD was fluent in Spanish, and he couldn't believe what he was reading. Already aghast, JD moved on to the next one. At first he thought it was a list of contacts, until he started reading the annotations. He recognized a few of the names, but the last one shook JD to his very core. "Oh my God!" JD exclaimed. "We're in deep shit."

He immediately placed a secure call to the one person he knew he could trust without question.

"Are you absolutely sure this link is secure?" JD asked.

"Rock solid," General Jeffries assured him. "How did the mission go?"

"I'm almost sure they were tipped off, but the attack was a complete success. However, that's not why I called. When we captured the general we confiscated his safe. We managed to decrypt a couple of files we found on his laptop, and I need to get them to you ASAP."

"Can't you just fill me in?"

"I'll risk telling you this much. It details a conspiracy between a foreign government and the SASR, as well as—"

"Say no more. I'll dispatch a courier to pick up everything you've got. Once I've had time to go over it, I'll get back with you. This is now strictly need-to-know, and make sure you keep Escobar under wraps. I'm going to have the Air Force hit the villa with everything they have, and if we get lucky, they may think everything was destroyed in the strike."

The courier arrived just after midnight. After General Jeffries had read the note JD included, he poured a stiff drink, and sat down to go through the material.

He'd just finished, when one of his aides rushed in with an ultra top-secret message from the British MI-5.

After he'd read the message, he called his aide in. "Get Admiral Zacharias on the NSA video channel."

"I'll need an authorization code."

The general opened up an encrypted folder on his laptop, and gave him the code of the hour.

Steve Zacharias, the chief of naval operations (CNO), was one of his oldest friends. His great grandfather had been CNO before him, and like him, Steve was a no-bullshit kind of a guy.

By the time he got the admiral on the line, it was 0400 in Washington, DC.

"Good to see you, General," the admiral said as he rubbed his eyes. "Couldn't this have waited until morning?"

"You tell me when we're finished. Is there anyone else with you?"

"No, I'm in my quarters, and since Linda died, I'm all there is."

"I'm sorry I couldn't make the funeral."

"No matter, old friend, we both knew you were there in spirit."

"I've got several pieces of information to share with you, but I'll share the most urgent first. I've just received a heads-up from a dear friend of mine in MI-5, and he thinks China may be considering a preemptive nuclear strike on our forces in Central America."

"I've got two questions," Admiral Zacharias interrupted. "Why would they send something of such importance to you, instead of directly to the president, and why would the Chinese be helping the SASR?"

"My contact hadn't been able to verify it, but he felt it was credible enough to give me a heads-up. Your second question brings me to the other pieces of information I've received, and why I'm absolutely convinced the tip is true. During Colonel Drury's raid on the SASR command center, they obtained information that details an alliance between the SASR and the Chinese government."

The admiral didn't respond, so he continued. "The documents contained a list of moles embedded throughout our government and the military. I won't get into any details on a comm link, but some of them are high enough to compromise the security of the United States."

The admiral put his head down on the desk.

"Are you all right, Steve?"

"No, not really. If even a fraction of this is true, we're screwed. Did he give you any time frame?"

"No. Like I said, he hadn't been able to corroborate it."

"I've got a meeting with the president at 1500, so I'll pass this by him then. However, I know he's not going to act on a random tip, without further verification." After the admiral had contemplated their options, he asked, "Have you still got the NSA laptop I sent you?"

"I do."

"Get one of your techs to plug it into the secure channel on your router."

When the downloads finished, General Jeffries asked, "What is all this stuff?"

"It's the launch codes for the navy's nuclear arsenal. There's also a version of 'The Football' and the encrypted VPN tunnel you'll need to get into the NSA servers."

"What am I supposed to do with it?"

"I hope nothing, but you'll know if the time comes."

"Do you want me to send you a copy of the documents?"

"Absolutely not!"

When they'd finished, General Jeffries made a series of calls before he reached out to Colonel Drury.

"I need you out of there ASAP. There are SUVs waiting outside your location, and I've got a couple of CIA jets standing by at the airport."

"Yes, sir, but what's the hurry?"

"We'll talk when you get here. Now get moving."

The SUVs never got below a hundred on the way, and when they arrived at the airfield, the guards waved them through the checkpoints. The pilots had the engines running on the two Gulfstreams, and when they were on board they closed the doors and left at high speed. As they were climbing away from the airport, JD went forward to talk with the pilots.

"Sorry to bother you, but what's our flight time to DC?"

"We're not going to DC."

"That's not going to work, I'm supposed to meet with General Jeffries ASAP."

"Relax, we're taking you to him. Now if you'll go back and sit down, we'll be there in a few hours."

What difference does it make to the dead, the orphans, and the homeless, whether the mad destruction is wrought under the name of totalitarianism or in the holy name of liberty or democracy?

—Mohandas Gandhi

PART 7

CHAPTER 1

As Colonel Drury and his team were streaking across the open ocean, the weather had turned unseasonably cold in Washington, DC.

An intermittent mix of freezing rain and snow had been falling all day, but it hadn't hurt the turnout for a gathering of President McDonalds's biggest supporters.

The Secret Service had set up a room on the fifth floor for the president's use on breaks.

"We've got a great turnout," President McDonald commented when he got to the room.

"It sure is. I was afraid the weather would hurt us," Willem Martell said.

"I've got some of your favorite tea brewed," Major Mullins, the marine carrying the football, told the president.

"I think I'll drink it on the patio."

"Suit yourself, but it's still spitting snow, and it's colder than crap."

"I won't be very long."

A few minutes later, Major Mullins came out and handed the president the secure satellite phone. "Admiral Zacharias needs to speak with you."

"Yes, I understand," President McDonald, said quietly.

"How long until impact? Oh my God. Thank you, and God bless you as well." The president's face was ashen when he hung up.

Willem Martell had followed the major outside, and when the president hung up, he asked, "What's happening?"

"NORAD is tracking a massive missile launch from the Chinese mainland. The attack is targeted at our forces in Central America, and first impact will be in fourteen minutes."

"What's been done so far?" Willem Martell asked.

"General Little's aware, but they're pretty much screwed. However, they're not going to die alone, because I'm going to nuke the sneaky bastards off the face of the earth," President McDonald growled.

Major Mullins turned to the vice president. "Sir, please step back." The major opened the titanium briefcase, and placed it in front of the president. "Please place your right eye up to the sensor," the major instructed. Once the machine had verified the president's identity, it powered on and displayed the launch options.

As the president read down the list, the major reminded him, "Once you've decided, just say the option number clearly. You'll be asked to repeat it, and give the six-digit code beside the option."

The vice president was still hovering close by. "Mr. President, think about what you're doing. Do you really want to kill over a billion people?"

"No, I don't, but I'm not going to stand by and do nothing while they commit mass murder."

The president faced the horror every modern-day president feared, the decision to launch a nuclear attack. While President McDonald took a moment, Willem slipped on a pair of rubber gloves, and literally ran back inside to chain the door shut.

"I select option two," the president said as clearly as he could.

The machine responded, "You've selected option two, maximum response on mainland China. If that's correct, please repeat your selection, and give the authorization code to confirm."

President McDonald took a deep breath. "I select option two, confirmation code Alpha, Six, Oscar—"

Before he could finish, Willem put his pistol to the side of Major Mullins's head, and pulled the trigger.

"My God, Willem, what have you done?" the president screamed.

Willem just smirked as he put a bullet between the president's eyes.

He hadn't used a silencer, so he knew the Secret Service detail would reach them in seconds. He put the gun into the dead marine's hand, and squeezed off another round into the president.

He heard the Secret Service detail breaking through the door. He closed the football so it would power off, removed the gloves, and stuck them in his coat pocket before he started screaming, "Oh my God, he's assassinated the president."

Earlier, JD and his men had landed at a private airfield outside of Benitez, Puerto Rico.

"I wonder where the hell we are?" Colonel Drury asked when they landed.

The planes taxied to the end of the runway and spun around. When the copilot opened the door, JD was the first one down the ladder.

"Colonel Drury, welcome to Puerto Rico. I'll take you to the general, and the bus will take your men to their quarters."

Even though he was dressed like one of the locals, JD

could tell by the way he carried himself he wasn't just a driver.

"So, how long have you been with the company?" JD asked.

"Sit back and we'll be there in a few minutes," the driver said, ignoring JD's comment.

When the SUV pulled up in front of a native shack, JD thought for a moment he'd been set up. He'd started to pull his sidearm, when the driver said, "Relax. Just go on in, and they'll take care of you."

JD got out and walked across the dusty yard to the front door. When he opened it, a gust of refrigerated air hit him in the face.

The sergeant had his back to the door. "Close the damn door, you're letting all the cold air out." When he turned around, he said, "Sorry, sir, I thought it was Jeremy. He's always holding the door open to piss me off."

"Follow me, the general is expecting you," Jeremy instructed. He opened a crude thatched door, revealing a highly polished elevator door. JD rode the elevator down to the sixth level, a hundred feet below. When he stepped off of the elevator, General Jeffries was waiting.

"When did you relocate to Puerto Rico?" JD asked.

"A couple of weeks ago. Come on in. Would you like a drink?"

"You got any beer?"

"Just the local swill, but it's cold."

THEY'D BEEN TALKING for about twenty minutes when the news of the Chinese attack started coming in.

After the general had read the NORAD assessment, he told JD, "China has launched an ICBM attack against General Little's army."

"Have we retaliated?"

"It doesn't look like it, but I'm going to check."

When Admiral Zacharias picked up, he put it on speaker so JD could listen in.

"Why haven't we launched yet?" General Jeffries demanded.

"President McDonald has been assassinated, and the whole situation is FUBAR."

"Holy shit, what about Martell?"

"He's fine, and they've already sworn him in as president."

"He doesn't have time to waste on that, he's got to hit them back."

"Not gonna happen. I just talked with the secretary of defense, and he said President Martell believes it would be an overreaction, and that we could work it out diplomatically."

"Now I know why his name was on the list." General Jeffries snarled under his breath. "What are you going to do about it?"

"I can't do a thing. He's already ordered the secretary of defense and the Joint Chiefs of Staff to stand down. I'm afraid you're our last hope."

The general was about to respond, when the satellite link went down.

"The shit has hit the fan for sure," General Jeffries said.

"What did the admiral mean, when he said you were our last hope?" JD asked.

"It's better if you're not involved."

"What makes you think they'll let me live when they find out what I know?"

"Good point. The admiral gave me the navy's launch codes."

General Jeffries walked over and unlocked the safe where he'd stored the laptop. He'd watched the tech plug it into the router, so he plugged it in and booted the laptop. Just like the football, the various response options were predetermined. He scrolled down to the same option President McDonald had been going to use. The two-man rule still applied, but the admiral had been working with the head of the NSA, and he'd provided the links and the software to spoof the process. The VPN tunnel led directly to a computer buried deep inside the NSA secure network, and from there it was a simple matter to transmit the president's launch authorization and the secretary of state's confirmation.

The laptop program wasn't voice activated, so General Jeffries selected the option and hit send. Within minutes, every nuclear-armed submarine, aircraft, and surface ship around the world had received their verified launch orders.

CHAPTER 2

President Martell was in a private meeting with the chief justice of the Supreme Court, when the Air Force major, who was now carrying the football, rushed in.

"The CDRUSPACOM (Commander, U.S. Pacific Command) just sent a sit rep on our counterattack. The Pacific fleet's missiles will strike the Chinese mainland in just under three minutes, and the Atlantic fleet's will be there ten minutes later."

"What the hell are you babbling about, we haven't launched any missiles," President Martell asked.

"Sir, the missiles were launched a few minutes ago, under President McDonald's authorization code."

"Impossible, he's dead. I need to know how this happened."

"Yes, sir, right away, sir," the major stammered, clearly confused by the turn of events.

When he'd persuaded President McDonald to install a hotline in the Oval Office, he would have never guessed how badly he would need it. When they saw President Martell start sprinting down the hall, the major, and his Secret Service detail followed. The group was shocked when President Martell activated the hotline speaker-phone and started screaming in Chinese.

"I'm telling you the first wave of missiles will hit in"—President Martell glanced at his watch—"less than thirty seconds."

President Martell could hear several excited conversations in the background, as he waited for a response. He was still waiting when there was a sharp squeal, and the line went dead.

The president attempted to reconnect several times, but with no luck.

Caught up in the moment, he'd been oblivious to anything else, until he realized he wasn't alone. When he turned around and saw them, he almost panicked, but he quickly recovered. "I thought that we owed them a heads-up, but it looks like I was a little late."

None of them knew how to respond, but the president broke the tension when he bellowed, "I need the damage assessments from our strikes, and a report on how General Little's command has fared, and I need them now."

They hadn't ever seen Willem that worked up before, but before they could respond, he got an urgent call from the Taiwanese president.

"We don't have much time left, but I wanted you to know we've launched everything we had," President Hue reported.

"Why would you do that?" President Martell asked.

President Hue had expected a different response, but he continued. "Since the silly warmongering bastards have finally managed to get us all killed, I figured we would do our part."

Bile filled President Martell's throat as he fought not to say what he was really thinking. "I wish I could have prevented this, but you'll be remembered for your courage." He paused to let President Hue respond, but the line had gone dead. "Well, I guess that's that." He turned to the group and ordered, "Everybody out." The head of his Secret Service detail started to protest, but the president cut him off. "I don't think anyone is likely to break in here, do you? Wait, there is one thing that you can do for me. My briefcase is in my office, would you mind getting it for me?"

"No problem."

Once he had his briefcase, he didn't want to chance being overheard again, so he walked over and locked the door. He retrieved a secure satellite phone from his briefcase, took a couple of deep breaths, and placed his call to General Sung.

General Sung didn't interrupt, as President Martell tried to explain what had happened. When he finished, General Sung didn't respond right away. Then in a very quiet, calm voice, he said, "I should have you executed, but you might be of some use yet. I'll give you further instructions once I've figured out where we're at. Right now, I need you to find out who's responsible for this mess."

When the General had finished with him, President Martell sat trembling for several minutes. Once he'd managed to calm his nerves, he called the staff back in.

"Have you located General Jeffries?"

"We don't have a location on the general, but we did receive a short sit rep. They had a reconnaissance aircraft overfly General Little's position, and it reported extremely high radiation levels, and no signs of life."

The president didn't comment, because he already knew how much firepower the Chinese had unleashed.

At 2130, President Martell received an update from the NSA, and the latest satellite images. After he'd read their assessment, he spent a few minutes perusing the photos. Much of Central America was obscured by the towering clouds of steam generated by the searing heat from the explosions, but a few areas were partially visible, and they didn't show any outward signs of the cataclysmic events. The lack of physical damage wasn't a surprise, because the Chinese and Americans had converted their nuclear arsenals to ERW (Enhanced Radiation Weapons) or neutron bombs, a full decade before.

When President Martell finished, he addressed the group. "I'd hoped to have some good news for you. However, after reading NSA's preliminary assessment of the attack, that's not the case. "The effected areas are showing catastrophic radiation levels, and it's highly unlikely there will be any survivors."

"Surely some of them survived?" Admiral Zacharias asked.

"I suppose there's a remote possibility. However, we don't have any way to reach them.

"Luckily the prevailing winds are sweeping the radiation clouds out over the Pacific, and we believe they'll dissipate before they reach any significant population centers."

CHAPTER 3

After several days of frustration, President Martell was pushing his team to find out what had happened.

"We've discovered how they did it, but I can't tell who it was," James Driscoll, the director of the NSA, informed President Martell.

"Your agency is charged with maintaining our security, and I find out that they used your assets to carry out the attacks? Can you tell me why I shouldn't sack the lot of you?" President Martell asked angrily.

"You do whatever you need to."

To hell with him, the president thought to himself. "I'll call you if I need anything else," he said as he hung up.

THE NEXT MORNING, General Sung took President Martell by surprise, when he came strolling into the Oval Office, accompanied by six heavily armed bodyguards.

Oh shit, this can't be good, the president thought to himself. *How the hell did they get by the Secret Service?* More than a little worried, the president tried to put on a good front. "It's good to finally meet you in person," President Martell said.

"I'm afraid you'll be singing a different tune before very long," General Sung replied.

President Martell tried to brush the comment aside. "As I said the other day, I'm terribly sorry about the unfortunate incidents last week."

"Incidents? So you're calling the deaths of more than two billion of our countrymen an unfortunate incident?"

"I meant no disrespect, and I can assure you that I did everything I could to prevent it." By now President Martell was visibly agitated, even though it was only seventy degrees in the Oval Office. He was sweating profusely.

Desperate to make the general understand how hard he'd tried, he started explaining. "I even killed President McDonald in an attempt to stop our response. We've discovered that they used the NSA computers to pull it off, but we haven't been able to find out who did it."

"I'm already aware of details of what transpired. I purposely delayed my trip until I could identify the perpetrators. It took some extreme measures, but we've ascertained the attacks were initiated by General Jeffries."

"Impossible, that's way out of his pay grade!" President Martell said.

"No doubt, but Admiral Zacharias gave him the codes, and tools to circumvent the fail-safe procedures."

"How can you be so sure?"

"The admiral's chief of staff is one of our people, and he put us on to him. After we discussed the matter with the admiral, he was more than happy to confess."

The president had gotten to know Admiral Zacharias fairly well, so he knew it hadn't been a voluntary confession. "Is he still alive?"

"Certainly, do you think I'm a barbarian? He'll receive a fair hearing, and then he'll be executed."

"The public will never stand for it. They're going to see him as a hero."

"Whatever. They've grown too soft to be much of a

threat. As long as their bellies are full, they'll fall into line," the general said cynically.

The general sat down at the president's desk, put his feet up, and asked, "So, what do you think I should do about you?"

"What do you mean? I've spent over twenty years doing as I was told, and I think I've done a damn good job for our country."

"Good job! They're all dead, and you're a damn fool to think that I would ever tolerate a traitor like you around me." The general waved one of his bodyguards over. "Get this asshole out of my sight. Lock him in his rooms, and make sure he doesn't escape."

"You can't come in here and pull this kind of shit," the president yelled as he activated the panic alarm he wore on a chain around his neck.

"You can push that all you want, no one is coming."

As they led President Martell away, he could see the Chinese soldiers roaming the halls of the White House. He'd worked as a deep-cover operative for most of his adult life, and he'd always expected to be caught and executed at some point. However, he'd never thought it would be at the hands of his own people.

Before he left the West Coast, General Sung had arranged a prime-time TV broadcast for that night. He hadn't wanted them to question his request, so he'd told them the president would be giving a national security update. When General Sung's image filled every TV screen in the United States, he was standing behind a podium in the Oval Office. He was wearing his best dress uniform, and he cut a dashing figure. His silver hair sparkled in the high-powered lights they'd set up for the broadcast, and many of the people watching the telecast thought that he was an actor at first.

"Who the hell is this?" the producer for the White House press pool demanded.

"I believe it's General Sung, the commander of the UN peacekeeping forces," the assistant producer informed him.

"Good evening, ladies and gentlemen, I'm General Sung, the supreme commander of the UN peacekeeping forces. These are perilous times, and I realize that many of you are terrified by the horrific events which have transpired. Our best estimates place worldwide casualties at approximately two-point-five billion so far, but we need to move past that. While I'm reluctant to call anything about the events good, we were fortunate that both sides used enhanced radiation weapons or neutron bombs, as they are more commonly known, and we expect the radiation levels to dissipate in a few months. Both of our nations have suffered horribly, but if we keep our wits about us, we should be able to limit future casualties. However, to achieve that, it's imperative we maintain order. There have been far too many incidents of violence and civil disobedience, and my patience is at an end," the general said as he slammed his fist on the podium.

"From this moment on, disobedience will be considered an act of treason. To emphasize what that means, I'm going to make an example out of a couple of traitors. What you are about to witness will be distasteful to most of you, but let it be a lesson to all of you."

The general paused to let the guards drag Admiral Zacharias and President Martell into the room. The general motioned to the guards, and they forced them to their knees on the carpet.

"What the hell is going on?" the producer screamed.

The general stepped away from the podium, and slowly walked up behind the prisoners. The cameras zoomed in on their faces, and the entire nation held their breaths, as they contemplated what came next.

President Martell was whimpering and begging for

his life, when the general drew his sidearm and shot him in the back of the head. The bullet's impact sprayed blood and brains all over the presidential seal in the carpet.

Horrified, the producer yelled, "Shut the cameras off." The camera operator didn't have time to respond, before one of the soldiers shot the producer and motioned for them to keep the cameras on.

As the general slid in behind Admiral Zacharias, he looked up at the cameras and screamed, "Long live America, death to the invaders."

The general had to admit the admiral had balls, but he shot him anyway. When his body hit the floor, General Sung motioned for the soldiers to move back. He left the bodies lying where they would be in full view of the cameras, as he returned to the podium to finish his speech.

"So that there won't be any more pretenses about what's going on, the United States is now under my direct control. To ensure an orderly transition of power, I'm immediately dissolving the UN, Congress, and all state legislatures. You'll be receiving more instructions in the coming weeks, but if you follow the rules, you can lead long, productive lives."

The general motioned for the cameras to be turned off, and for the first time since they'd thrown the British out, the United States was under foreign control.

As General Sung was about to leave, one of the guards asked, "What do you want us to do with the bodies?"

"Throw Martell in the Dumpster, and make sure the admiral is buried with full honors in Arlington Cemetery."

General Jeffries and Colonel Drury had watched General Sung's speech, and when the general shot Admiral Zacharias, General Jeffries bowed his head in prayer for his friend. JD did the same, and while he was at it, he asked God for the strength to free his homeland.

"He certainly lives up to his reputation," General

Jeffries said as he wiped the tears from his eyes. "We've got to make sure he burns in hell for this."

"I'd be happy to send him," JD offered.

The general shook his head in agreement. "But we don't need to go off half-cocked. It's going to take time to organize a resistance."

The soldier above all others prays for peace, for it is the soldier who must suffer and bear the deepest wounds and scars of war.

—Douglas MacArthur

PART 8

CHAPTER 1

Within hours of General Sung's declaration, riots had broken out across the country.

When Admiral Zacharias's last defiant words reached the fleet, Admiral Gentry, the commander of the Pacific fleet, immediately assumed command of what was left of the United States fleet.

The Chinese fleet had never been much of a threat, but after decades of budget cuts and neglect, neither was the American's. Admiral Gentry realized that time was of the essence, so an hour later, he made a worldwide broadcast to the fleet.

"Today we lost a great shipmate, and a true patriot. In honor of Admiral Zacharias, and to take the first step to drive the invaders out, we're going to sink every damn Chinese ship we can find." The admiral had to call for quiet before he could continue. "This order is to anyone who is still in command of a United States vessel or installation. You are guns free, and hereby authorized to sink any Chinese ship, and kill any member of the Chinese military you find. Communications are limited, and likely to become even worse, so each of you is on your own. "Good luck, good hunting, and long live America, death to the invaders."

The rest of the commanders took the admiral's words to heart, and within a matter of weeks, the US fleet had fought a series of vicious engagements with the Chinese.

"I'VE JUST FINISHED analyzing the radio traffic, satellite images, and the VLF communication logs," Lt. Commander West reported. "As far as we can tell, our forces have finished off the Chinese fleet."

"Great news." General Jeffries whooped and slapped him on the back. "Any news out of Admiral Gentry's task force?"

"I'm afraid they didn't make it. They engaged the main Chinese fleet in the Sea of Japan, and one of the Chinese submarines managed to bracket them with its nukes."

"Sorry to hear it, he was a good man. Other than the admiral's task force, how many ships did we lose?"

"I'm afraid we've suffered catastrophic losses. This is still a tentative count, but we've only been able to contact forty-four submarines and one carrier, CVN 78 (*Gerald R. Ford*), and it's badly damaged, but still underway."

"That's it?"

"The numbers are tentative, but I don't think the count is going to climb very much. The *Ronald Reagan* is in dry dock in Newport News, but when the Chinese seized control, the captain flooded the ship with radiation to keep it from falling into their hands."

The general thought for a moment. "Have the survivors rendezvous in Guam."

"They mothballed Guam years ago."

"I'm aware of its status, but most of the facility is intact, and as remote as it is, they should be relatively safe for a while."

* * *

As THE WEEKS passed, the riots had continued to rage across the country.

"How bad?" General Sung asked when he saw Major Ma come in with the daily status report.

"Thirty-two riots, with eleven hundred civilians killed," Major Ma reported.

"Damn it, I was hoping that they would have come to their senses by now. I've been patient enough. Give the order to shoot the rioters on sight."

The Chinese security forces were absolutely ruthless, and the death toll had been horrendous, but by the end of the ninth month, the violence had started to abate. As General Sung struggled to consolidate his hold on the country, he decided to begin limiting the information flow to the people. TV, radio, etc., it didn't matter. He either seized control of them, or in the case of the Internet, he decided to shut it down.

"You're asking for trouble if you do this," Colonel Su, his chief technology officer warned.

The general was visibly frustrated that the colonel was continuing to push back on the issue. "I'm tired of your excuses. I'm ordering you to shut it down immediately," the general screamed.

The colonel knew that just shutting it down was a risky proposition, but he could see that the general was clearly done talking about it, so he pulled the plug.

A few hours later the general discovered that they'd turned it back on, and he was furious. "Get Colonel Su in here immediately."

"General, you don't understand, I had to turn it back on," Colonel Su tried to explain. "Once we disabled it, we discovered that the national power grid and the fail-safe infrastructure for the nuclear power plants run off of it. We came within minutes of melting down one of the reactors."

The general was still furious, but he could tell by the look on the colonel's face that he was telling the truth.

"OK, I get it, but how do we keep the people from doing mischief on it?" General Sung asked.

The colonel had already briefed him twice on the subject, but he hoped that he would actually listen this time. "We'll make the content filtering programs mandatory, and we'll force the ISPs to monitor all the traffic for keywords and patterns. I believe that by allowing more open access, it will let us ferret out the traitors more quickly."

"Sneaky, I like it. Just make sure you keep a handle on it, because I'm expecting more trouble out of those damn militias."

When the Internet had first gone dark, General Jeffries had thought it was one of the many interruptions they suffered through every week.

"The Internet's back up," Larry Lindsey, better known as the geek, announced.

"Good job," General Jeffries told him.

"It wasn't anything I did. One of my friends back in the States just told me that the Chinese had forced all the ISPs to power down."

"I don't know why they changed their minds, but I'm glad they did," General Jeffries said. "How are you coming with setting up a secure communication channel?"

"I've finished the programming, and I've sent a copy of it to one of my old running mates in Idaho, and he'll take care of the distribution."

"How did you manage to get the programs to your contact, since they're monitoring everything?"

"I embedded the code in a set of vacation photos that I e-mailed him last night."

"If they find out, they'll kill him."

"There's no way they're bright enough to figure out the code is even in there. I know everyone in their cyber squads, and while they're good, they're not as good as they think they are."

"Great, when you're ready, here's the first group of messages I want to send."

CHAPTER 2

Previously, General Jeffries would have derided anyone who suggested that the ultimate fate of the United States might depend on people who he considered to be on the very fringe of society.

Once the word had gotten out, General Jeffries had been shocked at the sheer number of responses. After he'd done his initial assessments, he sat down with Colonel Drury to lay out his plan.

"I've compiled a list of the organizations I want you and your team to work with," General Jeffries said.

"Great, do you think there's going to be enough men to make a difference?" Colonel Drury asked.

"I don't think that's going to be an issue. We only sent the original message to thirty-one groups, but we've already received responses from a hundred and seventy, and there's more coming in every day. I'd always known there were a great number of people who weren't comfortable with the way the country was being run, but I had no idea the militia movements were so widespread."

"Me either, but when can I get started?" JD asked.

"I've got a submarine coming for you and your men next Wednesday. The group I want you to focus on is near Hidalgo, Texas."

"I know the area well. Who are we going to meet up with?"

"They call themselves Texans for Independence."

"These guys are for real, right?" JD asked, clearly worried about working with some sort of radical fringe group.

"Most definitely. Their leader is a Texas billionaire by the name of William Sheldon, and he runs a tight operation. They're headquartered on his fifty-thousand-acre ranch just outside of Hidalgo, and not even the local sheriff is allowed out there without an invite."

"Anything else I should know about him?"

"I wish I could tell you more, but he's a bit of an enigma."

"No problem, I'll figure it out. So you don't think we'll have any problem with the Chinese patrols?"

"No, it's far too remote of an area to have drawn any real scrutiny."

THE SUBMARINE DROPPED them off without a hitch, but when they reached Hidalgo there was a huge crowd crossing the McAllen-Hidalgo-Reynosa Bridge.

"See if you can find out what's going on," JD told Corporal Ramirez.

The corporal was only gone a few minutes. "They're headed to BorderFest in Hidalgo."

JD studied his map and said, "There's a Ryder truck rental two blocks over." He pointed to the map. "Get over there and rent the biggest truck they have."

When Corporal Ramirez returned, JD ordered, "Sergeant, you and the men load the equipment, and get in the back. Corporal, you drive and I'll navigate."

It was slow going for the first couple of miles, but once they got past the festival crowd, the traffic thinned out. As they approached Sheldon's ranch, JD told the corporal, "The road should be coming up on the right."

"Got it," Corporal Ramirez said, as he slowed to make the turn. "Looks like they've got a guard house."

When they stopped, a guard walked out to see what they wanted. "What can I do for you?" the guard asked.

"I've got business with Mr. Sheldon," JD told the guard.

"What's your name, hoss?"

"I'm Colonel Drury."

The guard flipped through the sheets on his clipboard, and said, "You're not on my list. Are you sure you're in the right place?"

"I'm sure. Why don't you get your boss on the horn, and ask him?"

The guard started to refuse, but he took another look at JD. "OK, fine," the guard said, as he slowly walked back to the building. A couple of minutes later the guard came out of the shack, except this time he was in a real hurry. He raised the pole barring their way and instructed, "Just stay on this road, and you'll run into the main house. Sorry for the confusion, I meant no disrespect," he stammered, as he snapped JD a salute.

They followed the winding lane for a couple of miles before JD caught sight of the sprawling ranch house and outbuildings. They pulled into the circular drive and stopped in front of the massive entryway. Standing on the steps waiting for them was one of the biggest men JD had ever seen. As JD got down out of the truck, he could see the film of sweat on the man's ebony skin. It wasn't particularly hot out, and JD was wondering what had him so worked up, until he realized how excited the big man was to see them.

"Damned glad to meet you, Colonel Drury, I'm William Sheldon," the big man bellowed.

JD knew Sheldon was in his sixties, but when he grabbed JD's hand, he couldn't help but grimace at his viselike grip.

"Thank you for seeing me, Mr. Sheldon."

"It's just William to you. You got anyone else with you?"

"The rest of my men are in the back of the truck."

William motioned to one of his men, and ordered, "Get that door open, and show those boys where they're going to be staying." He looked at JD and explained. "I've got a whole wing set up for you and your men. Now come along, and we'll talk about why you're here."

When they reached the den, it reminded JD of a scene out of one of the old cowboy movies that Leroy had loved to watch in the evenings. From the chandeliers, to the rough-hewn wooden floor, it was the perfect Western room.

"Make yourself comfortable. What would you like to drink?" William asked.

"A cold beer, if you've got one?"

"Boy, this is Texas; of course we've got cold beer. Coors all right?"

"You bet. I grew up drinking Coors."

"Where you from?"

"I grew up in the Oklahoma panhandle, about a hundred and seventy miles north of Amarillo."

"I know the area well. I used to go up there to buy cattle."

When they had their drinks, William motioned for him to take a seat.

"Let's get to it. You and your boys here to stir up them damn Chinese?"

"Yes, sir."

"What do you need from me? Men, guns, vehicles?"

"Depends, what have you got?"

"You name it, I got it, or I can lay my hands on it."

They'd been talking for several hours when William remarked, "I could eat a horse, let's get some chow."

They continued their discussions over a feast of ribs and steaks, and when they finished, they retired to the patio for a drink.

"I've missed these sunsets," JD said, as he sipped a tumbler of straight bourbon.

William nodded in agreement, and told him, "From what you've told me so far, I'm confident I've got everything you need." He paused before he asked, "I hope you're not naive enough to think this is going to be an overnight success."

"We know it's likely to take years. I don't know whether you'd agree, but I think the first thing we've got to do, is figure out how to get the American people out of their comfort zone, and willing to make the sacrifices necessary to drive the Chinese out."

"I've got faith in America, but I couldn't agree more. How are you going to get started?"

"Do you remember when the Chinese turned off the Internet?"

"I sure do. They ended up cutting the power to half the country, and almost melted down a reactor."

"That's what gave me the idea for our first move. I intend to drop as much of the national power grid as I can."

"To what point? It won't take them any time at all to repair whatever damage you do."

"I've got two messages I'm trying to convey. I want to show the people that there are still patriots, who aren't going to stand by and let our country fade away into history, and I want General Sung to understand we're coming for him."

"I just hope you don't end up like the mouse giving the eagle the finger, as it swoops down on him."

The night before they took off, William threw them an old-fashioned Texas barbecue. They had horse troughs filled with ice and beer, and picnic tables stacked high with rib eye steaks, and trays of smoked brisket.

"Have a good time, but remember we leave at 0400," JD said.

William and JD fixed their plates, grabbed a couple of beers, and sat down at one of the vacant tables.

"I still don't get the plan," William admitted.

"Due to the budget cuts, they've never addressed the redundancy and capacity issues in the power grid, and I intend to take advantage of it. They're forecasting the hottest day of the year, so everyone will be running their air-conditioners. The grid's capacity will already be strained, and when we drop the interconnects, the massive overload should cause a cascading failure throughout the system."

"That makes sense," William agreed. "How are the people supposed to know it wasn't just a system failure?"

"The geek is going to hack into the major news Web sites to post our message."

"Here's to success," William said as they bumped their beers together.

CHAPTER 3

All the teams were using the same plan of attack, and at precisely 1700 the four-man sniper teams shot the sentries, and moved in to plant their charges.

JD's team was in New Mexico, and when they finished planting the C4, and programming the time-delayed detonators, JD ordered, "All right, men, let's mount up.

"Slide over, I'm going to drive," JD instructed.

JD was really pushing it, and as the SUV roared down the narrow two-lane road, his mind flashed back to his days of driving for Rex Allen, and he wished he'd gotten to see him one last time before he'd been murdered.

"WHAT'S GOING ON with the power?" General Sung asked.

"At first we thought it was just a power failure," Major Ma explained. "Until a hacker posted a claim from some militia group taking credit for it. They've challenged the American public to stand with them to drive the Chinese forces from American soil."

"The fools! Find out who did it, and kill them all."

* * *

THE NEXT DAY, JD was sitting with William Sheldon, watching the six o'clock news, when they broke in with a news bulletin.

"We're now taking you live to the Phoenix area, where rioting has broken out. This is Harry Fossey, reporting live from the Channel 14 news copter. We're approaching the scene of the riot, and the smoke you're seeing is from a combination of burning buildings, and vehicles."

Harry paused to listen to a new message on his headset. "We're now going to Sally Prentice, on location in the Channel 14 news van."

"This is Sally Prentice, reporting live from the Intersection of Grand Avenue and West Glendale Avenue. Sir, can I have your name and a description of what you saw?"

"I'm Hank Skinner, and I'll go you one better, I've got a video of it."

"Billy, could you upload this to your laptop so we can show it to the viewers?" Sally requested.

"Sure, boss, give me just a minute."

"While Billy is doing that, would you recount what we're about to see?"

"Sure. I was standing here watching the demonstration, when the UN troops forced one of the low riders in the parade to stop."

"So they were causing issues?"

"Not really. They were honking their horns, and yelling, but they weren't causing any problems."

"I've got the video," the video tech interrupted.

"Thank you, and now we'll show what just took place."

As the low-resolution video played out, the viewers could see the first cars roll by. Even though the temperature had again soared to 115, and most of the city was still without electricity, the mood of the participants seemed lighthearted. When the first of the gang members' convertibles passed by, one of the Chinese soldiers stepped in front of it. They could see that he was yelling something, but they couldn't make it out. When he started pounding on the hood, one of the men shot him in the face. Mortally wounded, the soldier fell to the pavement. The next thing they heard was the Chinese commander yell, "Kill those animals."

They watched in horror as the soldiers' machine guns shredded the car. When they saw their friends being slaughtered, several carloads of the gang members jumped out and joined the melee. As the violence escalated, the Chinese commander sent in reinforcements and it quickly turned into an all-out firefight.

The video cut off at that point, when Hank dove for cover.

"Wow, that was intense," Sally commented.

"You ain't telling me anything," Hank agreed. "I peed my pants."

Sally quickly cut him off. "On that note, back to you, Harry."

"Thanks, Sally, we're going to move over the area and try to show you some of the fighting that is still going on."

The news helicopter was showing the action in real time, and within minutes they could see hundreds of gang members and normal citizens scrambling to join the fight. As the fighting raged below, the helicopter kept circling, trying to catch all the action.

After almost thirty minutes, one of the Chinese commander's men asked, "Sir, did you know that this is being broadcast on TV?"

"Oh, hell," he exclaimed, as he looked up at the helicopter circling overhead. "Shoot the damn thing down."

"Oh dear God, there's a missile tracking straight for us," the pilot screamed as he tried to turn away.

The last thing the viewers saw was the missile heading straight for the camera.

A minute or so later the picture returned, but this

time it was the station's normal news anchor in the studio.

"I'm sorry to report that our news helicopter has been destroyed in the fighting. Sally Prentice's crew has just reached the scene of the crash, and they're reporting no survivors." He paused to listen to an update. "I've just received a report of rioting in the Scottsdale area, not too far from the Penn Foster College. As we get more information we'll break in with updates."

"General Sung won't be pleased that his men were on national TV, slaughtering people in the streets," William Sheldon commented.

"I intended to get people stirred up, but this isn't what I expected," JD told him.

"It's regrettable, but this may be what it takes to wake people up."

Even though he was exhausted by the time he got to bed, JD didn't sleep very well, as he dreamed about the slaughter he'd caused.

It took the Chinese over a week to restore power to portions of the West and to quell the riots. By the time the power was fully restored, there had been almost three hundred heat-related deaths, and the fighting in the Phoenix/Scottsdale areas had killed over four thousand people.

JD had been struggling to coordinate with General Jeffries, until Corporal Lindsey came up with an innovative technique to stabilize their communications.

"Are you sure this is secure?" General Jeffries asked.

"I wouldn't pretend to know how Larry did it, but he swears it's not only secure, it's virtually untraceable," JD explained. "Something about splitting the bandwidth into parallel data streams and sending them by way of multiple IP addresses, whatever that means. I guess you saw the mess I caused?"

"You can't put that on yourself," General Jeffries

admonished. "The Chinese commander overreacted, and I imagine it's giving General Sung nightmares. If a relatively minor event can lead to that much bloodshed, think of what a real uprising could cause. I'd hate to think where we would be if the Supreme Court hadn't come out for a citizen's right to bear arms. Between the private citizens and the militias, there's a buttload of guns in the people's hands."

"True enough, particularly in that part of the country. So what's up, or did you just call to talk about Phoenix?"

"No, I wanted to talk about what comes next," General Jeffries said. "Do you still have forty-four men, counting yourself?"

"No, I'm down to forty. I had four men killed in a car wreck. Why do you ask?"

"What would you think about dispersing your men to organize and train some of the larger militias?"

"I'm all right with the training programs, but until I'm sure we can control them, I'd rather not use any of them for direct action."

The uncomfortable silence that followed let JD know the general needed more. "OK, how about this as an interim step? I've gotten comfortable with TFI and their abilities. I could use them as a support group while I mount a few attacks here in Texas to keep them riled up."

"I'm OK with whatever is short term, but when it's practical, we've got to hit them as hard and as often as we can."

"Understood."

I can no longer obey; I have tasted command, and I cannot give it up.

—NAPOLEON BONAPARTE

PART 9

CHAPTER 1

Their progress had stagnated, so General Sung decided to make some changes.

"I'm promoting you," General Sung announced.

"Thank you for your confidence," General Cheng replied. "I'll do my best for you."

"I wouldn't accept less. I'm giving you everything west of the Mississippi, and I don't want any more Phoenix debacles."

"Yes, there was a regrettable loss of life."

"Let's not misunderstand each other," General Sung interrupted. "I don't give a shit if you've got to kill a few of them, just keep it out of the press."

While General Sung was struggling to get the country under control, JD was hoping to keep it stirred up.

After JD had briefed his men, they spread out across the country to train the militias.

Once they were gone, JD went over to the main house to meet with William Sheldon.

"I've decided to stay here and stir up some trouble," JD said.

"Excellent, what do you need from me?" William Sheldon asked.

"I need a couple of your men to provide logistical support, and some way of getting around without drawing any attention."

"If you don't mind me asking, what are you up to?"

"I'm going to try to demoralize their troops by killing as many of their officers as I can."

"I've got just the men you need, and we can use the cattle truck I modified to smuggle operatives across the border."

Smuggle operatives? I wonder what that's about, JD mused.

THE BARN WHERE he had the truck parked was over two hundred thousand square feet, and it was jammed with everything from pickups to the largest eighteen-wheelers.

"This is the one I was telling you about," William said as they walked up to a cattle truck.

"Perfect, but where am I supposed to hide? It doesn't even have a sleeper."

"It's not in the truck, it's in the trailer," William said as he led him up the ramp. When they reached the nose of the trailer, he told him, "Watch this."

He pulled down on a bolt in the front panel, and a doorway silently slid open, revealing a three-foot wide hideaway. "I know it's not very large, but it's as big as we could make it without being obvious."

"I would have never guessed it was there," JD admitted.

THE TFI HAD a large number of members in the Dallas–Fort Worth area, so William tasked them with identifying JD's potential targets.

"I guess I'm going to get going," JD said. "I can't begin to thank you for all of your help."

"No thanks needed, just make sure you kill a couple for me," William Sheldon said, as they shook hands.

"You can count on that."

Once JD and his team got to Dallas, they quickly fell into a routine. Every day before dawn, Stan Waters would drop JD off at one of the predetermined locations to take out the targets of the day. However, by the fourth week, JD was growing dissatisfied with their progress.

"This isn't getting it done," JD complained.

"What have you got in mind, boss?" Stan Waters asked.

"I don't know, but working from a stationary position isn't cutting it. I only get to kill one or two before I have to either hide out, or make a run for it."

"Umm, I may have a solution if you can give me a few days."

"No problem. I need to make a run out to William Sheldon's place anyway."

When JD returned, Stan had modified a van to replace the cattle truck. As they walked around it, Stan started explaining what he'd done.

"I've exchanged the glass panels in the back with reflective one-way glass, and added strategically located gun ports, so you can shoot without being seen."

JD took a few moments to climb in and check it out. "Stan, this is great," JD complimented. "What's on tap for today?" he asked.

"We just got a tip that they're holding an emergency strategy meeting at the Adolphus Hotel, and I think we should swing by and see what's going on."

"Perfect."

As luck would have it, there were three of the area commanders walking into the hotel when Stan drove by.

"Slow down," JD instructed. He slid his rifle through the gun port and shot them in the head.

"You'd better get going," JD urged.

"That should give them something to talk about," Stan said as he accelerated away from the hotel.

* * *

COLONEL LIANG HAD been trying to handle the situation on his own, but after JD shot the three senior officers at the hotel, the news of the killings had caught the national media's attention.

"What the hell's going on down there?" General Sung demanded.

"Someone has been targeting our officers," Colonel Liang explained. "I've already lost twenty-two, including eight of my senior group commanders."

"What have you done about it?" General Sung asked, pissed that he hadn't been brought into the loop.

"We've rounded up the normal suspects, but I don't believe any of them were involved."

"Damn militias again," General Sung said.

"Possibly, but whoever's behind it definitely has a military background. All the kills have been head shots, and my forensic experts tells me they're using a military-grade sniper rifle."

"You'd better get a handle on it, or I'm going to send Colonel Chu down there to take care of it," General Sung threatened.

Colonel Chu was the general's dirty little jobs' officer, and whenever he had a particularly distasteful job to be done, he sent the colonel. Chu wasn't even Chinese; he was a Vietnamese national. The general had first met him when he was cleaning up the Indonesian insurrections, and over the years the general had used him many times.

After the general had thought about the conversation, he called Colonel Chu in. "I need you to go down to Texas and resolve a situation."

"What am I looking at?" Chu asked.

"Someone is killing our commissioned officers, and I want it stopped."

"Understood, and do you want me to do anything with the local commander?"

"I think he's a good man, he's just in over his head. Unless he gets in your way, let him be."

"Could I have a few days before I go? I've got a couple of things that I need to wrap up."

"No problem."

Colonel Liang definitely didn't want Chu messing around in his command, so when he got off the phone, he told his aide, "Effective immediately, I don't want any officer traveling without a security detail, and they've got to use armored transportation."

The colonel's mandate had an immediate effect, and for the first time, JD went three days without a kill.

On the fourth day, JD and Jesse Ortiz, one of the locals, were sitting at a Starbucks in Las Colinas, having a cup of coffee and a muffin.

"It looks like they've finally smartened up," Jesse commented.

"It does. Can you get me into the gated community where Colonel Liang is living?"

"Sure, I'll get them to drop you off in the morning."

"It needs to be today."

"What's the hurry?"

"There was an article about Liang in yesterday's paper, and he's leaving town on Friday to go deep-sea fishing in Florida."

They used a landscaping truck to sneak JD through the gates, and dropped him off a couple of blocks from the colonel's home.

The Chinese had gotten into the habit of just taking what they wanted, and the house that Colonel Liang had confiscated was a million-dollar-plus mansion in Forest on the Creek.

The colonel had told the reporter how much he loved to swim, and that he tried to swim at least two miles every day. So JD decided to take him when he went for his evening swim.

The mansion's pool was built on the top of one of the rolling hills in the backyard, and it overlooked a winding pathway that led down through the trees to a stream that ran through the community.

The colonel was still at work, so JD hid in the tree line until he got home.

JD had intended to just shoot him in the head, but when he saw him come out for his evening swim, he decided to take a different approach. Since the pool sat above the stone walkway, JD was able to crawl up beside the pool without being spotted. He waited patiently until the colonel grabbed the side of the pool to rest. As he pounced on the colonel, he flipped his Special Forces knife open and hooked his arm under Liang's chin.

Terrified, the colonel struggled as best he could, but JD pulled him partially out of the pool, jerked his head back, and slit his throat. JD thought about the statement he was trying to make, and used the razor-sharp knife to sever the Colonel's head. As the colonel's body sank to the bottom, a crimson cloud billowed into the pristine water.

JD cut off a section of the rope in the pool, and used it to tie the colonel's head to the stone mailbox in the front drive. When he finished he called to Jesse, "You can pick me up."

As he waited, he thought about what he'd just done. It wasn't that he lacked compassion; he simply viewed the act as a means to an end.

When Jesse pulled up he spotted the severed head. "Damn, that's cold!"

As they pulled away, JD placed an anonymous call to the local TV station.

* * *

"I THINK YOU'D better see this," Major Ma told General Sung, as he turned the TV on.

The news crew was broadcasting from in front of the colonel's house, and the first thing the general saw was the colonel's head hanging from his mailbox.

What really pissed the general off, was the message JD had painted on the base of the mailbox.

Long live America, death to the invaders.

Completely disgusted with the turn of events, the general growled. "Turn that damn thing off, and find out if Chu has landed yet."

"He just landed, would you like to talk with him?" Major Ma asked.

"Hell no, I was just asking to see if he had a nice flight, you nitwit."

"HAVE YOU HEARD what happened?"

"I just caught the news report on the TV in the FBO."

"This is getting worse by the minute," General Sung complained.

"How would you like me to proceed?"

"I want you to kick some ass until you find the people behind this, and then I want you to kill them, and every member of their family. On second thought, kill everyone who even knows them, and I want you to make this very public. They need to learn that this kind of crap isn't going to be tolerated."

"No problem, I'm on it."

THEY'D SENT A car for him, and the driver asked, "Where to, Colonel?"

"Take me to the Dallas County jail."

When he walked in, the guard saluted, and asked, "How may I help?"

"I need to see your commander, ASAP."

"Yes, sir, right away sir."

"SORRY, I WASN'T expecting you," Major Dong, the jail's commander said.

"Don't worry about it. How many prisoners did you round up?"

"Several hundred, but what's your interest?" the major asked, concerned that someone from General Sung's staff was poking around.

"It's none of your business. I'll need a list of the prisoners, and any information you've gathered," Colonel Chu ordered.

"Right away, Colonel."

After he'd gone through the list, Colonel Chu selected the most promising ones, and spent the rest of the day interrogating them.

Several hours later, Major Dong stopped by to check on the colonel.

"This was a waste of time," Colonel Chu said.

"I don't know why you even bothered to pick them up. None of these people know anything."

"How can you be so sure?" Major Dong asked. "They might be lying."

"Trust me, when I'm done with someone, they'll have told me."

As the major glanced around the interrogation room, he noticed the blood splatters on the walls, and that the drain was clogged with what looked like bits of raw meat. He was holding it together until he saw an ear under the bench on the wall. He managed to reach the sink before he upchucked, but Colonel Chu didn't cut him any slack.

"Been at this long? I want you call the TV stations

and set up a press conference for 0900, and here's a list of things I need you to take care of."

By morning, the accounts of Chu's brutality were flying around the Dallas–Fort Worth metroplex.

"I heard he killed three men while he was interrogating them," Jesse Ortiz said.

JD closed the dossier on Colonel Chu. "Colonel Chu's a piece of work all right."

"Chu's holding a press conference this morning. Do you want to stay and watch it, or are we going hunting?" Jesse asked.

"We'll watch. General Sung sent him down here to take care of me, so let's see what he has to say."

At 0855 Major Dong herded the prisoners outside, and lined them up in front of the jail, where the press was gathered.

"Everything is in place," Major Dong reported.

"Good morning, I'm Colonel Chu. I'm a man of few words, so today's events won't take very long. General Sung has tasked me with stopping the criminals murdering our officers. The men you see before you have been arrested on suspicion of aiding the criminals carrying out these acts. I've interviewed a few of them, and I don't believe any of them were involved."

"Oh thank God, he sounds like a reasonable man," Jesse said.

"Unfortunately for them, I'm going to use them to make a point to the people carrying out these heinous acts," Colonel Chu announced. He nodded to Major Dong.

The machine gun fire almost deafened the reporters, and seconds later, the prisoners lay dead in the street.

The news crews wouldn't have broadcasted the colonel's brutality, but he'd caught them by surprise.

"That animal murdered them all," Jesse said.

"He wouldn't view it as murder; it's a message to me," JD explained.

"What are we supposed to do now?"

JD pondered the situation for a moment and said, "Given their new security procedures, and the colonel's actions, it's time that we move on."

"We're going to turn tail and run?"

"I know some will say that, but we need to pick our spots. I've heard some good things about the militias in the Houston area, so we'll try our luck down there."

CHAPTER 2

After a week had passed with no reported incidents, General Sung called Colonel Chu.

"Well, done. It looks like they didn't have the stomach for it."

"I wouldn't be too quick to declare victory," Colonel Chu warned. "I seriously doubt they've given up."

"I'll take what I can get. Hang around there for a few more days, and if nothing else happens, you can come on back."

After General Sung finished with Colonel Chu, he met with Major Ma for their daily briefing.

"There have been several more reports of riots and killings in the Houston area," Major Ma reported.

"I can't believe General Feng hasn't stopped that shit already." Even as he made the comment, General Sung knew it was probably his fault. He valued officers that would do whatever it took, and General Feng was by far the most ruthless commander he'd ever seen. He'd promoted him to a one-star general after he'd wiped out the South Koreans in 2021, but the promotion had spurred him on to such new heights of savagery that he had to censure him.

"Get General Feng for me," General Sung ordered.

* * *

"I KNOW I put you on a short leash, but the situation has changed, and I don't care what sort of methods you use. Just get it under control."

"Consider it done," General Feng said, chuckling to himself, because he'd intentionally let the situation deteriorate to force his hand. Several weeks before, he'd obtained the membership rolls of several of the south Texas militias, and he intended to exterminate them. General Feng launched the crackdown at midnight, and he used over ten thousand men in an attempt to eradicate them in one fell swoop.

"Major Ye is here to see you," General Feng's aide announced the next morning.

"Send him in."

"We've completed the operation," Major Ye reported.

"Excellent. Give me a rundown."

"We killed three hundred and ninety militia members, and we've taken thirteen hundred prisoners."

"What were our casualties?"

"A hundred and two dead, and forty-four wounded."

"More than I had expected, but well worth it. Where are you holding the prisoners?"

"They're still in the trucks," Major Ye told him. "I wasn't expecting this many, and I haven't been able to find anywhere to put them."

"How about the Harris County jail?"

"I already checked, it's full."

"I'd like to keep them all together, so just empty it out, and put them there," General Feng ordered.

"What do you want me to do with the convicts?"

"I don't care, hell, just turn them loose."

SEVERAL DAYS LATER, JD and his team arrived in the Houston area, where Sergeant Jerome Brown met him. The sergeant was one of his men, and he'd been training the area militias, and helping them plot their attacks. The sergeant had arranged for him to stay in a bunkhouse on one of the horse farms outside of Houston.

Once JD had gotten settled in, Jerome and a couple of the locals spent almost an hour briefing him on General Feng's crackdown.

"So they just kicked all the crooks loose?" JD asked.

"That's right, and then they locked our people up down there," Larry Scribner, one of the local militia commanders said.

"Are you going to start killing their officers like you did in Dallas?"

"Probably, but right now, I want to break those people out."

"I was hoping you'd say that."

"I've already been scouting it out. I've got the troop dispositions, shift changes; you name it, I've got it. How soon do you think we'll be able to attack?"

"Slow down, first things first," JD cautioned. "How many men do they have on a normal shift?"

"If you include the cell block guards, there are usually around two hundred on nights, and roughly seventy more on days."

"How about Sundays?"

"About the same."

"OK, let me have everything you've got, and when I've had enough time to study it, I'll give you a call."

It took JD three days to formulate a plan, and when he finished, he called Sergeant Brown to set up a meeting for the next morning.

Since it was only two in the afternoon, JD decided to go outside to get some air. As he sat on the bunkhouse porch soaking up the warmth, he allowed himself a small hope it would all end someday, and that he could make some sort of life for himself.

Get over it, he thought to himself. *You're a soldier, and that's probably all you'll ever be.*

SERGEANT BROWN AND Larry Scribner were there the first thing in the morning, and eager to get to work. JD spent two hours covering the details of the attacks.

"Any questions?" JD asked.

"Can you give me a couple of days to pull my end together?" Sergeant Brown asked.

"Sure, that'll work."

THREE DAYS LATER, JD and forty of Jerome's best men were staged around the holding facility. They kicked off the assault by setting off a series of smoke grenades they'd hidden in the building's air ducts. When the building started filling up with smoke, the fire alarms and the sprinkler systems went off. The guards did just what they'd been trained to do, and immediately locked the facility down.

"Evacuate all the guards," Captain Singh, the watch commander, ordered.

"What about the prisoners?" Lieutenant Wong asked.

"Just leave them. They'll either be here when we return, or they'll all die. It doesn't really matter either way."

When JD thought that all the guards were out, he ordered, "Blow the charges." They'd planted IEDs along the building's perimeter, and when they detonated, they took a terrible toll on the massed guards. They had armored SUVs strategically spotted outside the building, and they opened fire shortly after the last IED went off. The SUVs were outfitted with General Electric M134DT mini-guns on the roof, and they poured torrents of machine gun fire into the shell-shocked guards. Three minutes after the firefight began, it was over, and the street looked like a slaughterhouse floor.

"Move it," JD ordered. "We need to be out of here in twenty."

Each team had a section to clear, and as they ran into the building, the buses started arriving. When they led the prisoners out of the building they herded them onto the waiting buses.

"You'd better get a move on, they're ten miles out," Larry Scribner reported.

"I ESTIMATE THAT we're about six minutes away," Captain Ho, the commander of General Feng's elite rapid response force reported.

"Understood. We've just received several reports that they're using buses to move the prisoners, so get a move on, and make sure they don't get away."

Captain Ho's vehicles were similar in design to the old Humvees, but with a lot more horsepower. There were twenty of them in the convoy, and they were closing on the jail at a hundred miles per hour.

They were just two miles from the jail when JD's men started triggering the massive IEDs they'd planted. Their vehicles were lightly armored, and the explosions turned the lead vehicles into fiery pinwheels as they tumbled down the street. The remainder of the convoy jammed on their brakes to keep from ramming into the inferno ahead of them.

"We've been hit," Captain Ho reported. "We'll regroup and go around, but it's going to take a few more minutes. Turn around and follow me," Captain Ho ordered.

The column had just gotten moving again when they started detonating the rest of the hidden explosives. The blasts were throwing Captain Ho's vehicles around like toy cars.

"We're under heavy attack, send me some air support," Captain Ho requested. When he saw their path was blocked, he reported, "We're abandoning the vehicles, and we're going to try to find some cover in the nearby buildings."

As the survivors broke for cover, they didn't get very far before the militia snipers cut them down.

Twenty minutes later, General Feng found out about the ambush, and immediately scrambled a squadron of helicopter gunships.

"I've had one of my men land and check it out, but they're all dead," the squadron commander reported.

"Any sign of the rebels?" the general asked.

"No, sir, they're long gone."

"To hell with them. Get over there and check on the prisoners."

A few minutes later, the squadron commander reported back in.

"The jail has been destroyed."

"I don't give a shit about the jail, where the hell are my prisoners?"

"Not a clue."

"You've got to find those buses. I don't want those bastards getting away."

Twenty minutes later the commander checked in with an update. "We've swept a thirty-mile radius, and they've disappeared."

"Keep looking," the general ordered.

THEY FOUND THE buses the next morning, in an abandoned warehouse.

When the general got the news he yelled at his aide, "Get Major Wang in here, right now.

"I've got a job for you," General Feng told the major. "I need you to find out who's behind this."

Major Wang worked tirelessly, but after two weeks he had to admit defeat.

"I've worked every source we have, and I simply can't

get a handle on who is behind the attacks," the major reported.

"I find it hard to believe that some ragtag bunch of buffoons can make us look like rank amateurs," the general complained.

"Yes, sir, I know it reflects badly on us, but this wasn't some group off the street," Major Wang told him, as he slid his report across the desk. Their attack was well planned, and flawlessly executed."

The general couldn't mask his distaste, but he knew if the major couldn't find them, it was a lost cause. "Double the patrols, and I don't want any officers going anywhere without an armed escort, and make sure they all have one of the new armored cars."

JOHN DAVID STILL wanted to kill as many of the Chinese officers as he could, but like Dallas–Fort Worth, their enhanced security measures were making it almost impossible.

After several weeks of futility, JD realized they needed a dramatic shift in their strategy. He spent three weeks gathering his research, but he'd finally concluded it wasn't simply a matter of killing the Chinese. After he had a plan worked out, he contacted General Jeffries.

"I need the schematics for the miniature IEDs," JD requested.

"Sure, what are you up to?" General Jeffries asked.

After JD finished his explanation, the general told him, "I'd be surprised if you don't get some push back."

"Understood, but it's the best I could come up with, given our limited resources."

"I'm not saying it won't work, but many of them won't think it's the American way."

CHAPTER 3

JD called a meeting to walk the militia leaders through his new strategy, and when he finished, they started peppering him with questions.

Larry Scribner was the first to comment. "I'm a bit of a history buff, and this resembles the tactics the Iraqis used against us."

"Close, it's a combination of the Iraqi and Afghan insurgents' tactics. They caused us an immense amount of pain, and even though history might say otherwise, I believe it's why we eventually pulled out of both countries."

"This seems like the coward's way out," one of the commanders complained.

"Look, I realize none of you like what I'm proposing, and if one of you has any other thoughts, I'd be happy to listen." After what seemed like forever, JD told the group, "All right then, let's get to work."

IT DIDN'T TAKE them very long to start adapting the smaller IEDs to their new missions. They used them as car bombs. They hid them in mailboxes. They even developed one that resembled a lightbulb, and was designed to explode when the power was turned on.

As their losses had continued to mount, General Feng

grew tired of the daily casualties. "I've had enough of this bullshit," General Feng told Major Wang. "They need to learn that they can't kill my men and not pay a price for it. Round up a hundred people off the street, and bring them down here."

Once the major had gathered up the required number of people, General Feng called the TV stations and told them to get their news crews down to City Hall.

When the news crews arrived, the general had Major Wang herd the unfortunate individuals into the Martha Hermann Square in front of City Hall. The prisoners were standing beside the reflecting pool, discussing what was going on, and it presented a deceptively benign scene.

"You'd better watch this," Rex advised.

"What now?" JD asked.

"General Feng is holding some sort of press conference."

"Shit, that usually means trouble."

When the news crews saw the general and his entourage come out of the building, they panned their cameras to follow them. When he reached the gathering, he got right to the point.

"As you know there have been a number of attacks on my officers, and to the criminals behind these attacks, this is on your heads," General Feng proclaimed.

"From this moment on, whenever one of my men is killed, we'll round up a hundred people at random, and execute them."

Before anyone could react to his words, the general nodded to Major Wang, and his men machine-gunned the men, women, and children they'd rounded up. Many of the victims' bodies fell into the pool, and as everyone stood frozen in horror, the reflecting pool turned red with their blood.

The general didn't utter a word as he turned on his heel, and strolled back into City Hall.

JD wasn't shocked by the mindless brutality, but he didn't say anything for almost a minute as he contemplated his response.

Finally, Rex asked, "Are you all right?"

"I'm fine, but I'm not going to rest until he's been made to pay for that. Find out who those people were, and where you can, help out their families."

"I'm on it, anything else?"

"See if you can find the architectural plans to the courthouse, and someone to interpret them for me," JD ordered.

"What on earth for?" Jerome Brown asked.

"I'm going to kill General Feng, and I want to send the rest of those bastards a message when I do it."

It took him a few days, but Jerome managed to find the right man for the job.

"This is Ray Finger," Jerome explained as he led the middle-aged man into JD's office. "His granddad, Joseph Finger, was the architect who designed the building. He's an architect as well, and he has a copy of the original building plans."

JD shook his hand and said, "Have a seat. I've got a few questions for you."

After JD explained what he wanted, Ray told him. "Give me an hour or so, and I'll show you where you need to plant your devices. My best friend, and his wife and kids, were in the group that General Feng slaughtered, so I'll do anything I can to help kill the murderous bastards."

JD wanted to make sure General Sung got his message, so he arranged for the news agencies to receive an anonymous tip that there would be something going down that Thursday at noon.

General Feng was holding his daily staff meeting in a fifth-floor conference room, when he glanced out the window. "Somebody find out what's going on down there."

JD knew that many of the building workers took their lunches to the park to eat, so he'd planned the attack at 12:15 to try to mitigate the civilian casualties. When it looked like most of them had left the building, JD said, "We can't afford to wait any longer, hit it."

The canisters of VX nerve gas were strategically hidden in the building's air handling systems, and they started spewing an aerosol cloud of the deadly nerve agent. The colorless, odorless gas was virtually undetectable, so the general and his staff had no inkling they'd been attacked. At first the general thought his allergies were acting up. His eyes were watering and his nose was running, but when his chest started to tighten, he became concerned. He wiped his eyes, but when he tried to blow his nose, he found himself gasping for air. Terrified, he tried to take a deep breath, but all he could manage was a couple of quick shallow breaths. His lungs felt like they were on fire as he gasped, "Quick, call an ambulance. I think I'm having a heart attack."

His aide never answered, as his own lungs contracted violently.

By then they were all having convulsions, and a few seconds later they'd all passed out.

One of the security guards in the lobby had managed to stumble out the front door, but he didn't make it very far. When he went down, he pitched face forward, and slid about halfway down the stairs in front of the building.

"What's going on?" Steve Bullock, one of the TV station news anchors, asked when he saw the guard fall.

His camera operator zoomed in on the guard's horribly contorted face, and exclaimed, "God, that's gruesome. For his sake, I hope he's dead."

"Give me a second and I'll get a team up there to check it out," Steve's assistant, Sally Wooly told him.

Luckily for them, they were still gathering their equipment when a small plane flew overhead dropping leaflets. Sally picked one up, and started reading.

"What does it say?" Steve asked impatiently.

"I can't believe they had the balls to do it," Sally said. "It says they've used VX nerve gas to execute General Feng and his men."

"Executed! Does it say who's behind it?" Steve asked.

"A group calling themselves Texans for Independence is claiming responsibility for the attack, and says that this is just the start of their push to free the United States." When Sally noticed one of the other news teams approaching the building, she screamed, "Stay away from the building, there's nerve gas in there."

Steve wanted to get the news out, but he had his crew back away to a safe distance before they went on the air.

"Ladies and gentleman, this is Steve Bullock, reporting live from the Houston City Hall. We haven't verified their claims, but a few minutes ago a small plane dropped leaflets which detail a purported VX nerve gas attack on City Hall. The group, known only as Texans for Independence, claims to have executed General Feng and his staff, in retribution for their murder of innocent civilians. The pamphlet states that their ultimate mission is to drive the so-called peacekeeping forces from our shores, and return America to Americans. I've personally witnessed only one casualty, but I have no reason to doubt their claims."

"General, we've just received word that General Feng's headquarters has been attacked," Major Ma reported.

"I haven't received any reports of an attack. Where did you get your information?" General Sung asked.

"I just watched a news broadcast out of Houston," Major Ma explained. "They reported that a little after noon today, a group calling themselves Texans for Independence executed General Feng and his staff with a VX nerve gas attack."

"What the hell were they thinking? Don't they realize this will only strengthen our resolve to eradicate them?"

"I've tried to warn you about going too far, because at some point, we'll incite them to rebellion," Major Ma reminded him. "The general's tactics were particularly harsh, and I imagine it's what got him killed."

"Whatever. Who's the next in line down there?"

"Colonel Du, but I think you should promote Major Wang instead."

"Why would I put a major in charge?"

"Two things. He was General Feng's chief intelligence officer, so he already understands the situation, and second, he's even more ruthless than the general."

"I can't believe that's even possible."

After the general had considered it for a few seconds, he told the major, "I don't know either one of them, so if that's what you recommend, I'll go along. Make him a general, and turn him loose. Just make damn sure that he understands that I want these people found and eradicated."

General Wang was every bit as ruthless as he'd been portrayed. He'd rounded up and brutally tortured hundreds of people, but he was unable to gain any real insight into the Texans for Independence. After six weeks of some of the most brutal tactics imaginable, General Wang was forced to admit failure.

"I've been unable to garner any useable information about the Texans for Independence," General Wang reported.

"Have there been any more incidents?" General Sung asked.

"None. It's like they dropped off the face of the earth."

"Knock on wood, maybe they've decided to quit while they're ahead."

AFTER THEY'D TAKEN General Feng out, JD expected General Sung to make an all-out effort to track them down. As he watched General Wang's savagery unfold, there wasn't anything he could do about the collateral damage.

"I think we need to disappear for a while. I'm hoping things will settle down if they can't find us," JD said.

"You're the boss," Sergeant Brown said. "I'll get the boys ready to move."

"We need somewhere to lay low," JD said.

"I've got a little place in northern Mexico that should work," William Sheldon said. "Just hold tight until I can get you picked up."

The little place was eighteen thousand acres. It had a barracks and a main house that was outfitted with the finest communications gear that money could buy. It didn't take long for them to get settled in, and as JD had hoped, their attacks had emboldened people from all over the country to begin striking out.

"You need to see this YouTube video," Rex proclaimed.

The cell phone video was a little grainy, but they could see a Chinese officer slowly strolling down the sidewalk in Santa Fe, New Mexico. A car suddenly swerved across the street and up onto the sidewalk. The old woman driving had a look of grim determination, and both hands on the wheel, when her car struck the officer with such force that his body was thrown completely over the roof.

"The video has already gotten over three million plays, and it's only been up a little over forty-eight hours," Rex said.

"I sure hope the Chinese haven't seen it," JD said.

"I'm afraid they have," Rex admitted. "They arrested

her yesterday afternoon, and they hung her in the square an hour later."

"Bastards."

"Without a doubt, but when they did, a massive riot broke out. They had to declare a citywide curfew, and they ended up killing several hundred protesters before they got it stopped."

"I'm sorry about the old woman, but this is exactly what we need to happen if we're going to have any chance against them."

CHAPTER 4

As the discontent spread across the country, the instances of everyday people striking out had increased dramatically.

"We've had thirteen hundred and forty casualties this week," General Wang reported.

"How many of those were just wounded?" General Sung asked.

"All dead."

"They don't leave much to chance."

"So it seems. Have you read the recommendations I sent you?"

"Yes, and I'm fine with them, although I do have a question. What do you hope to gain by rounding up a bunch of academics?"

"They encourage the young people to think for themselves, and they're impeding our attempts to adjust the curriculums."

"Fine, do whatever you think is necessary, but I'm expecting results."

A FEW DAYS later, Dr. Douglas Lassiter was about to board a bus in Kansas City, when the Chinese moved in to arrest him. The doctor was the head of the Kansas

City University of Medicine and Biosciences, and a well-known figure in the community. He'd been quite vocal in his opposition to the Chinese occupation, and often spoke out against their methods.

"Professor Lassiter?" the Chinese lieutenant inquired.

"I'm Dr. Lassiter," he said as he handed the officer his identification.

"You're under arrest."

"You're kidding, right?"

"Afraid not. You're going to have to come with us."

The professor realized that very few people they picked up were ever heard from again, so he began to protest as loudly as he could. "I haven't done anything wrong, and I'm not coming with you."

The lieutenant motioned to his men, and they grabbed the professor by both arms and started dragging him away.

"Leave me alone you bastards," the professor screamed, hoping that someone would help him. When he continued struggling, the lieutenant struck him on the back of the head with his pistol.

Jeff Kelley, a massive all-pro defensive end with the Kansas City Chiefs, saw what was going on, and yelled, "Let's get the bastards." When the other passengers heard his plea, several of them rushed to help out. Jeff grabbed the lieutenant and growled, "Let's see how you like this," as he drove the lieutenant's head into the side of the bus. The impact shattered his skull and broke his neck. Jeff slung his lifeless body to one side.

Several of the lieutenant's men rushed Jeff to try to stop him. Jeff fought them like the madman he could be, but they'd finally managed to put enough bullets in him to bring him down. As he was going down, he managed to snap one last man's neck, before he fell facedown on the terminal floor.

In the confusion, one of the passengers had grabbed

the lieutenant's pistol, and opened fire on the soldiers. He managed to kill three of them, before they gunned him down.

"Holly shit, do you see what's going down in concourse A?" the security guard monitoring the bus terminals security cameras yelled to his partner.

"I called nine-one-one."

"There's no one there anymore."

"That's right, I'd forgotten. We need to do something."

"What are we going to do? We don't even have weapons, and I'm sure as hell not getting into that mess."

Several passengers from the other buses had joined in, but most of them were unarmed.

It was a one-sided fight, but by the time the guards got the situation under control, they'd lost twenty-two men, and killed seventy-three passengers. The professor was still out cold on the ground, so unfortunately for him, he survived.

"They'll cover this up for sure," the security guard told his partner. "I'm gonna post this on the Web."

"You'd better hurry, because they're headed our way."

He'd just finished uploading the video when they broke in and killed them both. By the time the Chinese managed to get the original video taken down, the massacre had been downloaded millions of times.

THEY'D TRANSPORTED THE hapless professor to Fort Leavenworth, Kansas, where they were holding the rest of the prisoners they'd rounded up.

During Professor Lassiter's brief incarceration, they tortured him every day, until he died of his wounds.

Sickened by what they'd done, one of the guards smuggled out the video of the torture sessions, and a copy of the journal the professor had secretly compiled. He posted them on one of the file sharing sites, along with his account of what happened, and within a matter of hours the material had gone viral.

One of the Chinese cyber analysts had discovered the material during one of their sweeps. After he'd taken it down, he sent General Sung a copy.

When the general got around to looking at it, he called General Wang for an explanation.

"How the hell did this get out?" General Sung demanded.

"The same way everything else gets leaked. I'm sure some of it's coming from our own people. I'm afraid that many of them don't agree with what we're doing."

"We've got to get shit like this stopped."

"The day is long past where we can keep any of this a secret. I tried to warn you when you asked me to crack down on them that we might make it even worse."

When General Sung didn't respond, General Wang was afraid he'd just signed his own death warrant.

Finally, General Sung asked, "How many more teachers do you have left to pick up?"

"We're done, and we're in the process of moving our people into place. By the time the spring semester starts, our people will begin teaching the new curriculums. We've already closed West Point, Annapolis, and the Air Force Academy, but I think that we need to close several of the larger universities, because we don't have enough people to staff them."

"Do whatever you think is necessary."

THE NEXT DAY, General Sung contacted Vasily Makarov; the president of what had once been the USSR.

"Vasily, I need your help."

"What sort of help?" President Makarov asked. "You know that we don't have much in the way of equipment."

"I've got plenty of equipment, I just need men."

Vasily had a vast army, but he was having a hard time keeping them fed. "How many are we talking about?"

"All you can spare."

After a brief negotiation, they agreed on a million to start, with more to follow if needed.

GENERAL JEFFRIES HAD suspected the Chinese were up to something when the news of the teachers' disappearances started trickling in, but it was several months before they understood the full extent of it. Terribly concerned, the general reached out to JD to discuss the situation.

"We have a count of the teachers they've picked up, and it's mind-boggling," General Jeffries said. "They've already grabbed a hundred and twenty-four thousand professors and teachers, and replaced them with their own people. Along with the military academies, they've closed several of the larger universities, and all the Ivy League schools. The ones they're leaving open are staffed with their people, and the new lesson plans are laced with misinformation and propaganda."

"To what end?" JD asked.

"They've finally realized that they have to do something to change public opinion, and this will be just the start of it. You'll start seeing public service announcements, and I imagine the TV shows are being rewritten as we speak, to try to spin a better image for them. But enough of that for now. How are you holding up?"

"Compared to what?

"Some days it seems like it's all a waste of time."

"I know it's been slow going, but believe it or not you're making a difference. I just wish that we could get you some more help, but it's difficult to know who to trust after the incident in Houston."

"Thanks, but luckily Houston turned out to be an aberration. What have you got for me this week?"

"We've managed to decode a series of General Sung's communications to their European allies, and they've started moving in reinforcements."

"How are they coming in?" JD asked.

"They've commandeered every wide-bodied jet they could, and it looks like they've already moved several hundred thousand troops."

"Great, more of the bastards to deal with. How do we get them stopped?"

"I've just sent you the plans for some ordnance that should allow you to take care of the aircraft."

JD opened the file and scanned the summary and the schematics. "Simple, but effective. So we should be able to drop these into the plane's fuel tanks, and either remote detonate them, or set them on timers?"

"You got it. We've tried to keep them simple, but you need to hurry, because they've been moving troops for weeks."

The Chinese had commandeered almost five hundred aircraft, so it was a big task.

To minimize the civilian pilot casualties, the plan was to destroy as many aircraft on the ground as they could.

A few days later, General Sung was relaxing in his quarters, when Major Ma called. "What now? You know that I don't like to be disturbed when I'm reading."

"I thought you needed to be aware of something," Major Ma told him, wishing that he'd waited.

"Well, spit it out, or do I have to guess?"

"We've received multiple reports of the troop transports blowing up."

The general let out a deep sigh. "How many?"

"It's too early to say for sure, but at the rate the reports are coming in, it may be all of them."

The general put his bookmark in place, and slowly closed his book. He was a dedicated soldier, but sometimes he wished he could just go home. As the thought crossed his mind, he was again struck by the almost overwhelming grief of knowing that his home didn't exist anymore, and that he would never see his loved ones again. He yearned for his beautiful young wife, and the sounds of his children's laughter, and in spite of himself, he closed his eyes for a few seconds to savor their memories.

He opened his eyes, and told Major Ma, "Call every airfield we're using and get me a count. Then get General Wang for me."

"CONGRATULATIONS, IT LOOKS like you got them all," General Jeffries said.

"Yes, we did. Unfortunately, a hundred and forty-nine of them were in the air," JD said.

"That's too bad, but you've saved many lives. I suspect that they've already started rounding up the ground crews, so they can find out who was behind the attacks."

"We've already gotten our people out, but I imagine they'll kill a bunch of innocent people trying to find out who we are."

"You're probably right, but I've already sent a message to the major news services, announcing it was the Texans for Independence, and reiterating our demands to leave our country, or die."

"Did you rename William's group?"

"I decided we needed a name that better conveyed the breadth of our movement."

"What if they track it back to you?"

"I'm not worried about it.

"This was a huge win, but my guess is that they'll try ships next, so I've already put our subs on alert. If they try to move anything toward the mainland they're under orders to sink them."

"I thought they'd expended their ordnance?"

"Just the missiles, they've got plenty of torpedoes, and besides, there was an old ammo dump full of them on Guam."

IT HAD TAKEN them a month to make the arrangements, but the Chinese were again moving large numbers of troops.

"I'm afraid I've got more bad news," Major Ma reported.

General Sung sighed and asked, "What now?"

"The American submarines have sunk a large number of our troop ships, and we don't have any way to stop them."

"Shit. You might as well turn the rest of them around. Now get out."

THE NEXT DAY General Sung called Major Ma back in to assess the situation.

"What a debacle this has turned out to be," General Sung said. "How many troops did we get moved?"

"Just over a million two."

"It'll have to do. Not counting the Russians, what's our current headcount?"

"Two million three."

"If I remember correctly, at one time we had over two-point-five million. I guess I've lost touch with the casualty counts. Have you identified who's pulling the strings for them?"

"Not yet, but we're getting closer. We were able to intercept a series of satellite conversations that took place just before the latest attacks, but we haven't been able to decipher them."

"Why not?"

"They're using a highly sophisticated military grade cipher."

"So why did you bring it up?"

"Because we've got a fix on one end of the conversation."

Suddenly energized, the general demanded, "Show me."

"It's coming from a remote section of Puerto Rico," the major said as he pointed it out on a satellite photo.

"Do you think General Jeffries could be hiding there?"

"There's no way to tell for sure. We have a few operatives in the country, but everyone we've sent into the area has disappeared."

"It's the best lead we've had so far, so I'm going with it," General Sung said.

"Were you able to persuade Professor Jacquelyn's team to reactivate any of the ICBMs?"

"Two, but then one of our nitwitted commanders killed them all, when they tried to escape." When he saw the fury in the general's eyes, he quickly explained. "Before you ask, I've already had him executed."

"Damn, they were our last real hope of reactivating the rest of the nukes. I still can't believe that Admiral Zacharias managed to hide the fact that he'd given General Jeffries the codes to disable the remainder of the nuclear weapons."

Feeling full of himself, Major Ma told the general, "I guess you should have waited to kill the president and the admiral like I asked you to. With a little more time, I would have discovered the rest of the information he hid from us. He might have even known where General Jeffries was hiding."

As soon as the words had spewed out of his mouth, he knew he'd made a mistake, but he would have never suspected the result would be so swift, or brutal. The general needed his services, so he didn't kill the major. After he'd shot him in both knees, the general walked out of his office and told one of the clerks,

"Get a medical team in there ASAP, the major needs some help."

Several weeks later, they were back in the general's office. Only this time Major Ma was in a motorized wheelchair. As they resumed their last conversation, the major was choosing his words carefully.

"We'll continue trying to decipher the transmissions, but I'm afraid it's beyond our capabilities."

"What are the odds the general's hideout is in Puerto Rico?"

"I would say a little better than fifty-fifty."

"Close enough."

The next day JD almost missed his weekly videoconference with General Jeffries. "Sorry I'm late," JD said. "There was a situation in South Dakota that I needed to handle."

"Anything serious?" General Jeffries asked.

"Tragic would be a better way to term it. We had one of our men run amuck up there. The Chinese arrested his wife in a sweep, and after they'd raped her, they killed her, and dumped her body on the side of the road. When he found out, he walked into City Hall and machine-gunned everyone he met. They killed him, but not before he'd slaughtered the local commanding officer, and most of his staff."

"God, that's hard to hear. We've got to drive these bastards out. How is the training coming?" the general asked, trying to change the subject.

"We've got seventeen training videos online, and what's left of my team is still plugging away."

"I almost hate to ask, but how many men do you have left?"

"Six, including myself." JD was about to continue,

when the image on the screen exploded in a blizzard of light and sound, before the connection dropped.

"See if you can find out what's wrong with the damn thing," JD told the technician helping him.

After he'd tried to reconnect for several minutes, the technician reported, "I can't find anything wrong with our equipment, or the satellite. I'll get the geek to take a look."

Fifteen minutes later, Larry Lindsey came rushing in. "It's definitely not in the equipment. It could be weather on the other end. Let me see if I can still access the NSA servers where they store the satellite surveillance videos."

He'd installed a back door the last time he was there, so it only took a few seconds to log in. He didn't want them to discover he was hacking in, so he worked quickly.

"Got it."

He disconnected before he opened the file. After several minutes, the geek still hadn't said a word.

"Did you spot the trouble?" JD asked.

"I'll put it up on the screen so you can see for yourself," he said quietly.

As the video played out, they watched in horror as the missiles de-orbited and detonated.

"No one could have survived that," the geek declared. "Those were two high-yield ICBMs."

"Who could have done this?" JD asked.

"I'm afraid they were ours."

"Damn, the general told me he'd disabled them all."

JD spent the rest of the day sitting in the dark, thinking about the general, and the challenges that lay ahead. He had no allusions that any of them were likely to survive, but as he sat there feeling sorry for himself, he realized the general would expect him "to keep on keeping on," as he liked to say.

He said a short prayer for him, and all the people who had already lost their lives, before he walked out, and went back to work.

Some are born great, some achieve greatness, and some have greatness thrust upon them.

—William Shakespeare

In peace sons bury their fathers, but in war fathers bury their sons.

—Croesus

PART 10

CHAPTER 1

After General Sung nuked Puerto Rico, he flooded the southern states with reinforcements, to quell the rising tide of resistance.

Meanwhile, General Wang's strategy for winning over the younger generations was starting to show progress.

On the first anniversary of General Jeffries's death, JD had come to the realization they were losing the fight, and needed to shake things up.

Their Internet connections had become unreliable, but JD got lucky, and everyone was online for a change.

"To put it bluntly, we're getting our ass kicked," JD told the group. "We've lost over two hundred men in the last three weeks, and have nothing to show for it. We're going to have to try something else, or we're done for."

"I doubt many of you understand our situation up here," Jeremy Love, the leader of the combined Michigan militias declared. "The fact is that we've got more members than the rest of the country combined, and we've managed to stockpile a shitload of equipment over the years."

"That's good to know, but we've had even less success in your areas," JD challenged.

"That's true, but the Chinese forces saturated this

part of the country from the get-go. Given the amount of pressure we're all under, I'd like to suggest that we consolidate our resources into Montana."

JD pulled up the current troop counts, and after he'd added them up, he realized Jeremy wasn't exaggerating. "How did you manage to recruit so many members?"

"The economy up here has sucked for decades, and we've provided the men with a sense of self-worth, so it was an easy proposition."

As JD thought through the possibilities, he quickly realized Jeremy's suggestion had real merit. "I'm going to take Jeremy's recommendation," JD announced.

"I'll send out your orders when I get them worked up."

William Sheldon had located a stockpile of Iraqi War–era AH-64D Longbow Apache helicopters that had been mothballed in the Nevada desert. So before they left, JD had them moved to Montana, so they could start refurbishing them.

It hadn't been easy, but after almost a year, they'd managed to consolidate the bulk of their men and materials to Montana.

JD knew he was taking a terrible risk, but he called a meeting of all the surviving militia leaders. The remote ranch where they were meeting was a few miles north of the North Chinook Reservoir, and could only be reached by four-wheel-drive vehicles or on horseback.

An eccentric billionaire had built the lodge back in the 1980s, and the sumptuous decor and the roaring fireplaces belied the dire straits they were in.

As JD looked around the great room, he was saddened to realize how many faces were missing from the group. The years of almost continuous warfare had extracted a heavy toll. With no end in sight, JD knew that if they couldn't come up with a more effective strategy, they were going to end up as a footnote in the history books. He'd used the time it had taken them to relocate to work out a daring, and extremely risky new strategy. As he was about to address the group, he found himself hoping that he was enough of a statesman to sell them on his new approach.

"Thank you all for coming," JD said as he opened the meeting. "Before we get started, I'd like to take a moment of silence to remember Jeremy Love, and all the other people who have made the ultimate sacrifice to defend our country.

"Thank you, and now let's get to work. We've arrived at a pivotal moment in our fight for survival, but we need to be honest with ourselves. The education curriculums they've instituted are starting to convince our children that democracy was an interesting experiment, but an abject failure. I believe the time has come for us to either drive them from our land, or accept the fact that the United States of America is no more."

"Fine words, but what the hell do you want us to do about it?" Jim Jackson, the leader of the Idaho militia, asked angrily. "We've killed over a hundred thousand of their men, and I can't say that they're one damn bit weaker than when we started."

"True enough. Look, I don't pretend to have all the answers, but it does bring me to why I asked you all up here. If you'll bear with me for an hour or so, I'm going to lay out a strategic plan to begin launching more conventional attacks on their forces."

"That would be suicide," William Buckley, the leader of the Montana militia, exclaimed.

The room erupted into chaos as they all started trying to shout over one another. JD let them go for several minutes, before he used the microphone to regain order.

"All right, if you've gotten that out of your systems, let's get down to work. The packets being handed out detail the strategy we're going to discuss." After they'd all received their packets, JD continued. "Now, if you'll open your handouts, I'll walk you through our first campaign."

It took him three days to persuade them, but after much cussing and discussing, they agreed to follow his lead.

"Good, it's settled. We'll launch our first attack in six weeks," JD told the group. He was about to dismiss them for the day, when he saw William Sheldon raise his hand. William had taken on the role of elder statesman, and he'd grown to be one of JD's greatest supporters. "Mr. Sheldon, what do you have for us?"

"The other militia leaders and I have decided it's time to formalize our command structure."

Thinking he was in for another marathon session, JD reluctantly asked, "Fine, how would you like to proceed?"

"We've already come up with the structure, so if you wouldn't mind, I'd like to present it to the entire group."

"You've got the floor," JD said as he took his seat, not knowing what to expect.

William had just turned seventy, but as he stepped up to the microphone, he was still an imposing figure of a man.

"Except for General Jeffries, our senior officers were either killed in Costa Rica, or rounded up and executed. When General Jeffries's command was wiped out, it left our movement without a seasoned flag officer. We've known for some time that we had to address the leadership vacuum. So we've spent almost six weeks mulling over who we wanted to assume command of our combined forces."

William turned to JD. "Colonel John David Drury, please rise.

"John David, I'm pleased to announce that we've selected you as our first four-star general. You've been doing the job ever since General Jeffries was killed, and we thought that it was time we recognized your stellar leadership."

"I'm humbled, and I hope that I can be half the commander General Jeffries was."

"You're far too modest. General Jeffries had made a point to speak with several of us about what to do if he was killed, and it was his strong recommendation that you get the job. We didn't want to burden you with developing the starting command structure, so we've decided that the leaders of the six largest militias would be one-star generals, and that the rest would be colonels. I know this is a lot to throw at you at one time, but what do you think?" William asked.

"Obviously I'm honored," JD told the group as he rose to his feet, but he paused and looked over at William.

"Please know that you will be free to change the roster if you want," William assured him, afraid that he might be uncomfortable with their picks.

"It's not that. I've got no problem with what you've done. It's you and your men who are going to bear the brunt of the upcoming combat. None of us can know how this will all end, but I promise you that I'll do my best to lead us to victory."

"We never doubted it."

"Is that all you had?" General Drury asked.

"Don't you think that's enough?"

The next day General Drury held his first working session with his senior staff.

"The same situation that allowed our military such success over the years, is now our biggest problem," General Drury said. "We've managed to refurbish a good number of the helicopters we salvaged, but we don't have any fixed-wing aircraft, and that gives General Sung's forces complete air superiority. We've got to do something about it, before we can have any realistic chance of success."

"What have you got in mind?" General Waverley asked.

JD motioned for the first slide in his presentation. "Here are the schematics to build the explosive devices that we used to stop them from ferrying in the Russian troops, and we're going to use them to even the odds a little."

"They seem simple enough," General Waverley commented. "Where and when?"

"In front of you is a list of the bases where their main squadrons are based, and I'd like to be able to launch our attack in thirty days."

General Waverley scanned the list and commented, "We've already got operatives at most of these. If you'd like, I can contact them to coordinate the attacks."

"Great. How about the time frame?"

"It's doable," General Waverley said.

TWENTY DAYS LATER their operatives went after the aircraft.

"We managed to get all the major squadrons," General Waverley reported.

"How many men did we lose?" JD asked.

"I'm afraid we lost them all."

"Do what you can for their families," JD instructed.

"Are you ready for Monday?"

"We are, I just hope we're not biting off more than we can handle."

"I'll admit there's risk, but I believe it's a good plan."

"Yes, it is, but I'm afraid my opinion on plans is a lot like the old-time boxer, Mike Tyson."

JD laughed and said, "I know. Everyone's got a plan until they get hit. Let's just hope we're still standing when it's over."

The sun was just coming up when the Apache helicopters struck. The Chinese's armored vehicles were lined up in neat rows, so they made easy targets as the helicopters swooped in.

As they'd hoped, the Chinese troops were slow to respond, and with no support vehicles, the helicopters' miniguns cut them to ribbons within minutes.

Their infantry had followed close behind, and it had only taken a couple of hours to mop up what was left.

Both commanders had managed to report the attacks before they were overrun, and when General Sung finished reading the Wyoming commander's report, he called Major Ma in for an explanation.

He almost felt sorry for him when heard the hum of his wheelchair approaching. However, he quickly brushed the thought aside, and bellowed, "What the hell is going on in Wyoming?"

"I'm afraid Wyoming isn't our only problem," Major Ma said. "I've just received a report that we've lost Montana as well."

"Shit. Use whatever resources you need, but make damn sure you take care of the situation quickly. We don't need them thinking they can attack us and get away with it."

Major Ma guided his wheelchair over to a computer terminal and started checking their troop dispositions.

"I've got to admit that I'm more than a little surprised they would try something so brazen," the general said.

The major just nodded in agreement, and continued working through the logistics of the situation. He worked feverishly for almost a half hour before he spun his chair around, and said, "They wiped out the only assets we had in that quadrant. I've dispatched strike forces from Kansas City and St. Louis, but it's going to take a few days to launch a counterattack."

"Whatever," General Sung said disinterestedly. "Just make damn sure that you don't leave any of them alive."

Be not dishearten'd—Affection shall solve the problems of Freedom yet; those who love each other shall become invincible.

—WALT WHITMAN

PART 11

CHAPTER 1

"Congratulations on a great victory," JD's aide Sergeant Jerome Brown said.

"The first of many, I hope, but now the real work starts," JD cautioned. "We surprised them this time, but now we'll have their full attention. General Sung is going to hit back fast and hard, so I need to make sure we're ready. "Get one of the Black Hawks warmed up; I'm going over to see General Waverley."

Along with the Apaches, they'd rebuilt sixty-five UH-60L Black Hawks. They'd added several upgrades to their aged fleet of helicopters, but one of the more significant was the addition of the terrain-following radar they'd appropriated from the last generation of cruise missiles.

Flying at less than fifty feet off the deck, the trip had been uneventful, and scary as hell, as the terrain zipped by at almost two hundred knots.

When they landed, JD was met by a twenty-three-year-old lieutenant by the name of Molly Spitz. She'd been in her senior year at the Air Force Academy when the Chinese had seized power. On the night that General Sung had slaughtered President Martell and Admiral Zacharias, the school's commandant had released all of them, and told them to try to disappear. It had been good advice, but the Chinese had managed to track down and kill most of them.

As JD slid into the passenger seat, he had to admit that Molly was the best-looking woman he'd ever seen. Her long blond hair flowed over the collar of her field jacket, and the fatigues she was wearing, did nothing to hide her voluptuous figure.

JD's career had consumed him, and except for an occasional hooker, he hadn't been with a woman since he'd broken up with Susan. He tried not to, but he couldn't keep his eyes off of her, as she drove him to the command center.

It didn't take long to line out General Waverley, and when JD was finished, he decided to stay in town for a couple of days.

As Molly was driving him to the hotel, JD decided to ask her out. "I know this is probably in poor taste, but would you like to have dinner?"

"I sure would," Molly said.

JD met her in the lobby when she returned to pick him up. To JD's delight, she'd changed out of her fatigues, into a short, low cut black dress, which didn't leave much to the imagination.

"What do you have a taste for?" Molly asked.

As he struggled not to blurt out what he was really thinking, he managed to say, "Anything you'd like. It's been awhile since I've had a decent meal."

She took him to a small Italian restaurant she'd found a few days before. The restaurant wasn't very crowded, and the owner met them at the door. "If you'll please follow me, I've got the perfect table for you two."

As they sat down at the candlelit table, JD still couldn't believe how beautiful she was. They'd made an immediate connection, and they spent most of the time laughing and sharing stories about themselves. By the time they were served their desserts, JD couldn't believe how comfortable he felt with her.

"I don't mean to sound too stupid, but I feel like I've known you forever," JD told her.

Molly reached across the table and took his hand, and smiled. "Me too."

As they were getting back in the car, she asked, "Would you like to stop for a drink?"

"Sure." JD figured they were either going back to the hotel bar, or one of the nearby clubs, but a few minutes later they pulled up in front of a small frame house.

"I don't have anything but beer, but it's cold," Molly said.

He thought to himself, *I don't care if it's horse piss, as long as you come with it.* "Beer's great. Is this your place?"

"I'm just renting, but yes, it is. I hope you don't mind, but I thought this would give us a little privacy to get to know each other a little better."

Molly unlocked the door and they went inside. After she closed the door behind them, JD took her hand, and gently pulled her to him for their first kiss. He'd half expected her to slap his face for being so pushy, but Molly responded with more heat than he'd ever experienced from a woman. In seconds, their first kiss had turned into them almost ripping each other's clothes off. As they continued kissing, she was slowly guiding him toward the bedroom, but they ended up making love for the first time on the couch in her tiny living room.

"Damn girl, that was incredible," JD gasped.

"Wasn't it?" Molly purred. "Let's move to the bedroom where we can be a little more comfortable."

He managed to come up with several reasons to hang around, but after three days he couldn't put off leaving any longer.

"I would love it if you'd come back with me," JD

offered hopefully. "I've already talked with General Waverley, and he's fine with it."

"Of course he is, silly. You're the head honcho," Molly's blue eyes sparkled with glee as she picked her head up off of his chest, and gave him a long, wet kiss. Which led to another round of extremely hot sex.

On the helicopter ride back, Molly commented, "I'm glad you asked for me, because I would have just followed you."

"That would be desertion. I might have to put you in chains, like in the old days."

"Promises, promises."

CHAPTER 2

Molly wanted to stay on active duty, so JD decided to make her his aide.

When they landed, he pulled Jerome aside and explained what was going on.

"I hope you're all right with this?" JD asked.

"Hey, I get it, and I sure don't blame you," Jerome said. "She's a hell of a lot smarter than me, and maybe a little prettier. Since you're making changes, I would like to return to a field unit."

"Whatever you'd like, Colonel."

"Whoa, that's quite a promotion. How are the other officers going to feel about it?"

"Trust me, they're not going to have a problem with it. You've got more combat experience than all of them put together."

"What now, boss?" Molly asked after Jerome had left.

"Now we get down to the hard work. We caught them by surprise the first time, but General Sung will try to put a quick end to our little uprising."

"That might explain the two-hundred-thousand troops they've pulled out of St. Louis and Kansas City."

"How about aircraft?"

"Mostly helicopters, but we've got reports that one squadron of fighters is getting ready to deploy."

"They don't have that many left, so you can bet your ass they'll be headed our way. Do we have anyone in the area?"

She did a quick search. "Yes, there's a small contingent in the St. Louis area."

"Do they have any Stingers?"

"The system shows that they've got three dozen."

JD grabbed a laptop off the conference table, and laid out what he needed. When he finished, he told Molly, "Have Larry Lindsey encrypt this, and get it to whoever's in command."

Molly scanned what he'd written. "This doesn't say anything about how they're supposed to make their escape."

"I didn't want to mislead them. I don't think there's much chance they'll survive."

When Jacob Michaels, the local commander, got JD's instructions, he gathered up everyone he could find on such short notice. "OK, that's the plan," Jacob said. "Does anybody have any questions?"

"You didn't cover our escape routes," Jenny Welsh observed.

"All I can tell you is that after you fire your missiles, run like hell."

Each team loaded six missiles, and hauled ass toward Lambert–St. Louis International Airport. They'd been waiting for almost an hour when the spotter, Jenny Walsh reported, "They're moving the aircraft into position."

"Roger that. Everyone prepare to fire, and Godspeed," Jacob told the teams. Jacob's team was covering the longest runway, 12R/30L, and their target aircraft had just passed the airport boundary when he ordered, "Fire, fire, fire."

The aircraft on the left disintegrated into a ball of fire, but the other one crashed into a nearby interstate. The roadway was packed with rush-hour traffic, and as the jet cartwheeled down the roadway, it cut a fiery path through the oncoming vehicles.

"I just got an update from St. Louis," Molly reported.

"How'd we do?" JD asked.

"They got them all."

"Great news. What about the team?"

"All dead, except for the spotter who made the report."

"That's a shame, but at least they didn't die in vain."

As Molly listened, she wondered what kind of toll it was going to take on him, as he had to continue sending people to their deaths.

"Do we have the routes and ETAs of the reinforcements?" JD asked.

"Just got them," Molly said, as she put the map up on the screen. "The largest group is out of Kansas City, and they're halfway between Lincoln and Scottsbluff, Nebraska. The detachment from St. Louis is about a day and a half behind them."

"Get Colonel Weinstein for me.

"Harvey, I've just forwarded you all the intel we have on the contingent out of Kansas City. The column is made up of roughly eighty thousand men, sixty-two tanks, a hundred and twenty-three armored personnel carriers, and over a thousand trucks."

"What do you need from us?"

"I need you to hit them with everything you've got."

"No problem, but I've only got thirty birds ready to go, and we're having a hard time keeping them flying."

"It's a wonder to me that any of them can fly; they're all older than we are. Just do your best, and try not to get killed."

Harvey laughed. "I'll do what I can."

* * *

IT WAS DUSK the next day when Harvey's choppers intercepted the column. They were flying nap of the earth, and when Harvey caught sight of the convoy he ordered, "Alpha group, check your spacing and follow me in. Bravo group, slow to eighty knots and wait until we've cleared the other end of the column to make your run."

Their choppers were carrying a variety of Hydra-70 warheads to maximize the impact of the attack. The first wave was carrying antitank warheads, and the second's missiles were tipped with antipersonnel flechette canisters. They caught the column by surprise, and destroyed several tanks and armored personnel carriers without any effective return fire. The column immediately stopped and deployed their infantry, allowing the second wave's flechette rounds to catch them out in the open. The flechettes cut a bloody swath through their ranks, and sent them scrambling for cover. However, they were battle-hardened veterans, and once their officers regained control, they started mounting a ferocious response. Their shoulder-fired missiles represented the greatest threat, and Harvey could see several streaking up through the growing darkness. Their countermeasures took care of most of them, but a few struck home, sending the aircraft spinning to a fiery death. Running low on fuel, and out of ammo, Harvey radioed, "Break it off, were done for tonight."

It was almost 2200 when they landed, but Harvey personally inspected every aircraft. JD had sent one of the Black Hawks along to take video of the skirmish so they could assess the results of their attacks. When Harvey finished his inspections he wrote up his sit rep, and had the Black Hawk deliver it with the video. Harvey had another sortie scheduled at 0630, but JD contacted him just before they took off.

"Well, done," JD said. "It looks like you put a real ass kicking on them. I know you lost six birds, but how many more are too damaged to go again?"

"I've got five that need major repairs."

"Not too bad, considering what they were throwing at you. "How many of the AB49s do you have?"

The missiles were outfitted with the latest generation of their fire-and-forget guidance systems, but they'd never been used in combat.

"I don't have an exact count, but there's a bunch, why?"

"I want you to rearm your ships with them. That way you can stand off at a safe distance when you hit them today."

"Understood, but it'll take us an hour or so to swap them out."

"Take your time, they'll still be there."

Harvey paused for several seconds before he asked, "Did I screw up?"

"Not at all. We're in for a protracted conflict, and we don't need to lose any more choppers."

Day after day, Harvey's squadron kept up the pressure as the enemy advanced across Nebraska and into Wyoming. JD had intended to make a stand at Cheyenne, but the terrain didn't lend itself to the type of warfare they needed to wage. When the Chinese column moved into Cheyenne, the commander was ecstatic that they'd abandoned the city.

"Yes, sir, that's correct," General Duan, the commander of the Kansas City contingent, reported. "We've driven them back into the area they call Yellowstone."

"Good job, I'm dispatching General Tang's forces from California to block their retreat, and General Ni's group out of St. Louis should reach you by tomorrow evening," General Sung said. "I'm putting you in command of the joint operation; however, I want you to hold your positions until General Tang is in position, and don't let them trick you into following them into Yellowstone."

General Sung's move had caught JD by surprise, and he was scrambling to understand what they were up to.

"They've moved General Tang's forces out of California, and if they maintain their current pace, they'll have us surrounded within the week," Molly Spitz reported.

"That makes it easier to decide which direction to attack," JD said. "Let me see what you've got." After he'd read her report, he said, "Get ahold of General Waverley and General Thomas and set up a staff meeting for 0600, and while you're at it, have them send me their current situation reports."

"I'll have to bring them in tonight, if you want to meet that early."

"There's no need for them to travel, we can do it on videoconference."

CHAPTER 3

"Hurry up, or we're going to be late," Molly implored.

"Oh well, they'll wait, and besides it was more than worth it," JD said.

"It sure was." Molly giggled as she dropped the sheet she was wrapped in, and walked out to take her shower.

"If you don't stop it, we're going to be even later," he yelled, as he jumped out of bed and ran after her.

"Sorry we're late, but something came up," JD said as he squeezed Molly's thigh under the table.

JD just ignored the smirks, and continued. "I've gone over your reports, and it looks like we're in good shape. We've got a little over two hundred thousand troops and plenty of supplies, but now comes the tricky part. Did you get the files I sent?"

"Yes, we did," General Waverley affirmed. "However, I'm definitely confused. First you had us retreat, and now you want us to take the fight to them."

"I just hope the enemy commander is as confused as you are. We've got to get them moving again, before they can bring in more reinforcements." JD had Molly put up the presentation, so he could walk them through the strategy. When JD finished he told them, "I know this is a lot to ask of you and your men, but if we pull it off, it will give us a chance to achieve our ultimate objective. Do either of you have any comments or questions?"

"Is there any chance we can get a few helicopters to help out?" General Thomas asked.

Molly handed JD a folder of their current assets, and pointed to one of the pages. "There are fifty helicopters due to finish refurbishing next week," Molly said.

"I'm going to let you have all fifty. Just remember we can't replace them."

"Thanks, we'll put them to good use. Could we have Harvey Weinstein too?"

"Sure, but I'll need him back."

SEVENTY-TWO HOURS LATER, Major Ma handed General Sung a dispatch from General Duan.

"It's about time. Get General Duan on the line, and I'll get him lined out," General Sung ordered. "Have General Tang deploy his men along their western and northern flanks, and have General Ni cut off their southern escape routes. Once they're in position, move your men into the Yellowstone area and wipe them out. You'd better be quick about it, because winter will be on us before you know it," General Sung warned.

GENERAL DUAN TASKED a young hard-charging general by the name of Diem to lead the expedition to eradicate the American forces. General Diem and his men were fifteen miles outside of Cheyenne when the Americans made their first strike.

General Waverley's task was to wage possibly the most difficult military maneuver ever conceived, a fighting retreat. He wanted to inflict as many casualties as possible, while minimizing his exposure, so they'd planted several large IEDs along the route they'd take.

General Diem had six heavy tanks, and twelve APCs on point, with the rest of the column stretched out for miles behind them.

As the enemy column approached, Sergeant Lindale exclaimed, "Damn, that's a lot of firepower." When the tanks reached the mines, he punched the remote detonator, and they disappeared in the cloud of fire and smoke. By the time the smoke had cleared, the commandos had picked off several of the first responders, and moved on.

Later in the day, Colonel Weinstein's squadron flew its first sortie against the column. When Harvey slowed to a hover behind the foothills, he ordered, "Spread out and wait for my command." When the column came rumbling by their position, Harvey ordered, "Let's get them, boys." The squadron rose above the ridgeline, and let loose a barrage of missiles. "OK, let's get the hell out of here," Harvey ordered.

Their hit-and-run tactics allowed them to escape unscathed for almost a week, but General Diem had finally gotten lucky and managed to flame three of Colonel Weinstein's choppers.

That evening, after Harvey had made his nightly report to General Waverley, the general told him, "I'm pulling your squadron off the line."

"Why, haven't we done everything you've asked?" Colonel Weinstein asked.

"More, but I can't afford to sacrifice any more of your ships. We'll need you even more once we draw them into the mountains. Colonel Brown, your teams are going to have to pick up the slack," General Waverley ordered.

"Understood."

The next morning Colonel Brown had just finished

briefing his team. "How do you think the men will do?" Colonel Brown asked.

"They're still green, but they're willing," Sergeant Wilcox remarked. He was a retired marine sergeant major, and Jerome valued his opinion.

"I think so too, but keep an eye on Edmonds. There's something about him I don't like."

"He's a little strange, but he can sure as hell shoot."

As Colonel Brown's men moved into position, they were hiding in the cracks and crevices of the mountains. The Chinese were getting better at spotting the buried IEDs so they'd changed tactics, and strapped the IEDs to the trees.

Jerome was perched on a ledge, about fifteen hundred feet above his men's position, and when the column reached the kill zone they triggered the IEDs.

Since they weren't buried, the IEDs didn't do much more than scorch the tanks, but they ripped through the sides of the first six armored personnel carriers. The burning carriers had the road blocked, so they deployed several squads of soldiers to provide cover while they cleared the way.

"Fire at will," Captain Brown ordered. His men didn't bother concealing themselves, since the enemy's weapons couldn't match the range of their Barrett M88 fifty-caliber sniper rifles. They'd fired about twenty rounds each, when the top slid back on several of the APCs, and up popped 14.5mm OJG 04 heavy machine guns.

Colonel Brown immediately radioed his team, "Take cover."

As the Chinese gunners swept the hillside, they were shredding everything in their path.

As he watched the slaughter through his binoculars, he spotted Corporal Edmonds. He'd taken up a position in a particularly rugged section of the hillside, and he was calmly picking off the machine gunners.

As Jerome watched him work, he could see the old sergeant had been right about his marksmanship. He'd killed eight of their gunners before they managed to bring enough firepower on his position to keep him pinned down.

Colonel Brown called to him on his headset. "Edmonds, cease fire, and keep your head down."

They kept firing until they'd shoved the burning vehicles off the road.

"Warn the other teams that they've got heavy machine guns concealed in the lead vehicles," Colonel Brown reported.

"What's your status?" General Waverley asked.

"We've taken heavy casualties, and the column has moved on."

"I'll get the word out. Just hang tight, I'm sending you some help."

As General Diem's column moved deeper into the Yellowstone wilderness, General Sung was growing impatient.

"How much longer is it going to take?" General Sung asked.

"It's hard to say," General Duan explained. "General Diem's column is only making a few miles a day, and the terrain is growing more rugged by the day. To make matters even worse, the weather bureau is predicting a major snowstorm next week. If it's as bad as they're predicting, we may be forced to stop."

"Damn it, I was afraid of that." General Sung muted the call while he conferred with Major Ma. When he came back on he ordered, "You're going to need some time to dig in for the winter, so stop and consolidate your positions, and we'll finish them off in the spring."

"It looks like they've stopped," General Waverley reported.

"Great, how are you coming with your preparations?" JD asked.

"We should be done in plenty of time. I just hope we don't have a warm winter."

"I think we may be in luck, because our weather guy's predicting one of the worst winters on record."

THE FIRST SNOWSTORMS hadn't been too bad, but they'd gotten progressively stronger. By mid-December there was over a hundred inches of snow on the ground, and it was still snowing.

A few days before Christmas, General Duan made an unannounced visit to the front.

"Does it ever stop snowing?" General Duan asked.

"Not once it starts, and I'm afraid that we've not seen the worst of it yet," General Diem said.

"There's what the locals call an arctic express, swooping down through Canada, and they're predicting at least three days of severe blizzard conditions."

"Let's get this over with. I'd like to get out of here before the weather gets much worse," General Duan said, as he glanced up at the darkening skies.

The valley where General Diem had decided to winter over was some of the most rugged terrain in Yellowstone. He'd foolishly believed the mountains afforded some measure of protection, when all they really did was limit his ability to maneuver.

They were using a half-track to tour the camp, and General Diem was pointing out the key points as they went. "These are our officer quarters. I managed to get enough of the prefab buildings put up to shelter all of our officers."

"How about the enlisted?" General Duan inquired.

"That's why I wanted the ditch-digging equipment. We've ringed the camp with trenches, and covered them with the acrylic panels. It lets them stay warm, and provides decent visibility."

"Won't that limit their ability to respond to assaults?"

"Maybe a little, but we've installed heavy machine guns every hundred yards, and the overlapping fields of fire should allow us to fend off most attacks. Besides, I doubt anyone would be crazy enough to attack in this weather."

They'd set up the motor pool in the center of the camp, and as they drove around the extensive collection of vehicles, General Duan asked, "Why have you allowed the snow to cover so many vehicles?"

"At first we tried to keep them all uncovered, but the snowfall has just been too heavy. We've even had to stop our regular perimeter patrols due to the conditions."

"You should at least try to keep a portion of your armor where you can use it," General Duan advised.

"OK, we'll try, but I doubt they'll start."

As the wind-driven snow swirled around them, General Duan said, "I'd better get my ass out of here. Call if you need anything, but by the looks of that sky, I doubt we'll be much help."

As General Duan hurried across the clearing to his helicopter, he was struggling to walk against the gale-force winds. He was only halfway, when his pilot stopped him.

"I'm sorry, sir; we're not going to be able to get out of here tonight."

"Damn it," General Duan exclaimed.

Seconds later, a piercing alarm cut through the howling wind.

"What the hell is that?" General Duan asked.

"It's our motion sensors. We got the perimeter wired, but they don't work when it's snowing this hard," General Diem said. He turned to his aide. "Have them turn the damn things off, and triple the sentries."

* * *

JD HAD SET the alarm for 0400, but he woke up a few minutes before it went off. He turned it off, and took a few seconds to contemplate what the day might bring.

If they succeeded, they just might have a chance of retaking the western United States, and if they failed, they would be dead.

They'd left the bathroom light on, and as he sat up in bed, he could see Molly's perfectly sculptured body, as she lay naked in their bed. As he took a moment to enjoy the view, he couldn't believe how much he loved her. He'd spent most of his life alone, and he'd never dreamed that he would find someone as perfect for him as she was.

She was tough, intelligent, and the most gorgeous woman he'd ever seen. What was even more amazing, since the first day they'd met, it was like they'd known each other their entire lives.

He was supposed to wake her so she could go with him. Instead, he got dressed and tiptoed out. He left her a note on the nightstand, but he knew she was going to be mad as hell that he'd left her behind. He was only going as an observer, but experience had taught him that you could never tell how things would turn out.

When he arrived at the airstrip, he noticed his helicopter was already running. "Sorry, If I'm late," JD said as he climbed on board.

"You can't be late, you're the boss," the pilot assured him. "I had to keep it running after we pushed it out of the hangar, or it would have frozen up. It's almost ten below, and if the engine ever cools down, it won't start again."

Their Black Hawks had been specially modified for high altitude, and were outfitted with the terrain-following radar, but it was still a hazardous flight.

It was a short flight, and the pilot left immediately after he'd dropped JD off.

"I thought Molly was coming with you?" General Waverley asked.

"I didn't want to risk getting her hurt, so I didn't wake her up," JD said. "Before you say anything, I know she's going to be pissed, but oh well. At least she's safe. Is everyone ready?"

"They are, and I've got a snowcat over here for you. It's loaded with communications gear so you can keep up with what's going down."

It was just after sunrise when General Waverly's men launched the first attack.

Colonel Brown had led several hundred snipers down the slopes toward the Chinese perimeter, and the white-out conditions had allowed them to advance undetected.

The darkness and the snow had given them cover, but as they sat hiding in the trees, they were about to freeze to death.

"We should've been able to see them by now," Colonel Brown said. "We've got to move closer."

They were only eighty yards out, when they finally caught a glimpse of the sentries through the occasional gaps in the blowing snow.

Colonel Brown ordered, "All right, boys, take them out."

Their fifty-caliber Barretts were deadly accurate at over a thousand yards, so at that range, it was sheer slaughter.

Colonel Brown let them fire for almost a minute before he gave the signal for the second phase of the attack. "Snowcat One, go, go, go," he ordered.

Normally the roar of their engines would have echoed across the canyon walls, but the howl of the wind drowned it out, as the snowmobiles started down the mountainside. Behind the snowmobiles, they had ten thousand troops waiting to charge down the mountain. They were all expert skiers, so they could deal with the conditions, but General Waverley didn't want to commit them until he was sure they'd breached the enemy's perimeter.

"WE'RE UNDER ATTACK," General Diem announced as he rushed into General Duan's quarters.

"In this weather?" General Duan asked.

"This is just the opportunity I've been waiting for. There's no way they can fight us head-on. You should get to the command center. I'll be right behind you, and make sure you've got a situation report ready for me."

AS SNOWMOBILES WERE making their way down the mountainside, they were supposed to be laying down covering fire with their M134 7.62mm miniguns.

"We can't see a damn thing," Sergeant Mallory reported.

"We'll mark the targets with flares," Colonel Brown said. "Just fire at the flares, and keep moving. My men are about eighty yards from their lines, so be careful."

JD couldn't see a thing from his vantage point, but he was trying to follow the action by listening to the radio traffic. The attack had been going on for almost an hour, when he heard General Waverley kick off the next phase. "Bring up the grenade launchers."

JD couldn't believe their good luck, when William Sheldon sent them seven railway cars full of Heckler & Koch XM25 grenade launchers.

When the grenade teams were in place, Colonel Brown ordered, "Set your rounds for air bursts, range three hundred yards, and you can fire when ready."

"WE'RE TAKING A lot of casualties," General Diem reported. "They are using some sort of air burst weapons, and the men are starting to panic."

"Have the tanks blast them off the slopes," General Duan ordered.

"It's too cold; we can't get the damned things started."

"Then contact Cheyenne, and have them scramble some air support."

"I've already tried, but they said they couldn't fly in this weather. They're supposed to start launching sorties when it clears."

"Did they give you an idea when that might happen?"

"Weather central is forecasting three days of this weather."

"Damn, we could be in real trouble. Get me a situation report, and we'll try to figure out if we have any options left," General Duan ordered.

The Chinese's heavy machine guns were firing blindly, for the most part, but they'd exacted a heavy toll on the American forces.

The tide of battle had ebbed and flowed throughout the day, but when darkness fell, both sides paused to take stock of where they were.

CHAPTER 4

At 1900, General Waverley held an officers' call to discuss their tactics for the next day.

JD was still just observing, so he sat in the back of the gigantic tent they were using as a command center.

"What's your status, Colonel Brown?" General Waverley asked.

"Five hundred and ninety-three men dead, sixty-two wounded. We had a hundred and eleven snowmobiles destroyed, and another forty that will require significant repairs."

"How many can you put in the field for tomorrow?"

"I kept a fifty percent reserve, so we can do the same as today."

"How many does that leave in reserve?"

"Fifty-five."

"How about your sniper teams, Major Gump?" the general inquired.

"A hundred and seven dead, thirty-three wounded. We also lost seventy-two men off of the grenade teams, but we'll be ready to go."

It took the general another twenty minutes to finish tweaking the plans for the next day. "Good job everyone, and that should wrap it up for tonight. Try to get a little rest, and we'll hit them again at first light."

THE NEXT DAY went much as the day before, as the tide of battle went back and forth.

At 1400, Colonel Brown's snowmobiles had pulled back to refuel and rearm, and he contacted the general to give him an update.

"I think we can break through with the next attack," Colonel Brown reported.

"Great, I'll send the infantry in behind you. How long before you go again?" General Waverley asked.

"At least another thirty minutes."

"What's the status of the infantry?" the general asked.

"The troops are loaded and ready to go," Major Williams reported.

"Damn it, I didn't realize what time it is," General Waverley commented when he checked his watch. "It'll be dark soon. Colonel Brown, hold up on sending your men back out. Major Gump, have the grenade teams keep hitting them until dark. Major Williams, you can have your men stand down."

JUST BEFORE DARK, General Diem called down to the motor pool, "Are you nitwits ever going to get those tanks started?"

"We've got three running, but there's too much snow to get out," Captain Loo said.

"Understood, but all I need is for you to start putting some fire on the slopes to the north."

"Roger that."

Captain Loo called to the tank commanders, "Target the slopes to the north, and fire for effect." The tanks pivoted and started lobbing shells into the mountainside. One of them was armed with a pod of rocket tubes, and when it fired its first barrage of missiles, a hundred-yard-wide section of the mountain erupted. They'd been firing blindly, but the rockets had bracketed the tent General Waverley was using as a command post.

They continued exchanging fire until the Americans pulled back for the night.

"Cease fire, it looks like it's over for today," General Diem ordered.

"Is there any chance my chopper can get out of here?" General Duan asked.

"Not until the weather lets up, and we'll have to fly in a replacement, because yours got blown up in the morning attack," General Diem said.

"Damn, another night in this godforsaken place."

"Given the circumstances, I think you need to spend the night in the headquarters building," General Diem advised.

General Duan knew the answer, but he asked anyway. "How bad is it?"

"It's not good. We've taken heavy casualties, and the morale is so bad that we're starting to see a lot of desertions."

"Don't worry about that right now, we'll deal with them when this is over. What are our chances of making it through another day?"

"Problematic. I'm sure we still outnumber them, but they're really hammering us. I don't see how they can keep up the levels of their attacks. They've got to be running low on fuel and ammo, but if not, we're screwed."

General Duan didn't say anything for a few seconds, and then he asked, "Do you think you could get one of the vehicles started, and if so, what's the chance of making it out of here?"

"We had a little luck today, so we might get something started, but even if we did, you aren't going to get very far in these conditions." He looked General Duan in the eye. "I shouldn't have stopped here. I was over-confident, and I'm afraid that I've gotten us all killed."

"It's too late to worry about that now," General Duan said. "What have you told General Sung?"

"I haven't updated him at all," General Diem admitted. "Why, do you want me to?"

"No, I suppose not.

"You need to go ahead and deploy your reserves, because I'm sure that they're going to hit us early, and hard tomorrow."

"What makes you so sure?"

"It's what I would do. I'm going to try to get some sleep, and I suggest you do the same."

It was almost 2300 before General Drury managed to get them together to go over the day's events. They'd pulled three of the snowcats together to break the wind, but it was almost unbearable.

"It's colder than hell out here, so we'll make this quick," JD said. "How's General Waverley doing?"

"We airlifted him out about twenty minutes ago, and he was still holding on," Colonel Brown said. "The corpsman thought he had a chance."

"How did the medevac chopper fly in this weather?" JD asked.

"They didn't, Harvey had one of the specially equipped Black Hawks, and well, you know Harvey."

"He's a wild man all right."

"I assume you're taking over?" Colonel Brown asked. "We've got another big tent, so I'll get it set up for you."

"I am taking over, but don't bother with the tent. I'm going to use the snowcat as a mobile command center."

"Good deal. Do you want to modify General Waverley's orders for tomorrow?"

"I do, and this is what I need to happen." He quickly explained what he wanted, and said, "That's all I have, now we just need to go out and execute."

THE SUN WASN'T quite up when Colonel Brown's men hit them with everything they had left.

General Drury knew it was go big or go home time, so the snowmobiles were followed by the snowcats, filled to capacity with infantry. They'd pooled their remaining resources for a concentrated attack on the HQ building. Once they were inside their lines, they unloaded the first wave of infantry, and stormed the HQ building.

Colonel Brown was leading the assault team, and they laid down a withering barrage of machine gun fire, and rocket-propelled grenades as they charged the entrances. "Follow me, and don't kill them all, I need some prisoners," Colonel Brown ordered.

JD was listening intently to the radio traffic, but he was having a hard time following the fast-moving action. Frustrated, and desperate to get a better sense of how the battle was going, he kicked his snowcat into gear and moved over to the edge of the snow-covered ledge to see if he could catch a glimpse of the action.

When the MRAPs finished unloading the troops, the snowmobiles broke away on a high-speed firing run along the camp's perimeter.

Up to that point, the Chinese troops had been warm, and relatively safe in the trenches. However, with the Americans behind their lines, they were forced out of their bunkers, to try to repel the assault. As they streamed out of the trenches, the snowmobile's miniguns were really chopping them up.

The Chinese still vastly outnumbered them, but fifty minutes of close-quarters combat, the brutal conditions, and the Americans overwhelming firepower had taken its toll. As the Chinese troops broke ranks and started making a run for it, several of the American commanders ordered their units to pursue them.

JD immediately broke in. "Let them go. They won't last very long out in the open." He switched over to the command channel. "Colonel Brown, make sure you set up a perimeter while we sort this out, and I'll be right down."

"Yes, sir, will do."

JD slid into the driver's seat, but when he put it into gear to back up, the rock ledge started crumbling. When he felt the cat lurch forward, he gunned the engine to try to back away from the edge, but the ledge gave way. As his snowcat tumbled down the steep mountainside, it triggered an avalanche, and by the time the massive snow slide reached the bottom, JD's snowcat was buried under thirty feet of snow.

As the battle wound down, Colonel Brown tried to contact JD to tell him they'd taken at least one high-ranking officer prisoner. When he couldn't raise him he ordered, "Take a squad and find out why General Drury isn't responding." After the squad left, he walked over to the hut where they were holding the prisoner.

"Who do we have here?" Colonel Brown asked.

"No idea, I can't get him to say a thing," Lieutenant Sharp said.

Colonel Brown took a picture of him with his satellite phone, and forwarded it to Molly, to see if she could identify him. Seconds later, he felt his phone vibrate, and he clicked it to open a video chat.

"So now you want something from me," Molly said sarcastically. "Oh sorry, Colonel Brown, I thought it was JD finally answering my calls. What can I do for you?"

"I just sent you a picture, can you do a quick search to identify the prisoner?"

"I don't need to; it's General Duan. How did you end up with him?"

"No idea."

"Is JD around? I'd love to have a short conversation with him," Molly asked.

"Join the club. I just sent a team out to try to locate him."

"He's missing?" she asked, as her anger turned to concern.

"I imagine he's just having radio trouble, but I'll call you if it turns out to be anything else. I wouldn't worry; he wasn't taking part in the attack, and he's damn good at taking care of himself."

When they finished, Colonel Brown walked over to General Duan, and sat down across the table from him. "So General Duan, what do you think we should do with you?"

"Why ask me, Colonel Brown?" the general asked in impeccable English.

"How in God's name do you know who I am?"

"We know everything there is to know about General Drury and his team. Although I thought you were a sergeant."

"I got promoted. Now that the formalities are out of the way, I would like to ask you a few questions."

"Ask me anything you would like, but I'm not going to answer."

"Look, the war's over for you, so you might as well cooperate."

"Fool, my men will be coming for me as we speak."

"Maybe, but from what I just observed, the ones who survived aren't going to stop running until they hit Cheyenne."

The general didn't respond, but he saw a hint of doubt, as his words sank in. Colonel Brown spent almost an hour talking with the general, but he couldn't get anything out of him. Fed up, he called one of the guards over. "Hold him here until I can arrange transport, and if he gives you any trouble, tie him up."

Colonel Brown moved to one of the other officer billets, and held a staff meeting.

"Has anyone located General Drury yet?" Colonel Brown asked.

"No, sir, but we've put three more squads on it. Don't worry, we'll find him."

Colonel Brown was worried, but he couldn't let it show. "All right, I need an update on our situation."

"I'll start with vehicles," Lieutenant Sharp volunteered. "We've lost eighty-two snowmobiles, and twenty-one snowcats."

"That's not as bad as I'd feared. How about casualties?"

"It's still a little sketchy, but we've confirmed 2,873 killed, and 1,101 wounded. The medevacs still can't land, so we're using the snowcats to move the casualties to the other side of the mountain."

They were just finishing up the briefing, when Molly walked in.

"What the hell are you doing up here?" Colonel Brown asked. "JD will kick my ass for letting you come."

"I'll take care of that. Have you found him yet?"

"No, not yet, but we've got several squads out looking. Don't worry, we'll find him."

By then it was pitch dark, and the temperatures were dropping like a rock. Although the storm was making it extremely hazardous to keep looking, they had plenty of volunteers.

Around midnight, Colonel Brown finally persuaded Molly to try to get a little rest. She finally fell asleep about 0300, but she kept dreaming that JD was lying dead in the snow. Unable to get any real rest, she got back up at 0600.

* * *

"HAVE YOU FOUND anything yet?" she asked, as she tried to fight back her tears.

"We haven't found a trace of him, or his snowcat," Colonel Brown said.

"Snowcat! They have a transponder and a GPS in them, don't they?"

"I'm not sure."

"I'm almost sure they do. Let me make a quick call. Get me the geek," she instructed.

"What's up?" Corporal Lindsey asked.

"Don't the snowcats they're using up here have transponders and GPS?"

"They sure do. Why, did you lose one?"

"JD's missing, and he was in one of them when he was last heard from."

"If it still has power, you should be able to locate it by scanning this frequency," he told her, as he texted it. I tell you what, I just saw Harvey come in, so I'll come up there and help you find him."

Harvey Weinstein was still the only one crazy enough to land at their forward base, and they met Corporal Lindsey when Harvey dropped him off. They didn't get a chance to thank him for coming, before he started talking a mile a minute.

"I modified one of the receivers on the flight over, and if he's out there, this should be able to pinpoint his location. I amped up the circuit, and it's about twenty times more sensitive than it was."

"Thank you for coming," Molly said, as she gave him a hug, and broke down in tears.

"Hey, it's going to be all right," Larry said. "He's the toughest SOB I've ever known."

They loaded up in one of the snowcats and started up the mountainside, toward JD's last known location. It took them over an hour to make their way up the mountain, but they finally reached the spot where the ledge had broken off.

"Look over there," Molly said, as she pointed to where the ledge had broken away.

"It's too dangerous to drive," Colonel Brown said. "We're going to have to get out and walk."

The conditions were horrible, as they slowly inched their way across the treacherous mountainside. When they reached the spot where JD had gone over, it was easy to see what had happened.

"It's too dangerous to go straight down," Colonel Brown advised. "We need to go back down and come up the valley." They moved as quickly as they could, but it took them all night to reach the area where the avalanche had come to rest.

"Everybody spread out, and be careful," Colonel Brown instructed.

Several minutes later the geek screamed, "I've got something. It's really weak, but it's definitely nearby." He was sinking up to his knees in the wet snow, as he attempted to pinpoint the location. "It's directly below me."

"Lieutenant Sharp, I need as many men with shovels as you can round up, and I need them right now," Colonel Brown ordered.

The loose snow made it slow going, because it kept caving in on them.

"Go and rip out some planks from one of the buildings, and bring back some ropes as well," Colonel Brown ordered.

Once they had the boards in place to hold the snow back, they started making progress. However, it still took them almost three hours to reach the cat.

"We've found it," one of the soldiers yelled out.

"How's it look?" Corporal Lindsey asked.

"It's lying on its side, and it's torn all to hell."

When they heard the call, Molly and Jerome struggled through the snow to where they were digging.

"Get that door open," Colonel Brown ordered.

When Molly saw them open the door, she slid down one of the ropes, and hit bottom with a thud.

"Be careful, we don't need you getting hurt too," Jerome yelled.

She ignored him as she pushed the soldier out of the way, and lowered herself through the door. She found JD lying in a heap of debris against the far wall. As she bent down to check him out, she was scared to death he was dead. "Oh, thank God," she exclaimed, when she felt the pulse in his neck. She gave him a kiss on the cheek, and yelled, "He's alive, but I'll need some help to get him out of here."

Colonel Brown was the next one through the hatch, followed quickly by a corpsman. The corpsman did a quick evaluation, and said, "I've put a brace around his neck as a precaution, but I don't think he's broken anything. He probably has a concussion, but we can move him when you're ready."

Jerome picked JD up and shoved him through the hatch. They rushed him back to the helipad where Harvey had just landed, and within minutes they had him on the way to the field hospital.

It turned out that the corpsman was right, and by the next afternoon JD was awake and champing at the bit to go back to work.

"Oh no you don't," Molly admonished. "The doctor said that you needed to stay in bed for at least three days, and that's what you're going to do."

"OK, but I need to talk with Jerome."

She handed him a satellite phone and said, "Good idea. He probably wouldn't admit it, but he was as worried about you as I was. He was the first one down, when I called for help. I couldn't believe it. He picked you up like a small child, and literally threw you out of the hatch."

"What do you mean, you called for help? What the hell were you doing up there?"

"Don't you yell at me! I was supposed to be there all along, but you snuck off without saying a word. Besides, I would have gone to the middle of hell to find you, if I'd needed to."

She was definitely the most gorgeous woman he'd ever known, but he could tell by the fire in her eyes, she meant every word. "As I would for you. Since I have to stay in bed, how about climbing in here with me?" he said with a wink.

"Think you're up to it?" She giggled as she started unbuttoning her blouse.

An hour later, he got around to calling Colonel Brown.

"Good to hear your voice," Jerome said.

"Good to be heard. I was very lucky, wasn't I?"

"You think? You tumbled down that mountainside for over a thousand feet before you hit bottom."

"How are you coming out there?" JD asked.

"Not too bad, but we took a lot of casualties. We're a little shorthanded, but don't worry; I'll have the replacements in place by tomorrow night."

"Cancel the replacements, you're not staying."

"Aren't we moving on to Cheyenne?"

"Nope, we're going to regroup, and go after General Tang's army. I don't think the group we just mauled will be any threat for a while, and it's imperative that we take the West Coast back."

"You're the boss. We'll be ready to move as soon as we can get loaded."

"Good, but I do want you to salvage everything you can, before you take off."

"You got it."

JD could hear him take a deep breath before he

continued. "Look, I hate to dump this on you, but I think you need to make the call on this."

"Let's hear it."

"We had a rather ugly incident while we were mopping up the resistance."

"What happened?"

"There were eleven Chinese soldiers who surrendered to one of our forward units, and it seems that once they'd disarmed them, they lined them up and gunned them down in cold blood."

"Damn it. How many men were involved?"

"Six. It turns out that they're the only survivors from a small town in Montana. The Chinese executed the entire town's population in retribution for killing one of their officers."

"They were all involved?"

"They were all there, but I think it was their sergeant who pulled the trigger."

JD didn't say a word as he mulled over his options. "I know this may not be politically correct, but I don't want you to punish them."

"Fine by me, I was afraid you were going to have them shot."

"I considered it, but I'm not sure I wouldn't have done the same thing."

CHAPTER 5

The weather made it brutal work, as they worked feverishly to salvage everything they could. With no way of verifying what the Chinese were up to, and with their meteorologist forecasting clearing conditions, JD became convinced they were out of time.

"I'm afraid they could be on you at any moment, so wrap it up, and get the hell out of there," JD ordered.

The Chinese didn't get there until the next morning, and the carnage from the battle was all they found.

"Yes, sir, that's right. They're all dead. The headquarters building has been burned to the ground, and there are bodies everywhere," Major Xie reported.

"Any sign of Diem or Duan?"

"We've found General Diem's body, but we haven't located General Duan."

"I need you to do a quick assessment, and send it in," General Duan's aide told him. "I've got to let General Sung know what's happened."

When he received Major Xie's report, General Duan's adjutant forwarded it to headquarters.

Shaken by what he'd read, Major Ma considered the best way to present the bad news to the general. After he'd reread it for the third time, he decided that putting it off wasn't going to make it any better. He handed the dispatch to General Sung, quickly powered his wheelchair back a few feet, and waited for the explosion. When the general finished reading the first paragraph, he bellowed, "Get me General Duan, he's got some explaining to do."

This would have been a lot easier, if he'd bothered to read it, Major Ma thought to himself. "I would, but General Duan is missing. He'd gone to the front to inspect the troops, and got weathered in."

"Shit, how about General Diem?"

"He's dead."

The general leaned back and didn't say anything for several minutes as he contemplated his next move. Finally, he picked up the dispatch and read it. When he finished, he realized that if the initial projections held up, their losses had been staggering. "Get my plane ready. We're going to Cheyenne."

When they landed, General Sung had Major Ma start digging for answers. Major Ma interviewed Major Xie, but he didn't know why General Duan had gone to the front, or what had gone wrong.

Frustrated by the lack of information, the major was getting ready to check out the site of the battle himself, when six survivors came straggling in. Major Ma grilled them for hours, but their stories didn't make much sense. Supposedly, when the order to retreat had been given, they'd managed to get one of the troop carriers started, and in the confusion, they'd lost touch with the main body. The truth was that they'd made a run for it, the night before the final attack

"There's no way these dip-shits should be the only ones who made it out of there," Major Ma said. "Throw the cowards in the brig until I can figure this out. That bullshit story of theirs just doesn't add up."

They'd immediately dispatched a relief column, but the immense snowfall had made it slow going. They'd gotten within forty miles of the battle when they started picking up the other survivors. Less than eight thousand troops had made it out alive, and by the time they reached them, several hundred more had frozen to death.

Two weeks later, Major Ma gave General Sung his final report on the battle.

After General Sung had spent an hour trying to figure out what it meant to his future strategy, he called Major Ma in to discuss their next moves.

"Before we get started, I want you to call down to the brig and have those six cowards from the motor pool shot," General ordered.

Major Ma keyed the radio built into his wheelchair, and gave the order. "Done. Now, what did you want to discuss?"

"I'm now convinced *we* made a mistake when we moved General Tang's army. Work out the logistics, and get him started back to California, because I'm convinced General Drury is going to try to regain control of the West Coast."

"What makes you think they won't move east?"

"Because he doesn't have enough resources, and if he's able to regain control of a deep water port, he can bring in supplies and fresh troops."

For once he found himself agreeing with the general's assessment of the situation. As he listened to how "we" had made a mistake, he managed to keep his sarcasm to himself. "I'll take care of it immediately."

"Very good, Colonel, that will be all."

Colonel? I wonder when he promoted me, Ma thought. After he'd drafted the orders for General Tang's army, he checked the files to see if he'd been promoted. Sure enough, the general had promoted him the previous day, but hadn't bothered to tell him. *Oh well, my new wife will appreciate the extra money.* As he thought of her, he thought of his first wife and family, and how much he missed them. They'd been killed in the American counterstrike, along with over two billion of his fellow countrymen. He sat there for almost ten minutes, before he wiped the tears from his eyes and went back to work.

THE WEATHER HADN'T allowed them to move out right away, so JD had spent the time working on his tactics for the coming move toward the West Coast. He'd gotten up extra early to put the final touches to the plans, and he'd just saved the final updates, when Molly came in to check on him.

She'd been putting it off for days, but she finally asked, "So, what was the idea of sneaking off without me? If I'm going to be your aide, you can't treat me like the girlfriend."

JD could see the fire in her pretty blue eyes, and had to laugh in spite of himself. He'd prepared an elaborate story, but he decided to go with the truth. "I couldn't stand it if anything were to happen to you. So you're just going to have to live with me trying to protect you, and about the girlfriend thing, I think it's time you married me."

"Yes, sir, General, sir," she said, as she threw him a mock salute. "That had to be the lamest proposal of all time, but I guess I'll accept."

She ran over and gave him a big kiss.

"You'd better stop it, or we'll be late for the briefing."

She let him go, and went to lock the door.

THEY WERE BOTH grinning like schoolkids when they walked in.

"If I dare to ask, what have you two been up to?" Colonel Brown said.

"We've decided to get married," JD announced.

"It's about time. There's sure no reason to wait, because none of us know how long we may have."

"True enough, but it looks like you have something else you need to say."

"General Waverley died this morning."

JD's smile was replaced with a scowl. "Damn it to hell, the doctors said he was going to make it."

"They said it was a blood clot, and that it just happens sometimes."

"I told him to stay out of the line of fire, but he wouldn't listen."

"Look who's talking," Molly scolded.

"We sure couldn't afford to lose him," JD said. "Got any idea who we should promote?"

He'd expected a recommendation from Colonel Brown, but Molly jumped in first. "I think you should take a look at Colonel Connelly," Molly suggested. "General Waverley spoke highly of him, and from what I've heard, he's one tough customer."

"I've heard of him," Jerome said. "If I'm not mistaken, he led SEAL team six at one time?"

"That's right," JD said. "I don't know how I could have forgotten him. He gave us a lecture on guerrilla tactics while I was in OCS. He's got to be getting up there in years, but he'll damn sure do. Get him on the videoconference, and we'll get him started."

JD promoted him to general, and gave him command of Waverley's battalion.

"Why don't we put the briefing off for a day? It would be better if you had some time to get up to speed before we go over the battle plans," JD said.

"Thanks, and I'll be ready by tomorrow," General Connelly said.

JD KICKED OFF the meeting the next day. "Are your men in position and ready to go?"

"Yes, sir, they are," General Connelly said.

"Do you have any comments, questions, or concerns about the operation?"

"I do, and if you'll bear with me for a few minutes, I'd like to show you what I'm thinking." He put a map of the area up on the screen. "The heavy snowfall is going to force them farther south, and I know the area like the back of my hand. "Here's the route I think they'll follow. If I'm right, we should make our move when they enter the St. Anthony Sand Dunes."

It took General Connelly three hours to finish explaining his plans for the operation, and answer General Drury's questions.

"Bob, this looks damn good. Is there anything you need from us?"

"Could you spare Colonel Weinstein and his choppers?"

JD laughed and said, "Damn, old Harvey sure is a popular request. I'll let you have him and his birds, but I'd like them back when you're done."

When General Tang started his retreat, he made sure his small squadron of helicopters was overhead anytime they were moving, to try to mitigate the inevitable ambushes.

General Connelly had intended to have Harvey Weinstein's choppers harass the Chinese column, but when he saw their air cover, he decided to hold them in reserve.

"We can take them," Colonel Weinstein said.

"I believe you," General Connelly said. "You'll get your chance, but not yet. I need your squadron intact when we spring my trap, so just be patient."

They lacked the firepower to go head-to-head with General Tang, but they had several hundred off-road vehicles that they'd outfitted with advanced night vision, rocket launchers, and miniguns.

*   *   *

Each morning, General Tang held a briefing in his armored trailer before they broke camp.

"What was the damage from last night's attacks?" the general asked.

Colonel Li, his XO, checked his PDA and said, "Two hundred killed, and fifty-five wounded. We also lost six personnel carriers, and three transport trucks."

"That's not as bad as the previous night, but why aren't our helicopters picking them up before they hit us? I know they're running dark, but we've got night vision too."

"I've interviewed the flight commander, but all he could tell me is that they just appeared out of nowhere. We did manage to destroy two of their vehicles in last night's attack, but we lost two choppers, and there's another one that's on its last legs."

"We can't stand losses like that! Ground the helicopters when it gets dark," General Tang ordered.

"That's going to leave us wide open."

"Deploy the heavy tanks on the perimeter. They haven't had much luck taking them out."

The next morning General Connelly was going over the results of the previous night's operations. "Captain Stallworth, you can go first," General Connelly prompted.

"There wasn't any air cover last night, so we couldn't shoot down any aircraft."

"That means we can get into the action," Colonel Weinstein said.

"Not so fast, it could have been a onetime occurrence," General Connelly said. "Besides, I don't want them to know we have aircraft. Continue, Captain Stallworth."

"Even without air cover, we had a rough go of it. They had their heavy tanks on the perimeter, and none of our weapons can penetrate their armor. We destroyed a couple of trucks, but we lost eleven vehicles, with seven killed and two wounded."

"I know it's going to be tough, but I need you to hang in there for a few more days."

That night General Connelly briefed General Drury on the situation.

"I'll reach out to William Sheldon and see if he's got another trick up his sleeve," General Drury said.

When JD told William what they were running into, he said, "I may be able to lay my hands on some stuff that might help."

Three days later William had acquired a thousand German PARS 3 antitank missiles and ten Tiger helicopters.

The Tigers were fitted with mast-mounted sights, and when the terrain allowed it, they could launch their fire-and-forget missiles without exposing themselves to enemy fire. William dispatched four semis with the missiles, but they decided to bootleg the helicopters through Canada.

THE TRUCKS ARRIVED two days later, but the helicopters didn't show until a few hours before their attack.

"Sorry we're late, we had a hard time scrounging fuel," Colonel Hans Kruger said.

"I'm just glad you made it. However, I'm going to have to throw you into action right away," General Connelly said.

"No problem, that's why we're here. Just let me know what you need us to do."

General Connelly put a map on the screen, and walked him through the mission.

As the column had moved westward the terrain was changing.

"I didn't realize there were sand dunes in this part of the country," Colonel Li said.

"I'd seen the notations on the map, but they're a lot

more extensive than I'd expected," General Tang said. "They're kind of neat, in a desolate sort of a way."

Once the enemy column was in the sand dunes, General Connelly had his sappers mine the road behind them. They'd already laid the mines in front of them, and by the time their point vehicles drove into the minefields, they'd cut off their path of retreat.

When the lead vehicles started exploding, the column stopped and prepared for the expected attacks. General Connelly knew they would deploy men to both sides of the road, so they'd mined one side of the road to force them in the direction they wanted them to go.

When the mines started exploding, Colonel Li ordered, "Pull back, they've got mines on that side." As the explosions continued, the colonel screamed into the radio, "Move your men to the other side of the road, you idiots."

General Connelly gave them enough time to begin moving, before he launched their next attack.

What was left of General Tang's helicopter squadron was flying cover for the column, so when their off-road vehicles started popping up out of the pits in the ground, they radioed a warning. "You've got a large body of vehicles headed your way from the east," the squadron commander said. "We're moving to cut them off."

As the squadron banked to try to break up the attack, Colonel Weinstein's choppers popped up from behind the large sand dunes where they'd been waiting.

The Chinese helicopters were fixated on the off-road vehicles, so they never saw the missiles coming until they started getting missile warnings.

Harvey's men destroyed all but one of the enemy helicopters with their first salvo. As the lone survivor tried to turn to meet the new threat, seven missiles hit him.

"We've finished off their air cover," Colonel Weinstein reported. "You can launch the second wave." As the next wave left their bunkers, Harvey had his men turn their attention to the main body of the column, and called to the Tigers. "Light them up, Kraut," Harvey ordered.

Kraut was their code name for the ten German Tiger helicopters that were still hovering behind the sand dunes.

GENERAL TANG COULDN'T believe it when he saw the first volley of missiles come streaking over the sand dunes.

"Where are those damn missiles coming from?" General Tang asked.

"No idea, we haven't been able to get a bead on them," Colonel Li said.

THE AMERICAN'S FIREPOWER was taking a heavy toll, but they were running out of time.

"They'd better start moving, because we're almost out of ammo and fuel," Colonel Weinstein said.

"Same here," Captain Billy Elliot, the leader of the ground assault, said.

AT THE LAST moment, Colonel Li called to General Tang.

"They're cutting us to ribbons sitting here, but there seems to be an opening to the West."

"Give the order," General Tang said.

"THEY'RE FINALLY MOVING," Harvey reported. "We're out of time, but will be back ASAP."

Captain Elliot's men kept pressing their attacks, but several of them made their last runs with no ammo.

* * *

"I think we can stop here, it looks like we've beaten them off," Colonel Li said.

"It's about time," General Tang said. "Get me a damage assessment."

General Connelly's strategy had been to get them inside the four-miles-long-by-three-miles-wide rectangle, which represented their predetermined field of fire.

A couple of miles away, he'd hidden 500 M270 MLRS (Multiple Launch Rocket Systems), and 501 M777 Howitzers. When their first barrage hit, General Tang thought that hell had opened up to swallow them.

"My God, where is that coming from?" General Tang asked.

The colonel didn't respond because he was already dead, and before General Tang could call again, the second barrage turned his trailer into a brilliant fireball.

The American batteries were really pouring it on, and after thirty minutes, General Connelly ordered, "Cease fire. Captain Elliot, are your men ready?"

"Yes, sir."

"You can attack at will."

When Captain Elliot's men came over the last sand dune, and caught sight of what was left of the Chinese column, the carnage took their breath away.

"My God," the captain exclaimed. "It's hard not to feel sorry for the poor bastards, but better them than us."

It was 2030 before General Connelly had time to make his report to General Drury.

"Yes, sir, that's right, we've destroyed the entire column," General Connelly reported. "From the documents we've recovered, I would put their losses at around two hundred thousand men."

"Congratulations, you've won a tremendous victory,"

General Drury said. "How long before you can be ready to move out?"

His question caught General Connelly by surprise. He muted the call, and checked with his adjutant, before he responded.

"Sorry, I was figuring on stopping for a few days. I think we could be ready to move in forty-eight hours. What's the rush? There shouldn't be any effective fighting forces between here and the coast."

"There isn't, and I don't want to give General Sung any chance to redeploy his troops. I'll send you your orders as quickly as I can, but for tonight, enjoy your victory, and let's hope it's just the first of many."

When JD hung up he turned to Molly. "You were right, Connelly is a good man. His plan worked to perfection."

"Do you have any idea what comes next for the general and his men?" Molly asked.

"Yes, I'm going to send him west, but I need a little time to work up the specifics."

JD had been working on the strategy for several hours, when Molly came back in to check on him.

"Have you finished the new orders for General Connelly?"

"I'm close. I hate it, but I'm afraid his men are going to have to bear the brunt of the fighting for the next few months."

"That sounds tough all right, but you might want to take a look at this note from General Sanchez before you finish up."

"Who the hell is General Sanchez?"

"I believe he's the head honcho with the SASR."

"I'll read it, but I can't imagine why he'd be contacting me."

After JD had read the note, he asked, "You think this is legit?"

"I had our techs trace the IP address, and it's definitely out of Venezuela. General Sanchez took control of the SASR after the Chinese attack, so as far as we can tell, it's on the up-and-up."

JD paused, as he weighed the risks and rewards.

"I'm going to take the meeting. I know it's a stretch but we desperately need the help. See if Harvey Weinstein can get me to Sheldon's place. He's got a Gulfstream that can reach Caracas nonstop."

"I'm coming with."

"No, you're not, young lady. It's far too dangerous, and I need you to stay here and keep an eye on things for me. I'll only be gone a couple of days. If you'll give me a few more minutes, I'll have General Connelly's orders ready."

WHEN JD'S PLANE landed in Caracas, the general and fifty of his bodyguards were there to pick him up.

"You expecting trouble?" JD asked as he shook the general's hand.

"Always, it's why I'm still alive. The damn Chinese have people everywhere, and it's not hard to buy friends down here."

As the armored SUV was pulling away, the general said, "I appreciate you taking the risk to meet with me, and I intend to make it worth your time."

After a short drive, the general's men escorted them inside the magnificent villa the general was using.

"How much do you know about our situation?" JD asked as they sat down at a table on the veranda, overlooking the pool.

"I know you've just defeated a fairly large group of General Sung's men, and that you're about to make a move to retake the West Coast, and that you'll be hard-pressed to keep up the pressure." The general could see JD was concerned. "Before you ask, I've got people inside of General Sung's operation. I'm going to get right to the point, if it's all right with you."

"Please do."

"I'm not sure that anyone remembers why, but our countries have been mortal enemies for some time. However, I think it's time we put aside our issues, and unite against our common enemy."

"I couldn't agree more. What have you got in mind?"

"We lost most of our manpower in Central America, but we have a significant amount of arms and equipment, which we'll contribute to your cause. However, for us to be effective, you'll need to open up a seaport."

"Say I do manage to seize a port. How much help are we talking?"

"As much as I can lay my hands on, but at a minimum, I can supply you with helicopters, tanks, and at least a few aircraft, although most of them are outdated. Also, I can supply you with all the food and ammunition you need. Along with an ample supply of antitank and antiaircraft shoulder-fired missiles." He paused to let JD absorb what he was proposing. "To put it another way, I'm prepared to expend every resource I can muster, to help you wipe the sorry bastards off the face of the earth. Which includes reaching out to any other country that's willing to help."

"I've got to admit that we could use the help. Let's see what we can work out," JD said.

They talked well into the night, and by the time they took a break to get some rest, they'd hammered out an agreement.

After a short nap and a meal, the general accompanied him to the airport.

"What's this?" JD asked, when the general handed him a faded leather pouch.

"It's been in my family for generations. I'd intended to hand it down to my son, as my father did to me, but my bloodline will end with me, because he was killed in Central America."

JD opened it, and saw an ancient, razor-sharp dagger. "What do you want me to do with it?"

General Sanchez leaned in and whispered in his ear.

"I promise you, I will if I can," JD said.

"If I were a younger man, I would take care of it myself," General Sanchez said with a quiet, but undisguised fury. He patted JD on the back, and said, "Good luck, and may God go with you."

ONCE GENERAL CONNELLY had received his orders, he called a staff meeting. "It looks like we're going to Seattle," he told the group.

"I'm glad we're headed to the coast, but why aren't we going for San Francisco, or even farther south?" his XO asked.

"To paraphrase Lord Tennyson, 'ours is not to wonder why, but to do or die.' Besides, it's got to be warmer, so let's get the hell out of here."

CHAPTER 6

General Sung had gone ballistic when they received word of General Tang's defeat, but the rage had soon turned to introspection. "Damn, I never thought it could get this bad. Get Colonel Ma in here."

"Yes, sir, is there something you need me to do?"

The general almost made his normal rude comment, but instead he told the colonel, "Yes, there is. I've decided Washington isn't safe anymore. We're moving to Manhattan."

"How is that more secure?" Colonel Ma asked. "They don't like us a damn bit better up there."

"I don't give a shit if they like us. You'll have to coordinate with General Hsieh, but I want the island cleared of locals."

The colonel almost popped off, but he held his tongue.

"Yes, sir, I'll get them started right away, but it's going to take awhile, there's a lot of people in Manhattan."

THREE WEEKS LATER, General Sung called General Hsieh for an update.

"Yes, sir, we're working as fast as we can, but there are a great many people who are refusing to leave," General Hsieh said.

"Who gives a shit, get them moved," General Sung ordered. "I'll be there in two weeks, and you'd better be done, before I get there."

At first they'd managed to keep the relocation out of the national news, but shortly after General Sung's ultimatum, the shit hit the fan.

"Have you heard yet?" Molly asked.

"Heard what?" JD asked.

"General Sung is taking over Manhattan, and they're moving everybody off the island."

"That's a buttload of people."

"Almost two million at last count. I just watched a local news report, and they were showing video of them going door to door booting people out of their homes. If they resist, they're shooting them. They even had footage of them dragging bodies outside, and throwing them into trash trucks."

"Isn't anyone fighting back?" JD asked.

"A few, but they're not very well organized. What are we going to do about it?"

"I'm afraid my hands are tied, we're already spread too thin."

When General Sung relocated, he set up shop in the Westin Hotel in Times Square. The move had gone off without a hitch, but he hadn't been sleeping well. After several sleepless nights, he finally broke down and took a sleeping pill. The pill had put him to sleep, but when he woke up from his nightmare, he was drenched in a cold sweat. He'd dreamed they were surrounded, and that he was faced with either surrendering, or committing suicide. The dream had felt so real that he pulled his right arm out from under the covers, to see if he was holding his pistol.

"Thank the gods, it was just a dream," he exclaimed. "I might as well get up and try to get some work done."

He wasn't prone to self-doubt, but he realized the dream could easily come true. He sat down and started sifting through the large stack of reports on his desk. After a couple of hours, he sighed and leaned back, rubbing his tired eyes.

The documents had painted a grim picture, and left his mind swirling with a myriad of thoughts. He was having a hard time focusing, so he decided to start by listing the challenges and potential fixes. When he finished, it was four thirty in the morning, but he called Colonel Ma to begin work on fleshing out his thoughts.

While he sat waiting, he had to admit he was still a little awestruck by the panoramic view of the city.

He heard a quiet cough behind him. *I must be getting old,* the general thought to himself. *I never heard him come in.* "I'm going to put a bell on your wheelchair, so you'll stop sneaking up on me."

"What can I do for you?" Colonel Ma asked, clearly perturbed.

"I couldn't sleep. So I've put together a list of issues, and potential solutions, and I need you to help me turn them into actionable items."

Normally the general's attention to detail was lacking, but in this case, Colonel Ma was surprised to find that his list was lucid, and well organized. It only took him a couple of hours to turn the general's thoughts into a series of orders.

"That should take care of your list. Is there anything else you need, before I go back to bed?" Colonel Ma asked.

The general almost said no, but the report of increased militia activity was eating at him. "Have you been able to locate any more of the militia family members?"

"We've positively identified fifteen hundred, and another two thousand probable."

"Excellent, that'll be more than enough. Can you pick up a couple of families by tomorrow night?"

"It shouldn't be a problem. Can I ask what you intend to do with them?"

"I'm going to use them to make a point to the resistance fighters. If they're going to continue causing me problems, they're going to learn that there's a price to be paid."

Colonel Ma almost told him he'd stir up more problems than he could handle, but he remembered the last time he'd popped off, and held his tongue.

They'd just finished eating dinner, and JD was sitting in his office going over the day's situation reports.

"General Sung has preempted prime-time programming for some sort of urgent message," Molly told him when she came in.

"That can't be good," JD said.

"I hope it doesn't have anything to do with the roundup of family members we've been hearing about," Molly said, as she turned the TV on.

"Oh God, I just read your report, but I'd figured it was just their normal harassment."

JD had scheduled a briefing with Colonel Brown, and when he came in, he asked, "Are you going to watch the general's speech?"

"Of course, why don't you sit down and watch it with us."

Colonel Ma had set up the hotel's grand ballroom to hold the general's press conference. There were over a hundred reporters and TV news anchors in the room when General Sung entered with his bodyguards.

As the heavily armed bodyguards fanned out around the room, they were an imposing group. Two of them took positions on either side of the general as he walked to the podium.

"Good evening. This won't take very long, but it's imperative that each of you pay close attention to what I'm about to tell you. As I stand here tonight, I'm thinking back to the very first time I addressed the nation. It shocked most of you when I executed President Martell and Admiral Zacharias during the broadcast. However, I must warn you now, that tonight will shock you even more. If you have any children with you, I would advise you to make them leave the room immediately." He paused for almost a minute before he continued. "I hope that you've done as I advised, because what I'm about to do is distasteful even to me. Remember this night, and that the murderous traitors fighting against our forces have forced me to take these extreme measures."

General Sung motioned to the men holding the two families off camera. It took ten guards to drag the two young mothers and their children in front of the podium. As the soldiers forced them to their knees, they were crying hysterically.

"My God, surely he's not going to kill innocent women and children," Molly gasped.

They were frozen in horror as the general came forward with his pistol drawn. As he walked down the line, he methodically shot each one in the back of the head. In seconds, he'd slaughtered the two women and their six children. When he'd shot the last one, a little, six-year-old, blond-haired, blue-eyed doll of a child, he turned, and walked back to the podium.

"From this moment on, we'll be executing two families every Thursday night, until all the militia units in the United States stand down. If you criminals value your families, you'll do as I ask."

Once she was able to stop sobbing, Molly wiped her eyes, and demanded, "You've got to do something."

"I'm afraid there's not much that I can do, other than continue down the path we've set. Surrendering wouldn't stop him; he'd just find some other pretext to kill our families."

"I understand, I guess, but that was horrible."

He pulled her to him, and held her close for several minutes.

"Thanks, I'm better now," she said.

"I need you to schedule a video conference for 0500," JD told her.

"No problem, do you have an agenda?"

"We need to discuss how we are going to keep the men from deserting."

TRUE TO HIS word, the general's men started picking up families and executing them on national TV. However, it was just a couple of weeks before they started having serious issues.

"Why did you cancel tonight's execution?" General Sung asked.

"They're already dead," Colonel Ma said. "When they went to pick them up, they started shooting when the soldiers kicked in their door. We lost four men trying to take them. To give you an idea of how bad it was, one of our men was killed by a ten-year-old child with a butcher knife."

"I hadn't even considered they would fight back. Most people would try to cling to life as long as they could."

WITHIN DAYS, THE word of what had happened had gone viral on the Internet. So every time the general's soldiers tried to pick up a family, they were fighting to the death, rather than being led meekly away to the slaughter.

In some cases, entire neighborhoods had attacked the soldiers, resulting in a tremendous loss of life on both sides.

"This isn't working," General Sung complained. "We've only had one execution all month, and they were already half dead. I still can't believe mothers would sacrifice their children."

In spite of himself, Colonel Ma vented. "You sadistic bastard, what the hell did you think they would do? You were going to slaughter them anyway." The colonel fully expected the general to kill him this time, but the more he thought about it, he really didn't give a shit.

However, the general didn't respond at all, as he turned and walked away.

THE NEXT AFTERNOON Molly was preparing the notes for JD's daily briefing, when she read a report out of New York.

"It looks like they've decided to stop the executions," Molly said. "They've contacted all the networks and told them they could resume their regular programming."

"I'm glad that nightmare is over," JD said. "Did you ever get the number of desertions that I asked you for?"

"I did, but the commanders didn't want to turn the names over, and I seriously doubt that this is everyone. If their numbers are anywhere close to right, there were only a couple thousand deserters."

"Then it wasn't as bad as I'd feared."

"Several of the commanders reported that many of them would come back if they could. They're also asking how you want to deal with them if they're caught, or return on their own."

JD knew history, and more importantly, his men, would judge him by his answer.

As he thought about what he would have done if they'd taken Molly, he knew what his answer had to be.

"Tell them we're granting complete amnesty. I can't find fault with what they did. If they'd been after my family, I'd have gone myself."

His scowl turned to a grin as he took Molly's hand and asked, "Speaking of family, are you ready to get married?"

"Any time you are, General, sir." She giggled.

SINCE NEITHER OF them had any family to invite, they had one of the chaplains marry them the next day. At everyone's urging, JD agreed to take a few days off.

"Well, Mrs. Drury, where would you like to go for your honeymoon?" JD asked.

"How about the mountain cabin we stayed in at Yellowstone?"

"Fine with me, but it'll be too cold to do much sightseeing."

"Oh well, I guess you'll just have to make do with me for entertainment."

Shortly after the ceremony, William Sheldon called to wish them well. "You guys need to think about nothing but yourselves while you're away, because it's going to be all you get for a long time. "I can still remember when Reba and I got married, and you need to savor every moment you have together. Because you never know how long you've got."

"Thanks, and we're going to do just that," JD said. "Oh, by the way, thanks for the equipment. I don't know how you do it, but you're a lifesaver."

"It's little enough. You two go and enjoy yourselves, and forget about this nightmare for a little while."

HARVEY WEINSTEIN FLEW them back to the cabin, and as they were getting out in the several-feet-deep snow, he told them, "Enjoy, and just give me a call when you're ready to leave."

"Thanks, Harvey, and be careful, the weather looks like it's getting worse."

The next few days seemed like heaven, as they put

aside the horrors going on around them. In what seemed like minutes, their time was up, and it was time to go. As they were flying toward General Connelly's location, JD and Molly were going over the situation reports.

"When we land, I need you to get a message to General Sanchez," JD said, as he continued leafing through the reports. "Tell him we should have control of the port in Seattle by the middle of March, and ask him to forward a list of what's in the initial shipments."

"Do you have a wish list, or does he already know what we need?"

"Good point. We talked in generalities when I was down there, so it wouldn't hurt to be specific. I just sent you General Connelly's most urgent needs. I can't seem to find General Thomas's list, so you'll have to give him a call."

They'd only been gone for a short time, but with General Tang's forces out of the way, General Connelly had made tremendous progress.

When they landed, JD went straight to General Connelly's rolling command center.

"How was the honeymoon?" General Connelly asked.

"Wait, that's the stupidest question of all time. What could be better than spending a few days with the woman you love, particularly one as gorgeous as Molly?

"You've made great headway," JD observed.

"We have. The weather has cooperated, and we haven't run into any real resistance. If nothing unexpected happens, we should hit Seattle in three days."

"I read an intercept on the way, and if they deciphered it correctly, General Sung has ordered all the units from Sacramento, north, to consolidate into the Portland, Oregon area," JD said.

"That makes sense. They'll want to engage us as far from their Southern California base of operations as possible. You don't intend to go after them right away, do you?"

"No, not until we've had a chance to get our feet back under us. Your men have done a great job, but I know that they've got to be tired as hell."

"True enough. I've been pushing them pretty hard."

"We'll hold in Seattle until we've received our first shipments from General Sanchez. That should give your men enough time to recharge, and give General Thomas enough time to get here."

As they entered Seattle, they were greeted by hundreds of thousands of well-wishers, and General Connelly's men got their well-deserved R & R.

The next week, the first shipments started arriving.

"Here's the list of ships from the harbormaster," Molly said.

As JD scanned the list, he was amazed at the number and variety of ships and cargoes. "Damn, he even sent three supertankers loaded with gasoline. I never even thought to ask for fuel."

The ships kept coming, and three weeks later, JD decided they were ready to move on to Portland.

As they went over the battle plans, General Connelly said, "The I-5/Columbia River bridge could present a problem."

"It's a possible bottleneck," JD agreed.

"What would you think of dropping a strike team in to take the bridge?"

"It could work, but it's going to be one hell of a job."

"I've got just the man for it," JD said.

He turned to Molly. "Get Colonel Brown in here."

"Yes, sir, what can I do to help?" Colonel Brown asked.

"Sit down, Jerome," JD said. "Bob and I were just going over our plans, and we need you to put together a team to take and hold the Columbia River bridge."

"How many men can I have, and how long do I have to hold it?"

"Whatever you need, and if our current timetable holds up, it could be as much as thirty-six hours."

"Damn, that's a long time."

"We'll get there quicker if we can," General Connelly said, "but I can't guarantee anything."

"Hell, I can't live forever. How long have I got to put the team together?"

"Six days," JD said.

"OK, I'm on it," he said as he headed out the door.

"He seems like a good man," General Connelly said.

"The best. He was my top sergeant when I was leading a team, and he's all that's left."

"We've all lost a lot of good men. If you don't have anything else for me, I'd better get to it as well."

CHAPTER 7

The mission to secure the bridge was by far the most hazardous they'd undertaken. The plan called for Colonel Brown's men to be dropped off by a squadron of UH47F Chinook helicopters, with Harvey Weinstein's squadron providing air cover.

They were scheduled to take off at 0430, and there was a light rain falling when JD arrived to see them off. The aircraft lights were reflecting off the rain-covered runway, and they made it difficult for JD to spot Colonel Brown. Finally, he caught sight of him, and rushed over to where he was about to board his chopper.

"Good luck, and we'll relieve you as quickly as we can," JD yelled over the roar of the rotor blades.

"Thanks, and we'll hold it, or die trying," Jerome yelled back.

JD slapped him on the back and stepped back from the aircraft. When the chopper disappeared into the overcast, JD turned and went back to his jeep.

"I sure hope they make it," Molly said.

"That's in God's hands, but Jerome will do what needs done."

The Chinese commander, General Cheng, knew the bridge was the key to how long he could hold Portland.

So he'd deployed sixty-five hundred crack troops to defend it.

It was still dark when the first wave of Harvey's choppers arrived. The visibility was limited by the low clouds and the driving rain, but their MTS (Multispectral Targeting Systems) let them see as well as the conditions would allow. As they hurtled down toward the bridge, all the enemy could hear was the thump of their rotor blades, and the roar of their engines.

The guards hunkered down behind the crude fortifications they'd set up, but the helicopter's miniguns and rockets devastated over half of their force in their first three passes.

The weather made it impossible for the soldiers to catch more than a glimpse of the attackers, as time after time they circled back to hit them again.

The defenders had lost 80 percent of their men, when the choppers turned to make their seventh firing pass.

As the Chinese commander watched his men break ranks and run, he screamed to his officers, "Shoot the cowards if you have to, but you've got to hold this bridge." When his officers refused to shoot their own men, he ordered over the radio, "Captain Si, fall back to the south end of the bridge and blow the charges." He had no way of knowing that Captain Si was already dead, and as he was about to radio headquarters that they'd lost the bridge, a missile hit his position.

"WE'VE GOT THEM on the run," Harvey radioed to the choppers carrying the troops. "You can come on in."

Colonel Brown had eleven hundred and fifty-three men on board the choppers, but as he deployed his troops, he realized just how thin they were going to be spread. "We're down, and the bridge is secure," Colonel Brown radioed.

"Good work," JD said. "General Connelly is on the move, and they should reach you in no more than thirty-two hours.

"We'll get Harvey's choppers turned around ASAP."

"Roger that, Delta One out."

When the bridge's security detail didn't check in, they sent a small detachment out to check on them. As they came into sight, Colonel Brown ordered, "Hold your fire. Jacobs, I want you to target the lead vehicle, Mason, your target is the trailing vehicle. The rest of you don't fire until I give the order." When the lead vehicle was within a hundred yards, Colonel Brown gave the order to fire.

When the two missiles struck the Chinese version of the Humvees, they exploded and went tumbling end over end. The other five vehicles skidded to a stop on the rain-slick road.

"We're under attack," Lieutenant Sol frantically radioed back to headquarters.

"Pour it to them, boys," Colonel Brown yelled.

The rest of the squad fired their missiles, and the remainder of the vehicles disappeared in a sea of fire.

"Cease fire, don't waste your missiles," Colonel Brown ordered. "Ramirez, take two men and make sure they're all dead."

GENERAL CHENG HAD pre-staged a full brigade near the bridge, in anticipation of their attack, and he was pissed that the officer of the day hadn't already pulled the trigger.

When he walked into the command center, he screamed at Captain Peng, "Get your head out of your ass, and have Colonel Chou clear them off the bridge."

AS THEY LAUNCHED their counterattack, the weather was continuing to deteriorate.

"Damn, this sucks," Lieutenant Jamison said.

"True enough, but we wouldn't have had it this easy if it didn't," Colonel Brown said.

"I'm afraid we're in for it, because Harvey's not going to be back for another forty minutes. Is everyone in place?"

"Everything's ready. We've got plenty of missiles, and Ramirez's squad has finished deploying the new IEDs."

They'd known time would be short, so they'd made rolls of three-inch-thick plastic explosive that was camouflaged to look like pavement. All they had to do was roll it out, insert a detonator, and get out of the way.

Colonel Chou's detachment was ten thousand men strong, and had fifteen heavy tanks to back them up.

The colonel knew they would be dug in by the time they got there, so he had his tanks take the lead as they approached the bridge.

Colonel Brown had lookouts positioned along the only approach.

"They're two miles out, and I count fifteen heavy tanks in the lead," one of the lookouts reported.

"How many troops?" Colonel Brown asked.

"Too many to get an accurate count, but at least several thousand."

"After you blow the charges, hustle back, before you get cut off."

When the lead tank reached the far end of the improvised IED field, they triggered the explosives. Almost fifteen hundred feet of the roadway disappeared in a thunderous explosion. The blasts were so powerful that several of the massive tanks were thrown several feet in the air. The secondary explosions took several minutes to subside, and the searing heat from the fires could be felt from over a hundred feet away.

The rest of the column had come to an abrupt halt when the explosions had erupted. Once the fires had subsided, Colonel Chou screamed at his XO, "Get me a damage assessment."

"There's no need to do an assessment," Major Leao said. "The armor is gone, and they're all dead. Nothing could have lived through that."

"Very well, push that mess out of the way, we need to get moving," the colonel barked.

"Too hot, we'll have to go around them, but we'll have to be careful because the ground is soft from the rains."

As the colonel's SUV was making its way around the still burning tanks, he put his hand on the side glass. "Damn that's hot. I wonder what they used; I didn't think an IED could take out a main battle tank like the ZTZ99A2."

He considered his options, and ordered, "Move the APCs to the front, and have them pick up the pace."

As the APCs accelerated toward the bridge, the spotter called, "We got their tanks, but there are fifty APCs headed your way."

"Hold your position," Lieutenant Jamison ordered.

Colonel Brown verified they were ready, and thanked God for William Sheldon. When William had heard about their mission, he'd sent them two skid-mounted General Electric GAU-8/A Avenger Gatling guns that he'd salvaged from a couple of A10 aircraft.

As the enemy vehicles approached, it was raining so hard that Colonel Brown had to judge the distance from the sound of their engines. When he was sure they were within range, he yelled, "Fire."

The depleted uranium rounds spewed out of the gun at over three thousand rounds a minute, and they ripped the APCs to shreds. When the first gun ran out of ammo, the second one took over while they reloaded. By the time the second gun ran out of ammo, the APCs were nothing more than highly perforated, flaming pieces of junk.

"Cease fire," Colonel Brown ordered.

He still hadn't seen the vehicles, but from the amount of flames they could see through the swirling rainstorm and the lack of engine noise, he knew they'd gotten them stopped.

MAJOR LEAO WAS monitoring the APCs' progress, and when they went up in flames, he rushed back to update the colonel.

"What do you mean the APCs are gone?" Colonel Chou asked. "What'd they do, get up and fly off?"

"I don't know what type of weapons they're using, but they're devastating. What do you want to do now?"

"Have Captain Han press the attack."

"Without any support?"

"Did I stutter? Give the order."

A SHORT LULL in the rain let them catch a glimpse of the blasted hulks, and when the infantry came charging around the debris, Colonel Brown couldn't believe they were being so foolhardy.

He didn't want to waste their heavy armament, so they used their M134 miniguns.

Colonel Brown was standing in the middle of the roadway gauging their advance, and Lieutenant Jamison was starting to get worried as they grew closer. When they were five hundred yards out, Colonel Brown yelled, "All guns fire."

THE TORRENTS OF fire from the miniguns made the fight terribly one-sided, but the Chinese troops showed a dogged determination to press their attack. However, after almost twenty minutes of savage combat, the attack fell apart.

As what was left of their forces scrambled past Colonel Chou's SUV, he screamed, "Cowards, why are they retreating? We've got to retake the bridge."

"We've already lost over ninety percent of our men, and all of our equipment," Major Leao informed him. "We've got no chance of defeating them."

"Bullshit, I'm going to take a look for myself." The colonel got out of his vehicle, and strode confidently toward the American position. The closer he got, the worse the devastation became. When he reached the area where the APCs had been destroyed, he couldn't believe the carnage. Whatever weapons they were using had punched holes completely through the APCs before they'd caught fire and incinerated the men inside. He slowly picked his way around the burning vehicles, but he had to stop and throw up, as the stench of burnt flesh filled his nostrils. He glanced around to see if anyone had seen, but no one had followed him. "I'm going to kick Major Leao's ass when I get back. He should have made sure that I had a security detail with me," he muttered. Finally, he reached the end of the blasted vehicles, and he peeked around the edge of the last one. It was a truly gruesome sight.

He'd been a soldier his entire life, and had seen combat on three different continents, but the scene before him was the worst he'd ever seen. Over seven thousand of his men lay slaughtered before him. There were body parts everywhere, and the rainwater rushing down the gutters was red with their blood. He decided that he'd seen enough, but as he turned to leave, one of the American snipers saw him, and put a fifty-caliber bullet through the back of his head.

"HAVE YOU SEEN the colonel?" Major Leao asked.

"I saw him about a half hour ago," Sergeant Pai replied. "He was headed forward. You want me to go find him?"

"Yes, and be quick about it. We need to get out of here before it gets dark."

A few minutes later the sergeant returned and reported, "I found him. I think."

"Did you or didn't you find him?" the major snapped. "Don't you know what your commanding officer looks like?"

"Most of his face was gone, so it was a little hard to tell."

"Oh! That settles it; we're getting the hell out of here."

For a moment, the major considered radioing in to report what had happened, but he decided it might be better to do it in person. It took them almost an hour to return to base, and as Major Leao entered the administration building, he was dreading making the report.

"Sir, Major Leao would like to speak with you," Lieutenant Ming announced.

"Who the hell is Major Leao?"

"I believe he's Colonel Chou's, XO."

"Very well, send him in.

"You'd better be here to tell me the colonel has retaken the bridge."

"No, sir, I'm afraid that we've failed," Major Leao said.

"Your dip-shit commanding officer failed, so he sent you to make his excuses. That's not going to cut it. I want you to go back and tell him that he needs to get his sorry ass up here, and do it himself."

"I can't do that."

"Why not?"

"Because he's dead, along with over seven thousand of our men."

"How is that possible? You were supposed to be facing a small group of commandos."

"I couldn't say for sure. We never managed to get close

enough to get a count. However, I can say that they have an amazing amount of firepower. After they ambushed our tanks, they shredded our APCs like they were made of papier-mâché."

"Get the hell out. Ming, get your ass back in here," the general screamed, furious at himself for overestimating Colonel Chou's abilities. "Who do we have ready to move?"

"Major Cao's detachment is about to leave," Lieutenant Ming said as he scrolled through their available resources. "They've already loaded their heavy tanks on the flatbeds, but we could get them unloaded in less than an hour."

"I'm not losing any more armor, just send Major Cao."

"With no support?"

"Yes, now get out."

Major Cao's forces had gotten to within fifteen miles of the bridge, when Harvey Weinstein's squadron returned. "There are fifty troop transports headed your way, but we'll take care of them," Colonel Weinstein said. "Let's get them boys," he ordered, as he dove to make the first pass.

Their missiles leaped out of the missile pods, and blazed a path of destruction through the line of closely packed vehicles.

"Like shooting fish in a barrel," Major Bingham, Colonel Weinstein's second in command yelled as he led the second wave in to continue the attack.

"Cease fire," Colonel Weinstein ordered as he looked down at the line of blasted piles of flaming junk.

"They've destroyed the column we sent," Lieutenant Ming reported.

"Damn," General Cheng said. "That's it, we're going

to pull back to San Francisco. Contact all the divisional commanders and let them know that we're moving out within the hour. Also, have General Sao start moving his army up from San Diego." When Lieutenant Ming didn't immediately respond, he asked, "What's the problem?"

"General Sung has ordered him to begin digging in."

"That's all I need, he's already second-guessing me."

JD HAD BEEN monitoring the battle, and when he received Colonel Weinstein's latest report, he called Jerome for an update. "How are you holding up?" General Drury asked.

"Surprisingly well," Colonel Brown said.

"I just got a report that Harvey's men destroyed a convoy of trucks that were headed your way."

"I heard, but I guess that means they're about to hit us again."

"I don't think so. Harvey made a quick pass down the coast, and he said it looked like they're pulling out."

"Damn, that's good news."

"It is, and even better, General Connelly's men will be there in eighteen hours to relieve you."

"Good deal, I'll pass the news along."

"Do that, and please convey my congratulations on a job well done."

"Will do, anything else for me?"

"No, but see me when you get back. I want to bounce a couple of ideas off of you."

CHAPTER 8

Three days later, General Drury had an interesting turn of events.

"I've got General Sanchez on the video," Molly said.

"What can I do for you, General?" JD asked.

"I've got a proposition for you, but first, congratulations on your great victory in Portland."

"Thanks, but I think we got lucky, and they underestimated us."

"No matter, a victory is a victory. I've just had an intriguing phone conversation with one of my contacts in Mexico. He's been talking with the drug cartel honchos, and they've offered to help."

"We're certainly not in any position to turn down help, but why would they help us? We've been trying to eradicate them for decades."

"The Chinese are bad for business, and they realize Mexico would be next in line."

"What are they proposing?"

"They have over a half million men positioned just across the border from San Diego, and they're prepared to move whenever you give the word."

"Excellent. Do I need to fly down there to work out an agreement?"

"I wouldn't recommend it. The Chinese have just gotten several F-35s back online, so it wouldn't be safe."

"First I've heard of it," JD admitted.

"They haven't put any in the air yet, but the first fifty are operational, and they've got another seventy, which are close."

"That's all we need. Other than a few old F-16s you sent us, we don't have any fixed wing aircraft, and they're no match for an F-35."

"No, they're not, but you might want to give William Sheldon a call."

"Will do. Anything else?"

"Not right now, but I hope to have something else for you in a few weeks."

WHEN HE HUNG up, JD told Molly, "Between Sanchez and Sheldon, it would be hard to tell which one has more surprises up their sleeve."

"True, but I don't know where we'd be without them."

"That's for sure, but speaking of William, I need to talk with him as well. Would you get him for me?" JD asked, as he playfully slapped her on the butt.

"Keep that up, and that's not all you'll get."

"IT'S GOOD TO see you again," William Sheldon said. "What can I do for you?"

"I've just finished talking with General Sanchez, and he suggested I give you a call. However, before we get to that, how do you know the general?"

"We first met at MIT. At one time he was the head of their intelligence organization, and we've swapped a few favors over the years. So, he told you about the F-35s?" William asked with a chuckle.

"Was I the last one in North America to find out?"

"Not quite, but let's get to why Sanchez told you to

call. You're probably too young to remember when they canceled the Raptor program."

"I remember reading about those. Wasn't it called the F-22?"

"Correct. It was intended to be the end-all of air supremacy fighters, and then the world changed, and it was serving a need that was no longer there, so they scrapped the program."

"Good history lesson, but how does it help me? Unless you've got a few in your hip pocket."

"It just so happens that I have six of them. They were some of the early preproduction prototypes, but they've got more whistles and bells than the production models."

"How the hell did you get ahold of aircraft like that? If I remember right, they spent billions on the program before they shut it down."

"Over sixty billion, but who's counting. I take it I've piqued your interest?"

"Piqued might be a bit of an understatement. How come Sanchez knew about them before I did?"

"He's the one that provided the spare parts to fix them. I didn't bother mentioning them before, because they weren't airworthy."

"I doubt you'll answer me, but who the hell are you, anyway? I know you're richer than dirt, but rich couldn't get shit like this done."

"If you play your cards right, the next time we have a drink together, I might just tell you. So, where do you want them delivered?"

"Is there any way you can get them to Portland?"

"Done. You need anything else?"

"Have you got any more of those Gatling gun sleds?"

"Nope, I sent everything we had, but I did manage to acquire several thousand surface-to-air missiles for your M270 MLRS (Multiple Launch Rocket Systems)."

"We'll take them. William, I'm sorry to cut you off, but I've got a staff meeting in ten minutes."

"No problem, and come visit when you get a chance."

TWO DAYS LATER, JD drove out to Portland International Airport to watch the Raptors land. Colonel Jesse James was the squadron commander, and he was the last to land.

"Colonel, I'm General Drury, and I sure am glad to see you and your men."

"Colonel Jesse James at your service, and yes, I'm distantly related to the outlaw."

"After reading your service record it would seem that you have a bit of outlaw in you as well," General Drury said.

"I've been accused of having a wild streak from time to time."

"Me too, so we should get along fine. Time is short, so let me get right to why I sent for you. The Chinese have managed to put some of the F-35s back in service, and I need them out of the way before we launch our next attack."

"Point them out, and we'll blow their asses out of the sky," the colonel said confidently.

"I like your spirit, but I've got to warn you that you're going to be badly outnumbered."

"Shouldn't be an issue."

MEANWHILE, DESPERATE TO hold on to the West Coast, General Sung had reached out to General Cheng to help him plan a counterattack. After several hours of debate, General Sung realized they faced certain defeat if something didn't change.

General Sung muted the call, and told Colonel Ma, "Once I get a count of their available aircraft, I want you and General Kao to put together a plan for an air-strike on the Americans.

"How many aircraft can you put up?" General Sung asked when he rejoined the call.

"We've got sixty-three F-35s, and a couple F-18s that we salvaged off of the *Ronald Reagan,*" General Cheng responded. "If you want to throw everything at them, I've also got almost a hundred attack helicopters."

"That should be enough for the task at hand. Our latest intelligence reports show they don't have anything but helicopters, and a few old F-16s. General Kao and Colonel Ma will work up a plan and get it over to you."

THREE DAYS LATER, General Kao held one last briefing.

"We're wheels up in thirty minutes. The helicopters are scheduled to reach the target twenty minutes before we arrive, and hopefully they'll distract them enough for us to be successful," General Kao, the onetime commanding general of the Chinese Air Force, told the group.

"No matter what the cost, it's imperative that you inflict maximum damage on their column," General Cheng reminded the group.

WHEN THE AMERICANS' radar picked up the planes from Edward's, the helicopters were only thirty minutes out, and closing fast.

General Connelly was holding his morning staff meeting when he heard the air-raid sirens go off. A few seconds later, he got a call from the command center.

He picked up the phone and bellowed, "What the hell is going on?"

"We've got a large number of incoming aircraft, at four hundred miles out, and closing fast.

"Damn it, they've beaten us to it. Scramble Colonel James's aircraft immediately."

"They're already rolling."

The general felt the ground shake, and then he heard the roar of their afterburners as they climbed straight up, off the end of the runway.

As they were rocketing upward, Colonel James caught sight of the ground-hugging helicopters, closing on General Connelly's position. "Heads up, you've got a large number of helicopters about fifty miles out," Colonel James warned.

The Chinese formation was at thirty thousand feet, and General Kao was flying lead as they closed on General Connelly's position at 600 mph.

Colonel James's tiny squadron was at maximum thrust, and within seconds of taking off, their An/APG-77 AESA radar systems picked up the incoming aircraft.

"Tallyho," Colonel James radioed. "They're two-fifty out, and we're moving to cut them off."

Since they were so close, the Raptors stayed at full burn until they were at altitude.

"Lock on and fire at will," Colonel James ordered, as they leveled out.

To minimize their radar profiles, the Raptors carried their missiles inside the aircraft. The weapons' bay doors were only open for a second at a time as the hydraulic arms pushed the missiles outside to send them on their way.

The F-22s only carried eight missiles each, so once their missiles were away, Colonel James ordered, "Switch to guns, and make them count."

Their M61A2 Vulcan Gatling Cannons could spew their 20mm rounds out at 6,600 rounds per minute, but it was definitely a weapon of last resort. Because at their maximum rate of fire, the 480 rounds they carried would only last for about five seconds. Their prototype missiles were stealth as well, so they hadn't triggered the enemy's missile warning systems. By the time they'd closed to gun range, there were burning aircraft spread all over the countryside. The survivors had scattered, and they never saw the Raptors until they swept in with their guns blazing. Their cannons inflicted devastating damage, but their limited ammunition only allowed them to shoot down eleven more aircraft. As they rocketed away from what was left of the attacking squadron, they'd shot down fifty-seven of the sixty-five aircraft in under thirty minutes.

"We've expended our ordnance, and are breaking off," Colonel James reported. "There's eight left, and they're headed your way."

"Well done, and we'll take it from here," General Connelly said. "Stay out of the area until you see it's over."

As COLONEL MA'S plan had dictated, the helicopter gunships arrived just before the main strike force, but as they swept in toward General Connelly's position, his missile crews were ready.

They had two hundred MLRS rocket launchers and when the helicopters came into range, their rockets filled the air like a swarm of malevolent wasps. The helicopters were at less than a hundred feet above the deck, so they had no chance to take evasive action before the missiles swept them from the sky like a fiery broom. The entire engagement lasted less than forty-five seconds, and it had left the countryside dotted with blasted, burning helicopters. Out of the ninety-seven helicopters that were attacked, not one survived.

"WHAT'S WITH ALL the smoke?" Lieutenant Jung asked, as the surviving jets banked and dove to make their attacks.

"Incoming," Captain Shelly, the missile team commander reported. He quickly checked the radar, and when he saw that there were only eight aircraft, he ordered, "Batteries one through fifteen, fire on lock."

As soon as the batteries got radar lock, they fired four missiles, and as General Connelly watched the missiles leaping out of the tubes, he remarked, "Poor bastards, they don't stand a chance."

KNOWING THAT THE fate of his army hung in the balance, General Cheng went to the command center to see how they were faring. "Have we hit them yet?" the general asked.

"The only communication we've had so far was from a Lieutenant Jung, and he reported that they'd taken heavy casualties from some sort of fighter attack."

"How is that possible, and why was a lieutenant reporting? What happened to General Kao?"

"No idea. The lieutenant was very excited, and he wasn't making much sense. He kept babbling something about Raptors. His last transmission said that they were about to initiate their attack on the main column."

Exasperated by the lack of useable information, the general asked, "How about the gunships?"

"When we last heard, they were ten miles out, and were preparing to make their first firing pass, but since then nothing."

The general closed his eyes for a couple of seconds, as he realized he was now faced with a dilemma. If he stayed to fight it out and lost, there wouldn't be anything between the American forces and the East Coast. However, if he retreated to conserve his forces, the enemy would be able to stream supplies and reinforcements in from their allies.

"I need to get a look at what's going on. Retask one of the surveillance satellites, and get me some pictures," the general ordered. "I'll be in my quarters, and when you get something, bring it to me immediately."

It was almost an hour before the general received the high-resolution photos. As he studied them, he could see their aircraft strewn about the countryside. He didn't even bother reading the assessment that accompanied the photos, because it was self-evident that they'd suffered a crushing defeat. He sat down at his desk, and established a video link with General Sung's headquarters in New York.

"I was hoping you had good news," General Sung remarked. "But by the look on your face, that's not the case."

"We don't really know what happened, but they evidently had some sort of advanced fighters, and—"

General Sung cut him off. "Cut through the bullshit. You got your ass kicked."

"That's putting it mildly. As you'd instructed, we sent everything we had, and there were no survivors."

"Shit." General Sung paused. "Here's what I need you to do. Pull all of your troops back to San Diego, and join up with General Sao. He's already dug in down there, so you should be able to hold out until I can get you some reinforcements."

A FEW MINUTES before sunset, General Connelly had Harvey Weinstein fly him around the countryside. As they flew over the battlefield, he started to get a sense of the devastation they'd just inflected on the attackers. The setting sun accented the plumes of smoke, which went on for miles, where the various aircraft had fallen.

Once he'd surveyed the scene, he landed and contacted General Drury. "I'm not sure what they have left, but we absolutely slaughtered them," General Connelly reported.

"Our spies tell us they sent everything they had," JD said. "What's your status?"

"They hit a few of our missile launchers, and we suffered twenty casualties, but we're in great shape. Unless they manage to hit us again, we'll be ready to move out by morning."

"I don't think that's likely. The latest satellite images show that they're pulling out."

"Great, we'll be hot on their trail."

"Go ahead and clear the San Francisco area, but hold there until you hear from me."

CHAPTER 9

As General Cheng retreated down the coast toward San Diego, they were taking a burnt earth approach, in an attempt to slow down General Connelly.

A few days after JD's conversation with General Sanchez, General Connelly contacted him with an update. "We're ready to go when you give us the word, but were' really going to struggle to have enough fuel. General Cheng destroyed virtually everything as they retreated."

"Just continue holding. General Sanchez has twelve supertankers headed your way," JD ordered.

"Shouldn't we be moving out?"

"I didn't tell you before, because I wasn't sure they were for real. The Mexicans are going to hit them in the morning, and if they have as big a force as Sanchez has led me to believe, you may not have to do much."

"That would be a nice surprise."

When the combined forces of what was left of the Mexican army and the drug lords launched their attack, it caught General Sao by surprise.

"We're under attack from the south," General Sao reported.

"What the hell do you want me to do about it?" General Cheng asked.

"Nothing, I just thought that you should know," the general said, thinking what an asshole Cheng was.

"How large a force?"

"The first reports were all over the board, so I sent our last remaining helicopter to check it out. It managed to send a few pictures back before they shot it down, and I would estimate that they have at least three hundred thousand men. They don't seem to have any armor, but they have a large number of what looks like pickup trucks, with heavy machine guns mounted on the roofs."

"I didn't think the Americans had any troops south of you."

"They don't, I think they're Mexican."

"Unlikely, most of their armies were wiped out in Central America."

"I heard the same thing, but they got more men from somewhere, and we're under heavy pressure."

"Do the best you can. We'll get there as fast as we can, but it will be several more days before we can reach you," General Cheng advised.

After he'd hung up with General Sao, General Cheng told his XO, "We're going to hold here until we see how this is going to play out."

THE BATTLE RAGED for three days before General Sao called back. "This may be my last transmission," General Sao reported. "We're cut off, and I don't think we're going to last much longer. In fact, I'm thinking about asking for terms."

"If you do, you'd better hope Sung doesn't ever get ahold of your sorry ass," General Cheng admonished. "You know how he feels about surrender."

"I know, but I don't think that I have any options left.

I've already lost over seventy thousand men, and the twenty thousand or so I have left are worn out."

"Understood. Good luck, and thanks for the heads-up. I guess we'll turn east."

Armando Castillo, the dominant drug lord in Mexico, was commanding the Mexican forces. Since Castillo had more men and material, the commander of what remained of the Mexican army had been more than happy to follow his lead.

After General Sao had surrendered, he and his men were taken to the San Diego Chargers stadium.

As General Sao and what remained of his men stood on the field, he wondered how it was going to turn out. There were over a thousand heavily armed soldiers guarding them, so he knew they had no chance of escape if they changed their minds.

General Sao had never been in the stadium before, and he had to admit it was impressive. As his mind wandered back to better days, he remembered watching the NFL games on satellite, and he could almost hear the cheering crowds as he looked around.

They'd been standing outside for several hours, and it was starting to get dark. When the stadium lights came on, he thought they might be bringing them some food, and maybe some blankets. Because even though it was Southern California, the nights could get chilly.

A few minutes later people began streaming into the stadium, and in little over an hour, the stadium was filled to standing-room only.

By then, General Sao was concerned. He was about to walk over and ask the officer in charge what was going on, when Armando Castillo came walking out onto the field, flanked by more than a hundred of his henchmen.

The general could hear them snarling and cursing as

they pushed through the crowd toward him. When he finally got a good look at Armando's posse, their massive, long-haired, heavily tattooed bodies struck fear into his heart. "My God, they look like Satan's spawn," the general muttered under his breath.

JD had been following the action all day, but he hadn't heard anything for a couple of hours.

"You'd better come and watch this," Molly yelled from the next room.

"What's up?" JD asked.

"One of the San Diego TV stations is broadcasting from Charger stadium, and it looks like something's going down."

A bit of a showman, Armando was wearing a wireless microphone so the TV audience would be able to hear what was about to take place. The cameras were following him as he made his way toward General Sao. He walked with a bit of a limp, from an unsuccessful assassination attempt by the Chinese. The explosion had shattered his leg, and killed his wife and kids. He'd never been a benevolent man, but their deaths had left him filled with an all-consuming black rage toward the Chinese, and General Sao in specific.

He walked up to General Sao. "So, General. We meet at last, you sorry bastard."

Taken aback by the vehemence of his words, General Sao asked, "Have we met?"

"Only by your cowardly actions. Your people slaughtered my family, and I mean to return the favor."

"When we agreed to surrender, we were promised fair treatment."

"And fair treatment you shall receive," Armando told him, as he nodded to his men.

Two of his massive bodyguards grabbed the general from behind, and pushed him down on his knees. They forced his head down as Armando drew his machete, and struck a savage blow to the general's neck, beheading him with one stroke. As the general's head fell to one side, the blood gushed out of his neck and sprayed Armando.

"A pig even in death," he growled. He wiped the blood off of his face, and then he spit on the general's still twitching body. "Behead the rest of these animals, and make sure that the cameras record each one," he said, as he turned on his heel and walked away.

"My God, he means to slaughter them all," Molly said.

"So he does," JD said. "He's always been noted for his cavalier attitude toward brutality, and they did murder his family."

"You can't stand by while they slaughter those people in cold blood."

"The hell I can't," he said. "I'm not sure that I wouldn't do the same thing in his place."

"But they're murdering defenseless people."

"How is it different from them murdering our families on national TV? Don't expect me to feel sorry for them."

Their eyes met briefly, before he turned and left the room.

She'd only rarely seen that side of him, and even though she loved and trusted him completely, he could be scary as hell.

The next morning JD got a call from General Sanchez.

"I'm sorry about what happened yesterday."

"Shit happens. Do you think you can control that animal?"

"Control! No, I don't believe anyone can. However, I may be able to reason with him now that he's extracted his revenge on the man who killed his family."

"Is Castillo going to follow up his attack?"

"Not likely, I believe he'll try to consolidate his hold on Southern California."

"So he thinks that we're going to let him keep Southern California?"

"He knows that you've got more than you can handle, so he's going to take full advantage of it. I know you don't like it, but if it were me, I would ignore him for the time being," General Sanchez advised.

"I will, but at some point I'm going to circle back and deal with him. I'm not going to allow an animal like him to enslave our people."

"I think you'll find that he's not interested in killing his customers, but we can worry about him later. What are you going to do about General Cheng and his men?"

"I'm going after them. However, it's going to be a week or two before we can be ready to give chase."

"A few weeks one way or the other isn't going to matter in the long term."

THAT NIGHT, AFTER they'd made love, Molly and JD were lying in bed talking.

"What's bothering you?" JD asked. "Are you still fretting about what happened?"

"No, I've got something else that I need to tell you, and I'm afraid you'll be upset with me."

"Silly, there's not much you could do that would get me upset with you."

"I'm pregnant," she blurted out.

"What!"

"See, I was right. You're upset."

"Not upset, but I am surprised. I thought you were taking something?"

"I am, but the doctor said sometimes it just doesn't work. I'm about nine weeks along."

He pulled her on top of him and gave her a long kiss. "I couldn't be happier. I just wasn't expecting it."

"Oh goody, I've wanted to tell you all week, but you always seem to have some disaster going."

"I'm afraid that's not likely to change in the near future, but this is wonderful news."

Just before he fell asleep, JD thanked God for Molly and their unborn child, and asked him to help keep them safe.

Life is eternal; and love is immortal; and death is only a horizon; and a horizon is nothing save the limit of our sight.

—ROSSITER W. RAYMOND

PART 12

CHAPTER 1

JD was on his way to a staff meeting, when Harvey Weinstein pulled him aside. "If you've got a minute, I'd like for you to listen to what Joseph Enos has to say."

"Sure, no problem, Harvey."

"Thank you for taking a couple of minutes to hear me out," Joseph Enos said. "I'm the president of the Intertribal Council of Arizona, and I'd like to offer my people's help."

"What did you have in mind?" JD asked.

"If you'll give us weapons, we'll make the Chinese's lives miserable as they try to cross our lands."

"You'll just end up getting a lot of your people killed."

"What's so unusual about that? We've been getting kicked around for over a century. Besides, it's our country too."

"I get it, and anything you can do to help will be much appreciated." JD wrote out a quick note and handed it to Harvey. "This will let you draw the weapons he wants out of the armory. I'm sorry to cut you short, but I've got a meeting."

WHEN GENERAL CHENG'S column left Flagstaff on I-40 moving east, Joseph's snipers started picking them off.

Three days later, General Cheng was holding a morning status meeting before they moved out. "We lost another twenty-two men yesterday," Colonel Guo reported.

"That's better than yesterday. Have your snipers managed to kill any?" General Cheng asked.

"None that we can verify. We've found a couple of blood trails, so we think they're dragging their dead away with them. We need to do something, because the men are afraid to be out in the open. We've caught several of them taking a dump in the back of the APCs."

"Disgusting pigs."

You're one to talk, you've got a toilet in your trailer, the colonel thought to himself.

The general could see the colonel's contempt, but he let it pass. He'd lost his last three aides, and he didn't feel like breaking in another one.

The last item on the agenda was their equipment status. "Weren't we supposed to receive twenty helicopter gunships?" the general asked.

"They should be here by tomorrow afternoon, did you have something in mind?"

"Don't let them join the column. Have them land about thirty miles in front of us. The next time the snipers hit us, I want to see if we can take them by surprise for a change."

Two days later, Enos's snipers attacked as General Cheng's men were getting started for the day.

"Air six, we're under attack from the east," Colonel Guo called to the helicopters.

"Roger that, we're on our way."

The two man sniper team was firing from a small mesa, and they never had a chance when the gunships opened fire.

"The sniper team has been naturalized."

"Retrieve the bodies and bring them to us. The general wants to show the men that we're taking action," Colonel Guo instructed.

When the helicopters landed, the general rushed out to inspect the bodies. "Is this supposed to be a joke?" he screamed. The younger one looked like he was twelve, and was wearing a T-shirt, jeans, and sneakers. The second sniper was probably seventy, and was dressed in the battle dress of his ancestors.

"What did you do, shoot up a day care and a carnival?" As the general turned away, disgusted at the turn of events, he told them, "Just bury them; I'm not going to let the men see that we're being terrorized by old men and boys."

As they continued eastward, General Cheng's army was finding it slow going, because Enos's men were blowing up the bridges.

"This is taking a lot longer than we'd planned, and where the hell is the convoy with our fuel?" General Cheng asked.

"They just left Albuquerque, New Mexico," Colonel Guo said.

Colonel Wong knew General Cheng's column was running low on fuel, so he'd decided to drive straight through. His command vehicle was bringing up the rear, and he could see the brightly lit trucks stretching out in front of him. The lead tanker was almost to the top of the steep grade when the side of the mountain erupted.

"My God, what was that?" his driver exclaimed when he saw the cloud of fire. As Colonel Wong watched in horror, a quarter-mile-long strip of the roadway collapsed. As the fuel tankers tumbled into the rugged gorge below, they were exploding into pinwheels of fire.

"Stop, you damn fool," Colonel Wong ordered.

It took almost five minutes for the thunderous

explosions to die down, and by then the rugged gorge was engulfed in a river of fire.

Caught up in the moment, Colonel Wong and his men worked through the night, as they frantically searched for survivors.

It was almost dusk the next day when General Cheng cornered Colonel Guo. "Shouldn't those fuel trucks be here by now?" General Cheng asked.

"The convoy was attacked last night," Colonel Guo explained.

"How bad?"

"They've lost a third of the trucks, and I-40 is impassable. Colonel Wong wasted an entire day looking for survivors, and now they've got to backtrack, and reroute."

"We need another plan."

"There's a refinery about seventy miles from here, and if it's still intact, we might be able to get fuel there."

"Send some of the APCs and three thousand men on ahead to make sure those damn savages don't blow it up," the general ordered.

IT WAS THREE hours before sunup when the main body caught sight of the refinery lights. The captain they'd sent to secure the site met them at the turnoff.

"It wasn't heavily guarded, so we didn't have any trouble taking it. I've set a perimeter around the refinery, and we're ready to start fueling."

"Great work, Captain," the general said, visibly relieved that something had finally gone right. "Great work, but too easy," he realized. He turned to Colonel Guo and screamed, "Send everyone you've got to reinforce the perimeter, and scramble the gunships."

The Indians' strike force was about to launch their attacks when the gunships caught them. They'd been counting on the cover of darkness, but the gunships were equipped with heat sensors and night vision, so it was like shooting fish in a barrel.

When the general received the reports, he gloated. "Finally, we managed to kick the shit out of someone. Even if it was only a ragtag bunch of savages."

GENERAL DRURY WAS holding his morning meeting when they received the news.

"We've just learned that General Cheng has wiped out most of Enos's men."

JD immediately called to verify the report. When Enos answered, JD was relieved. "Good, you're still alive. Sorry to hear about your men, but you can take heart that you've caused them a lot of pain."

"Thanks for the kind words, but I underestimated them, and I got a lot of good men killed."

"I'm afraid it happens, and it comes with the job. If you're open to it, I would like to offer you a position on my staff."

"I'd be honored, but could I have a few days to arrange a service for my men?"

"Of course, but be ready to work when you get here."

SINCE THEY'D MANAGED to acquire fuel, JD realized General Cheng was slipping out of his grasp.

JD decided to hit him one last time, as they were traversing the mountains on the other side of Albuquerque.

He called Jesse James in to explain what he wanted.

"About time. We've been sitting on our asses for weeks."

The mission was at the outer limits of their range, so Colonel James knew they couldn't loiter. When they were in range, they launched their long-range missiles, and started their descent toward the column.

When the missiles ripped into the column, General Cheng asked, "Where the hell did those come from?"

"We've got aircraft coming in from the west," Colonel Guo reported.

"All right boys, lets drop the rest of this shit down their throats," Colonel James ordered, as they dove toward the convoy.

"Shoot them down, you idiot," General Cheng ordered.

When the F-22s weren't carrying wing-mounted accessories, they were virtually undetectable. But with auxiliary fuel tanks and the wing mounts for the JDAMs, they presented enough of a radar signature for the Chinese to pick them up.

"Fire when you get a lock," Colonel Guo ordered.

In the excitement of the moment, the Chinese missile commander launched every missile they had loaded. As the hundred and seventy SAMs leapt out of the missile tubes, it was an impressive sight. Even with the extraordinary number of missiles coming at them, the F-22s managed to evade most of them, however, one of their aircraft got caught in the swarm of missiles, and was blasted out of the sky.

As he watched it spiral to earth, Colonel James was pissed. "Damn it, he wasn't paying attention. Hit the afterburners, and let's get the hell out of here."

The sixteen JDAMs they'd dropped had been deadly accurate as they traced a ribbon of destruction through the heart of the convoy.

"What's the damage?" General Cheng asked.

"Sixty-seven vehicles and eleven hundred casualties."

"Is it true that we managed to hit one of their aircraft?" the general asked.

"Yes, we did," Colonel Guo said. "We fired way too many missiles, but we did hit one."

"We've got a lot more missiles than they do aircraft."

"Give the missile battery commander a promotion, and set him up with some whores at the next town."

"We hit them hard, but we got sloppy, and lost an aircraft," Colonel James reported.

"Not good. I need you to stand down. We're going to need you when we go up against General Sung."

Disappointed, the colonel started to protest, but he realized JD was right. "You're the boss, but don't forget about us."

"Not likely."

The next day, General Drury laid out the next phase of their campaign.

"We're going to hold at the west side of Texas," JD said. "I want you to keep the pressure on them until you reach the border, and then I want you to stop and dig in."

"Understood, but why stop there?" General Connelly asked.

"We've got a lot of territory to defend, and while we've got an adequate supply chain for now, we're still desperately short of personnel."

As General Cheng continued retreating eastward, General Sung called with an update. "I know that we haven't done what we said we would, but I'm sending you a squadron of fighter aircraft to cover your retreat."

"How long can I hold on to the aircraft?"

"They're yours, use them as you see fit."

After he'd hung up, General Cheng turned to Colonel Guo, and asked, "Have you checked out that lead we received?"

"As far as we can tell, it's legit."

"Excellent. Here's what I want you to do."

The group JD was traveling with had set up camp at a small abandoned army base, and JD had scheduled a 0300 briefing.

JD and Molly had set the alarm for 0200.

"You all right in there?" JD asked, when he heard Molly throwing up in the bathroom.

"Yes, but you'd better go on, I'll be there when I stop puking."

Forty minutes later, Molly had just left their quarters, when six missiles vaporized the building. The explosions had knocked her down, but other than some ringing in her ears, she was unhurt. JD was holding the meeting in an adjacent building, and when he heard the explosions, he ran outside.

"Are you all right?" he asked as he helped her up.

"I think so, but what happened?"

"A sneak attack, and by the looks of it, they were targeting me."

Molly was visibly shaken, and JD was worried that the stress might hurt the baby.

A couple of nights later they were lying in bed talking, when he broached the subject. "I talked with William Sheldon this afternoon, and he's offered to put you up until the baby's born, and I think we should take him up on it."

"I don't want to leave you," Molly pleaded.

"I would feel a lot better if you were someplace safe." He could see that she was about to cry, so he pulled her to him. "Look, I don't want to be apart from you either, but I think it's a good idea if you stay with him for a while. I'll fly down and see you every chance I get, and I promise that I'll be there when the baby is born."

"OK, if that's what you want, but I don't have to like it."

CHAPTER 2

JD hadn't managed to get down to see her as often as he'd hoped, but when Molly gave birth to their baby girl, Tabatha, he was there by her side.

"She's beautiful, just like her mother," JD said.

When the doctor laid Tabatha on Molly's chest, she said, "I love both of you so much. I've never been happier."

Two days later they were feeling well enough to go back to William Sheldon's ranch. He'd set them up in one of the wings of his sprawling ranch house, and it was the nicest place either of them had ever stayed in.

"It's really sweet of William to take us in like this," Molly said.

"He's been a good friend and ally," JD agreed.

When Molly and the baby laid down for a nap, he stepped out onto the patio to watch the horses playing in the pasture.

I never tire of coming here, he thought to himself. He heard the baby rustling around, and as he looked in at them sleeping, he thought, *And I know William will take care of you guys.*

* * *

TABATHA WAS ONLY sleeping a few hours at a time, so after dinner, Molly and the baby both turned in for the night.

"Let's go out on the veranda and have a cigar and a drink," William Sheldon suggested.

The only light was coming from a couple of torches they had burning to keep the flies and mosquitoes away. As they sat sipping the fine Kentucky bourbon, JD asked, "Would this be a good time for some answers?"

"Sure. Like you, I started in the military, but I was recruited into a hidden, and darker side of our government. I've spent the last thirty years playing the part of the eccentric Texas billionaire, and while I am a billionaire, the seeds of my success came from the black project funding. Whenever our government needed to intercede, or take down a government, or even a criminal organization, I've been the one who took care of it. I've funneled money and arms to some of the worst despots and mass murderers of our time. Hell, I'm the one who provided the funding that enabled the SASR to seize power in South America."

Startled, JD asked, "What? How could you have backed a group dedicated to wiping out our way of life?"

"It didn't start out that way. I had an agreement with Raul Mascuranus, that after Hugo Chávez formed the SASR, he was supposed to have assassinated him, and take it over. Unfortunately, Raul was killed in a car wreck before he could carry out our plan, and well, the rest is history. Luckily, most of my other operations were a lot more successful."

"So that's how you get all the weapons, and know people like General Sanchez?"

"Him, and many more like him, including our new best ally, Armando Castillo."

They talked far into the night; by the time JD went to bed, he had a much better understanding of William.

JD stayed with Molly and the baby for several days, before he had to get back to work. "I'll call you every day, and I'll try to get back down here as often as I can," JD promised.

"You'd better," Molly said. "There are lots of cute cowboys running around here."

JD had the best intentions, but he didn't make back until Christmas Eve.

William picked JD up at the airfield, so they got to talk for a few minutes.

"I don't know whether Tabatha will still be awake, but Molly was trying to keep her up," William said. "Molly has been like a cat on a hot tin roof all day."

"I've missed them so much, I just couldn't get back any sooner. General Cheng is a tough adversary."

"At least you've managed to fight them to a stalemate."

"Unfortunately, at this point we're closer to World War I, than World War III, but we're holding our own."

William's wife was long dead, so he hadn't celebrated Christmas in years. However, with Tabatha and Molly staying with him, he'd gone all-out when he'd decorated his great room.

They'd set up a spare crib for Tabatha, and Molly was sitting on the couch, waiting for JD to arrive.

When they walked in, Molly squealed with joy, and ran over to JD. They kissed for almost a minute before they came up for air.

"You guys look so happy," William said. "I sure do miss my family, but I guess it's the penalty for living too long. There are a few things from me under the tree, and I'd love to stay and visit, but I'm feeling a little under the weather."

"Thanks so much for taking care of the girls," JD said, as he patted William on the back.

"It's been my pleasure. They've brought life back to

my home, and for that I'm eternally grateful. With all the crap we've gone through, it's nice to see that there can still be some semblance of normalcy." William excused himself for the night, and they had the great room all to themselves.

They couldn't have wished for a better setting. The Christmas tree was surrounded with gifts, and even though it was almost twenty feet tall, it looked small in the massive room. The gigantic rock fireplace had a roaring fire, and for the first time in decades, there was a light snow falling outside.

As Molly cuddled up to JD on the couch she said, "I can't imagine a more perfect Christmas." As they kissed, and then made love on the floor in front of the fireplace, life had never been better.

A FEW DAYS before, General Sung and Colonel Ma had been discussing their situation.

"So, have you got a handle on this General Drury?" General Sung asked.

"Yes, I have. He was a colonel in their Special Operations group, and a protégé of General Jeffries."

"Jeffries seems to have done an excellent job, because he's been kicking our ass. Have you found any weaknesses we can exploit? Friends, family, etc."

"He's an orphan, and the couple who raised him are both dead. However, he got married last year, and we've learned that his wife had a little girl not long ago. We were even able to obtain a picture of them."

"Give me everything you've got, and make sure you keep tabs on them." General Sung paused for several seconds before he asked, "Is there a chance he's going to try to see his family?"

"Since it's Christmas, I would assume so."

"OK, here's what I want you to do, and you'd better not screw it up," General Sung threatened.

* * *

A COUPLE OF hours before sunup, on New Year's morning, fifteen F-35s came roaring across the ranch's pastures at less than a hundred feet. Following close behind were four choppers, carrying eighty elite commandos.

JD was in one of the conference rooms, on an early morning staff call, and he never heard them approaching until all hell broke loose.

The missiles, and then a string of incendiary bombs, tore a path of fiery destruction across the compound, and when they hit the main house, it went up in a series of massive explosions.

As the ceiling began to collapse, JD instinctively took cover under the heavy mahogany conference table. The table protected him from most of the falling debris, but the massive concussion from the explosions knocked him out for over an hour.

The electricity was out all over the ranch, but as JD crawled out from the rubble, the light from the raging fires let him see just how bad it was.

Their rooms were just down the hall, and as he stumbled through the rubble, into what was left of the hallway, he was terrified of what he might find.

He could feel the heat from the fires ahead of him, but the smoke was so thick that he couldn't really see. The heat became too intense for him to continue, but he remembered there was a fire extinguisher on the wall. His eyes were burning, and he was struggling to breathe, as the pungent black smoke filled his lungs. He pulled his shirt up over his nose and mouth, and started groping blindly along the wall for the extinguisher. After what seemed like forever, his hand touched the glass cover, but as he struggled to break the glass, he passed out.

When he came to, they had him laid out on a tarp on the west side of the house. He pulled the oxygen mask off, and propped himself up on one elbow to try to figure out where he was. His heart felt like it was going to burst when he caught sight of raging inferno. As he struggled to get up, a large section of the roof caved in, throwing sparks high into the crisp clear sky.

"Lie still until I can check you out," one of the medics told him, as he pushed him back down.

"Get off of me, I've got to find Molly and Tabatha," JD demanded. JD pushed the medic away and struggled to his feet. "It feels like a mule kicked me in the chest."

"That's because we had to give you CPR after they dragged you out of there. Now lie back down, and let me see if we broke anything."

"I don't give a shit about that; I've got to find my family."

As he struggled to stay upright, what was left of the walls collapsed into the raging inferno.

"Lie back down and do as he asks, there's nothing you can do," William Sheldon told him in a raspy, barely audible voice. "We'll find them, but you can't go back in there," he said, as he gasped for breath.

They were still arguing about it when Jerry Judson, the head of William's security team, came rushing up. "We killed several, but the rest got away before we could stop them."

"What the hell are you babbling about?" William asked.

"There was a large group of commandos that landed right after the first strike. They went straight for the wing where General Drury and his family are staying. I'm surprised the general didn't run into them."

"The hall was impassable," JD explained.

"They were kicking our ass, but they suddenly broke it off, and made a run for it. We tried to stop them, but one of their gunships kept us pinned down until they'd made their getaway."

"Get my chopper warmed up. I'm going after them," JD ordered.

"It was destroyed, so we'll have to fly one in," Jerry Judson said. "Besides, they've been in the air for almost two hours."

William was struggling to stay conscious, but he managed to tell JD, "We'll even up with them, just don't rush off and get yourself killed."

Before JD could respond, William passed out.

Several more paramedics finally arrived from town, and started triaging the rest of the wounded.

"Check out Mr. Sheldon first, he's in bad shape," Jerry Judson told the EMT.

As they went to work on William, another team got JD to lie back down. The first thing they did was start an IV.

"What the hell do you think you're doing?" he asked. "Stop that shit right now, I've got things to take care of."

Ignoring his orders, the paramedic managed to get some painkillers and a sedative into the IV.

As he was about to pass out, JD warned, "I'll throw all of your asses in the brig if you transport me."

"What do you think?" the senior EMT asked after he was out.

"If it was me, I'd leave him be," Jerry Judson advised.

It was almost three in the afternoon before JD regained consciousness, and by then the fire had burned out enough for them to begin searching the rubble.

"Why isn't this man in the hospital?" the fire chief, Captain Fredrick, asked.

"My wife and baby are missing, and I need get in there and find them," JD said.

"We'll find them, but you need to let us do our job."

JD was still groggy, but he managed to tell him, "OK. The room we were staying in is roughly in the middle of the west wing."

"All right, son, I give you my word, we'll find them."

Although it was only two hundred feet long, it took over forty minutes for them to pick their way through the still-smoking debris.

The captain had suspected what he'd find, but it still stunned him to see their charred bodies. "I've got them," Captain Fredrick called out over the radio.

Their bodies were charred beyond recognition, but he could see that the baby was still clutched in Molly's arms, as she'd tried to shield her from the flames. He'd been a firefighter over thirty years, but he'd never gotten used to the horror of what a fire could do.

The captain could see that JD had struggled to his feet, and was starting toward him. So he called to his men, "Keep him over there. There's no reason for him to see them this way.

"Get over here with a body bag," Captain Fredrick ordered.

"I'm so sorry, but they didn't make it," Captain Fredrick said as he put his arm around JD. "Where would you like us to send the bodies?"

"I need to see them," JD begged.

"Son, you need to trust me on this; you don't want to see them."

JD could be a hard man, but he broke down completely, as the reality of what the chief was saying hit him.

"I'll make sure that they're taken care of," William promised, as he struggled to his feet and put his arm around him. "The captain's right, you need to remember them as they were."

William was trying to think of something that would get JD's mind off it, when Jerry Judson walked over and interrupted, "General, your replacement helicopter is here."

"Why don't you go on back and see if you can get a

line on the bastards that did this," William Sheldon said as he slumped to the ground.

JD bent down to help him. "I will, if you let them take you to the hospital."

"Deal, now get the hell out of here, before I pass out again."

As he promised, William had taken care of all the funeral arrangements. He even had a special casket made, so they could bury them just as they had found them, with Tabatha wrapped in Molly's arms for all eternity.

Five days later, JD buried Molly and Tabatha in the small rural cemetery, beside Leroy and Emma. After the preacher and the other mourners had left, JD had stayed until they'd closed the grave, and the workers had left.

A dense fog was rolling in as he kneeled beside their grave. The cold wet mist was swirling around him, as he was sobbing and praying to God to take care of them.

As he'd spent most of his life, he was again left alone in the world. As much as he wanted to, he knew that he couldn't go off and grieve, because he still had a war to fight.

When he was finished saying his good-byes, and asking God's forgiveness for what he'd done and what he was about to do, he got up off his knees, and stood shivering on the bleak Oklahoma plain.

As he peered through swirling mist, he vowed, with a white-hot fury in his heart, that no matter the cost, he would extract his revenge on the ones who'd killed them. He took one last look at their grave, turned on his heel, and returned to war.

When he landed back at his headquarters General Connelly met him.

"I can't believe that I let them get killed," JD lamented. "I thought they'd be safe at William's."

"It's wasn't your fault, they were tipped off."

"Who would do that?" he asked, suddenly furious.

"It was one of William's men. They'd taken his family hostage, and he was trying to get them back."

JD didn't say anything, so General Connelly said, "We have him in custody, what do you want us to do with him?"

"Not one damn thing. I know exactly how he feels."

The general nodded in agreement, but he didn't tell JD that they'd already killed the man's family, before they'd managed to turn him.

CHAPTER 3

The day after the attack, General Sung had called for a report.

"Well, did we get him?" General Sung asked.

"Unfortunately, no," General Cheng reported.

"How about the contingency plan?"

"Yes, that went just as you'd planned."

"Excellent, and you took care of the strike team as well?"

"As soon as they landed." General Cheng was about to tell him how he'd done it, when he heard a round being chambered behind him. He tried to draw his sidearm, but his aide's bullet struck him just behind the ear before he could get it out. The shot had been fired from close range, and when the bullet blew the side of his skull out, it sprayed blood all over the papers on his desk.

"Well done, Captain," General Sung said. "Contact General Chern and let him know that he just got a promotion."

WHEN JD LEARNED William was getting out of the hospital, he flew down to check on him. William was waiting for him when he landed. He wasn't fully recovered, so he had his driver bring JD over to his armored limo.

"Thanks for coming down, but it wasn't necessary," William Sheldon said, wheezing a little. "Sorry, this damned oxygen dries out my throat. The doc said that I'd probably have to use it for the rest of my life. I'm not trying to make excuses, but the murderous bastards caught us by complete surprise," William said.

"It's nobody's fault but mine. I should have never gotten married."

"That's bullshit, boy. I'd gotten to know Molly, and I've never seen anyone who loved more than her. If she were here, she would tell you that she didn't regret a minute of your lives together."

JD struggled to answer, but he broke down in tears before he could get the words out.

William pulled him to him with his one good arm. "It's all right, son. You cry it out, and then we'll figure out how to kill all the bastards."

During the ride to William's ranch, JD said, "This isn't the way to your house."

"I've decided not to rebuild the main house. I had it bulldozed, and I'm having a memorial park built to honor Molly and Tabatha's memory."

JD didn't say anything, but William could see he was about to break down again. William just let him be until they pulled up in front of the guesthouse.

It was over ten thousand square feet, and just as nice as the big house had been. He'd turned the den into a war room, and when they walked in, JD couldn't help but comment when he saw the array of flat-screen TVs and computers. "Damn, this has got more cool shit than any of my briefing centers."

When they sat down, William started his pitch. "I've been working on this since I got out of the hospital, and I'd like for you to hear me out before you say no."

"Of course, but why wouldn't you think I'd be open to anything you'd have to say?"

"Because it has many unknown implications."

"What doesn't these days? Lay it on me."

"I've spent the last two weeks working out an agreement with our new friend, and benefactor, General Sanchez. He's already gotten commitments from virtually every South American government to provide him with all the personnel he needs."

"To what end?" JD asked.

"He wants to open up a second front, and he thinks he can be ready within six months."

"That's great news, but what does he want in return?"

"That's what's really strange. I'd expected him to ask for control of the rest of South America. Instead, he wants us to annex South America, when the war is over."

"Huh?"

"That was my reaction as well. When I asked him why, all he would say is that he truly believes it's the only way our two continents will be able to maintain our freedom. He said that when the war is over, he will step aside, or fill a role in the new government, if we ask him to."

"Why are you telling me this? It's not my call. I'm a warrior, not a politician."

"I think you're selling yourself short. We've already discussed it at length, and we all feel you'll have another role to fill when this horror is over." William could see that JD was struggling with what he was proposing, so he moved on. "Look, we can cross that bridge when the time comes. How do you feel about the general's offer?"

"I've got no problem with anyone who wants to kill the Chinese."

"Good, now let's go over some of the stuff Sanchez has for us," William said, just before he started coughing up blood.

"That doesn't look good."

"The docs say it won't kill me. However, it is a little disconcerting."

William grabbed a sheath of papers off of one of the tables, and handed it to JD. "Here's a list of some of the stuff General Sanchez and I have rounded up for the operation."

As JD scanned the list, he whistled and said, "Damn, where did you manage to find Sukhoi Su-47 jets? I thought we destroyed them all."

"We did, but it seems the Russians were playing their normal bullshit games, and had given the plans for the aircraft to the SASR. They never built very many, but the general has thirty-two of them. He also has a few of the T-97 main battle tanks. The Russians never even built them for themselves, but I guess the SASR had more money, because they have fifty-two of the bad boys."

"What are these?" JD asked, pointing to the last entry on the page.

"This is where I got the idea to sled mount the A10 Gatling guns. The general has several hundred Volvo trucks outfitted with knockoffs of the A10's Gatling guns. He sent me a video of a firing test, and I've got to tell you it's a very impressive weapon system."

"I suppose they've got the depleted uranium rounds to go with them?"

"Of course."

"Where does he intend to launch his attack?"

"He's got a half million men staged in the Bahamas, and they'll make an amphibious landing in Florida, and then move up the East Coast."

"How is he going to move that many men without the Chinese blowing them out of the water?"

"He's got a thousand Stena HS1500 catamaran ferries, and the damn things will do over forty knots. With the Su-47s flying cover, he thinks they can pull it off."

"Impressive. Do you think he'd build some of those Volvos for us?"

"There are already twenty-five on the way to San Francisco. Now, if you're amenable, I'd like to get the general on the video and solidify our agreement."

"Let's do it."

Four weeks later, the ship carrying the heavily modified Volvo trucks arrived in San Francisco. JD just happened to be in town for a meeting with General Connelly, and when they finished, General Connelly said, "I think we're done, let's go down and take a look at those new trucks."

When they offloaded the first Volvo, they had them pull it over to a nearby empty parking lot. As they walked around it, JD commented, "Damn, this is impressive. They've replaced the cab with a Kevlar shell, and then armor plated that. The windows are bullet resistant up to a twenty-millimeter round, and the tires are solid rubber."

"I'll bet those things are lethal," General Connelly said, when he spotted the Gatling gun mounted on the roof.

"The Chinese commander in Portland found that out the hard way," JD said. "They've installed the ammunition drum in the sleeper, and if you need more capacity, they have an attachment that allows you to belt feed the gun from a semitrailer. I've seen the specs, but I would love to see it in action."

"Good idea, let's try it out on that tank over there. They dropped it when they were unloading, and it's unrepairable," General Connelly suggested, sounding a lot like a kid with a new toy.

JD slid behind the wheel and fired it up. When the diesel roared to life, he turned the truck toward the wrecked tank. "I think this turns on the heads-up display," JD said as he flipped one of the toggle switches. He used the joystick to train the gun, and punched the fire button.

The Gatling gun spewed the 30mm depleted uranium shells out at 3,900 rounds per minute, so it only took a few seconds to get a sense of its firepower.

General Connelly let out a shrill whistle and said, "Shit, I can see daylight through the son-of-a-bitch."

"That was quite a show," JD agreed.

They heard a commotion outside, as seventy-five heavily armed sentries surrounded the truck.

"I'd better get out and call them off," General Connelly said, as he climbed down.

A FEW WEEKS later, Colonel Ma walked in and handed General Sung a folder of satellite reconnaissance photos.

"What's this?" the general asked.

"Proof that General Sanchez is up to something. They've got a flotilla of ships in the harbor, and we've had reports of several hundred-thousand troops in the area."

"Invasion?"

"Without question."

"How are they coming with the aircraft?" General Sung asked.

"We have three squadrons available, with more on the way."

"Have them moved to, what was the name of that old Air Force base?"

"Homestead."

"Yeah that's the one. Make sure those Coast Guard cutters we commandeered are standing by as well. If Sanchez is foolish enough to try something, we'll be ready."

* * *

FIVE WEEKS LATER, General Sanchez's car stopped on the highway that ran along the beach. He walked down to the edge of the water, and looked out at the vast array of ships anchored in the bay. They'd just finished loading the troops, and everything was ready. He took a deep breath before he turned his aide, and ordered, "Launch the attack."

While his aide was forwarding his command to the flotilla, the general called JD on his satellite phone. "We're on our way, and God willing, we should have a beachhead by nightfall."

"Excellent, everything is ready on our end. Good luck, and Godspeed."

THERE WERE A thousand and sixty ships in all, and as they spread out and came up to speed, they made an impressive sight as they sliced through the water at forty knots.

The Chinese forces had been on high alert for weeks, so they knew almost immediately when the flotilla left the harbor.

"They're at sea, and we've just launched our fighters and the frigates," the Homestead commander reported.

"Excellent, and make sure you keep us updated," Colonel Ma instructed.

As GENERAL SANCHEZ stood watching the ships pull away, his aide reported, "They've launched their aircraft."

"Scramble the fighters. Let's see who surprises who."

Like the F-22s, Su-47s had been designed to be air superiority fighters, and their top speed was more than Mach 3. The F-35s were a close match for the Su-47s, but they were outnumbered by a three to one margin, and in less than twenty minutes, they'd been blasted out of the sky. As the catamarans swept past the burning fuels slicks that marked the aircraft's watery graves, their wakes spread the fire out behind them.

"THEY'VE LAUNCHED THE invasion," Colonel Ma said.

"Have Colonel Wong's squadrons hit them yet?" General Sung asked.

"They're up, but we haven't received any action reports yet."

Thirty minutes later, Colonel Ma came rolling back in, and said, "We've lost them all."

"What have you lost this time?" the general asked.

"All three squadrons we sent up, including Colonel Wong's command and control aircraft."

"What the hell happened?"

"Just before we lost contact, Colonel Wong had reported they were engaged with a large number of Su-47s, and that they were taking heavy casualties."

"Are you sure? I didn't think there were any of those left."

"The only thing I know for sure is that the radar showed the last of our aircraft went down a few minutes later."

"How about the frigates?"

"They dispatched them with the aircraft, but it's been over an hour since they heard anything from them."

General Sung felt a wave of futility sweep over him. "Keep me updated."

GENERAL CHERN HADN'T been able to pinpoint which of the fourteen deep-water seaports General Sanchez was targeting, so he'd taken his best guess and deployed his troops near the Ports of Miami and the Everglades.

"Move the troops into position," General Chern ordered when he was sure they were on their way.

"We've run into opposition," Colonel Chung, the leader of the Miami contingent radioed.

"What sort of opposition? Their fleet is still at least an hour out," General Chern said.

"IEDs, snipers, antitank missiles, you name it, they've hit us with it. Also, they've blown the canal bridge, and we're going to have to find an alternate route."

"Whatever, but you need to get your ass moving, because they'll reach the docks in an hour or less."

"We can't, the damn bridge is gone."

The general started to berate him, but he realized the colonel was in a tough spot. "All I can tell you is to do the best you can, but if you don't get there within the hour, we're going to lose the port."

"Understood."

When the general finished with the colonel, he contacted the detachment defending the Everglades port.

"No, sir, we haven't met any resistance. We've already taken up our positions, and are ready to repel the invaders."

He suddenly realized he'd made a huge mistake splitting his forces. "Forget about the port," General Chern ordered. "Fall back and rendezvous with Colonel Chung's detachment at these coordinates. Contact me once you've joined up, and I'll give you further orders."

The general immediately called Colonel Chung back. "I need you to form up with the Everglades contingent at these coordinates," General Chern ordered.

"Will do, but we're getting the shit kicked out of us at the moment. I'll try to disengage, but they're well-organized and well-armed, so I don't know what I'll have left, if we do get there."

After the colonel got off the radio, he called his XO over.

"Organize a small group of your best men. Take every antitank missile you can carry, and get your asses to the port. The general has ordered us to retreat, but I'm not going to give them the port without a fight."

When the column turned and started retreating, thirty of his men hid out in the trees until the column was out of sight. When they finally reached the docks, several of the ferries had already started unloading. They managed to hit six ships before General Morales called in an airstrike to wipe them out.

The general knew if the ships went down where they were, it would render 40 percent of the docks unusable.

"Get those damn ships out of there," he screamed.

They managed to get all but one out to deep water before they sank, which left plenty of room to continue offloading.

Two hours later, General Sanchez called for an update.

"We've finished offloading about a third of the ships, and I've established a perimeter around the port," General Morales reported.

"Good work. About a half hour ago the local militia commander, David Ledbetter, reported that the Chinese's reinforcements had turned back. However, just to be safe, I'll have our aircraft overfly your position to see if there's anything else headed your way."

IT HAD BEEN two hours since he'd received an update, so General Sung summoned Colonel Ma.

"How are we doing in Florida?" General Sung asked.

"Not well. I just got off with General Chern, and they've lost the Port of Miami, and the rebels have started unloading."

"What's his assessment of their potential troop strength?"

"He'd only received one report from the squadron's commander before they lost contact, and he'd reported seeing hundreds of ships headed their way."

"I reviewed his tactics, and I was sure General Chern had a credible plan to defend the ports. What happened?" the general asked.

"I don't think he knows for sure, but the Miami contingent was jumped by a large group of rebels."

"Damned militias. Did General Chern have any idea what his next move was going to be?"

"He's pulling all of his forces back to consolidate them for a counterattack."

The general pondered for a few seconds. "What would you recommend?"

Colonel Ma knew the general might be setting him up, but he knew he had to respond. "It's obvious that we've lost the ports, so I think we should pull back, and try to hold them around Savannah, Georgia. They'll follow the coastline to make sure they have a viable supply route, so we may be able to stop them there."

"Make it so, but you and I need to sit down and map out our next moves, or we're going to be out on our butts before the year's done."

The colonel was surprised by the general's candor. "I couldn't agree more. We should bring all the generals in for a face-to-face."

"Do it, but make sure you frisk them before you let them into the meeting."

The colonel thought it was rather odd that the general didn't trust his own senior officers, and then he thought, *Hell. I'd kill him myself if I ever got the chance.*

CHAPTER 4

When the generals arrived at the Westin, Colonel Ma met them in the lobby.

"I trust you had a pleasant journey. Each of you has been assigned an aide for the duration of your visit, and they'll take your bags to your rooms."

Once they'd handed off their luggage, Colonel Ma said, "If you'll follow me, I'll take you up to where we'll be meeting." The colonel motioned to the guard, and he opened the door to the express elevator. As the elevator rushed upward, the colonel couldn't help but reflect on how much their circumstances had changed.

When they had first stepped off the plane in DC, there had been twelve generals, and now there were only five. Some had been lost to enemy action, a couple General Sung had killed, and one had died in a car wreck. At first they'd been viewed as protectors, and the people had welcomed them into their homes, but now it wasn't even safe to go out in public.

When the doors opened, several heavily armed sentries and a group of lab techs met them.

One of the gowned attendants said, "Welcome. If you'll follow me, I'll show you where you can change into the clothes you'll be wearing for the meeting. Each day you'll come back here to be prepped, before we take you upstairs for the conference."

"What the hell is going on?" General Chern asked.

"Protocol," Colonel Ma said. "It's my job to ensure the safety of General Sung, so you'll be going through a complete decontamination process. I simply can't risk you inadvertently infecting him with some sort of bacteriological agent that the militias might have planted."

When General Sung walked into the sumptuous meeting room, he was surprised to see his generals sitting around the table in white jumpsuits.

"Where are your uniforms?"

"You should know. It was your man who did this to us," General Chern said.

"Colonel Ma, what's the meaning of this?"

"We've had reports of the militias using biologic agents, and I didn't want to present them with the opportunity to wipe out our entire leadership."

General Sung knew the story was pure bullshit, but he had to admit it was fairly believable. "Whatever, let's get down to business," he said as he motioned for them to take their seats. "We've suffered a series of setbacks in the last few months, and if we can't turn it around, we'll either have to surrender, or turn tail and run." He paused to let his words sink in, before he continued. "Obviously, neither of these options works for me, so we aren't going to leave here until you come up with a plan."

They worked at it for days, but they weren't getting anywhere. Finally, on the eighth day, the general addressed the group again.

"Every day I've come and listened to you debate our situations, but I haven't heard a single viable idea. You're supposed to be the brightest minds we have, but this is a sorry state of affairs."

"We haven't heard any brilliant ideas from your team either," General Chern said.

Colonel Ma was shocked at the general's temerity. He'd ended up in a wheelchair over a much less inflammatory remark. You could have heard the proverbial pin drop, as everyone in the room waited for the explosion.

"Good point, although if I were you, I'd watch my mouth," General Sung said, in a surprisingly calm manner. "I already had a plan, but I'd hoped you could come up with something better." He motioned for Colonel Ma to put his presentation up on the screen. "I've mapped out your individual troop movements, and, unless my math is off, you should be able to reach your assigned positions in less than three weeks."

They took a few moments to study the map, and the routes they would have to take.

"I've been fighting them all the way across the United States, and I don't think there's anything I can do to buy enough time to reach those coordinates," General Chern said.

"That's where the Russian conscripts come into play. When you resume your retreat, I'm going to have them launch a counterattack, which should buy you enough time."

"There's no way that rabble can defeat the Americans," General Chern sneered.

"True, but they should last long enough for us to achieve our real objectives."

"So you're willing to sacrifice over a half million men?"

"Sure, as long as they're not ours."

The meeting continued for several hours, and after they'd finished for the day, General Sung and Colonel Ma stayed to discuss the day's events.

"If you don't mind me asking, why did you wait so long to throw out your plan?" Colonel Ma asked.

"I was honest about that. I'd hoped they would see something I'd missed. Unfortunately it didn't happen."

"How long do you think the Russians will last?"

"I'm hoping to get five weeks out of them, but who knows, at times they've turned out to be more competent than I expected."

CHAPTER 5

"They're up to something," General Thomas conjectured, as he put the surveillance video up on the monitor.

After they'd reviewed the footage, JD said, "I can't believe it, but it looks like they're massing their forces for a counterattack."

"Why would they attempt that now?"

"A better question would be, why use only the Russians? "At one time they had some crackerjack outfits, but they're ill equipped, and in most cases, we outnumber them."

"Connelly may outnumber them, but we sure as hell don't," General Thomas reminded him.

"If they hit us in force, I'd be hard-pressed to hold. Is there any chance you can send me some help?"

"Give me a couple of minutes," JD said. After he'd reviewed his available resources, he looked up and said, "About all I can spare is Harvey Weinstein's squadron."

"That's better than nothing." General Thomas was about to continue, when his orderly handed him a flash message. "I need a moment." After he'd read it, he said, "They've broken through our southern flank, and I've got to go."

"Take care, and I'll get Harvey headed your way."

* * *

Colonel Thorp's brigade had been headed down Highway 287, toward Dallas–Fort Worth, when the Russians jumped them.

"We've destroyed their forward elements," Captain Levkova reported.

"Send your sapper teams forward while the rest of your group digs in," Colonel Vladimir Putsch, the Russian commander, ordered.

"Major Sarnoff has already dispatched a hundred reinforcements, along with the sandbags and heavy machine guns."

The sappers' mission was to place IEDs and cause as much havoc as possible, without engaging the main body of Colonel Thorp's column.

When General Thomas left the meeting, he contacted Colonel Thorp, to get his assessment of their situation.

"They caught us with our pants down, but I'm almost ready to launch a counterattack," Colonel Thorp reported.

"That's quick work, but you've got to make sure they don't get past you," General Thomas said. "If they punch through you, there's nothing between them and Amarillo. I don't need them taking control of Pantex."

"I thought they'd closed the facility several years ago."

"They did. There aren't any functional weapons, but they could use the bulk plutonium to make dirty bombs."

"Good to know."

When they were finished, Colonel Thorp called his XO in. "How are you coming?"

"We've launched a drone, and you should have some video of what we're facing in a few seconds," Major Mathers reported.

"My God, there are a thousand men down there," Colonel Thorp said as he watched the video feed. "If we let them take the high ground, we'll be in deep shit. Let's get the Volvos fired up. They should be able to punch through the roadblock."

The Volvos' Gatling guns had proven to be brutally effective, as they raced toward the dug-in Chinese. The hail of depleted uranium slugs tore through the Russians' barricades like they weren't even there, inflicting heavy casualties.

Colonel Thorp was watching the engagement on the drone's video feed, and for a few moments, it looked like they were going to blow through the roadblock. However, the Russian sappers had planted a string of IEDs in front of their position, and when they detonated them, the massive explosions turned several of the onrushing Volvos into tumbling fireballs.

"Push on through, boys," Sergeant Musgrave screamed at the other drivers.

The survivors had closed to seven hundred yards before Captain Levkova sprang their next surprise.

Hidden about six thousand yards down the road, the Russians had seventy-five 155mm self-propelled howitzers, and when they fired, the concussions from their muzzle blasts reverberated down the valley.

Captain Levkova had a team painting the targets with pedestal-mounted laser designators, and the 155mm laser homing rounds were deadly accurate.

When their first volley destroyed most of the Volvos, Colonel Thorp ordered, "Abort, abort."

Colonel Thorp tallied up his losses and called General Thomas with the bad news. "I've lost most of my Volvos in our counterstrike, and I'm deploying my men into defensive positions," Colonel Thorp reported.

"What happened?" General Thomas asked.

"I screwed up. I didn't realize they had artillery."

"What's your situation?" the general asked.

"I think we can hold them, at least for a while, but we're severely outnumbered."

"Do the best you can, and I'll try to scrounge up some help."

Meanwhile, Colonel Putsch was holding an officers' call.

"We stopped their counterattack, but teams operating the roadblocks were hit hard," Major Sarnoff told the group.

"Send up some more reinforcements, and remind them not to move forward until I give the order," Colonel Putsch ordered. "Also, make sure you set up a good perimeter. I don't want those damned Americans sneaking in here and slitting our throats during the night."

Still angry with himself, Colonel Thorp was desperately trying to determine a plan of attack, but he needed better intelligence. They'd just shot down their last drone, and the replacements wouldn't reach them in time.

"Major, I want you to put together a team for a reconnaissance mission."

"Objective?" Major Mathers asked.

"I need a complete rundown of their troop strength, how they're deployed, and anything else you can get."

"I'll get right on it, but we're more than a little screwed up at the moment, so it may take me a little while."

"I hear you, but you need to get a move on, because, we're attacking again at 0500."

The recon team moved out at 2200, and as they slithered through yucca, mesquite, and sagebrush, they made very little noise.

"I'm damned glad it's cold, because I hate snakes," Sergeant Felix Juarez said.

It was after midnight before they reached a vantage point where they could properly survey the Russian positions.

"Damn, they've got more men than we thought," Sergeant Juarez mumbled under his breath.

"Did you say something, Sarge?" Corporal Fazio asked.

"Nothing important. You and the rest of the boys spread out. When I'm done with my drawing, we're going to kill a few of these bastards before we take off." When he finished, he told them, "Pick your targets carefully, and try to get the officers if you can. The Russians don't do very well if they don't have someone to tell them what to do."

They had to get a little closer than they would have liked, because their night-vision gear and silencers limited their range. The sergeant only let them shoot for ten minutes, but they'd managed to kill thirty-five.

"All right, let's get the hell out of here, before they figure out where we are."

TWENTY MINUTES LATER, an urgent knock on his trailer door woke Colonel Putsch from a sound sleep. "This had better be important."

"Someone has killed thirty-five of our men."

"I assume that by someone, you mean the enemy?"

"Yes, sir, of course," the young lieutenant stammered.

"What would you like me to do about it? Get Major Sarnoff to take care of it."

"That's not possible."

"Why not? He's the XO, you imbecile."

"He was one of the casualties."

"Oh shit. I need all the officers in the headquarters tent in twenty minutes."

Once they'd gathered, Colonel Putsch announced, "I'm sorry to report that Major Sarnoff has been killed. Major Efim, you're my new XO. I'm expecting an attack before dawn, so when we're done here you'll need to get the men ready."

* * *

As Colonel Putsch had suspected, the American's launched a counterattack at 0500.

Colonel Thorp had lost most of his armored trucks in the first attack, but he still had a few left, so he put them in the lead. As they roared toward the enemy positions, their MRAPs and supply trucks were tucked in behind them.

The drivers were using night-vision gear, so they didn't have to show a light, as they sped through the night. They didn't get very far before they had to slow down, because much of the road had been shattered by the artillery. As they picked their way around the craters, and the blasted vehicles containing the charred bodies of their buddies, not a word was spoken.

The Russian guards were on high alert, so they spotted them while they were still over a mile away.

"There's a large body of men moving our way," the guard reported.

"Open fire, you idiot," Major Efim ordered.

The Russians' tracers immediately filled the night sky, so the Americans started returning fire. When the Volvos finally made it out of the debris field they accelerated, and as they rushed hell-bent through the night, the aluminum alloy shell casings were flowing off the sides of their vehicles.

The Russians were hardened combat veterans, but there's something about not being able to see what's killing you that terrifies people. The guards managed to destroy all but two of the Volvos, but the survivors devastated their ranks and breached the roadblock. As the Russians turned to run, the Volvos simply ran down many of them, and cut the rest to ribbons with their side-mounted machine guns.

"We're through the roadblock, bring it on," the sergeant driving the lead truck screamed over the radio.

As they accelerated down the hill, the Russians' artillery commander ordered, "Prepare to fire on my command."

Before they could fire, Harvey Weinstein's squadron began launching their missiles. The barrage of missiles blew holes in the tightly packed artillery batteries, and made them forget about firing their first salvo.

"Cut them down, boys," Harvey screamed as he dropped down to less than fifty feet and opened up with his miniguns.

While Harvey's boys were strafing the column, the Tiger helicopters that Harvey had brought along began targeting what was left of the Russian artillery. They launched a fusillade of missiles, and the ground shook as the massive explosions erupted, lighting up the canyon. The savage attack broke the gunners' spirit, and many of them broke and ran into the night.

"Make your move, Colonel, we've got them ducking for cover," Harvey yelled.

As the remainder of Colonel Thorp's men swept down the hill, they were firing as fast as they could. The tracers from both sides filled the night air like fireflies on a dark summer's night, and the din of combat was deafening.

COLONEL PUTSCH FINALLY managed to regain some measure of control over his troops, and as they rallied to meet the Americans' onslaught, he caught sight of the glow of afterburners in the night sky.

"Let them have it, men," Colonel James ordered.

As the F-22s launched their missiles, and dove to drop their JDAMS, the Russian commander realized he was screwed.

Colonel Putsch turned to his radio operator and ordered, "Give the order to fall back," just before his command vehicle exploded like a Roman candle.

Major Efim reached the same conclusion when he saw

Colonel Putsch blown to bits. "We're going to bug out, give the order," he said as he jumped back into his APC. Terrified, he gunned his vehicle back onto the highway, and as he did, he ran over a couple of his own men. He was doing almost eighty, when one of his own APCs accidentally ran him off the road, killing him instantly.

In the confusion, many of the Russian subcommanders never got the order to retreat, so they continued fighting.

When Colonel Thorp's men charged out of their MRAPs, they were met with a barrage of bullets, grenades, and missiles.

"Air One, I'm going to mark your next target with the laser designators," Colonel Thorp called to Harvey.

"Roger that."

Colonel Weinstein yelled, "Got it, we'll be right there."

Harvey's squadron swooped in low over Colonel Thorp's position and launched their phosphorous-tipped missiles. As the ground shook around Colonel Thorp, it looked like the gates of hell opened up in front of him.

"That's all we've got, but we'll get back as quickly as we can, Air One out."

The air attacks had blown a large breach in the Russians' defensive perimeter, and Colonel Thorp realized it was do or die time.

"Go go go," Colonel Thorp screamed into his radio headset.

The tide of battle ebbed and flowed for over an hour, but by sunrise, the Russians were in full retreat.

Colonel Thorp drove to the top of one of the surrounding hills and climbed on top of his MRAP. The scene before him was pure chaos. He could see hundreds of Russian vehicles trying to escape down both sides of the highway. Many of them were mostly empty, while others were packed and had men desperately hanging on to the outside as they picked up speed.

"All commanders hold your positions, and report," Colonel Thorp ordered.

After he'd talked with most of them, he radioed, "Set a perimeter, and there will be an officer call in twenty."

WITH COLONEL PUTSCH and the new XO dead, command of the Russian contingent fell to Major Krill Bahanoff.

He tried valiantly, but he didn't manage to gain control of what was left of their column until they were seventy miles south of the battle. When he finally got them stopped, it took him the rest of the afternoon to assess what he had left. Since he had no idea what to do next, Major Bahanoff placed an urgent call to General Sung's headquarters in New York.

By then it was 1930 in New York, and the general was eating dinner, so Colonel Ma took his call. After the major had explained his situation, Colonel Ma ordered, "Hold your current position, and make sure you set a good perimeter. Go ahead and send me a complete list of the men and material you have left, and I'll get back to you before morning."

Colonel Ma and his staff spent most of the night studying the situation, and by 0500 he'd formulated a plan for the young major.

"Good morning, Colonel Bahanoff, I trust that you got a least a little sleep," Colonel Ma said.

"It's Major Bahanoff, sir."

"Not anymore, Colonel. I've just sent you your orders, and if you have any questions, give me a call. Otherwise get to it."

"Yes, sir, I will, and sir, thanks for the promotion."

GENERAL SUNG AND Colonel Ma had gotten into the habit of taking breakfast together. That way they could go over the events of the previous day, and make sure that the colonel understood whatever new thoughts the general had for him.

Colonel Ma had placed the Russians' action report beside the general's plate, and as he sat down, he asked, "What's this?"

"It's the action report from Colonel Putsch's division."

"Isn't that the southernmost Russian division?"

"It is."

"Just net it out for me, I don't feel like reading that shit this morning."

"The colonel and most of his senior officers are dead, and the survivors have retreated to just north of Wichita Falls, Texas."

"I expected more," the general said. "Who's in command now?"

"A young major by the name of Krill Bahanoff was next in line. Except, he's a colonel now, because I thought a division should be led by at least a colonel."

"Whatever, it doesn't make any difference; he probably won't live out the week anyway. What's their status?"

"They got their asses kicked, but after I looked over the satellite photos, it looks as though they mauled the Americans."

"Good, that's all I was really hoping for. I need them to hold out for at least another week, after that I don't give a shit what happens to them."

No more than you care about any of us, the colonel thought to himself, as he tried to find a comfortable position in his wheelchair.

"Colonel Thorp has stopped the Russian advance," General Thomas reported.

"Great news," General Drury said. "How long before he gets going again? I'd like to get 287 opened up to at least the Dallas–Fort Worth area."

"It may take them a few days. They got the crap beat out of them, and Harvey Weinstein's squadron lost almost a third of his birds."

"What the hell, they weren't even supposed to be involved."

"You know Harvey. He heard the radio chatter when their first attack went so badly, so he seized the initiative and jumped in to help." He could tell the General wasn't pleased. "Before you come down too hard on Harvey, Colonel Thorp told me they wouldn't have made it, if it hadn't been for him."

"Understood, but it looks like we need push-up delivery on the rest of the replacement helicopters. I'm going to be in Albuquerque tomorrow night, and we can discuss it then."

CHAPTER 6

The weather was decent for early December in New York City, and General Sung was enjoying a leisurely stroll through Central Park. Since arriving in the city, he'd gotten in the habit of taking at least a five-mile walk every day. He still found it hard to believe there was such a wonderful park in the middle of New York.

Although there wasn't anyone left on the island, other than his troops, he never ventured outside without his bodyguards. The light snow that was falling had already left a light dusting on the grass and trees. The serenity of the moment caused him to let his guard down, and for just a few moments, he allowed himself to think back to better times. He remembered taking his young son for a walk in the woods outside their vacation home in the Heilongjiang Province. When he'd first reached a position of power, he'd used some of his newfound wealth to pursue one of his passions in life, skiing.

His palatial home had been only minutes from the slopes at the Yabuli Ski Resort. He'd chosen Yabuli because it averaged 170 days of snow coverage, and it was the premiere ski destination in China. He'd visited as often as his schedule would allow, and it was one of the few places on earth where he had felt truly at peace.

The sound of an emergency siren interrupted his musings, and jerked him back to reality. Angry with himself for allowing the memories to sneak into his conscious thoughts, he turned to the lead guard and said, "Call the car. I'm done for today." He looked over at the extremely cute, nineteen-year-old blonde he'd selected to accompany him for the day, and told her, "My dear, let's get you out of this cold."

I'll bet that's not the only thing you want me out of, she thought to herself, but at least she was being well taken care of, and rarely did he ask for the same girl twice. She was one of a hundred or more young girls who they'd ripped away from their families before they slaughtered them. They kept them on a separate floor at the hotel, so they were close at hand when they were needed. The senior officers used them for their own pleasures, and when they were tired of them, they would take them across the river and dump them off to fend for themselves.

As they drove back to the hotel, the streets were deserted, except for an occasional military vehicle. The once-vibrant scenes that had played out every day in Times Square were long gone. The massive electronic billboards which had once touted the excesses of the American culture were dark most of the time, except when they'd turn them back on to flash notices to their troops.

General Sung decided to have dinner downstairs in one of the hotel's restaurants. It, like the streets of the city, had once been filled with beautiful, powerful people, but now the only people who frequented it were the Chinese officers, and their ladies of the evening. Even the waiters had been replaced by enlisted personnel.

When Colonel Ma rolled into the room, the general motioned for the waiter to bring them their meals. The general rarely invited him to dinner, so the colonel knew something was up. They were seated in front of a massive floor-to-ceiling window, and the view of the city was magnificent.

"Thanks for joining me," General Sung said cordially.

When he was this nice, he knew the general needed something out of the ordinary. The general made light conversation throughout the meal, and the colonel was beginning to think he'd misjudged his intent. However, when the waiter brought them their desserts, and coffee, the general finally got around to what he wanted.

"I need you to find this man for me," the general said, as he handed him a photograph.

"It shouldn't be a problem, but why the interest?"

"Not your concern. Can you take care of it for me?"

"Of course, but with nothing more than a picture, it may take a few days."

"Not a problem, I'm going to take a few days to tour some of the northern provinces of Canada. Their president invited me to his place outside of Edmonton, and I thought it would be a good opportunity to try to mend my fences with him. While I'm gone, I need you to make sure that no unauthorized people go onto my floor. The only people allowed up there are the cleaning crew and the waiters who deliver the meals."

"No problem. Would you like for me to check up on your guests while you're away?"

"No, stay out of there, they'll be fine."

The general left early the next morning, and as he always did, Colonel Ma made a point to track his every move. The general's aircraft spent the night at Edmonton, but at 0430 the next morning, it took off, moving north and east. Colonel Ma tracked it until it landed on the northeastern tip of Ellesmere Island.

What the hell, I don't show that there's anything there

that would interest the general, Colonel Ma thought to himself. *I wonder what the devious bastard is up to this time.*

It took him several minutes to ferret out what little information there was about the site. The facility was listed as the Canadian Forces Station Alert. The name didn't tell him much, so he looked it up in their intelligence database, and saw that it was a signal intelligence intercept station.

It didn't seem to make any sense for the general to stop there, but his plane spent most of the day on the island before it returned to Edmonton.

He knew the general was going to expect action on his request, so he'd put several of his best men on it. It had taken them longer than he'd expected, but they finally located their target in Brooklyn. He owned a dry cleaning shop, and the colonel couldn't figure out what the general wanted with him.

When the general returned, Colonel Ma considered asking him about the side trip, but he decided that discretion was the better part of valor.

When the general saw the man he said, "Good job. Who knows we picked him up?"

"Just the security team. They grabbed him on his way home last night, so his family doesn't have any idea where he is."

"Good, keep it that way," was all the general said, as he had the man led away.

CHAPTER 7

When JD was finished in Albuquerque, he flew down to Miami to meet with the rest of his team.

"OK, what's next?" General Thomas asked. "We've finished clearing the Russians out of everywhere west of the Mississippi. Sanchez's people have taken Florida, and all the Gulf coast states, back to the border of Texas."

"I know we've got General Sung hemmed in, but we need to make sure that we can hold what we've taken," JD said. "He's still a dangerous adversary, and there's no reason to move until we're absolutely sure we can finish him off."

"I hear you, but I dislike leaving the rest of the country in his hands," General Thomas said.

The look on General Thomas's face told JD there was something else on his mind. "Is there something else going on? You don't seem yourself."

"I just found out they killed my sister and most of her family. However, I think my niece is still alive, and that they're holding her prisoner somewhere in Manhattan."

"I can't begin to tell you how sorry I am, but I'm not going to chance moving too soon."

"Do you have any idea how long it might be?"

"I wish I could give you an exact date, but I just finished talking with Sanchez, and he's got some of the new aircraft and a large quantity of heavy armor headed our way. Once we have that, we should be able to move quickly."

What he didn't share, was that not long after Armando Castillo invaded California, William Sheldon had acquired the only full set of engineering plans for the F-22s still in existence.

When William delivered them to General Sanchez, he had Embraer tool up their Brazilian manufacturing plants, and begin production.

"I understand," General Thomas said, "but if you don't mind, I'd like to change the subject for a moment. I've got an old friend, who's on the president of Canada's staff, and he told me that General Sung met with their president a few days ago."

"Did he have any idea what they talked about?"

"He said it really didn't amount to much. The general apologized for sinking several of their frigates. He assured the president that he had no intention of threatening them in any way, and asked the president for the same assurances."

"The Canadians are in even worse shape than we were. They've been busted for years. Hell, they couldn't beat the Eskimos, let alone the Chinese. So I don't see why he'd worry about them."

"That's what my friend said, but he also mentioned General Sung met with some sort of Russian dignitary."

"I don't suppose he knew who it was?"

"Not a chance. He said that they were very careful not to let him be seen. The only reason he found out they were even there was that one of the guards commented about having the damn Russians around."

"Thanks for the info, and I'll reach out to my intelligence analysts to see if they've heard anything."

* * *

With winter approaching, and his meteorologists forecasting an unusually harsh season, JD decided to continue marshaling their forces, and wait until spring to make his move.

As he sat there thinking about what came next, the pain came flooding back.

It had been a little over four years since Molly and Tabatha had been killed, but the pain was as strong as the day they died. As he thought back to his time with Molly, his emotions overwhelmed him.

For months after their deaths, he'd considered ending it all. But he'd remember her words when he got on to her for risking her life to save him, and realized he could never dishonor her memory by taking his own life.

In late March, the first shipments of the F-22s were scheduled to arrive by high-speed catamaran, and JD decided to fly down and meet the first shipment.

"How would you like to meet me in Miami on Thursday?" JD asked.

William Sheldon's health had improved enough for him to travel, but his doctors had warned him not to overdo. "Sure, I think I can work it into my busy schedule," William said.

"Great. I'll pick you up when you land."

JD was waiting when he landed, and pulled up beside his jet as it came to a stop. As JD watched William walking slowly down the ladder of his Gulfstream, he yelled, "You look like shit, I shouldn't have had you come."

"I feel like shit, but the doctors keep reminding me that I should already be dead. Hell, I can suffer here just as well as at home. Besides, home will never be the same anyway."

JD didn't comment, but he knew exactly what he meant.

After a short drive, they parked on a hill overlooking

the yard where they were storing the shipments from Sanchez.

"I guess it's been longer than I realized since I was down here," JD said. "That's an unbelievable amount of stuff."

"Sanchez is a madman, but before he's done, we're going to have a better equipped military than we did before the Chinese wiped us out. I pulled a tally sheet just before I landed, and they've already delivered seventy F-22s, fourteen hundred helicopters, and four hundred M1A3 battle tanks."

"I thought the M1A2 was the newest generation of the Abrams?"

"It was the most current ever built, but I just happened to have the plans for the next generation. It's got depleted uranium armor, and all the bells and whistles. Hell, the new gas turbine engines crank out over four thousand horses."

"Impressive, Sanchez has definitely come through for us," JD said as he surveyed the storage lot.

"I'm very reluctant to bring this up, but I've got one other thing that I need to share with you," William said.

"Shoot."

"I've identified General Sung's current location."

"Why didn't you tell me first thing?" JD asked.

"Because I was afraid that you'd go and get yourself killed trying to take him out."

"Tell me!"

"He's staying on the top floor of the Westin, in New York."

"How did you find out?"

"One of our operatives was interrogating a severely wounded soldier last week, and the man said he used to take him his meals when he was stationed in New York."

"I want to talk to him."

"He died of his wounds."

"Damn."

* * *

WHILE JD WAS busy plotting their next offensive, General Sung was struggling to get a handle on their deteriorating situation.

"Here are the latest satellite photos," Colonel Ma said.

General Sung pitched them on the table. "So, what's it look like? Is the SASR still pouring equipment into the country?"

"Definitely. Sanchez has really stepped up for them. We should have pulled him out of there before we hit Central America."

"I know, you told me, but it's too damn late now, and since I killed his son, I don't imagine he holds any fond memories of me."

"Along with most of the rest of us," the colonel muttered.

"Do you have a feel for when they'll make their next move?" General Sung asked.

"They don't seem to be in any hurry, but if I had to hazard a guess, I would say late spring."

"Good, that'll give us a little more time to prepare. Have you redeployed the units?"

"Of course. General Chern had the farthest to go, but he's been in place since last Thursday. I know we can bleed them some, but you do know that with the addition of their new allies, we don't stand a chance in hell."

The general paused to consider the colonel's pronouncement. "Probably true, but I refuse to believe that we can't defeat a bunch of ragtag militias."

"Maybe so, but that doesn't speak very well of us, because they've kicked the shit out of us all the way across the country. The best we've ever done is to fight them to a standstill a time or two. Before I forget, I do have some good news. We've managed to retool a couple of the old US auto plants, and we should have a hundred heavy tanks ready by spring. Also, the Russians have managed to ferry in a hundred and seventy of the Sukhoi Su-47s and General Borski has promised another fifty."

"Good deal," the general said. "They're the only thing with any sort of chance against those . . . what the hell do they call them?"

"Raptors."

"Yes, that's it, Raptors. I just finished reading the report you gave me last night, and they must really be something. How come it's taken us this long to figure it out?"

"We could never document what was happening, because no one had ever survived an encounter with them. This time we got lucky, and one of our pilots managed to bail out. When I interviewed the pilot, he kept saying how he couldn't believe how they moved, and that the Raptor's radar signature was too faint for their weapon systems to get a lock on them."

"Do you think if we put up larger squadrons we could hold our own?"

"We could try it, and they probably could hold their own against the knockoff Su-47s they're using. However, when you factor in their stealth capabilities, advanced weapon systems, along with their speed and thrust vectoring technology, even the real Su-47s wouldn't stand much of a chance."

Colonel Ma sat there patiently as the general tried to sort through his rather meager options. After several minutes of uncomfortable silence, Colonel Ma was considering how to break the silence, when the general made a grunting sound and said, "I know it blew up in my face the last time, but I want you to resume picking up the known militia family members."

Oh hell, here we go again, Colonel Ma thought to himself. "I'll get right on it, but if you don't mind me asking, why?"

"Insurance. If push comes to shove, I don't think they

have the balls to sacrifice large numbers of their people
to kill us."

"This doesn't sound like a man in control," Colonel
Ma muttered, as he rolled away.

ALBUQUERQUE NORMALLY DOESN'T get an extraordinary amount of snow, but right after JD had landed
for an inspection tour, they got hit with a hundred-year
storm.

"Damn, it's really snowing out there," JD said.

"Sure is. We've already gotten eighteen inches, and
the weather bureau says it's going to snow for at least
another twenty hours," Colonel Weinstein said.

JD started to shake Harvey's hand, but his right arm
was in a sling from a bullet he'd taken through the shoulder when he'd gone on another unauthorized mission. JD
gave him his sternest look and said, "Once again, you and
your men saved the day, but if you ever disobey a direct
order again, I'll have you shot."

Harvey's face looked like JD had punched him in the
balls, before JD laughed and patted him on his good
shoulder. "Just kidding, but I wish you'd be a little more
careful. I can't afford to lose you."

"Damn, you had me going for a moment. I almost
believed you would really shoot me."

"I would, if had to, but not for taking the initiative."

When JD was finally able to leave, Harvey drove him
back to the airport. On the way, JD took the opportunity to ask him for a favor. As JD was about to board
his aircraft, he turned to Harvey and confirmed: "Now,
you understand what I expect when I call, right?"

"I do, and you can count on me."

"I know. That's why I asked."

CHAPTER 8

General Drury had intended to launch their final push on April 1, but a freak spring snowstorm had caused them to postpone.

"The weather bureau says that we can expect the latest storm to clear by next Tuesday," General Thomas reported.

"Good deal, is everything ready?" JD asked.

"Everything is in place, and when you give the word, we're a go."

JD took one last look at the map on the screen and said, "I guess it's a go. I can't believe it's taken this many years to get back to this point."

"It has been a long, hard road, but we should be getting toward the end of these sorry bastards. I'd like to ask a favor, if I may?"

"Shoot."

"I want to lead the first division into New York."

"You're a general, and it's not your job anymore. Your sole mission is the same as mine. We're supposed to make sure that everyone else does theirs."

"I understand, but this is something I've got to do. I've found out that my niece was caught up in one of their roundups, and I'd like the opportunity to try to rescue her."

"What makes you so sure she's in New York?"

"I've got a friend who used to be with the CIA, and he just confirmed she's alive. He was also able to verify that they're holding her, and several other hostages, at the Westin Hotel. She's all the family I have left, and I couldn't live with myself if I don't at least try."

"Let me think about it, and I promise that I'll get back to you before we make our move on New York."

WHEN TUESDAY ROLLED around, the Americans launched what they hoped would be their final push.

"They've hit us with overwhelming forces on all sides," Colonel Ma reported.

"Take a deep breath, and calm down," General Sung said. He gave the colonel a few seconds to compose himself, before he asked, "Now, would you care to explain what you mean by overwhelming force?"

"I mean they've hit us with several squadrons of F-22s and over three thousand tanks."

"We've got more tanks and aircraft than that, what's the problem?"

"They've already shot down over fifty-five percent of our aircraft, and their tanks have some sort of enhanced armor, which has rendered our tanks completely ineffectual."

The general took a few minutes to look over the situation reports before he responded. "Move the rest of the reserves up. They should be enough to stop Sanchez's army outside of DC."

"Will do, but what about the group moving on us from the west? That doesn't leave anything to help out there."

"They're going to have to fall back to the defensive

positions that I had you prepare in Pennsylvania. If they can reach them, we should be able to hold them there as well."

"THEY'VE STARTED RETREATING," General Thomas reported.

"I imagine they're headed to Pennsylvania. They've got a fairly robust defensive perimeter set up on the border," JD said. "Push them hard until they get there, and then back off."

"You want us to stop? I think we can bust through, if you'll let me."

"I'm sure you can, but I need a little time, so hold up and wait for orders."

GENERAL CHERN HAD managed to collect the remainder of the Russian forces as they'd retreated, and by the time they reached the Pennsylvania border, he had almost six hundred thousand men.

"We've reached the fallback positions, and I've got to say that I'm pleasantly surprised," General Chern said. "I think with this much firepower, they'll have a hard time getting through us."

"Excellent, General Sung has had us preparing those positions for over a year," Colonel Ma said.

"Along with the prebuilt bunkers and weapons, you'll find that there's supplies for a protracted siege."

"You can count us to hold out as long as we can.

"Do you know where their main force is right now? I'd like to know how much time we've got."

"You're in luck. I just finished debriefing the reconnaissance flight before I got on with you, and they've stopped about ten miles from your lines."

"That doesn't make any sense; they've had us on the run for days."

"Don't look a gift horse in the mouth. Take advantage of their timidity, and use the time to get dug in."

"Timid my ass, there's something else going on. Can you keep checking on them for me?"

"I'll do my best, but the pilot that I debriefed was the only plane out of twenty that made it back."

THE NEXT DAY, JD's helicopter landed at General Thomas's forward command post.

The general was holding an officer's call when JD walked in with a couple of MPs.

"What are you doing up here?" General Thomas asked. "You're always getting on our asses for taking too many chances, and yet here you are."

"Is Will Jackson capable of taking over?" JD asked.

"Of course he is. Are you relieving me?"

"I am."

"Your call, but can I ask what I've done to deserve this?"

"No. Please go with the MPs."

After General Thomas had left, JD called Colonel Jackson over. "Colonel, I've relieved General Thomas, which makes you the next in line."

"You can't be serious. He's the best commander I've ever seen."

JD ignored his comment. "I'm promoting you to general, and it's your command."

"Thanks, I think. What are your orders?"

JD handed him a jump drive and said, "This will explain everything. It details the next phase of your campaign."

JD and General Jackson continued talking for over an hour, before JD told him, "I've got to get going. If you have any questions, coordinate with General Connelly, or if you can't reach him, General Sanchez."

"Connelly or Sanchez, got it. Where are you going to be?"

"Need to know, but I'll see you in New York."

General Jackson's new command had over three thousand motorized cannons and tanks pointed at the enemy's lines, and when they began firing, it turned night into day.

JD had delayed his departure so that they could witness the start of the offensive.

"My God, that's impressive," General Thomas commented, as they orbited nearby in JD's helicopter.

"It certainly is. I just hope that we can blow through their defensive positions without losing too many men."

After they'd watched the bombardment for several minutes, JD yelled to the pilot, "I've seen enough, let's get moving."

As THE MASSIVE barrage of artillery shells swept thru the Chinese lines, many of their troops panicked and ran.

"Shoot the cowards," General Chern ordered.

"What for? We need to get moving ourselves," the general's aide told him.

The general pulled his pistol and shot his aide in the head. Then he turned to the wild-eyed young lieutenant standing nearby, and said, "All right. You're my new aide. Do you have any problems carrying out my orders?"

"No, sir! I'm on it."

The general's extreme methods had turned the tide for a few hours, but the artillery bombardment was followed by wave after wave of aircraft, dropping bunker-busting bombs.

For a time, there were so many planes in the air that they had to turn on their running lights to keep from running into each other. What few aircraft General Chern had left, had been swept out of the sky in the first minutes of the battle, giving the Americans complete air superiority. As General Chern watched them lining up to make their bombing runs, it looked like they went forever.

"Give the order to retreat; we're not going to be able to hold here," General Chern instructed. After the order had gone out, he placed a quick call to headquarters. "I've given the order to retreat."

"General Sung is not going to be pleased," Colonel Ma, warned. "We spent a fortune on those positions, and you should have been able to defend them."

"I don't give a shit what you spent," General Chern said. "I need some help. They've blasted the bunkers, and they're moving this way with thousands of tanks."

"Understood, we'll send what we can, but most of the reserves have already been committed to the DC area."

Colonel Ma found General Sung in his office.

"They've broken through on the western front," Colonel Ma said.

"So soon?"

"What are your orders?"

The general didn't say anything right away, and after a several minutes, Colonel Ma asked, "Are you all right? We've got to do something, or they'll be here in two days, tops."

"You can leave. I'll get back to you when I've figured out what I'm going to do."

Great, the asshole needs to meditate or something, Colonel Ma thought to himself.

He'd left thinking it'd be an hour or so, but the general didn't call for him until the next morning.

"What's the status?" General Sung asked.

"We're holding Sanchez at DC, but General Thomas's army is within a hundred miles of here," Colonel Ma said.

"What do we have left?"

"One understrength division, and a couple of hundred aircraft."

"OK, blow the bridges and tunnels, and deploy the troops under the plan X100."

"What good will that do?" Colonel Ma demanded. "We'll be trapped." The colonel had just looked down at the computer in his lap, when the general shot him in the back of the head.

"I should have killed the whiny little bastard the first time," he muttered. The general called down to the command center, "Blow the bridges and tunnels, and execute order X100, and I need a cleanup crew up here right away; Colonel Ma has had an accident."

"THEY'VE BLOWN THE bridges and tunnels," General Jackson said.

"That seems a little shortsighted," General Drury said. "When you reach New York, I want you to deploy your troops like we discussed, and then you can go ahead and contact General Sung."

A COUPLE OF hours later, General Wang was updating General Sung on their situation.

"We've executed X100, but there must be two hundred ships out there, and we don't have any way of getting off the island," General Wang reported. "Also they've just sent a demand for our surrender."

General Sung read the terms and remarked, "Screw them. We're not going to surrender. Pass the word, no surrender. Never mind responding, I'll take care of our response."

"NOT ONLY HAVE they refused to surrender," General Thomas said. "They're threatening to kill over ten thousand of our family members if we attempt to enter the city. You don't think that they'd really go through with it? Surely, they know we'd slaughter every last one of them if they did."

JD knew in his heart the general would do exactly what he'd threatened. "No, of course not. He's not insane, it's just a bluff."

They continued talking for a few moments, and then JD said, "I've got to go, close up your lines around the city, and wait for further orders."

As he was walking out, JD called Harvey. "It's time."

Revenge is a confession of pain.

—LATIN PROVERB

PART 13

CHAPTER 1

Much like the Raptors, Harvey's new chopper was virtually invisible to the Chinese radar. In addition, it had been outfitted with a state-of-the-art hush kit, so it could slip through the night sky undetected.

When Harvey put them down on the roof of the Westin, he said, "Good luck and call me when you want to be picked up."

General Thomas and JD hit the rooftop at a dead run, and JD took out the two guards with his silenced HK45.

"They're supposed to be on the forty-fourth floor," JD informed him as they entered the elevator. "I'll help you take out the guards, and then you can lead them back up here."

"How long have you been planning this?" General Thomas asked.

"Ever since you told me your niece was being held," he lied.

"You'd take a risk like this for a few youngsters?"

"It's not just about them; I've got something else that I need to take care of."

The general didn't really care, as long as he could rescue his niece. "Shouldn't we have brought a Spec Ops team?" General Thomas asked.

"They would have caused too big a ruckus. The only chance we have is to get in and out before they realize we're here."

When the elevator opened, JD was dismayed to see that there were several officers roaming the hallway.

"Look sharp, I didn't expect this many soldiers," JD said as he unlimbered his HK-G36 assault rifle. He could have picked a more powerful weapon, but its hundred-round magazine made it perfect for the job. As they moved into the hall they were firing two-round bursts at what turned out to be mostly unarmed officers. Even though they were supposed to be on full alert, twenty of them had taken the opportunity for one more pass at the girls. As their shots reverberated down the hall, two heavily armed guards came running up the hallway. JD calmly took a knee, and cut them both almost in half, with a burst of full automatic fire.

He reached behind him to retrieve another magazine, and said, "I think that's the last of them. Let's get the girls out of their rooms, and then you can lead them back to the roof."

The girls were locked in their rooms, so it took them a few minutes to kick in the doors. They didn't find the general's niece until they kicked in the next-to-last door. "Oh my God, it's you," the general's niece screamed when she saw him. She ran over and gave him a big hug.

He pushed her away and said, "Honey, we can catch up later. We've got to go."

They had to use all the elevators, including the freight elevators to move the girls, but as the last group was leaving, JD said, "I've called the choppers, and they should be landing about the time you hit the roof."

"How are you getting out?"

"Don't worry about it; just get the girls to safety."

When the elevator door closed, JD opened the emergency door and started sprinting up the stairs. When he reached the door to the penthouse level, it was locked as he'd expected. He quickly placed his charges and blew the door.

When he rushed through the still-smoking door frame, four heavily armed bodyguards met him. He wasn't in the mood to screw around, so he triggered his weapon on full auto and blasted the guards to bloody bits.

He'd taken four rounds to the chest, but his body armor had stopped them.

He shot the lock out of the door and kicked it open.

When General Sung jumped to his feet, JD shot him in both knees, and he slammed into the floor face-first, screaming in agony.

He'd rehearsed what he was going to say to him a million times, but he didn't utter a sound as he drew the ancient dagger General Sanchez had given him. When he reached the general, he rolled him onto his back, and drove the razor-sharp blade through his heart.

As JD stared into his cold, dead eyes, he noticed his right eye was blue. When he looked closer he could see the brown contact lens in the other one. He'd studied General Sung's dossier, and he was supposed to have dark brown eyes and a large birthmark above his right nipple.

He ripped the general's shirt open, but there was no birthmark. "Shit, it's not him."

Still determined to find and kill him, he started ransacking the penthouse in search of a clue. He could tell the general had left in a hurry, but the penthouse had been stripped bare of any personal belongings. Frustrated, he smashed one of the dressers against the doorjamb. As he kicked pieces out of his way, he spotted a photo that had been wedged behind one of the shattered drawers.

As he looked it over for clues, he thought was hallucinating. He fell to his knees and began weeping uncontrollably when he realized it was a picture of Molly, and that it had been taken on the roof of the Westin.

As he studied every detail, he decided the little girl standing beside her had to be Tabatha.

"Thank you, Lord," JD exclaimed.

His hands were shaking as he stuck the picture deep inside his pants pocket for safekeeping. He'd lost track of time, and when he checked his watch, he exclaimed, "Oh shit."

He radioed Harvey for pickup, and made a mad dash for the roof.

"Well, did you get him?" Harvey asked.

"No, I killed some poor son-of-a-bitch who was made up to look like him."

CHAPTER 2

Shortly after General Sung had murdered Colonel Ma, he'd taken their last helicopter, and left the city. He'd set up his exit strategy during his visit to Canada, and the secretive Russian he'd met with had been the Russian president.

In exchange for a huge bribe, he'd agreed to provide transportation, and turn over his government to the general.

They had a plane waiting at an airstrip just over the border.

"We're ready to go when you are," the Russian pilot told him as he came on board.

"Let's get the hell out of here, before they figure out I'm gone."

As he was winging his way across the Bering Sea to mainland Russia, he was congratulating himself for thinking ahead.

He looked over at Molly and asked, "So my dear, how's your Russian?"

"Bastard! Someday JD will catch up with you, and I just hope I'm there to see it."

"Temper, temper, you'll scare the child. How are you doing, my dear?"

"I'm good," Tabatha answered. "Am I going to have my own room like you promised?"

"Of course you are, sweetie."

Several hours later, they landed in Moscow, where the Russian president met them. "Good, you made it," Vasily Makarov, the Russian president said.

"Not a moment too soon, if I'd delayed any longer, they would have gotten me. Is everything ready?"

"It is. I've arranged for a press conference tonight, so we can announce the transition."

"How is an alliance between our people going to be viewed?"

"After you sent all that food last year, I don't believe anyone will complain when you take charge. As long as you can fulfill your promises, there shouldn't be any issues."

"It's already taken care of. There's a hundred and fifty million in your Swiss account, and your villa in Spain is waiting on you."

"Wonderful, I can't wait to get out of this godforsaken weather."

EARLIER, WHEN GENERAL Sung's bodyguards hadn't checked in, they'd gone to investigate.

"General Sung has been murdered."

"Lock down the hotel," General Wang ordered. "I'll be right up."

When he got a look at the body he said, "I don't know who this poor bastard is, but it's definitely not the general."

On his way back down, he stopped on the forty-fourth floor to check on the girls. When he got off the elevator, he saw several of his best officers lying dead in the bloody hallway, and that every door had been shattered. "The bastards took the bimbos. Too bad, I really liked the little redhead in 4402," the general muttered. "I'd better get this shit ended, or we're all going to die."

"This is General Wang, and I'd like to discuss the terms of our surrender."

"Unconditional surrender, and only if you haven't harmed any prisoners," General Jackson warned.

"I give you my word, no one has been harmed, but earlier today someone broke in and freed several of them."

"I wonder who that could have been." The general chuckled. "OK, here's the deal. We'll be outside the hotel in one hour. When we land, you need to lay down your weapons, and walk slowly outside with your hands clasped behind your heads. If there's any funny business, we'll kill you."

"Understood."

Three days later, they all met in General Sung's old command center to celebrate, and discuss what came next.

"I don't have the words to express my gratitude," General Thomas said.

"I'm just glad it worked out," JD told him. "If I'd known that shithead Sung had already bailed, we could have waited, but I was afraid he'd carry out his threat."

"Did you figure out who you killed?"

"Yeah, he was some poor schmuck from Brooklyn. Has anyone got a location on Sung?" JD asked.

"This is a proclamation that was shown on Russian TV last night, and it explains a lot," William Sheldon told the group. William connected his laptop to the wireless network feeding the big screen.

After they'd watched it, JD said, "He's a tricky bastard. Now he's the premier of Russia."

"Big whoop," General Jackson said. "They haven't been much of a threat for decades. Hell, they're more broke than us."

"True, but Sung managed to move many billions of dollars, and over half a million troops before he bugged out," William Sheldon informed the group. "However, I'm more concerned that he controls their nuclear arsenal."

"Even a madman like him wouldn't chance another nuclear conflict, would he?" General Connelly asked.

"Probably not. However, he knows we won't either. So, much like the previous cold war, we're left with few options."

They continued talking for over an hour, before JD asked for quiet.

"As many of you know, I was reluctant to take this job to begin with, and now that the fighting is over, I'd like to step aside."

His declaration set off conversations all over the room. The resulting chaos had continued until William Sheldon finally called for quiet.

"Gentlemen, given what JD has sacrificed for our nation, I think we should honor his request. We have several good men available who are more than competent to address the new tasks at hand."

THE NEXT MORNING, JD had asked William to meet him on the roof of the Westin.

"It's cold up here," William complained. He saw the look on JD's face. "Yeah, I know I've turned into a real wimp, but I can't stand any sort of temperature variation."

"Understandable, but you do look a little better."

"Fortunately, or maybe unfortunately, they tell me I'll probably live for years. How about you, what are you going to do now?"

"That's why I wanted to talk with you. Can you get me into Russia?"

"Probably, but what's up?"

"I don't want anyone else to know, but when I came to kill General Sung, I found out that he's been holding Molly and Tabatha."

"They're alive?"

"They are, and I think he took them with him," JD said, as he pulled the picture out of his pocket.

"The little one sure has grown," William commented as he studied the picture. "You know you've got no chance, don't you? Molly wouldn't want you to throw your life away for nothing."

"Probably true, but they're alive and I'm going to get them back, no matter what the cost."

"I understand, but I sense it's more, and revenge is a dirty business."

"I do know, but it changes nothing. As long as he's alive, I'll never rest."

"Look, I know you're in a hurry, but can you give me a few days to pull some things together?"

"Hell, it's been so long now, a few more days won't make any difference."

Three weeks later, William had his plans put together.

"I'd like to introduce Cynthia and David Gerardo," William told JD. "They're both research scientists from the Mayo Clinic, and they're going to be part of the team that'll be working on you."

"You mean working with me, right?"

"No, I meant working on you."

Next, William introduced the final member of the team.

"This is Leslie Stall, and she's the preeminent plastic surgeon in the US."

"OK, I've got to ask. What the hell are you up to?"

"Cynthia and David will be working on your pigmentation, and hair and eye color. Leslie will be working on feature modifications."

"Huh?"

"General Sung knows what you look like, and if you're going to be wandering around in that part of the world, you don't need to look so damned American."

Six weeks later, William walked into JD's hospital room, just as they were removing the bandages covering most of his body. They'd turned out most of the lights before they'd started, so it was a little hard to see. They'd kept his head completely wrapped in bandages the whole time, and even though there was very little light, when he opened his eyes, he exclaimed, "Ouch, the light is really hurting my eyes."

"That'll pass; just give your eyes a minute to adjust," Leslie Stall advised.

"Wow, I doubt that your own mother would recognize you," William said.

Once his eyes had adjusted to the light, they turned on some more lights, and Leslie Stall handed him a mirror.

"That's me?"

"It is, and unless they do a DNA test, you should be able to pass as a Tatar from the northeastern Gobi region."

"What's so special about the Gobi?"

"Nothing, but it was the farthest thing away from what you were before we could come up with, and it's an area that will fit into the culture you're trying to infiltrate."

"Am I always going to look like this?"

"No, it's fully reversible, although it may be somewhat painful," Leslie Stall assured him.

"It's not foolproof, but it'll give you a much better chance to move around undetected," William said.

"Thanks, and it looks like all that foreign language training is finally going to pay off."

THREE WEEKS LATER, JD was fully healed, and ready to get started.

"I'll contact you if I can," JD said. "Don't go sending anyone after me. There's no need in getting anyone else killed over my obsession."

"Hey, I get it. If I were in your situation, I would do the same," William said, as he gave him a bear hug.

They finished saying their good-byes, and JD went to catch his ride.

"IT'D BE A lot closer if you'd just let me fly you across out of Nome," Harvey Weinstein said.

"True, but the area is heavily guarded," JD said.

It took them several hops, but after refueling at an old navy base on Adak, in the Aleutian Islands, Harvey dropped JD on the cold, wet, windswept coast of the Kamchatka Peninsula.

Harvey marveled at the transformation as he helped JD unload his gear.

His appearance, clothing, weapons, food, and even his speech patterns had been crafted to withstand the closest scrutiny. JD could speak eleven different languages fluently, and they'd spent many hours perfecting the various accents he'd need to fit in.

"Good luck, my friend, and I hope we meet again one day," Harvey Weinstein said as they shook hands.

"Not likely, but thanks for your help, and stay low, so they don't get you on the way back."

After Harvey's chopper had disappeared into the swirling mist, JD picked up his weapons, adjusted his backpack, and went to meet his fate.